WYNTERTIDE

Also By Andrew Caldecott

Rotherweird

WYNTERTIDE

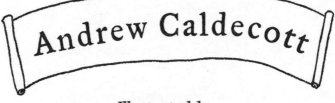

Andrew Caldecott

Illustrated by
Aleksandra Laika

Jo Fletcher
BOOKS

First published in Great Britain in 2018 by

Jo Fletcher Books
an imprint of Quercus Editions Ltd
Carmelite House
50 Victoria Embankment
London EC4Y 0DZ

An Hachette UK Company

A CIP catalogue record for this book is available
from the British Library.

HB ISBN 978 1 78429 802 9
TPB ISBN 978 1 78648 991 3
EBOOK ISBN 978 1 78429 801 2

10 9 8 7 6 5 4 3 2 1

Typeset by CC Book Production

Printed and bound in Great Britain by Clays Ltd, St Ives plc

For my mother and in memory of my father

PRINCIPAL CHARACTERS

Outsiders from wider England

Jonah Oblong   A historian

The town of Rotherweird

Rhombus Smith	Headmaster
Professor Vesey Bolitho	Astronomer and Head of South Tower Science
Hengest Strimmer	Head of North Tower Science
Vixen Valourhand	A North Tower scientist
Gregorius Jones	Head of Physical Education
Godfery Fanguin	Former teacher
'Bomber' Fanguin	His wife
Angela Trimble	School Porter
Sidney Snorkel	The Mayor
Gorhambury	The Town Clerk
Madge Brown	Assistand Head librarian
Hayman Salt	Municipal Head Gardener
Marmion Finch	The Herald
Boris and Bert Polk	Co-owners of *The Polk Land & Water Company*

Orelia Roc	Owner of *Baubles & Relics*, an antique shop
Aggs	A cleaner
Estella Scry	A clairvoyant
Gurney Thomes	Master of the Apothecaries

Rotherweird Countrysiders

Bill Ferdy	Brewer and landlord of *The Journeyman's Gist*
Ferensen	A nomadic close neighbour of the Ferdys

The Elizabethan and Stuart Age

Sir Robert Oxenbridge	Constable of the Tower of London
John Finch	Rotherweird's Herald
Geryon Wynter	A mystic
Calx Bole	Wynter's servant
Tyke	An enigma
Mel	
Estella	} Child prodigies
Nona	
Sacheverell Vere	A wealthy bachelor
Benedict Roc	Master Carver

Rotherweirders Abroad

Tancred Everthorne	An artist
Pomeny Tighe	A mathematician

Old English

Brother Hilarion	A monk and naturalist
Harfoot	His lay companion

CONTENTS

ILLUSTRATIONS

The Heron

p. v

Incus Major

'Harfoot would like to bottle these clouds.
Nobody will believe them otherwise.'

p. 7

The Kraken

'. . . a pantomime horror lumbers from the cave, spikes proud of
the back like a flustered porcupine . . .'

p. 81

The Tarot

'Someone you knew ended badly . . .'

p. 134

London

'Keep to the river, Fortemain had said, and you cannot miss it . . .'

p. 149

The Cat-Boy

'. . . a grisly jigsaw of cat and boy . . .'

p. 208

Old History

Caligatae is the name they have coined for themselves – 'foot-sloggers', men who march the known world, anywhere that's worthwhile.

He eyes his *caligae*. More than a Roman soldier's sandals, *caligae* are an emblem of Empire, their hobnailed soles stamping the alien earth. Yet practicalities matter too: they serve well in his homeland, and in Africa, where the sand flows through, and on any road anywhere – but in this pathless backwater of Britannia, with its midges, ticks and leeches, *caligae* let in the natural enemies. The woollen foot-sleeves help, but biting insects still climb the fibres to softer flesh. Here there are always *quid pro quos*.

His name, once Gregorius, is now Gorius: the army needs short names, shoutable.

He is the legion's *speculator*, the lead scout. He likes the word for sounding like the role it describes: a mix of looking, hope, guesswork and working alone.

Ferns tickle his ears; the helmet is off, lest it catch the light. He reads the land as those below will read it: the folds, the shifting skyline, the cross-hatching of bracken and earth. With his tanned skin, he blends in.

He has been here an hour. Time drags when a scene is familiar – the standing stones, the doomed men in white robes, the primitive huts fashioned with clay, animal dung and straw. Yet the idiocy of these particular *barbari* defies precedent, for they abandon the island, their one defensible position – some by coracle, others filing in full view through open meadowland – to converge on a wood which rises steeply to the valley rim: a trap of their own making.

Cavalry canter along the river, spearing the beached coracles to cut off escape by water. The infantry, dividing into three equal sections, descends from the north. The orders are short, the reaction instant.

Gorius admires the strategy, honed by months of similar operations and the perfection of Roman manoeuvre. About the slaughter of the innocent, he is more squeamish; he looks away. To the south beyond the river, an earthy prominence dominates the flat marshland. He thinks of a burial mound, although there is no path in.

He resumes his watch on the approaching battle. The *barbari* have retreated into the trees. This is child's play: skirmishers go in first, fanning out to seal the sides. Cavalry comb the grassland for covered pits, stabbing at the ground and finding none. The legionaries leave their shields and javelins beside the wood; in the congested trees, a short sword is quicker.

The nape of his neck tingles. Where are the cries of the women and children? He recalls the mix of unease and reverence this settlement generates in neighbouring communities. He hears only slashed undergrowth and soldiers' oaths; orders lose certainty. The legionaries drift out, as hounds might after losing a scent.

This is his task, Gorius with his hunter's eyes: finding the hidden ways, forestalling ambush. He marks their vanishing point, dashes to his tethered horse and gallops down.

'Now you can earn your bloody keep,' growls his tribune, Ferox by nickname and *ferox* by nature.

Gorius does not want the ground more trampled than it is. 'Call them all out, sir – leave this to me.'

'And when you find them, what then?' Ferox follows his *speculator* in, sword drawn.

Gorius pauses, points and moves on, like the dappled hunting dogs in Gaul. It is difficult translating unfamiliar ground seen from above to the place itself, but he narrows his search to a deep hollow whose upward slope is too severe to climb quickly; nobody has tried. Hobnailed *caligae* leave spoor, but smoother prints dominate here, bare feet. He crawls on all fours as Ferox mocks, and then he finds it: a lattice of twig and fern fronds, near invisible, held to the ground with pegs. He lifts them to reveal a white tablet, fine as any Roman marble, and incised with a flower. The workmanship is exquisite, surely beyond these savages. Ferox runs his sword across it, leaving not a scratch.

'A gate,' suggests Gorius. 'Has to be.'

The lines on Ferox's face map a man with little laughter, but now his eyes sparkle as he slaps his thighs, causing the leather thongs of his uniform to swing back and forth between his legs. He bellows like a bull: a gate for grown men, one metre square?

Gorius rests the palm of his hand on the tile. The dark hairs on his wrist stand proud, prickling with energy. Tentative now, he steps forward – and disappears.

Laughter strangling to a snarl, Ferox follows.

977 Anno Domini. A remote monastery.

By dint of one monk's remarkable chronicle of events, as impartial in its treatment of saints as of pagan kings, Jarrow is still reputed to be, two centuries on, the greatest centre of learning north of Rome.

Brother Hilarion in his humbler monastery nurses a like ambition, which brings him to his abbot's office.

'I understand you have an urge to set down like Brother Bede.'

'Yes – but not the history of men.'

'And what is wrong with men?'

Brother Hilarion does not say what he thinks. *If Man is made in God's image, God must be terrible indeed.*

'I prefer the gentler days of Creation – *flora*, *fauna* and celestial happenings.'

The abbot nods. 'They say you have a gift for description, and a special eye.'

This is true. No leaf or feather or star is quite like another to Hilarion. 'But I fear I seek my own renown – that I have fallen prey to pride.'

'Everyone talks of Jarrow, nobody of us – and who accuses Brother Bede of vanity?' The abbot crosses himself as a sign of respect. 'How far would you travel?'

Brother Hilarion feels his world turn from a cell three steps square to miles and miles of forest, marsh and pasture. An epic answer comes without thinking. 'I would journey from the southern sea to the northern wall.'

'All of *Britannia* that is! Take two horses, supplies, whatever you need by way of paper, quills and ink. A lay assistant will join you. Young Harfoot is strong. He can bear arms – and he has worked in the *scriptorium*.'

Brother Hilarion hangs his head as the abbot blesses him – a rarity reserved for the most demanding tasks. The abbot sees Hilarion to the door. 'When you return, you will dedicate this work—'

'To the monastery.'

'By name only?'

'I will include my humble and distinguished abbot.'

A wave and a rare smile. He has found the right response.

Within an hour of leaving they encounter a new butterfly: *papilio*.

'Pliny the Elder recorded them so why shouldn't we?' declares the monk.

Harfoot unpacks the instruments of record with a tidy eye. This is to be the first entry on the first page. He records the day, the month, the orange tips to the white wings and the insect's size by a wooden rule he has developed for the purpose. An hour passes before they move on.

They have an instant affinity. Harfoot's sunny disposition lightens the intensity of his master's vision. Their journey will end forty years later with a phenomenon that will make the sweeping events in Brother Bede's great chronicle look ordinary.

December 1017. The Rotherweird Valley.

Forty years on, and the mission has changed. Their early books filled too quickly with much that was commonplace and they bequeathed them to monasteries along the way. For the last decade, there has been but one book, home only to the local and the rare.

Word of mouth brings them to this escarpment rim.

The valley below keeps its own weather, a different degree of winter. A frozen river encircles an island, in appearance a bone necklace.

'What were those local mutterings?' asks Brother Hilarion. He is forgetful now, his voice feeble, speech an effort.

'A flying serpent.'

The monk needs only a cue. 'Ah yes: rare rocks and butterflies with blue-white wings, if we had time to wait a season.'

'And a plant that never flowers,' adds Harfoot.

The furrows in Brother Hilarion's face shape to a smile. 'Enough to hazard the journey then,' he says, 'even on the shortest day of the year.'

Their two ponies, refractory and apprehensive, pick their way. A huge rock stabs the sky from the island's summit like an accusing finger. A circular hole near the apex catches the light, suggestive of an eye. In the marshland to the southeast is a turfed prominence, apparently manmade, *terra firma* in the bog. Brother Hilarion feels beset by pagan images.

He notes the grey threads in his younger companion's hair, and the bald crown, which now matches his: Nature's tonsure is testimony to so many cliff paths, moors and mountains traversed together, as are their feet protruding through their sandals like tuberous roots. Age has deepened the bond between them, as it has altered the dependencies. Harfoot's tasks are multiplying. He describes for Brother Hilarion the finer details of the view, the stealthier sounds, and his vocabulary burgeons in consequence.

On reaching the valley floor, they look skywards and Harfoot points. 'You see the darkness in the blue, Brother.' Their *magnum opus* has a page devoted to Nature's more peculiar clouds.

'How are they shaped?'

'Like anvils in a forge, one south, one north.'

'Quill, good Harfoot,' calls the monk, although the familiar cry is unnecessary for Harfoot has already unwrapped quill, ink and parchment. 'We've never seen two at the same time.'

'These are different,' he suggests, 'portentous even.'

So they are: blacker, their edges sharp as quillwork, sitting like rival armies forming for battle.

Harfoot does the writing now the monk's crabbed fingers have grown rigid. Hilarion is ailing, his legs stiffening too, and his breathing is stertorous, like pebbles in a sieve – but as the body diminishes, so the spirit burns brighter. *So much to do, so little time . . .*

'We'll use your name for these: *incus maior*,' declares Hilarion; always eager to give his companion credit.

Lightning leaps from one cloud to the other: a strike from Vulcan's hammer. Harfoot would like to bottle these clouds. Nobody will believe them otherwise. However . . .

'Shelter?' he advises, in the respectful guise of a question.

'Ah, we have time,' the brother murmurs, staring upwards.

There are huts sprawling across the lower levels of the main island, but they see no one, despite the livestock tethered near the single bridge that runs to the flatter, less obvious island – until a man clothed in a muddle of pelt and hide bounds from the woods. He stops beside them – or rather, he continues to run, although stationary, muscles coiling in his arms and legs, ready to take off

'Harfoot would like to bottle these clouds.
Nobody will believe them otherwise.'

again at any moment. The skin is burnished, but it is the face which arrests. The eyes are welcoming, the mouth generous and the radiating lines humorous, but for Brother Hilarion, this pleasing mask holds suffering beneath.

His diagnosis is familiar. 'Are you baptised, my son?'

'*Sum Gorius.*'

Latin in this backwater? The mystery deepens.

'They talk of a rare plant,' interjects Harfoot.

The knees continue to rise and fall as he points to the flatter meadow. 'A plant so rare it fruits but once in a thousand years,' replies the man – Gorius – before slipping back into Latin. '*Sequi me.*' Follow me. He gives the command a near-religious emphasis.

He leads them at marching pace to the meadow, where, beneath a stand of scraggy oaks, spreads the evergreen, procumbent colony. In this blessed month of the Nativity, on the shortest day of the year, the flowers are gone, but the fruit, a rich blue-purple, still hangs at joint of stalk and axil. Beneath each round berry lurks a tiny red thorn.

'Pick but one,' advises Gorius. 'She is most jealous of her fruit.'

How quaint these country folk are, thinks Harfoot, but Brother Hilarion, still the better naturalist, is less dismissive. He has seen nothing resembling this plant anywhere from the southern sea to the northern wall.

The scratch of the quill sounds loud in the stillness, but not for long. The ponies feel it first, heads up, wide-eyed as they flick the frost from their muzzles. A knifing wind rises; the two *inci* close and ignite, flashing silver, and thunder booms as Harfoot, hands quivering in the cold, hurriedly wraps the book in layers of leather and sheepskin.

'Go back,' cries Gorius, pointing the way they have come. 'There is a holy house beyond the rim.'

Then he runs, and the hail erupts, swirling, the size of small pebbles, sharp enough to mark the skin. The ponies are too unruly to ride so Harfoot holds them fast as, step by step, heads bowed to the waist, they edge towards the upwards path. Thunder, hail and wind with their distinctive voices, the *roar*, *swish* and *howl*, batter the ears – but they are mere whispers set against the new noise: a grinding from the earth itself, Sisyphus pushing his rock. The ground beneath them, now white, shivers and slides—

—and abruptly, everything stops, leaving utter stillness in its wake. The hail softens to snow. Harfoot is holding the ponies with one hand and anxiously supporting Brother Hilarion with the other. The old monk's face is grey as stone.

At the rim of the valley they stop and turn to look back at the island – and now they understand. The henge with the eye atop the hill has vanished into thin air.

This is God's way of telling them this is journey's end.

Miraculum.

Brother Hilarion rests a hand on his companion's shoulder.

'You must build a church there – on the brow of the island. Upon this rock . . .'

Brother Hilarion dies peacefully on the eve of the Nativity.

Harfoot buries him in a field beside the monastery above the valley rim.

The following Mayday he takes his vows and, as soon as the abbot will allow, retraces his steps to the valley.

So long a pagan outpost, the community embraces the new, softer theology: love thy neighbour, a final judgement that favours the just and the poor, a bloodless sacrifice in a sliver of unleavened bread. Harfoot preaches on the island's prominence, the hill of the vanishing henge. It is, he says, a sign. Here, in Rotherweird, at this very spot, they must build a house for the true God.

He will call it the Church of the Traveller's Rest.

1035. Rotherweird Island.

The sky is clear and frost this sharp is colder than snow and more beautiful. The four circular holes in the ornate stone cross atop the church tower are chalked in, filled with white.

Brother Harfoot has found fulfilment. He inhabits a modest cell behind the church, a nighttime fire of applewood his single luxury; he inhales the scent like balm. In tribute to his friend, he finishes the book with a narrative of their last travelling day: the two battling *inci*, the running man, the vanishing henge and the flower that fruits once in a thousand years.

The new church has drawn men who turn wood, carve stone and colour walls, and Harfoot allows their energies to flourish as they labour for their afterlife. The fantastical scenes on the walls of the tower are uncomfortably real, but he does not ask their origins.

He knows the person interrupting his evening prayer as a local man of means, the weaver of stories who hired the men and directed the frescoes – which image on which wall; the mixing of colours; who will work on what. He holds a perfect sphere of rock, which neatly fills the palm of his hand, a swirl of colours like the painted wooden balls in a rich boy's toy chest.

Harfoot, the mighty traveller, has never seen its like before. 'Where's it from?'

'A peat-cutter found it nearby. He thought it should stay here.'

Harfoot weighs the stone in the palm of his hand. 'There was a henge where the church is now. It had a circular hole.'

'Locals called it *the eye of the winking man*.'

'What colour was it?' asks Harfoot.

'Veined rock, as I remember, and not unlike this.'

'And size?'

'There or thereabouts.'

'If it's the eyeball of the winking man, it should be kept in God's house,' he says as he accepts the gift.

In the marches of the night, a disturbing thought occurs. Did the sphere *cause* the vanishing? If so, to *where*? In the frescoes, the henge is there on one wall, on the next the church in its place – and then the henge again somewhere unrecognisable.

A puzzle best left, he decides.

OCTOBER:
FIRST FORTNIGHT

I

A Problem

How to thank Ferensen for that remarkable summertime feast?

Bill Ferdy, landlord of *The Journeyman's Gist*, under whose observant stewardship grudges were settled, prospective couples were
introduced, gloom dispelled and problems solved or softened, listened more than he spoke, treated all comers equally, respected
confidences, never served a drunk – and brewed that remarkable
beer, *Old Ferdy's Feisty Peculiar*. His approach in all matters flowed
from attention to detail and a desire to please, which was why this
small but tricky question troubled him considerably.

Ferdy knew what an effort the old man must have made, with
his Elizabethan theme, the restoration of his woodland maze and
clearing his tower of its miscellany of books and outlandish objects
to accommodate them. Ferdy pondered how exhausting near-
immortality must be. Ferensen, as Hieronymus Seer, had witnessed
the murder of Sir Henry, their childhood benefactor, only to suffer
with his sister under Geryon Wynter's rule, culminating in his
immersion in the mixing-point with consequences they could only
guess at. He likened him to the blasted oak at the border of his
farm: still in leaf, supporting nature in many forms, but wearing
the scars of his long existence.

Ferensen had declined all help, insisting that the feast would
be more than a thanksgiving. The company must still solve the
mystery at the heart of events: who was Robert Flask, the vanished
School Historian? Ferensen introduced the task as an after-dinner

game. The clues – a notebook, an address, a crossword anagram, the skull of Ferox the weaselman, the tapestries – all combined to reveal that Flask must be Calx Bole, Wynter's servant – and thanks to Wynter's abuse of the mixing-point in Lost Acre, a shapeshifter, and, like Ferensen, centuries old.

In the days after the dinner, as summer waned, Ferensen had changed. He turned monosyllabic, spending days on end immured in his tower. That, however, did not make him immune to the restorative effect of gratitude. *So, how to thank Ferensen?*

Knock-knock. Ring. Knock-knock-knock.

Cursing, Hayman Salt, Head Municipal Gardener and much else besides, tramped to the front door, where he was relieved to find one of the few men he considered worthy company.

'Bill!'

'Hayman Salt.'

One callused hand firmly shook the other.

'Come through.' Salt escorted Ferdy to his conservatory, where his dead Lost Acre cultivars had been swept into a corner to compost, innocuous as a spill of tobacco. More conventional blooms had replaced them on the wooden racks.

'I'm done with Lost Acre and adventure,' said Salt.

'You mean the Green Man changed you?'

Salt's brief merger with the Midsummer flower had deepened his affinity with trees and shrubs. Now he sensed their hidden illnesses, what boughs to lose, when to irrigate, drain or enrich. 'I'm a better gardener, that's for sure, and better morally, too.' Salt paused. 'But that's enough of me. To what do I owe this pleasure?'

'It's about . . .' Ferdy stopped, then mouthed the name 'Ferensen', whose existence and identity they had all sworn to keep secret.

'Ah.' Salt ushered Ferdy into his sitting room, and as his guest examined the botanical prints covering the walls, he produced

a bottle of *Feisty Peculiar*. 'They tell me it's rather good,' said Salt
with a wink.

Ferdy held his own brew to the light before passing it under
his nose. 'Last year's – thinner than the best, maybe, but not bad.'

'So: what about Ferensen?' asked Salt.

'He's in a poor way.'

'He shouldn't be – he masterminded everything.'

'We're not sure about that, remember?'

Salt did remember the unsettling thought that they'd all been
manoeuvred into saving Lost Acre to further some hidden design
of Calx Bole alias Flask alias Ferox alias who-else-besides?

Ferdy put his proposal. 'We haven't thanked him for that splendid
dinner. I thought a bag of seed would go down well – *Hayman's*
this, *Hayman's* that – he does so love plants.'

'Won't do,' Salt said, and explained that not only had Lost Acre's
cultivars all proved barren, but none had lasted beyond a single
season. 'I've cleared them all – turned over "a new leaf",' he murmured. 'Dust to dust.' He paused. 'What's his tower like in daytime?'

'You know the period: high windows, gloomy, scattered pools
of light.'

A flicker of affection lit up Salt's face. 'I do have one survivor –
and I'd like a good home for her.' He finished the last of the *Pecu-*
liar, smacking lips in appreciation, and took Ferdy back through
the house to the front hall. Climbing over a trellis set against the
wall was a thornless rose-like plant with pale green leaves and
small crimson flowers, even now in October. To mark his return
to normality Salt had removed the label.

'Years old,' said Salt. 'Don't ask me why she alone keeps going,
because I have no idea. I call her the *Darkness Rose*. Evergreen,
free-flowering, sweet-scented, and a creature of shadow.'

Ferdy smiled. Ferensen might see a gaudy pot plant as a rebuke
to his natural melancholy, but this retiring beauty would surely
cheer him up. 'I'll say it's from all of us.'

Salt bagged up the rose and heaved a sigh of relief as the door closed on her. He and Lost Acre had parted company. There was no going back.

'Ferensen?' he called, but there was no response. The evening sun heightened the orange-pink of the Jacobean brickwork as he tried the door. *Unlocked.* At first he could not see Ferensen – the single octagonal room had returned to its original configuration, but with a marked difference: a solitary candle sputtering in the dampness barely illuminated the glass tanks trailing weeds that now lined the walls and the reeds growing in brass buckets. He had entered an aquarium.

'Does the coolness bother you?'

Ferdy tracked the voice to the far corner.

Ferensen was sitting beneath a shelf cleared of books, away from the candle. Green fronds trailing from a long rectangular tank ran slick across his cheeks and head.

'Are you all right?'

'I'm laying up.' His words bubbled.

Ferdy brought over the candle. Ferensen's eyes looked glassy.

'I've brought a thank you from all of us.'

Ferensen's right arm snaked out and caressed the petals and leaves. 'A plant of shade. Of hu—' Ferensen briefly lost the word. '—midity,' he finally added.

'Salt calls it the *Darkness Rose.*'

'Ah, yes, Salt – one of us now.'

'I hope you like it.'

Momentarily the stems appeared to caress Ferensen's fingers, rather than the other way round. A semblance of normality returned to his voice, although the sentences still grew, word by word, like a child piling building bricks.

'Yes, I do, I do very much, and well named, so well named. Thank them – thank them all. Thank them all warmly.'

'*Thank you*,' replied Ferdy.

Ferensen raised his other hand in farewell. Ferdy placed the *Darkness Rose* on the floor beside the old man and withdrew.

As he descended the meadow to his home, he shook his head. If, God forbid, Bole made a move, Ferensen, their one-time leader and talisman, was in no fit state to oppose him; and Hayman Salt, who knew Lost Acre best, had hung up his boots.

Who was there to step into the breach?

Jonah Oblong, the School Historian and Rotherweird's one officially recognised outsider, judged himself 'acclimatised' as a person and 'arrived' as a personality. He knew the rickshaws to avoid and the best baker. He had grasped the rudiments of the town's circulatory system. He was even acknowledged in the street. His roots might be shallow, but at least he belonged.

Yet the excitement of his first six months, ending with the Midsummer Fair and Ferensen's feast, subsided as the leaves lost their lustre. Familiarity had not bred contempt, more a coasting approach: no strain on the tiller. Life was comfortable, pleasant and, yes, increasingly *familiar*.

Another symptom nettled: his poetry had been afflicted by *cosiness*. The inner voice lacked edge. Deeper down lurked another fault-line. In that frantic summer he had engaged with Miss Trimble, Vixen Valourhand and Orelia Roc; now he languished alone.

These cross-currents had an odd effect. Oblong found himself half-hoping that Calx Bole's manoeuvring presaged an outcome which nobody with an ounce of morality or sense would wish for: Geryon Wynter's threatened return.

He felt an urge to test the historical evidence – the arms of the Eleusians known as *The Dark Devices*, the account of Wynter's trial and the testimony gathered in advance of it – all held in Rother-weird's sole place of record, Escutcheon Place.

But its guardian, the Herald, Marmion Finch, never entertained visitors, so Oblong sent a letter, which might have been better expressed.

Dear Mr Finch,

　　You may recall a certain dinner with a certain person, at which we discussed whether a certain other person might return. I feel the historian's art would elucidate. I am free most afternoons in the week and most weekends and would be happy to work at Escutcheon Place.

　　Yours most sincerely,

　　Jonah Oblong

Finch's reply had been terse, even rude:

Too many cooks. F.

PS Careless words cost lives.

The reply hurt, but worse, Oblong felt becalmed.

If Oblong hankered for flirtation, Orelia Roc craved passion. To compensate for its absence, she invested her energies in *Baubles & Relics*. Every week she travelled outside Rotherweird, indulging Mrs Snorkel's *penchant* for blue-and-white pottery in return for permission to roam wider England, although her acquisitions were limited by the *History Regulations* and what she could carry. Orelia was convinced that Calx Bole had not been sated by the restoration of Lost Acre and Sir Veronal's destruction – she and Ferensen had been at the mixing-point that Midsummer Day, powerless prisoners, and Ferox-alias-Bole could have killed them whenever he wanted. Bole was not a man of mercy, so he must be playing a longer game in which she remained an active piece.

2

Deathbed

Beneath a formidable exterior, Angela Trimble, Rotherweird School's porter, had a sensitive side, which now prompted a restraining finger. 'I prefer the candle.'

The doctor, privately dismissing the sentiment that soft light could ease a man's passing and irked by an instruction from someone so low in the school hierarchy, nonetheless withdrew his hand from the gaslight. He cut a conservative figure in his three-piece suit, dark blue overcoat, brogues polished to a shine and a Gladstone bag.

'You a minister?' he asked drily.

Trimble read the subtext: *why her, and not Matron?* 'He foresaw his decline,' she explained. 'He called it "nature's way". He asked me to help.'

'You have professional staff.'

'And their diagnosis was "no diagnosis".'

The doctor did not share his puzzlement with Miss Trimble. 'Tell me about the relapse,' he asked.

A week earlier Vesey Bolitho, founder of the Astronomy Faculty and mixologist *extraordinaire*, had been his usual irrepressible self. Whatever the mysterious illness, he had appeared to be in remission, his pulse stronger, his colour restored.

She explained, 'Two days ago he retired to his bed. He weakened physically, but sharpened mentally. Yesterday he wrote the inscription for his gravestone and made dispositions for his funeral. This morning he gave me a hug and closed his eyes. He's remained mute and motionless ever since – which is not his usual state.'

The doctor held Bolitho's wrist and found a barely discernible pulse. 'Any time now,' he agreed. 'The body is closing down. I'd offer morphine, but he seems strangely . . .'

'Content,' she agreed. *Content with leaving us*, she thought. *Why doesn't he fight?*

'Should anyone be here?'

Again that unspoken message: the School Porter wasn't a suitable companion for a head of department on his deathbed. But she knew the school's web of personal relationships better than anyone – all human traffic docked at the porter's lodge: teachers, pupils, cleaners, gardeners. Bolitho was loved by everyone, but an intimate of few, so candidates for this final vigil did not spring readily to mind.

The enigmatic Gregorius Jones she vetoed as incapable of seriousness, and half in love with him, she could not face the complications. She had seen Valourhand grow close to the professor, despite the traditional rivalry between North and South Towers, but she had disappeared on sabbatical. Rhombus Smith, engulfed by the paper sea that preceded every new term, had already visited earlier in the day. Orelia Roc had her shop to manage, Boris would be on a charabanc run, Gorhambury would be embroiled in municipal business and Fanguin would drink.

She shrugged her shoulders.

'I'm sorry,' added the doctor before leaving. He had never removed his coat. It was that hopeless.

After showing him out, she sat beside the bed and opened the envelope the professor had left for her. The single instruction in Bolitho's once elegant but now stumbling hand had an unsettling directness:

Bury me in a traditional wicker coffin in my baggiest waistcoat and trousers.

He even left instructions for finding these clothes, right end of his dressing-room cupboard. The postscript warmed her:

Please remember me as I will you: a flicKer of light in a darK universe.

The note bore this very day's date, followed by the word 'Dusk'. Outside ribbons of cloud pinkened at their lower margins. She reached for his hand. No pulse now, at dusk, as if he had planned both the day and time of his death. Such orderliness did not fit the Bolitho she knew.

She bent her head, blew out the candle and kissed her dead friend's forehead.

3
Fliers

An anglepoise lamp in silhouette, the heron held its pose. Yellow eyes flicked open. By moonlight the reeds broke the surface of the water like tufts of hair on a scalp of glass.

On Rotherweird's southeastern frontier, treacherous marshland ran to a sharp escarpment carpeted in scrubby thorn where, as if ashamed by the surrounding desolation, the Rother plunged underground.

Light, stars, temperature, what calls, what sleeps, what the stomach says, these were the heron's timekeepers – but none had provoked this wakening. The bird did not move, because it sensed the unfamiliar. Eyes and ears reported nothing untoward – but the shadow on the water moved despite the windless night: left ahead, right to the side and in front, wheeling and slowly growing larger in a descent: a creature from another world, human in size, with leathery wings spread wide.

The heron lost its nerve and, launching from its toes, fled west, the wing-beats frantic, towards hedgerows and cover. The bird could not resist one backwards glance – and the image bit deep.

Never again would he venture this side of the running water.

4

Of Puddings

'I am Gurney Thomes, Master of the Apothecaries.' Burly in build, head almost square, with a goatee beard and piggy eyes, he wore a thin scarlet sash over the standard Apothecaries' black-and-white costume.

Mrs Fanguin gulped. Having followed her unsigned instructions religiously, east down Hamelin Way through the poor quarter to an anonymous side door in the Guild's Hall, she had expected a minor functionary.

The Master turned smartly on his heel and strode off into a labyrinth of dingy passages.

Poverty had brought Bomber here. After Snorkel had dismissed her husband from the School for not reporting Flask's several breaches of the *History Regulations*, she too had been dismissed as staff cook, despite support from a lengthy petition *and* the Headmaster.

'No – it's to mark the gravity of the offence,' Snorkel had declared, gleefully rubbing his hands. He disliked not only Fanguin, but *anyone* who liked him.

The Apothecaries' unexpected letter had been headed *Strictly personal, private and confidential*, a good excuse for keeping the adventure from her husband.

After a number of twists and turns, they reached a sparsely appointed kitchen with a cast-iron range and a table on which sat one pan, two empty bowls, two spoons and one small knife. A butler's sink sported one tap (cold).

'I have a signed reference from the Headmaster—'

He cut her off. 'We act on our own intelligence.' He pointed to a row of glass jars lined up on a shelf like a sweetshop, their contents strikingly diverse. At a glance she identified two sorts of beans – haricot and lima? – barley, or maybe wheat; she'd need to look closer. Chickpeas sat next to dried fruit – figs and apricots – and sugar. A cruet held rosewater, judging by the subtle scent pervading the room. 'The wherewithal,' he added.

Two unequal hourglasses, one marked 1 and one .33, stood like parent and child on the corner of the table. Thomes turned the largest as he left.

So, an hour and twenty minutes, and she must time herself: a test of her integrity as well as her speed.

She quickly confirmed the ingredients. Was she allowed to be selective? She suspected not, such was the Guild's reputation for stringency. A vestigial memory surfaced: a recipe she had never attempted, though the unusual name had lodged in her conscious-ness. Noah's pudding: how to achieve opulent simplicity when supplies are running low.

She reached for the larger bowl. *Seize the moment.*

The concoction filling the smaller bowl was tastier and more nutritious than it looked, and every ingredient had been used. She washed the pan, straightened the now empty jars and cleaned the hob. As the final grains tumbled through the neck of the smaller hourglass, footsteps could be heard, evenly spaced, *click-clack, click-clack*: another way of marking time.

Master Thomes shed his public face: his tongue darted in and out and his nostrils flared, readying the senses. He dipped the spoon and held it aloft, peering and sniffing before swallowing it whole. He licked his lips, which she found disconcerting – a Puritan voluptuary – but she nonetheless forced a smile. Cooks should appreciate being appreciated.

He placed a single page on the table. 'A covenant,' he said. 'You work only for me.' His fingers were seashell-pink, the cuticles near invisible: a Puritan with manicured hands.

She picked up the sheet and read. The pay was generous – more than the Town Council had ever offered – and the hours reasonable (Fanguin wouldn't notice her absence). Promptness and secrecy were absolute. She must enter by the same side door and keep herself to this room. The facilities would be improved, for he would expect variety and finesse. She could order ingredients as she saw fit; costs would be handled by the Guild.

He added an oral addendum: he disliked bitterness, and on no account should she ever use celery.

Bomber signed. They had to eat, so she had no choice.

5

Varnishing the Truth

Every five years the *cognoscenti* of the Artefacts Committee – the
Assistant Head Librarian, the Curator of the Rotherweird Art Gallery
(the only one of its kind in the town) and the Master of the
Woodworkers' Guild – inspected Rotherweird's more memorable
ornamentation: carvings, sculptures, paintings, the more ancient
books and other decorative arts. With a supporting cast of
ladder-carriers and note-takers, and a selection of telescopes, they
progressed from south to north over the course of several weeks.
Damp, dry rot, woodworm, bookworm, erosion, scars left by years,
weather and human agency – all were recorded, cures prescribed,
time limits imposed and, for the most fortunate, municipal grants
dispensed. No structure of any distinction escaped their prying
eyes, save for Escutcheon Place; inspecting the contents of the
Herald's place of residence would be to inspect *history*, and that
would be unlawful.

Most cherished a visit from the Artefacts Committee. Not so the
Guild of Apothecaries.

'Coffee would be nice,' said Madge Brown, the Assistant Head
Librarian.

'Coffee is for Guildsmen,' replied the Master curtly, 'and you've
already outstayed your welcome. *We* look after our heritage.'

Madge Brown had finished working her way through shelves of
leather-bound, gilt-edged scientific treatises, all immaculately maintained, while the Master of the Woodworkers admired the most

accomplished old carvings in town, an odd mixture of Christian parables and emblems of scientific endeavour.

The Curator had more joy. The town had no real-life portraits outside this room; the Apothecaries must have been powerful indeed to have secured an exemption from the *History Regulations* for this visual record of their ruling class. There were still limits, though, even for them: initials only, no names and no dates.

'This is odd,' said the Curator, pointing at the largest portrait, set in a most elaborate frame.

Madge Brown followed her finger. 'I've never seen anything like it,' she agreed.

Even Thomes was driven to admit that the Guild's founder had acquired an unpleasantly jaundiced veneer over recent months, but his response was accusatory. 'It's *nothing* to do with *us*. It appeared, just *like that* – I blame your last visit.'

The Curator did not rise to the bait, but she had been on the committee for a decade and had never encountered such a sudden decline. 'It'll take some shifting,' she said, 'but we have just the person.'

'Expensive work, no doubt,' Thomes responded, adding quickly, 'I expect a full subsidy.'

'My Guild never gets a penny, so yours certainly won't,' interjected the Master of the Woodworkers with feeling; everyone in Rotherweird knew the wealth of the Apothecaries dwarfed that of all the other Guilds.

'Misers!' Thomes interjected as he stormed out.

A week later the picture restorer arrived. She carefully manoeuvred the painting onto a specially strengthened easel. Perching precariously on the penultimate step of her high ladder, she addressed her apprentice, a callow young man of few words with fastidious hands. 'It's an unusual varnish, mostly copal and amber; it'll be the devil to remove. We'll need the Bunsen burner, the copper jug and the oil.'

'It's over the right bottom corner as well as the arms, the mouth and the eyes,' observed the apprentice. 'I wonder what lurks beneath?'

'To find out, we start at a top corner. We use the swabs gently; we clean after every double pass, so as not to put back what we've just removed. And remember: we don't press harder until we're sure we have the measure of it.'

They worked in relays, the demands on eyes, fingers, mind and temper uninterrupted by any show of interest or offers of hospitality from their hosts – until a young Apothecary, who introduced herself as Romilly, arrived on the third morning.

She was dressed like the rest, her skirt and smock unrelieved black, her chestnut hair savagely pinned back under a prim white bonnet. Yet her eyes twinkled, and half-smiles came easily. She brought coffee and offered biscuits with a beguiling flavour of marmalade and chilli.

'Master Thomes has a sweet tooth,' she confided, 'and a private cook. We're not meant to know, still less to share, but he's too busy to notice so she does us goodies on the quiet.'

She ate one herself, savouring it as if indulging in sin. The apprentice wondered how she might look with her hair down, in a tighter shirt and a colourful skirt swinging from the hips.

'I hear you're cleaning up the Founder,' she said, licking the last crumb from her bottom lip.

'We've done the left side,' the apprentice said, proudly.

'Half is enough to tell the rest,' she said, tracing a long aquiline nose and high cheekbones with her finger: an austere, intellectual face.

But the portrait held more. Twenty minutes later, tiny numbers crisply outlined in gold had emerged in the right bottom corner:

7.49

8.49

Lines of golden thread emerged around the upper arms of the black velvet gown, and the restorer had just caught another puzzling detail when Master Thomes strode in. When she pointed out the figures, he adopted the same accusatory tone he had used with the Curator.

'They weren't there before,' he said.

Romilly came to their defence. 'They were lurking beneath the varnish, Master – I saw them appear myself.'

'Odd numbers,' he said to nobody in particular, before delivering a dazzling sequence of observations: '7.49, 8.49 – multiply the first two numbers of each set and add the last to get 37 and 41, two consecutive prime numbers. The difference between them is 4, which is a perfect square, and the mean number between them is 39, the second number being the cube of the first.'

'Very clever, Master, how quick, Master!' was the liturgy Thomes encouraged and expected, but the apprentice, galled by the Master's lack of respect for his principal's skill, went off-script.

'That doesn't tell us much.'

Thomes glared at the whippersnapper. 'It tells us you *play* with brushes while we hunt down eternal truths.'

The restorer intervened. 'Your founder played with letters as well as numbers,' she pointed out. 'The gold filigree on the right sleeve holds the word "*vale*", and the left holds "*sum*": "Farewell" and "I am".' She traced the line with a brush before pressing home her advantage with an intuitive comment. 'I'd say it's a prophecy of some kind.'

Two days later, to Thomes' chagrin – it evidenced a serious breach of confidentiality by the committee – he received a most impertinent letter. Although initially inclined to ignore it, he changed his mind: anyone who presumed to educate the Apothecaries about their own artefacts deserved humiliation. He accepted the offer and made his preparations.

6

Two Consultations

For all his gifts for the darker political arts, Sidney Snorkel, Rother-weird's venal Mayor, feared the vagaries of chance. The beneficiary of this anxiety inhabited that shady hinterland where fortune-telling slips into the occult. Estella Scry's shop, *The Clairvoyancy*, sold Tarot packs, Tibetan prayer wheels, English hazel dousing rods, Indian incense and Native American dreamcatchers, alongside books on phenomena as diverse as ley lines, star signs and crop circles.

Scry did not dress the part – no bangles, hoop earrings or trailing scarves for her; more late-middle-aged respectable bordering on the prim: pleated woollen skirts, monochrome jerseys over cream-coloured shirts and well-polished sensible shoes. Nor did she fit the obvious physical archetype: her heavy features lacked spiritual presence. Only the eyes, with acquaintance, promised mystery: deep as wells, restless, intelligent. Vocally, she had variety, switching from rich to reedy, whimsical to firm: within the conventional lurked a performer.

Scry's more profitable business took place on the third floor of her private premises, a pencil-thin tower in Gordian Knot, the winding alley behind *The Clairvoyancy*. Unlike her artfully cluttered shop, her home lacked ornamentation or decoration save for a modern sculpture in her consulting room – hoops of sharpened steel, springs and bolts like an exploded mechanism haphazardly reassembled – with a single photograph of the same piece on the opposite wall.

A circular table overlaid with a white embroidered cloth sat between two plain wooden chairs. There were no crystal ball, cards or tea leaves here; this was a room for serious business.

Snorkel invariably visited at seven on a Sunday evening, slipping from a rickshaw, face dipped and shrouded by hat and scarf. On this particular evening Scry noted an uncharacteristically hasty step on the winding oak staircase: a Mayor on edge.

'I happened to be passing.' His standard movement followed his standard opening line: a Rotherweird ten guinea note slid across the table, which she slipped into her sleeve like a conjuror. She knew the eloquence of silence.

'Do I look anxious?' asked Snorkel, scrunching a fist into the opposite palm.

She grasped his podgy fingers and unclenched them. 'Humidity is building,' she replied.

A weather forecast, a comment on his clammy skin, or an approaching political storm? *Why was she so obscure?*

She shut her eyes.

Snorkel could contain himself no longer. 'I promised Father . . .'

Scry's eyes flicked open like a camera shutter, as if in sudden contact with Snorkel senior.

'The dynasty must continue and prosper,' hissed Snorkel.

'The people chose your father as Mayor,' she said calmly. 'Why would they not choose you?'

'Straight after *his* father's death – *he* had the sympathy vote,' Snorkel whinged.

'There was no vote – his two opponents withdrew,' she reminded him, adding, 'He had your political gifts.'

In the marches of the night Snorkel sometimes found himself fretting over Scry's troubling knowledge of the past. However . . .

'I don't pay you to witter. Just tell me – will there be – and will I win?' He *never* used that ugly e-word: *election.*

Scry's eyes flicked shut again. 'An old ruler will resume his reign.'

'*Will there be and will I win?*' Snorkel waggled his hands like a spoiled child.

'I say what I see.'

'So, there will be one!'

For a further half an hour he pressed, to no avail. Whatever her vision meant would happen, she explained; she could say no more.

The meeting ended as it usually did. 'I don't understand what you see in that *thing*,' he said, flicking a hand at the sculpture.

'I wouldn't expect you to,' she replied curtly.

Snorkel returned home a tortured soul. He had taken extensive precautions to keep democracy at bay, but this had been an inauspicious year. With the deaths of Deirdre Banter and the Slickstone boy, the fire in Mrs Banter's tower and an outsider tying for first place in the Great Equinox Race, the omens could not be considered promising.

Estella Scry listened to the funereal tempo of the Mayor's descent. He had come for unqualified reassurance and left disappointed, yet she had been merciful, sparing him the truth: he was but a pawn who thought himself a king. Her next appointment would be a different game.

She ascended to the top floor, another single room, each of the four windows with a small rail-less balcony attached like a landing stage, as if to provide moorage for attendant spirits: her bedroom.

She stripped off her make-up, removed her pearl earrings, buttoned her shirt to the throat and wound a silk pashmina around her neck. As she flipped through the hinged layers of her jewellery box, she recited the names of her forbears: Tiresias the blind seer, Cassandra, heard by many and believed by none, and the Sibyl, with her riddling ambiguities. One way and another she would have to play all three.

She re-read the letter.

Dear Miss Scry,

Two numbers, 7.49 and 8.49, have appeared during the cleaning of a portrait (of their founder) owned by the Apothecaries. As The Clairvoyancy sells almanacs and works on mystical numbers, we wondered if you might assist on their significance. Our chair thinks they may be co-ordinates, indicating the whereabouts of other lost artefacts.

Kind regards,

Madge Brown (for the Artefacts Committee)

She chose, and flicked the golden chain over her neck so the pendant rested on her cream shirt, where nobody could miss it: Pi, symbol of a never-ending but pre-ordained sequence of apparently random events, history in a word.

On her desk lay a copy of Rotherweird's *Popular Choice Regulations*, a piece of paper bearing the two numbers and a celestial almanac. The answer reassured her, but the existence of the puzzle did not. Another agency must be at work, meaning the whole truth had been withheld from her.

She had replied directly to the Master, knowing he would gather an audience to ridicule her unscientific trade. Why otherwise accept her offer?

The rickshaw pulled up outside the Hall of the Apothecaries – such a curious building, the core old and ornate, the wings later and severe. She neither knocked nor waited for the porter but strode in, seven o'clock to the second, to find her prediction confirmed. A full Court had been assembled. The Apothecaries had the air of a conclave of monks and nuns, until you read the faces – analytical, focused and resistant to distraction. She felt a surge of relief. This *was* part of the game. She could not think why, but that would come in due course.

At her entrance, a man hit the table with a gavel and cried, 'Any other business!'

Gurney Thomes rose portentously to his feet. 'There has been a bizarre suggestion by the Artefacts Committee that two numbers in the Founder's portrait may hold a prophecy or other message. Miss Estella Scry, a *clairvoyant*, has offered us her professional opinion. I insisted on a no-win, no-fee arrangement.' As he preened himself, a reciprocal shiver of approval washed back. *Clairvoyant*; no-win, no-fee: the Master was so amusing.

Scry went from face to face, finding scepticism leavened with contempt. She would enjoy the turnaround. She delved into her handbag and produced her magnifying glass with a snake in search of its own tail coiled around the handle. She held it to the painting, which, propped on an easel, faced the court like a witness.

She quickly caught a second intriguing detail while Thomes delivered his previous analysis of the mysterious numbers with the same smugness.

'Listing their properties as numbers tells us nothing,' she announced. 'We must start with the letters in the sleeves.'

Her bald certainty earned a perceptible shift in attention. Necks craned; eyes focused on her.

'We are not *blind*, Miss Scry. The letters say "*vale*" on one and "*sum*" on the other – "farewell" and "I am".' Thomes spoke hastily, to emphasise that *of course* he had seen them too.

'Yes – and no,' said Scry.

'There's no "no" about it. That's what they say.'

She ignored the rebuke, inhaled deeply, and walked around the portrait with eyes half closed. 'He founded your Guild to last, yes?'

'Talk about a statement of the blindingly obvious!'

Scry responded with a saccharine smile. '"Farewell" and "I am" – isn't that rather tepid as a legacy from the founding father?'

Nobody spoke to the Master like this. Thomes turned puce. '"I live on through you" – what's *tepid* about that?'

Scry now fully closed her eyes, mimicking an appeal for divine assistance. 'Put the last letter or letters of each word first and we

have *levamus* – "may we rise". Now *that's* not so limp, Master Thomes.'
Her mind was racing, engaged by her discovery and its staggering
implications. She had been naïve. She should have realised Wynter
would have thought of *everything*.

'Rise? To what?'

'Power . . . power in Rotherweird.'

The faces looked at her, looked at each other, looked at the
painting, looked at Thomes, looked at her, riveted. They were not
so supercilious now.

'*May we rise to power!*' Thomes could barely suppress his excitement. 'When?'

'Ask the numbers, that's why they're there.' She retraced her steps,
fingering her necklace as she continued, face as deadpan as her
voice, 'For 7.49, read seven hours and forty-nine minutes; for 8.49,
read eight hours and forty-nine minutes. The first is the length of
sunlight on the shortest day of the year; the second the difference
in time between that and the longest day of the year. The Apothecaries may rise at the Winter Solstice – *this year's* Winter Solstice.'

Thomes flapped his hands in irritation. 'We are *scientists*, Madam.
The times you mention are *variables*. This is mumbo-jumbo.'

'Of course they're variables.' She allowed herself a hint of irritation in her own voice. '*That* is the point.'

Thomes fumbled his way to the light. 'You mean . . . You can't
mean—'

'Every year the figures will differ, just as they differ at different
latitudes. They are as precise as two pins, one on a calendar and
one on a map. On this year's solstice, at this *precise* latitude, the
Apothecaries may rise.' She let her hand brush his arm, an offer
of truce, now she understood the game. 'You were right to ask
me. Thank you.'

Thomes sharpened his goatee beard with his right hand and
turned to the assembly. 'We would never disappoint the Founder,
now, would we?' he declared with a flamboyant gesture.

The outburst of applause surprised them both, as if a long-suppressed energy had suddenly blossomed: the moment a rabble turns into an army.

Thomes could not quite bring himself to muster an express invitation, but he did manage it indirectly. 'We make far better liqueurs than Vlad's, Miss Scry.'

She followed him through the twisting corridors to his study, which lacked the crude ostentation of Snorkel's private chamber in the Town Hall, but could not possibly be called Puritan. Carvings of the finest quality gave the wall panelling and furniture an air of refinement. An antique Turkish rug looked made for the room, a perfect fit, wainscot to wainscot, the opulent colours faded by age, but the thick wool, warp and weft, intact. Behind Thomes' walnut pedestal desk and high-backed chair an ornate display cabinet held scientific books and instruments on alternate shelves. Scry glanced through the titles, which covered the evolution of science from its very beginnings. She understood now: Wynter could not return alone. He would need assistants, administrators, enforcers. He would need the Apothecaries.

'The quince loosens everyone's secrets,' Thomes said with a piercing, almost predatory look at Scry. A young Apothecary appeared, pulled out Thomes' chair, and then a second for Scry. Thomes dismissed her with a lordly tilt of the wrist. 'We may agree,' said Thomes, 'that the Founder would not leave such an instruction with no policy in mind. Power to what purpose is the question.'

'I do agree – and that's why you have to trust me.' She had one card left, but she bided her time. 'Your founder has an ingenious face. Tell me about him.'

'The *History Regulations* apply to us too,' replied Thomes.

She could see Thomes had a card too. 'No traditions handed down?'

The girl returned with a tray. The air-twist glasses, a technique requiring the finest materials, mirrored the rug and carvings for style. The decanter, half filled with a mellow amber liquid, had a ribbed waist; the glass was centuries old.

Thomes poured as the girl offered pale biscuits glazed with sugar.

'It is said he was the first Mayor.'

The liquid smeared the glass like oil, but it warmed the throat. The rich autumnal taste of quince with a thread of apple lingered long on the palate.

'I see on your shelves a first edition of the *Popular Choice Regulations*. 1650, to be exact.'

Thomes took out the book. 'You mean he authored it?'

'As the first Mayor, it's logical.'

She opened the book and turned to the frontispiece. Tiny letters centred at the bottom read:

Excudebat Sacheverell Vere
For the populace of Rotherweird

'Vale Sum – a V and an S: might they not also stand for Sacheverell Vere?'

'They're in the wrong order.'

'But we mix the letters, remember. And 1645 would precede your foundation.'

Thomes gulped the remains of his glass, cheeks flushed. 'Occasionally – *very* occasionally – we elect honorary members,' he said.

She left, as her clients often left her company, half enlightened and half disturbed. Only Wynter could be behind these interlocking clues. Her task had been to find a retinue to carry out the many tasks his rule would demand, and so far, so good. But Wynter's execution had preceded the foundation of the Apothecaries by a good seventy years, so Wynter could *not* have arranged Vere's portrait.

A reassuring answer struck her: the traitor Slickstone would have had the same problem: as Mayor, he would have needed enforcers too. She remembered him glad-handing the townsfolk at the Mayday Fair. He had planned to stand against Snorkel in the coming election – he could have doctored the portrait to seduce the Apothecaries.

She hadn't needed to take on Slickstone, so she had kept well away. After all, Wynter had prophesied that his 'most special Judas' would return to Rotherweird and self-destruct, and Wynter never misspoke in matters of prophecy. The gore below the mixing-point testified to that.

But she nursed a residual anxiety that this analysis did not fit the Slickstone she knew. He believed in his own power; he had never been one to cultivate allies.

There were two other possibilities, but surely not after all these years – not without a single sighting . . .

Her mind turned to her next, even harder assignment: to find and kill Fortemain, if indeed he still lived.

7

Fieldwork

From Arctic explorers to astronauts, from bathyspheres to *The Beagle*, no scientist had studied in such conditions, concluded Vixen Valourhand after two months in the spiderwoman's lair. The early days after Lost Acre's Midsummer renewal had been tranquil; the surviving creatures slow to re-emerge into the wrecked landscape.

Even during this halcyon period Valourhand kept close to the spiderwoman's front door. She never went out after dusk. She never killed unless attacked and studied only carcasses, found on the ground or snared in the wiry remains of the spiderwoman's webs. She took to picking them up with the fire tongs after discovering that some played dead, sprouting a disturbing selection of eyes, teeth and fangs when disturbed.

She designed a whole new vocabulary and built family trees, the better to catalogue this new world. Some fauna approximated to terrestrial life, especially trees with heavy seed and underground animals, being less likely to find their way into the mixing-point, but others were so far removed from their origins as to be almost unidentifiable. She found hidden attributes in simple exteriors – poison sacs, retractable wings and claws – and startling realignments of fur and feather, beak and bone.

She became so engrossed that previous loyalties to the company and the coming term at Rotherweird School slipped away. But for the note, penned in an old-fashioned hand, she would have remained a student of Lost Acre until taken by age or a passing predator. It appeared on the front door mat one morning, but in her disconnected state she did not think to consider who the postman might be.

Rotherweird needs you. The enemy has an ingenuity you can only guess at. The attached may be of interest.

She unfolded the enclosure, from the *Rotherweird Chronicle*, and read the name beneath a grainy photograph. The concluding paragraph announced a funeral procession, to be held in Market Square. With difficulty she translated the day and date into real time, only forty-eight hours away.

She had no interest in the rest of the obituary, for she had her own memories, an improbable friendship, given the traditional enmity between the North and South Tower Science Faculties – enabled by her attendance at a Bolitho lecture about antimatter entitled 'The Evil Twin'.

Afterwards, Valourhand had put to Bolitho the case for an anti-periodic table. He read her well, eschewing patter for hard science. Thereafter they sporadically discussed the mysteries of particle physics in his rooms. Bolitho patted her forearms with the palms of each hand when she entered and in time she understood it as an embrace with no threat of follow-up: respectful affection. He greeted nobody else in this fashion, and she let it become their ritual. Then came the distractions of her encounter with Sir Veronal Slickstone, her experiments with lightning and her visit to Lost Acre.

The news of Bolitho's death flipped her rating of her present existence like a coin. At a stroke, cutting-edge work turned amateurish: a physicist trying out biology and advancing nobody's interests, including her own. She burned the carcasses, tidied the kitchen and sorted her papers as she re-engaged with reality. Who had delivered the letter? The front door was tight to the floor, yet the envelope showed no sign of friction. Who was the 'enemy' to whom the author referred? Wynter, Calx Bole – or someone else? How did the author know she was here? And why call on *her* to help Rotherweird? She finally remembered the new term. She had courses to plan.

She set off at noon in search of the white tile.

Rotherweird needs you. The letter felt like a call to arms.

8

Eulogy Dress

Absent-mindedness commonly accompanied the forensic precision of Rotherweird's scientific minds, and the post office catered for this frailty with its Delayed Action Service, where letters and parcels could be left for delivery weeks or months later. Within days of Vesey Bolitho's demise, the Service delivered a letter to Boris Polk.

A week before his death, his old friend had told Boris to expect the unexpected at his funeral, so the Professor's instructions came as no surprise. He was to collect a firework from the South Tower and install it on the eve of the funeral procession; the coordinates for location, the angle of lift-off and the time of ignition were all minutely specified. More immediately, he was to visit Bolitho's tailor for further orders.

Clasping a huge pair of scissors, which he sporadically snapped open and shut like a lobster, the tailor was out of sorts.

'I cut a mean cloth, Mr Polk, but I draw the line at all-in-ones.' Behind the tailor two racks held rows of baggy black overalls. 'There's a B guest list and an A guest list: you're to deliver to the As, I to the Bs. I fear the Professor went loopy at the end.'

While the tailor crammed one rack into two carrier bags, Boris scanned his list: the usual suspects – himself, Fanguin, Jones, Oblong – with two mild surprises in Gorhambury and Valourhand. Neither seemed natural Bolitho friends, Gorhambury for his lack of mischief and Valourhand as a rival from the North Tower.

'What about the B-list?' he asked.

'Favourite pupils, past and present. And you, Mr Polk, you alone are privileged to wear this number.' With a lopsided grin and another snap of the scissors, the tailor handed Polk an identical costume, save for an unbecoming belt encrusted with buckles and a large circle at the midriff. 'Turn the centre at 7.04 p.m. precisely,' said the tailor, adding wryly, 'Yes, *that* loopy.'

Boris left to last his most testing delivery – Snorkel had installed defences to shield his Town Clerk from common citizens during working hours.

'Ask Public Cleaning services, third floor, second left,' said Reception.

'Ask Licensing, third floor, second landing, first on the right,' said Public Cleaning.

'Ask Rent Collection, fourth floor, at the end of the long corridor,' said Licensing.

On being informed that his visit related to Professor Bolitho's funeral, the lady in Rent Collection, an amateur stargazer, relented.

Gorhambury's office lurked in a first-floor byway off the grander passages of the Mayoral Suite. With his reinstatement, his files had been returned to their former positions in cardboard drums with green plastic tops. They dotted the floor like mushrooms. On his desk, lines of paperclips, colour-coded by subject, awaited commitment to the fray.

He lowered his desk lamp closer to paragraph 3(1)(y)(iv) of the recently amended *Tower Refurbishment Regulations*:

> The cost of repairs to walkways between towers of different ownership shall be born in proportion to the height (2 points), circumference (2 points) and number of rooms (half a point each) of the respective towers, save where the repairs relate

to the entry point to a tower, when the costs shall be borne by the owner of that tower unless caused by subsidence or turbulence originating in the other tower, in which event the Tower Inspector shall exercise reasonable discretion in the matter.

Gorhambury felt a twinge of admiration at the clarity of his own prose, while regretting the lack of an immediate answer to the present appeal, which concerned an onset of dry rot away from the entry point, but in a beam that ran to the front door. What did *fairness* suggest? What about *policy*?

A solution was taking shape when a spectral figure glided in without knocking and sat in the solitary chair opposite Gorhambury's desk. Skeletal fingers grasped the armrests. Mors Valett, the municipal undertaker, looked agitated. 'The Mayor fears a disorderly procession,' he began. 'Knowing the lead mourners, I share his anxiety.'

The *Funeral Regulations* required the first two dozen mourners to be notified to the Town Hall forty-eight hours before the procession. Bolitho's cortège had more than a sprinkling of the artistic and unorthodox.

'I have had assurances – respectful music, no dancing, no carnival. The Headmaster will make a brief address in the Square. The internment will be private.'

'You do realise, Gorhambury, these "respectful" mourners include a trio of misfits: a sacked teacher, an outsider and a party-wrecker.' Gorhambury translated with ease: Godfery Fanguin, Jonah Oblong and Vixen Valourhand. 'I can also report that Boris Polk has been seen with a giant firework.'

'It's that time of year.'

'What's got into you, Gorhambury? Vulcan's Dance is weeks away.'

Vulcan's Dance, Rotherweird's annual firework day, fell this year in early December, but Gorhambury could hardly say that Valett's 'trio of misfits' had helped to save Rotherweird, or that Sir Veronal had not been what he appeared. Still less could he mention his own invitation to join the lead mourners. Gorhambury had navigated Bolitho's planning application for a planetarium through the shoals of the *Scholastic Building Regulations*, because he equated the workings of the heavens with how a town should be run: like clockwork.

Boris Polk, ear to the door, chose this moment to make his entry. 'One mourner's gown,' he announced, depositing the garment on Gorhambury's desk and shattering the parade-ground order of the paperclips.

'Gown?' queried Gorhambury, for whom gowns were vestments of authority requiring the highest sartorial standards.

'The Mayor is not wearing one of those. And nor am I,' declared Valett.

Boris parried the sideswipe. 'I should hope not. They're for family and friends.'

'*I'm* to wear this?' asked Gorhambury in pained surprise. When Boris grinned, he added, 'I suppose it's more inelegant than offensive.'

'Over your own heads be it,' punned Valett, now at ease. He and the Mayor would stand out: figures of dignity, apart from the riff-raff.

After Valett's departure, Gorhambury enquired about the giant firework.

'It's meticulously made to Bolitho's specifications,' Boris assured him.

Gorhambury quoted Richard II as he restored the paperclips to running order. '*I wasted time, and now doth time waste me . . .*'

Boris took the hint and retired. At the foot of the Town Hall steps a notice on the official board caught his eye.

THE SNORKEL ESSAY PRIZE

The Town Hall in its vigilant search for improvement invites essays on

'How government should work'

Open to ages from 21-30

1,500 words maximum

Closing date: 20th November

Prize to be decided

The implicit concession that improvement might be needed struck Boris as out of character for Snorkel, but then, in theory at least, a quinquennial election loomed. The old autocrat must be feeling uneasy.

9

The Winter Solstice Special

Bolitho had played shy of *Baubles & Relics*, peering in the window without entering, but occasionally slipping a shopping list through the letter-box. His last, delivered days before his death, followed the formula of its predecessors:

Find any of these on your travels and I'll double the money (cash):

1. The Savoy Cocktail Book by Harry Craddock (1930)
2. Plate 8, Mammals illustrated by Archibald Thorburn (1921)
3. Kepler's Mysterium Cosmographicum (any edition)

Orelia Roc had had no success with these recondite errands, and Bolitho remained a relative stranger. Deciding that such a vague acquaintanceship did not justify attendance at his funeral procession but that the shop could hardly be open as it passed, she set off for the library in the hope of making progress in the matter of Calx Bole.

Privately, she criticised the company for complacency since the dramatic events of Midsummer Day. Bole, the shapeshifter, was still out there and Wynter's last words from the official record of his trial – '*I will be back. Vengeance will be mine, and another will pave the way*' – jangled in her head. The Wynter of the tapestry, with his cold, angular face, did not strike her as a man who spoke loosely. The second and third of those prophecies had already been fulfilled with the arrival of Calx Bole and the destruction of Sir Veronal in the mixing-point; now only Wynter's own return remained. And yet everyone had gravitated back to their everyday lives as if the threat no longer mattered. According to Bill Ferdy, even the ever-alert Ferensen had retreated to his tower.

She walked against a steady flow of women with dark ribbons in their hair, men in black-banded hats, children with star-spangled flags, all flocking to pay their respects to a much-loved cult figure.

The funeral had drained the library of custom. She drifted from bay to bay without success, unsurprising given such a faceless enemy and the *History Regulations*.

Madge Brown, the Assistant Head Librarian, marooned in reception, looked in need of company. Orelia asked after her unlikely new friend.

'Gorhambury's horribly buttoned up, but I shall persevere.' She gestured at the *Rotherweird Regulations*, the valley's legal code, lined up on the shelf behind her. 'Spot the odd man *out?*' she asked with a wink.

'Volume seventeen,' replied Orelia – hardly a taxing question, given their arrangement in numerical order.

'The *Popular Choice Regulations* have been out for rebinding for *months*.' Another wink.

Orelia's blood boiled at Snorkel's chicanery. *Rebinding!* 'How do I get a copy?' she asked.

'Try the Hoy Book Fair – old Rotherweird volumes often surface there.'

'I've never heard of it,' she admitted. The *History Regulations* made antique books a difficult sell. Segregating the abstract novel from the historical had always been a challenge.

'There's a law against going – but as the law is out for binding . . .' This time Madge raised both eyebrows; Orelia was finding her less mousy by the minute. 'Try the barrows in the churchyard,' Madge suggested. 'You get all sorts there.'

Curiosity piqued, Orelia could not resist. 'When is this Fair?'

Madge's voice lowered to a whisper. 'Saturday week – but the gates will be shut.' Looking guilty, she returned to a card index and started diligently refiling.

Orelia tried the upper floor, but it shed no light on Rotherweird's electoral rules. However, a shelf labelled *Digressions and Diversions* included back copies of the *Rotherweird Chronicle*'s daily Puzzle Page, filed in date order.

Why had she not thought of it before? Calx Bole had set *Chronicle* crosswords under the name *Shapeshifter*. She had never had any aptitude for crossword clues and she loathed the way Bole used the craft to tantalise pursuers and trumpet his own cleverness. Now she discovered that Shapeshifter had compiled this year's Winter Solstice Special, a double-size puzzle already printed, with the solution to be published on the day itself.

She found two clues that stood out for their lack of any apparent connection with winter. The first was impenetrable: *Shown badly behaved flirt, Royal rages in empty house* (3, 5, 4, 5). The second, by contrast, could hardly have been easier: *Actualité stitched up* (4) – with two simple answers, *news* or *sewn*. At least this double anagram could not hide a third, there being no other word with the same letters.

She debated with whom to share these conundra. Ferensen's aloofness still unnerved her. Neither Fanguin, nor the Polks, nor Gregorius Jones could be relied on for gravity. Salt and Valourhand were unreliable in different ways, and she had no wish to resume any intimacy with Oblong. That left Finch, who had not been seen for weeks. She liked the Herald, but she suspected he would liaise with Ferensen and once again she'd lose control.

She postponed a decision on the speculative ground that the Hoy Book Fair might bring further enlightenment.

On her way out she tried Madge Brown. 'Do you do the *Chronicle* crosswords?'

'If I'm on the same wavelength, I manage about half on a good day, but I've never finished one. They're so bloody devious.'

'Who compiles them?'

'They alternate – *Cryptic, Crostic, Shapeshifter, Clever Soul* . . . and others; there are loads of them.'

'*Clever Soul?* How modest!'

'It's an anagram of "clue solver".'

Orelia could imagine the type. 'Who are they really?'

'Nobody knows. They're true *noms de plume*, so there's no risk of bribes or favouritism. The crossword world is fiercely competitive.'

A violent explosion rattled the windows. Vesey Bolitho was not going out with a whimper.

10

Last Rites

In the main School Quad, Mors Valett, immaculately attired in tailcoat and black top hat, was delivering a stream of orders through a loud-hailer. 'Five minutes and his Worship arrives, so let's have order. Some of you may be teachers, but today you're the class. Band – over here!'

Eighteen pupils shuffled into position in the middle of the Quad: strings first, then wind, with brass at the back, and, beside them, the solitary bass drum. Two strongly built boys carried a curious instrument between them: Bolitho's invention, a *stellarium*, which looked not unlike a chest expander with five strings attached to a metal strip at both ends.

Other pupils wore the dubious handiwork of Bolitho's tailor.

The Head of Music carried his baton and a lightweight music stand. Bolitho's final composition defied all rules, more *sound* than music. *Why not end with Rotherweird's traditional fare?* 'The Last Rick-shaw Ride' and the poignant 'Riverman's Lament' were favourites for a reason. Why tamper with the old ways? He could not wait for the whole event to be over.

'Lead mourners here!' shrilled Valett, placing them by his assess-ment of their social standing. Rhombus Smith, spared one of the tailor's creations, stood next to Gorhambury in the front row; Fanguin and Valourhand made up the last row with Oblong; the Polks and Gregorius Jones occupied semi-respectable middle ground. The remainder, mostly staff and a select few sixth-formers, tucked in behind their Headmaster.

Punctual to the minute, the mayoral rickshaw drew up at the school gate. 'The things I do for this town,' muttered Snorkel to his driver.

The Mayor's costume excelled even Valett's in pristine formality, and was enhanced by the ceremonial Malacca stick which only he was permitted to carry. Snorkel said nothing beyond, 'Keep it short, if you want to be here next term!' to the Headmaster, and, 'What the hell are you wearing?' to Gorhambury.

The drum called the pace as the procession wended its way along the Golden Mean and Snorkel heaved a sigh of relief. Paying respects *should* be respectful. Children gently waved their flags; adults inclined their heads – there was no applause, no rudery. His sense of a chore receded as he noticed most of the town had turned out to say their farewells. He puffed out his chest, a pose befitting the embodiment of Rotherweird's communal spirit.

As the procession passed, spectators abandoned the pavements to join on behind. Dusk fell and the shawl of the Milky Way glimmered. There was no moon, only the yellowish smudge of Saturn. *Planets don't flicker, suns do*: Bolitho's first nugget in his First Form guide to the night sky.

In Market Square, Valett reordered the procession before a temporary rostrum by the Town Hall steps: lead mourners directly ahead, musicians either side of them, the public behind rows of temporary barriers. As Rhombus Smith ascended the steps, the hands of Doom's Tocsin moved to ten to seven. Snorkel gave Valett and Gorhambury a cursory nod of approval: all orderly, all in place, all moving like clockwork.

A low sandbank where the tributary girding the Island Field rejoined the Rother provided a registered ignition point under the *Firework Regulations*. Vulcan's Dance, Rotherweird's firework day, fell on the last moonless night before the Winter Solstice, so today, Polk's giant firework and the large wooden tube containing it had no company.

At ten to seven, the timer took effect: seals broke, chemicals mixed and the ten-minute ignition programme began to run.

Rhombus Smith commenced his funeral address by raising a silver flask above his head like a chalice.

'I give you Vesey's finest creation, the Sea of Tranquillity – the most inappropriately named cocktail in the mixologist's lexicon.' The Headmaster took a swig. Eyes popped, his voice dropped an octave and he found eloquence. 'Light lives on centuries after the death of its owning star, as will Vesey in the memories of his pupils. Repeat after me: "*My versifying elephant . . .*"'

The audience accepted the cue, reciting with *brio* Bolitho's mnemonic for the order of the planets: '*My versifying elephant mixes jolly strong uplifting negritas pensively!*'

Mercury, Venus, Earth, Mars . . .

'Smith's bloody pissed,' hissed Snorkel over his shoulder, but irritation eased as the Headmaster moved smoothly to straightforward biography.

'Bolitho's parents sold our learning in Paris and he didn't return until late middle age to realise his dream of an Astronomy faculty . . .'

After a few choice anecdotes, the headmaster chose Tennyson to close:

> '*For tho' from out our bourne of Time and Place*
> *The flood may bear me far,*
> *I hope to see my Pilot face to face*
> *When I have cross'd the bar.*'

Doom's Tocsin struck seven of the evening: Bolitho's chime, the cocktail hour. Seconds after the final peal, Polk's rocket detonated to shattering effect, emitting a mass of dark and silver shapes. Across the sky these opposed particles hunted each other down, self-destructing on collision, causing secondary explosions: a spectacular battle between matter and antimatter, angels and demons. As the crowd cheered, Snorkel's outrage yielded to a desire to take credit for anything of appeal to potential electors. He nodded sagely.

Then there was silence; the Head of Music strode to the rostrum and raised his baton. He had not rehearsed this hotchpotch of notes – who could? Instruments were readied. The two musicians with the *stellarium* swayed, stretching the strings with one hand, lofting bows in the other. Snorkel glared at Valett, who glared at Gorhambury. What was going on? Had these people never heard of the *Funeral Regulations*?

The violins started precipitously high, an astral sound just short of where the human register gives way to the canine, then the cellos joined in, oscillating low, followed by the *stellarium* with an eerie note like a finger rubbed round the rim of a glass. The bass drum entered quietly, no more than a pulse, while horns and woodwind intervened with single held notes. To Snorkel, the resulting jangle sounded like the worst kind of modernism, but more receptive ears sensed a crescendo: *something* was about to happen.

7.04 p.m. Boris turned the medal-like ring on the front of his belt full circle. The music matched his cue.

'Gorhambury, what the hell's going on?' Snorkel had the frenetic look of a control freak with no control.

'It's just music,' spluttered Gorhambury, clasping his stomach to relieve what felt like a tremor of indigestion.

'Gorhambury!' Now scarlet, Snorkel pointed at Gorhambury's midriff, which was swelling fast and beginning to glow.

In the costumes a network of fine wire and chemicals activated, connected and reacted. At first Gregorius Jones feared his prize asset, his physique, had suffered an adverse reaction from years of training, but as his costume inflated and took him skywards, blessed relief overwhelmed him: *sartorial* forces were at work. Valett tried to hold Gorhambury down, but succeeded in rescuing only a shoe.

Snorkel shivered with rage as the Head of Music shouted, 'Play on!' and the orchestra, briefly stalled, recovered its poise.

'*Yes!*' cried Valourhand, clenching her fist in celebration of the posthumous reach of Bolitho's sense of mischief and the discomfort of the powers that be.

A deeper realisation dawned: the costumes now had single glowing letters on their chests – *p*, *n* and *e* – and as a waltz motif emerged, their movements cohered in a stately celestial dance. Valourhand glanced down at her own chest to see a red *e*. To her irritation she found herself orbiting a South Tower scientist, an unimposing young man with buck teeth. More groups of two formed, and two groups of six with two white *n*s and two red *p*s, orbited by two blue *e*s. The floating sixth-formers whooped with pleasure. It did not feel like a funeral.

We're playing atomic particles, concluded everyone except an ignorant Oblong: protons, neutrons and electrons, forming hydrogen atoms for the couples and helium for the groups of six. Bolitho had recreated the first two atoms in the periodic table, the early children of the Big Bang. Every face in Market Square peered up, transfixed, but Vixen felt unsettled as well as entranced – all this just for show?

'Bloody brilliant!' shouted her proton, floating around her.

'Bloody Bolitho!' she shouted back. They said nothing more as they continued circling each other in the eternal *pas de deux* of the hydrogen atom.

The tailor gawped, promotional slogans coming and going, 'the sky's the limit' and 'dress for the stars' among them.

Gregorius Jones, in a sextet with members of his class, found mid-air suspension ideal for new gymnastic exercises. 'Arms out!'

'Sir?'

'Legs akimbo!'

'Sir!'

His pupils caught on and followed suit, adding to the grotesquery.

Gorhambury found suspension strangely therapeutic, worldly worries ebbing away as Bolitho's astral music washed over him. The asymmetry of Rotherweird's tangle of towers and streets had a peculiar beauty.

A mellifluous singing voice intervened – Fanguin.

> 'A life on the ocean wave,
> A home on the rolling deep . . .'

'Fanguin, this is a funeral.'

Chastened, Fanguin stopped, but the spell was broken. Where he had seen perfection, Gorhambury now saw troubling details – a missing slate here, a crooked weathervane there. He made a mental note of their location as the orchestra picked up pace and the floating atomic particles spiralled ever faster above Market Square.

Oblong's unique costume bore no *e*, *p* or *n*, only a glowing representation of Rotherweird's skyline, and it held him stationary over Market Square not far above the sloping roof of Doom's Tocsin. Unfamiliar words tripped into his head – 'karma', 'transcendental', 'out-of-body experience' – he was high enough to be amazed, low enough not to be frightened, as an ocean of faces looked up from ground level, windows and walkways, a forest of arms beside them all pointing at *him*: Oblong, the privileged soloist, with Rotherweird emblazoned on his chest. Bolitho had in death endorsed him.

Oblong had no idea what the scientific symbols represented, only that Bolitho had bequeathed a message about the beauty of the universe: lucky to have lived in it, lucky to have understood it.

High above, the last stage of the rocket, still descending by parachute, released its payload: a silent volley of light and dark streamers which chased each other between the dancing atomic particles.

Oblong's costume juddered alarmingly in the nether regions. His skin prickled, seconds before an explosive *whoosh* propelled him high into space: a human cannonball corkscrewing as he went. The pitch of his screams diminished as he rose, a useful illustration of the Doppler effect, Valourhand noted, for future lessons on the subject.

Then peace and Bolitho's performers descended.

A sustained melodic chord and a tinkling effect from the *stellarium* accompanied the atomic particles to earth. Oblong too floated down. The glowing townscape on his chest faded, as did the letters on the other costumes.

Valourhand alone careered south over the walls into the deserted countryside beyond. Irritation at the malfunction morphed to apprehension as the suit rushed her past the Island Field to Rotherweird's borderland and into a sharp descent towards a roar of threshing water. Skin and hair turned damp: she was closing on the Pool of Mixed Intentions, where the Rother plunged out of sight and where coins were cast to the river god.

She tugged her sleeves and waved her legs, but the elasticated wrists and ankles and the clinging effect of the moisture frustrated any attempts to steer, until within feet of the water, the costume changed gear for the last time and veered away to land her on the western bank.

She looked east across the river to the marsh. Clouds were scudding in: it looked as if, with Bolitho's procession done, the night sky wished to veil her face. She could make out the cairn known as the Tower of the Winds atop the only prominence in an expanse of marshland.

The exhilaration of the flight had passed. Teeth chattering, she set off to town at a brisk jog, only to pull up minutes later at the sight and smell of excrement smearing the bank. The stench was vile and acrid, the colour grey-green, the surface flecked with fragments of bone. Valourhand gathered a sample in her handkerchief and resumed her progress home.

*

Boris Polk, Mors Valett and Rhombus Smith adjourned to the churchyard. The priest delivered a short service, which ended with a reading of Bolitho's self-authored funerary inscription:

'Earth to sky and sky to earth,
Matter matters in rebirth,
Sky to earth and earth to sky,
Life's mutations do not die.'

The wicker coffin lay on a low, wheeled wooden trolley, its sides carved with winged lions.

In the shadow of a yew a gifted pupil played a haunting nocturne on the alto sax. Boris affected to apply a handkerchief to the nose while drying his eyes.

Valett waited for everyone else to leave before summoning a minion to wheel the coffin into Rotherweird's underground mausoleum.

Rhombus Smith rarely defied the Town Hall. Harmonious coexistence between Rotherweird's leading institutions mattered. For Bolitho's funeral he made an exception. He had altered the text of his speech, added Bolitho's astral piece to the musical programme and, last but not least, authorised a transformation of Market Square – a wake on school premises would have been anathema to this man of the *boulevards*.

Within minutes of the last atomic particle returning to earth, a posse of well-rehearsed sixth-formers had set up school chairs and tables around the square, placing candles and cocktail glasses on blue and red checked tablecloths. Few present, including Rhombus Smith, had ever been to Paris, Bolitho's youthful hunting ground, but candles, *al fresco* drinking and street music represented their *idea* of Paris. Accordions and fiddles struck up as Jones filled jugs from a milk churn: Bolitho's late final cocktail, the Press Up.

The Square exhaled a heady mix of mango, Cointreau and gin.

Stale cake, tepid tea and platitudes formed the staple diet of Rotherweird post-funeral procession get-togethers. Bolitho's *fête* broke the mould. The Square echoed to two repeated questions: whose choreography, and what did it mean?

Oblong found neither table nor companion; instead, he stood alone and sulked over his ignominious descent in front of so many upturned faces disfigured by laughter. He caught – or rather, he *imagined* he caught – sidelong glances and smirks, hostile whispers or sarcastic jokes, all targeted at him. Nobody had commiserated.

He patted the rear of his costume, fearful of a second ignition.

Orelia entered the Square, despondent at having missed an unmiss-able occasion. Oblong looked as though he had missed out too.

'You look pale,' she said with what Oblong took to be a mocking smile, and a restraining chord snapped in his usually unexcitable mind.

'As if you're all so bloody marvellous,' he said with a sweeping gesture. 'Fanguin drinks too much. Finch always knows best. Boris never invents anything *really* useful. Valourhand is frankly mad.' He nearly added for good measure, *And Bolitho is dead!*

Orelia took a step back. 'And me?'

Emotions fanned by Press Ups, he found a stinging reply. 'Easy come, easy go.'

Orelia turned away, appalled that she had once harboured feel-ings for this rude, hapless outsider.

Oblong, no less hurt, stormed off.

Meanwhile Madge Brown, fresh from the library, collared her new friend Gorhambury. 'Did anyone land on a chimney? Get hooked on a weathervane?'

The librarian had a point, for everyone had touched down safely, many in the narrow streets leading on to Market Square. Bolitho had either been extraordinarily precise in his calculations, or his cast had been extraordinarily lucky – and if the former, statistically the favoured view, the Professor must have devoted *months* to his grand finalé, long before his illness had been declared.

The thought troubled Gorhambury. Deeper questions simmered beneath the surface.

In search of merrier company, Orelia sat down beside Fanguin, who, between gulps and refills, delivered an outline narrative and a verdict. 'I'm flummoxed.'

'You look flummoxed.'

'They're all hung up on the Big Bang: they think it was a demo, a cheery *envoi*, life born out of the dark. *But* . . .' Fanguin lifted his Press Up and steadied it as if to prove his sobriety. 'They overlook Oblong.'

'I only saw from a distance – there were people flying.'

'We played the particles which make up hydrogen and helium atoms – and most nuclear matter in the universe. And there was a big bang.'

'So far, so obvious,' muttered Orelia, bluffing. Educated outside Rotherweird, she had minimal physics.

'But why does Oblong with Rotherweird on his vest rocket up like a cork from a bottle?'

'Do tell – how high?'

'Almost out-of-sight high – he shrieked like a banshee, poor sod.'

'How awful,' giggled Orelia, infected by *Schadenfreude*.

'Quite. Bolitho liked Oblong – so what's he telling us? And why send Valourhand haring off into the countryside? Double flummoxed.'

Orelia remembered a comment by Oblong during their brief intimacy. She lowered her voice. 'Bolitho once gave Oblong a private demonstration in the planetarium. He hinted at a moment in time when prodigies were conceived and suggested a connection with Rotherweird's origins. He knew more than he let on.' She slipped in an illicit question prompted by Madge Brown's intelligence. 'What do you know of the Hoy Book Fair?'

Fanguin breathed in deeply, as if sampling another miraculous vintage. 'Think wider England. Think the 1640s.'

Orelia had not expected such a reply. She wagged a cautionary finger; he had slipped the leash. You did *not* discuss the deep past in Rotherweird – indeed, you shouldn't know about it.

He withdrew further into shadow, lowered his voice and continued, 'Democracy is baring her teeth; there's civil war and regicide. Rotherweird is not immune to these currents. An elected Mayor replaces the Herald and, to avoid the *History Regulations*, candidates go to Hoy to talk politics. Rotherweirders follow and Hoy folk, always a commercially minded bunch, sell them old things, forbidden fruit, especially books. The event evolves into a Fair, held before every Rotherweird election year. A new Mayor soon has second thoughts and amends the *Popular Choice Regulations* so now the Fair must do without Rotherweirders. But it remained a Hoy fixture and continues – and not just before Rotherweird's election, but every year.'

'How do you know all this?' she whispered, feeling conspiratorial, and better for it.

Fanguin gestured flamboyantly, as if it were natural genius, before owning up. 'Madge Brown tipped me the wink after Snorkel gave me the sack. She said I needed an away day. She recommended a local dealer called *Broken Spines* who sold me a history of Hoy.' Fanguin reacted to another wagging finger. 'All right, so it's history, but what can they do to me now? I've no job and no future.'

Poor Fanguin, cast aside for the sin of befriending Flask and for his insatiable curiosity.

'All library copies of the *Popular Choice Regulations* have been withdrawn by the Town Hall for *rebinding*,' she told him.

'The canny bugger!'

'Madge Brown suggested the Fair.'

Fanguin had the glint of combat in his eye. 'Mark my words: come Saturday week, the gate will be closed. Nobody in, nobody out.'

Fanguin's radical disregard for the law emboldened Orelia, and she shared with him the location of Salt's secret door in the outer wall and his hidden coracle. 'Six a.m.?' she suggested, her blood up too.

Fanguin considered. 'We'll need outsider currency.'

'A travelling buyer *always* has currency,' she said grandly. 'I do generous rates, no commission.'

Fanguin was beaming like a rewarded child when Boris joined them, looking uncharacteristically anxious. 'I've been burgled.'

Fanguin chuckled; Boris' untidiness was as legendary as his twin's sense of good order. 'How on earth did they find anything?'

'I created a sheet of invisibility film – not for export to the wider world, or here, just a frolic, but it's vanished . . . I think.' Boris came clean. 'The ingredients cost a pretty penny, and I haven't told Bert.'

Orelia could only smile – vanishing invisibility film was the point, surely. He had doubtless mislaid it.

'It'll turn up when you least expect it,' added Fanguin unhelpfully.

Oblong slammed the front door of his tower flat, fuming. He could not begin to fathom why he had been singled out for such humiliating treatment. How they had cheered and jeered! He penned a letter of resignation. If Rotherweird did not want him, he did not want them.

Then a cautionary voice broke in: in the outside world he had no qualifications, no job and nowhere to live. Rotherweird offered work and novelty, from subterranean passages to crewing a coracle, quite apart from their darker adventures.

His thoughts turned to Orelia and he realised she had been normally dressed, so not part of the celestial dance. Indeed, he had not seen her during the procession. And who would not look pale after being propelled into the heavens? He just might have been unfair. 'Easy come, easy go' had not only not been merited, it was plain rude. Shuddering, he replayed his onslaught. He had struck at his friends, one by one – Finch, Fanguin, Boris, Valourhand and Orelia.

Rage became wretchedness. He replaced his resignation letter with the following:

Dear Orelia,

Apologies – I really did not mean what I said. Consider me scrambled by space flight and press ups.

Jonah O x

Gorhambury, homebound, reflected on his aerial view of the town. He saw the body politic with the Golden Mean as the spine, the roads and lanes as limbs and arteries and the Town Hall as the head. This body was in perpetual need of sustenance, repair, training, self-discipline and governance – and without a head, the body could not administer such complex functions. Changing a head which worked struck Gorhambury as a precarious exercise . . . and yet, might change lead to improvement in unexpected directions? The founding fathers must have thought so.

Democracy or enlightened despotism? The argument raged in his head. Perhaps the people should choose.

Plop! Another miss as the ball of paper bounced along the carpet, soundlessly, so rich was the pile, to nestle beside its companions near a basket some ten feet from Snorkel's desk. Snorkel's despair deepened as he scrunched and threw another essay prize entry. They had, without exception, been unremittingly dim, bland and impractical, the products of honed academic minds without a glimmer of political nous.

The evening's events had cut him to the quick. His network of spies had failed to scent the chaos to come, and worse, the crowd had relished the occasion. Was his confidence in Rotherweird's conservatism misplaced?

He needed a kindred spirit, someone with energy and vision to nurture his destiny – and his dynasty.

Fanguin, homebound, made five mistakes, each a consequence of the one before. First, he could not resist recourse to his whisky flask. Second, he could not resist singing in a loud voice a ribald song entitled 'What the Dromedary said to the Camel'. Third, so rapt was he in the magnificence of his own performance that he did not see the Gatehouse guards walking towards him. Fourth, he misinterpreted their polite attempts to silence him as an attempted assassination. Fifth, he fought.

Estella Scry watched the procession and its aftermath from the north bedroom window balcony. She disliked the joshing cama-raderie on view – centuries of self-imposed solitude had drained her of empathy – but she admired in the pyrotechnics an unusual mind at work, a breaker of moulds. She had never met Professor Bolitho, who had kept to the School. The *stellarium*'s shimmer of abstract sound reinforced an intriguing thought ... Surely not? But why not? Her fingers worked at the silk cuffs of her shirt as concern slipped into ecstasy. *Oh please, do make it so.* Vengeance and fulfilment beckoned.

She descended to her sitting room and polished her sculpture. *Keep focus, keep discipline.*

Come the next stormy night, she would go exploring.

11

Hangover

Denzil Prim, Head Gaoler of Rotherweird Prison, had a fine line in gallows humour. 'Coming as a paying guest, Mr Finch? We 'aven't 'ad one of those since Mad Wally Herbert. Once he were out, he'd break another window just to get back in. He loved the nosh, he did.'

Marmion Finch, Rotherweird's Herald and sole denizen of the *archivoire*, the great library chamber in Escutcheon Place where the town's secret historical records were kept, raised his bushy eyebrows in recognition of Prim's wit, a throwaway price for his co-operation. The prison, set into the cliff at the northeastern edge of the town, languished in darkness and damp. Few others shared Wally Herbert's enthusiasm.

'I'd like a view of the old cells, if you have the time.'

'Time – there's a word; 'ere we *do* time, we don't 'ave it. And no point planning escapes, Mr Finch, a dog couldn't get through them windows. They're set in solid rock, and the bars go down and down and down.' Prim's voice descended as if to stress the point.

'Carvings are my business, Mr Prim. I have to record them all – whatever, wherever, and however ancient. I heard a whisper . . .'

'Ah, you'll be meaning Cell One – the oldest, the deepest, the dampest – I'd only put takers of life in there.'

Precedent there, thought Finch, but it being history, he kept it to himself.

Prim led Finch down a meandering passage. The first cells had modern steel doors with narrow grilles through which Prim and his underlings could check on the occupants.

'You timed your visit well, Mr Finch. We've just the one rowdy cooling off.' He rattled a grille as he passed. 'They gets a table and a nice lamp with a floral shade. Mind you, we're less accommodating on the sanitaries.'

The deeper they went, the danker the atmosphere became. Two cells with doors of ancient oak hunched round a circular chamber at the end of the final passage. The moisture prickled Finch's skin.

'Cell number one,' announced Prim, 'for the *crème de la crème*, or should I say, the *crimes des crimes*. And there be your carvings.'

A solitary window offered a faintly glowing parallelogram hatched with bars on the opposite wall. Finch blinked several times, then scuffed his shoe on the flagstone floor. It was slick with a covering of moss. He trailed his torch across the walls, which in the gloom had a patterned appearance. Up close he saw shapes everywhere, cut into the rock – shapes with a hint of the three-dimensional, abstract-looking, despite their age. Some repeated and some were more finished, suggesting a process of trial and error.

'We have postcards,' added Prim, 'but they never sell.'

'Yes, please, whatever you have.'

'Uh-oh,' muttered Prim, peering back down the passage, "ere comes trouble.'

'Trouble' took the form of a handsome middle-aged woman with a pale but pleasant face, scarlet lipstick, swathes of dark hair and a forthright stride.

'Good morning,' said Prim, cursing his assistant for allowing her in at such an early hour.

'Yours may be,' Mrs Fanguin replied. 'Where is the blithering idiot?'

'Sorry,' mumbled the cell door.

'Mercifully, Madam, orders are: ten guineas for overnight accommodation and a signed recognisance of twenty guineas for good behaviour. Of course, if he wants a full-blown trial, he can have one.'

'Done,' she said, handing over a ten-guinea note.

Finch extricated himself from Fanguin's pending retribution and resumed his analysis above ground. Only cells one and two were old enough and had the river view, but the symbols in cell one decided the issue.

Among Wynter's trial papers Finch had stumbled on a fragmentary report of his incarceration. The accused had shown 'strange tempers', calling through his cell window at night to the river below and carving the walls with the edge of his irons. Wynter's carvings had achieved remarkable precision for such a crude instrument. More disturbing, Wynter had been viciously attacked in his cell, suffering 'wounds most unnatural'. The perpetrator had such a striking likeness to the under-gaoler that he had passed through without challenge, only for the gaoler to be found days later, strangled in a ditch. Oxenbridge's report suggested the intervention of 'dark magicks'.

Finch had a more rational explanation: Calx Bole, shapeshifting, had been the intruder. But why would Bole, the faithful servant, attack his own master? For not the first time in recent months, Finch had the uncomfortable sensation that the talons of the past were clawing at the present, but he could not articulate why.

Old History

Fortemain has a head full of stars and this cerebral universe swarms with questions. How do they hang? Who or what sets their seasonal movement so exactly? Why do most oscillate when a few (the planets, according to Sir Henry) glow still as a lamp? In the other place the stars are inverted, yet their light and arrangement are otherwise the same – how can this be?

A quiet young man, he opposes Wynter more by action than words. Wynter knows he is hostile, but he and Bole agree: the other place's contrary sky holds secrets that only Fortemain can unravel. He is permitted to use Grassal's optical instruments in the Tower of Knowledge but his work must be shared, and his precious sheets of parchment are numbered to police this condition. For Fortemain, study is escape. He habitually works into the early hours.

On this particular winter's night, the anniversary of Grassal's death, Orion rides high beside a waxing moon. The golden door is open and the tube with the mirror follows as the sky unwinds. He is astonished at how fast the moon moves, a game of catch-up. Morval would catch the intricate shading on the moon's face, but she is not permitted here.

A sharp click triggers a tumble of lighter notes: a pebble bouncing down the slate roof below. He descends a floor and peers into the night to see a spectral figure beckoning. Wisps of mist hang above the frost, but Fortemain can make out bare feet in sandals, a grey robe with hem held above the grass and an oil-lamp lifted away from his visitor's face.

The figure walks away. It is Fortemain's choice to make. He hurries down, unbolts the door and follows the lamp bobbing and swaying north and east towards the island's higher ground. Fortemain guesses the destination well before they arrive: a building regularly attended by Sir Henry and never by the Eleusians, the oldest by centuries on the island: the Church of the Traveller's Rest. The figure raises his lamp to the carved stone inscription over the entrance: *Sub hanc petram*, an unusual variant of *On this rock I will build my church*. But nothing here is usual.

The deep-set windows choke the moonlight. The lamp dances in and out of the stone columns, then halts and a spark flares to a flame. His companion, now unmistakably an elderly priest, exchanges the lamp for two candles. 'To lessen the soot,' he says, his cavernous voice sounding as old as the stone itself. He unlocks a heavy oak door and leads the way up to the belfry.

Fortemain fumbles his way up, past walls teeming with figures and scenes, some homely and everyday, others outlandish. Sir Henry had shown him an illuminated book of the hours with the appropriate night sky in a semi-circular frame above seasonal workaday scenes like these, sowers to revellers, harvesters to skaters.

The priest moves his candle to a fragment of night sky with a tailed phenomenon – a comet, Fortemain would have said, but for the black pigment – but there, on the opposite wall, is its twin in white. A hill with a shadowy henge sits beneath the dark comet, again mirrored on the opposing wall, save the hill is bare; the henge has vanished. Beneath the summit is a cluster of men, raising rocks in leather slings: church-builders. There is even a table nearby where other men are mixing colours, wooden spoons in hand. The past engulfs him, for he recognises the hill's profile. These are the fresco-makers, in *this* very church: self-portraits.

'*Saeculum*,' says the priest. 'They say the dark comet comes every millennium.'

Fortemain squints, peering harder.

'*Sub hanc petram*,' adds the priest, quoting the inscription over the porch. He retreats back down to the nave, where he hands Fortemain a small bound book. 'This is our second treasure, a natural history recorded by the church's founders. It's copied from the original, *De Observatione Naturae*. Keep it, and more importantly, read it.'

'Why me?' asks Fortemain, bewildered by such largesse.

'Mr Wynter's experiments will worsen. He or his kind will enter the mixing-point and live on. Someone who knows must do so too, to resist when they return.'

The priest has not finished. He leads Fortemain to the altar and from beneath a square stone in the dead centre of the floor he produces a perfect sphere of rock with multicoloured seams.

'Tradition places this at the last millennium,' he says, showing it to Fortemain before returning it to its resting place. 'That book explains how the rock it belonged to miraculously vanished. We like to think the sphere was part of the miracle.'

They part in the porch. Trudging back to the Tower of Knowledge, with a layer of ancient natural history in the crook of his arm, Fortemain feels he has come of age.

June 1566. London and Rotherweird.

Wynter's experiments do worsen as the Eleusians 'progress'. More often than not their animal-bird-insect creations survive. They fashion familiars as pets, but Wynter tires of heraldic monstrosities with limited brain capacity and usefulness. It is time for the Sixth Day, the crowning act of creation: to merge humans with other life forms or elemental forces. There will be casualties, so he needs children who will not be missed. Coin will not catch, or catch safely; nobody gives coin for nothing. He needs a lure, an emblem of innocent charity.

Wynter the traveller has tasted what others have not. He fingers the twisted tuberous root as he heads for the kitchens to hook his line.

Master Malise pinches his nose in disgust: in the gutters of London fish offal splatters the quay; streams of excrement clog the cracks in the cobbles; dead animals litter the foreshore – scavengers scavenged, their innards picked apart by crows. Prospecting urchins sift the mud for coin and jewels and rifle nets for edible slivers left from the catch. The birds have the wherewithal to wheel away to open fields and clean air but these human scraps are doomed to scuttle through their lives like crabs. The river looks turgid and flat in the milky sunshine.

He cannot conceal his contempt for their feral talk and slow wits, but she, his fellow Eleusian, the one Wynter calls Mel, Latin for honey, knows how to smile. She feigns warmth, and they flock to her. He has lain with her and she feigns warmth there too. She is practised but cold: a born dissembler, and *almost* as clever as he.

Mel plays this game because it works. She holds out the long, flat biscuits and the urchins snap off fragments, licking before they bite. Soon, craving more of the luxurious, pungent sweetness of gingerbread, they follow her to the wagon – but one boy hangs back. He's taken the lure, but still he doesn't move. He has the same abject leanness, but without the hangdog look the others wear. He has a striking symmetry of face and body, one might almost say noble.

'You wish me to follow?' asks the boy, his voice calm, clear as an actor.

The suffering and sadness in his face passes Malise by, but not the faint sardonic smile. *I come as a martyr, not as a fool*: that is the message. This boy knows the promises are hollow.

'I *expect* you to follow,' hisses Malise.

Wynter does not blench at Lost Acre's monstrosities, but he draws the line at dirty children in the Manor. They are scrubbed and clothed in velvet and fur from top to toe. Suspicion lingers, but more gingerbread and steaming meat pies quickly dispel it. In the Manor's Great Hall they line up, booted and suited, to meet their benefactor.

Bole reads out name, sex, height and weight as each comes up. In days some will sprout claws or mandibles; some will learn to burrow or fly; some will die. In Malise's reckoning they have become worthwhile.

The last two catch the eye for contrast: a stunted boy with carrot-red hair and, always last, the boy without blemish. Wynter narrows his eyes as he too catches the message: *I come as a martyr, not a fool.*

'Vibes,' says Vibes, affecting a bow, off-centre like the rest of him.

'I will not have such names in the Manor,' crows Wynter. 'Spin the letters, Mr Bole.'

Bole spins. 'Bevis,' he says.

'Bevis it is. And who is this one?'

Bole looks at his paper. 'No name.'

'Friend of Vibes,' says the boy, returning the name Wynter has just banished.

The Eleusians close in from the shadows, the better to see the contest, but Wynter dismisses him with a single syllable. 'Tyke.'

There is ambiguity here: *tyke*, a childish mischief-maker, and *Tyche*, the female goddess of luck. The boy does not bow. *I am a martyr, but not a fool.*

The next afternoon Fortemain tracks down Bevis and Tyke beside the Rother. Bevis paddles in the shallows, entranced by the transparency of the water and the small spined fish which dart and stop, while Tyke sits on an outcrop, sunning himself, easy as you like.

'This does not last,' says Fortemain.

'What doesn't?' asks Bevis.

'They take you to a different place and they change you. Depending on the outcome, you may need this.' Fortemain finds this difficult; he wishes to warn without instilling panic. Tyke takes the tiny map and examines the arrows marking a path from a tree in a meadow to a stream on the edge of the forest. They end at a cross and a cave.

Fortemain takes the map back and points. 'You can hide here on your return.' He flips it over to reveal another plan, this time of the Rotherweird Valley. 'The house is close to the only road out.' By the house is a name: Tom Ferdy.

Tyke tunes the bell of Fortemain's voice: complex, dissonant at the edges, but the heart of the note is true. 'You are risking your life,' he says.

Fortemain blinks. The boy has a strange resignation to his fate. 'Anyone would.'

Tyke shakes his head. 'Anyone *should*.' He pockets the piece of paper. 'One day I may return the favour.'

Feeling heavy of heart, Fortemain retraces his steps to the Tower of Knowledge knowing he cannot prevent, he can only mitigate. He wonders where Morval is, and what she is recording in Wynter's terrible books.

June 1566. Lost Acre.

On the way to the tile, they are blindfolded. *A surprise*, Wynter tells them, *one too glorious to be diminished by clues, richer even than gingerbread*. They can feel underfoot the bridge over the Rother and hear the swish of the grass, followed by the wrapped-in sound of the bowl fringed by beeches where the white tile hides. Then, after a shaking of every sense and sinew, they face a strident new vocabulary of sound: the grass whirrs; birds or animals churr and shriek. Somehow, they have travelled to a different world.

There are other voices surrounding them: Mr Wynter's richly dressed young men and women and his corpulent servant. They catch the squeak of hinges as doors open and close, and the singing rattle of the winch, but nobody cries or protests.

There follows a cacophony of mocking laughter or applause or an intake of breath, and often the sounds of the chase – flapping, threshing, running, the squeal of animals in pain.

They cannot see the reason for the laughter when poor Bevis emerges with one hand like a lobster claw and his back plated, gifted by a companion crayfish.

The debate is brutal; only Fortemain and Morval Seer stand apart.

'We're not there yet,' says Wynter, 'not by some way.'

'Put that monstrosity down,' suggests an Eleusian woman, waving a stiletto in each hand. She has a penchant for 'putting down' the failures.

'He could wait at table – a lobsterman serving fish,' jests Malise.

'I wonder if he swims?' adds pretty Mel.

Wynter raises a hand. 'We cannot risk the over-monstrous. Only the pidgeboy comes back with us.' The misshapen bird, its human element barely visible, has already managed to fly despite the uneven limbs. 'The others stay here.'

'Bring on Tyke – bring on the ratwigs!' cry the men, who loathe the boy's innocent beauty; it rebukes their corruption.

The women, also mindful of that face and body, half-hope Tyke will be spared.

Wynter smiles. *I come as a martyr, and not as a fool* – so be it. Ratwigs as large as your fist, tailed and with furred armour, burrow and nest in Lost Acre's rotten tree stumps. Two are pulled out with tongs to accompany the boy. Tyke breaks precedent, flicking off his blindfold as the cage rises. He ignores the mixing-point and watches his watchers.

In swings the cage; out swings the cage – to silence. One ratwig with a face at front and back straddles the bars, but Tyke stands easy, as before.

Bole coins a new meaning from an old word. 'A pure,' he shouts. 'We have a pure!'

Tyke has never known quite who he is: a ghost ship without port of origin. There is no recorded parent, place of birth or teacher, and in this vacuum stories attach, even among the denizens of the mudflats – found in the reeds like Moses, bastard son of an earl. Do the stories beget the presence, or does the presence beget the stories? He knows only that he is different.

Others talk of his stillness, distance and insight, but such language falls short. *Still*, yes, but he is articulate. *Distant* too, in that he is apart from the crowd, but he cares for all, including the mangled ratwig, doomed to die. *Insightful*, yes and no: he has no feel for the future but he reads people, their voices as much as their faces.

A stiletto releases the ratwig from its misery as Wynter asserts his authority. 'Bevis and the "pure" will guard the cages.'

'That's a death sentence,' protests pretty Mel, who has her eye on the pure. A week earlier, cages had been broken open and their occupants torn to pieces.

But Tyke does not protest. He touches the changelings through the bars of the cages, as if the decision were his, not Wynter's. Fortemain feels vindicated as the Eleusians process away, the pidge-boy tethered to Malise's wrist. This boy is different.

Above Fortemain's head, the glow of the evening star, the planet Venus, intensifies. He prays for the pure and his charges, and as he looks up, a relieving dream takes root. In tribute to Sir Henry, he will build a tower in Lost Acre, fashion a telescope, observe and learn from its contrary sky. He will bring good science to the other place. Morval's twin might lack courage, but daily Hieronymus uncovers another terrestrial law of Nature. There must be celestial laws behind the sun's warmth, the way the stars move and hang in space, why Venus glows as she does. He has his grail.

*

The Eleusians gone, Tyke releases the changelings. They stand stock-still, here a claw hanging slack, here a dribbling mouth, here a single Cyclops eye. They are no larger than the children they were, but the gift of speech and understanding survives in their tangled brains. Tyke offers what comfort he can. Beside him stands Vibes, the least damaged in human resemblance, and the doglike Mance, so christened by Bole's twisted acrostic humour, a crude anagram of *canem*, a muddled dog.

'Your handicaps will have balancing enhancements, be it sight, strength or smell,' he tells them. 'Cherish these gifts, and guard your humanity too.'

The high-flown speech passes most of them by. Some mumble, some are weeping, still in shock.

'We can't stay in the open,' says Vibes, 'not at night. They talked about the creatures out there.' With his claw, he gestures to the forest edge.

'Nor can we use the tile by day; Wynter will surely set a guard,' adds Tyke. He consults Fortemain's map and finds the cave below, on the fringe of the forest. Fortune belatedly smiles too: Fortemain has left them a sack of supplies, which Vibes' claw lifts with ease.

At the cave's mouth they find the skeleton of a huge animal, presumably its previous owner.

'Kraken,' croaks a changeling – he has heard the name on the wharfs – and so it is christened. Its twelve hooked claws make excellent tools. Tyke does not command the changelings; he works with them: *Show, not tell.*

The lair has several chambers. They find glowing globes of rock in the rearmost chamber, and a vent in the ceiling. They seal the door with bones and branches and light a fire. They have ham, bread, fresh water and now a home, of sorts.

When the fire is spent and the others asleep, Vibes shares his strategy with Tyke.

'Does the map show where we came in?' When Tyke nods, he goes on, 'You say it's too perilous to leave by night – but suppose we too were monstrous?' The kraken's bones have given him the idea. 'We six can link arms for the body, and you'll play the head.'

Tyke nods again, and Vibes says firmly, 'Tomorrow then.'

And they do just that. They boil the remains of the kraken's skin, although the stench is foul, and at nightfall they daub their cheeks, legs and backs with the viscous oil. They wedge luminous rocks into the eye sockets of the kraken's skull and clean six paired ribs. Tyke finds a smooth horn from one of the kraken's victims, which he works with the point of a rock.

Come the next midnight, a pantomime horror lumbers from the cave, spikes proud of the back like a flustered porcupine, and crosses the stream towards the white tile. Tyke and Vibes whisper a refrain to keep their charges focused: '*Move as one. Think as one.*'

The scent of flesh and the soft, vulnerable footfalls quickly draw predators. They swoop and probe, but do not strike at first, baffled by the glowing head and the stink of putrefaction. They grow bolder when the beast neither attacks nor takes evasive action. A rib is seized and tossed aside.

In response, the belly of the beast emits a baleful moan as Tyke blows his horn: more precious minutes gained.

Move as one. Think as one.

In sight of the tile there is a loss of nerve and half the changelings cast aside their ribs, just as the grass comes alive with tentacles and claws. The skull collapses into the grass; the eyes dislodge and roll away as some run, some crawl. The Mance, first on all fours, then erect, snarls and bays, but they are fortunate: the hunters have flinched at the fracturing of their quarry into so many constituent parts and the Mance's ferocity wins precious seconds.

It is enough. They clasp each other and are through.

Wynter's guards have withdrawn to their soft beds, confident nobody can survive the other place at night.

'. . . a pantomime horror lumbers from the cave, spikes proud
of the back like a flustered porcupine . . .'

Stars blaze brightly through the beeches above them. An owl skims past, reassuringly ordinary. They clean up in the river.

The sky is lightening when they reach the farmhouse. The changelings are exhausted from the effort of coaxing mobility from unfamiliar limbs.

Tom Ferdy is a bull of a man with arms the colour of old walnut and a face fissured by the elements. His shock and sadness at their condition quickly give way to practicalities. To Tyke, the bass voice is beautifully rounded and true.

'It's too dangerous for you to stay in the valley,' he tells them. 'I'll take you to Wynter's abandoned house near Hirstoak. It's the last place he'll look and nobody else will go there, such is the man's reputation.'

They resupply and leave in Ferdy's covered cart. It's Sunday and the road is deserted; they have chosen well.

'You have children?' Vibes asks along the way.

'I had many, now but two,' Ferdy says. Later, he adds, 'And I had a wife.'

The voice brings an image to Tyke of a woman hanging from a tree, her mind broken by her loss.

The house is indeed abandoned, but Wynter has left the cruder furniture, along with anything else that might suggest lowlier origins, so as well as a pervading aura of neglect, there are cutlery, crockery and several beds.

'We're going up in the world,' says Vibes.

Ferdy speaks to Tyke and Vibes, the spokesmen. 'In time, we must find them work. You'll need to learn to feed yourselves; my son will bring seed and cuttings. I'll get word to Fortemain.'

A man of few words, Ferdy does not linger, but delivers a parting, heartfelt message. 'We'll find a way to bring him down.'

At dusk Fortemain stands in the Manor's rose garden, waiting for Venus' glow and fearing for Tyke and Vibes.

'You're a quiet one.' She has plaited her hair since their return and it accentuates the heaviness of her features.

'So much to ponder,' he replies.

'I come from an old family – maybe not quite a manor, but a fine house.' Her palm grazes his wrist. 'You do too, I think. Your looks say so.' She pauses, then says softly, 'I tire of Malise. He thinks only of himself.'

Fortemain feels uncomfortable. With Morval Seer, words flow as nature intended, as they did with his fellow Eleusians in the Tower, on the journey to Rotherweird and in the early days, but now, he cannot find words for her.

'I am no better,' he says at last, pointing at the sky. 'I watch only what interests me.'

'Have you been to the attics? Have you counted the children? At best they're half Eleusian and half ordinary, all of them. Suppose we were the first . . . imagine *our* children – imagine their minds.'

'Perhaps the ordinary bring balance.'

'You watch the peasant girl.' *Peasant*: the word is almost spat.

'She's not ordinary.' He paused, searching for a way to soften his refusal. 'It's just . . . we have an understanding.'

Her hand traces the vein in his neck. 'There are pleasures beyond *her* understanding – but not beyond mine.' Her other hand finds the small of his back.

Fortemain pushes her gently away and she tilts her head, her face hard as stone. 'You don't reject me without cost,' she snarls as she leaves.

Fortemain doesn't understand this turnaround, the way 'like' has transformed to 'loathing'.

January 1567. Rotherweird and Lost Acre.

The hour after sunset is when the servant girls light the bedroom fires. The days of dormitories have long passed. Fortemain has the smallest room on the Manor's northern side. Tonight brings a girl he has not met before. The flue is damp, and as his room is the last, she is left with a mix of the dry and the green.

When the fire stutters and fails he kneels beside her and they re-lay, sorting good from bad. He adds tallow ends saved from the Great Hall candles. She has chestnut hair, high cheekbones and a generous mouth. They blow, and the fire begins to take.

She turns to look at him. 'They say they make monsters, while you hide in the heavens.'

He reads sympathy, not hostility. They blow again, and a spark sticks in the soot, glows, spreads upwards, multiplies.

'How far will he go?' she asks.

Fortemain is unsure if she is talking of the spark, or Wynter, or both. 'As far as he can,' he admits.

Then she surprises him. 'I watch the heavens,' she says, 'and I see ice and fire there.' She moves away from the fire on her knees, her skin fading to dark. She gives him a smile. The wood is ablaze now. She stoops, takes the hem of her shift and lifts.

Then, it seemed natural, wonderful even, but now, two hours later, her presence no more than a warm imprint on the featherbed, he feels exploited. His visitor must be Wynter's agent, or Malise's, or sent by the Eleusian he rejected to break his bond with Morval – and yet there is no gloating, no word from anyone. It is his secret, yet guilt invades.

The priest's words chime in Fortemain's head: *You must enter the mixing-point to live on, to resist when they return.* This is to be his penance.

Wynter's library holds a slim volume entitled *The Art of Conjuration and Legerdemain*; another entitled *Abbadon's Potion Chest*. Wynter unwittingly assists, for he checks the presence of the stones in the bag at his waist, when not in use, by touch only. Balls of polished bogwood make excellent replicas; the two books, illusion and herbal science, do the rest.

He stands beneath a clear night sky. There is wind enough to sway the cage and make the winch sing. He has found and copied Bole's notes on the placing of the stones on Wynter's more private creaturing days, but he is taking a serious risk. He strokes the nape of his companion's neck. Will they become a monstrosity or, as he hopes, a dual being, ostensibly human, but not?

He lowers the cage, fixes the stones and steps in.

OCTOBER:
SECOND FORTNIGHT

I

Books, Books, Books

Via Denzil Prim's loose tongue, Fanguin's indiscretion made the Town Crier's evening bulletin, prompting Orelia to question the wisdom of recruiting him for the Hoy Book Fair. In the event, Fanguin obeyed instructions, secreting his bicycle beyond the North Bridge the previous day and appearing by the potting sheds concealing Salt's exit through the town wall at six o'clock precisely the following morning.

'Morning, co-conspirator,' he whispered, breezy words, but uncharacteristically subdued in delivery. They crossed the Rother in Salt's coracle, recovered their bicycles and set off uphill. A vigorous, if eccentric, cyclist, Fanguin's knees pumped out sideways with feet at right angles to the pedals. Orelia allowed him the lead. The air was chill and halfway there the light mist had thickened into fog.

Exercise loosened Fanguin's self-restraint. 'It'll be blazing sun up there, always bloody is when we're in the soup,' he boomed.

They laboured past the huge oak where Boris Polk picked up Rotherweird's supplies from wider England, as well as her very occasional visitors, and as predicted, mist gave way to sunshine over the escarpment edge, as well as a more advanced autumn: trees bare, all flowers spent. Fanguin drew Orelia's attention to a disconcerting sign, half buried in the hedge by an early turning. *The Agonies* had been scored into the wood. The drive snaked back to the valley rim before vanishing into an impenetrable stand of evergreens.

'Who would call a house *that*?' shouted Fanguin over his shoulder.

Thereafter the road flattened out and the approach to Hoy, hedged on both sides, proved uneventful. Once there, they divided the workload. Fanguin awarded himself the shops, leaving stalls and barrows in church and churchyard to his junior partner. There, he hoped, she would find Bevis Vibes, the owner of *Broken Spines*.

'He is beyond description,' said Fanguin, 'so I won't attempt one.'

Orelia had always disliked Hoy's tameness – there was no interesting architecture, no towers, no aerial walkways, no grotesque carvings, no Doom's Tocsin, no countrysider stalls trundling in and out at dawn and dusk, no bicycle rickshaws, no enveloping river. It was all that Rotherweird was not: pretty, she thought, damning with faint praise, but *ordinary*.

She was expecting a morning of drab, fruitless search, only to be confronted by a welter of sandwich boards, banners and posters advertising THE SPECTACULAR HOY BOOK FAIR! along the approach to the High Street. Images of monks, mediaeval presses, human organs, scientific instruments, maps and bestiaries jostled for attention in bewildering profusion. Wit surfaced in the event's main poster, a woodcut of an elegant girl reading a book: *A HOY FAIR MAID*.

All the High Street shops had been commandeered by dealers whose exotic banners hung over the names of Hoy's humdrum traders, from *Holzbucher of Leipzig* to *Bibulous Bishop Books*. *Beastly Bindings* had taken over the stationery shop, while *Vesper's Erotica* nestled on the top floor of Hoy's electrical store. Cars had been banished to accommodate a fleet of barrows tenanted by less affluent dealers.

Orelia chose 'crumpled' to define the barrow men and women, and not just their clothing – features, posture and hair too. Many warmed their palms with instant coffee in chipped mugs of doubtful hygiene and they were, to a man and woman, enthusiastic, whether negotiating, gesticulating, or comparing sales achieved and sales narrowly lost. Among them drifted serious collectors, more sober in manner and dress, but as alert and on the hunt.

Orelia spent half an hour searching for *The Popular Choice Regulations* inside Hoy Parish Church, where the fare had a superior feel, before moving to the more esoteric dealers behind another flotilla of barrows in the churchyard. She worked her way past *Treasure and Trivia*, *Hotch, Potch & Paper* and *Ramsden's Raving Miscellany* to *Broken Spines*, whose barrow stood shyly in the lee of an ancient yew.

But Bevis Vibes could never have been inconspicuous. More dwarf than man, he was stunted in build and bow-legged. Above a fleshy face, clean-shaven and smooth as a child's, fine silver hair curled from his ears as well as his head. He wore heavy shoes, an open over-large coat and nondescript trousers held up by leather braces. His oversized hands were gloved and he sported a coloured neckerchief. He looked like a character from a fairy tale – but for all that, he knew how to sell.

'Smollet, sir?' he was saying to a corpulent American. 'Take it from me – Roderick Random, Peregrine Pickle – they're your kind of heroes! I've a complete set, all first editions.'

'Cut to the chase, Mr Vibes,' the man responded, patting the pockets of his creased but expensive lightweight suit.

'Five hundred for the lot, sir.'

'Four fifty.'

'Sir, Mr Smollett was a Scot. He would find the very notion of discount upsetting. Let us respect his views.'

So it went on, until the American paid in full, but happily. 'Mr Vibes, I've combed book fairs from Boston to the Baltic and I know my bindings, sir, I surely do. And this here is rare stuff: ancient techniques with modern exactitude. I commend you, sir.'

He waddled off, beaming, and Vibes turned and stared at Orelia, an inquisitive look, gloved hands floating over his stock like a conductor calling for quiet. The barrow held unenticing stacks of dog-eared postcards, soiled paperbacks, Victorian prints and under-size books with – yes, broken spines; it looked more car-boot than book fair. Yet between them gleamed leather books with literary merit and bindings of exceptional beauty.

While she feigned mild interest, Vibes dipped into a canvas bag at his feet and extracted an ancient volume beautifully bound in dark maroon. The leather had a polished sheen. The gaps on the ribbed spine were embossed in gold with, in ascending order, a leaf, a caterpillar, a chrysalis and a butterfly.

Vibes opened the book. The frontispiece bore the unsettling title *Straighten the Rope* and, underneath, the date *MDXC*.

The opening printed pages featured four complex solid shapes, shaded differently and seen from a variety of angles, followed by page after page of manuscript calculations, sketches, doodles and more sketched pieces similar to, but different from, those at the beginning. The overall effect resembled a Leonardo da Vinci codex, although without his fastidious sense of good order.

'Before you lick your finger and dab, the later pages are live ink.'

'How much?' she asked, trying not to replicate the American's eagerness despite the improbability of her meeting the price.

'*Broken Spines* respects a discerning customer. Let's say a month on approval?'

The smile brought symmetry to his face.

'Uncommonly generous, Mr . . . ?'

'Bevis Vibes. It's a local book. I've researched it for many a year with no success, but I'm sure the answer lies in Rotherweird. You live there and deal in old artefacts, so have a good dig. But she's not to be sold, shared or parted with. And take my bag – it's immune to pox, water and sunshine.'

She hesitated – how could he know who she was, or about *Baubles & Relics*? Why loan a complete stranger a book of such obvious rarity and value? Why *trust* her? The binding was exquisite. And as for his request for research, he must know that in Rotherweird the study of history was prohibited. Something else troubled her too: *MDXC* meant 1590, which post-dated Wynter's death by a good fifteen years. Flask had used Hengest Strimmer to get *The Roman Recipe Book* to Sir Veronal and Hayman Salt to return the stones for the mixing-point to circulation. Was she to become another victim of Calx Bole's subterfuge? Had *Straighten the Rope* a hidden purpose? Vibes *must* know more than he was letting on.

'No clues at all?' she asked.

'The monogram is Hoy, an unusual local press. Maybe some of it is in code – the Elizabethans loved them. John Dee, Nicholas Bacon, Burghley. Up to you, Miss – adventure, revelation or wasted hours? I promise nothing except you will be intrigued, challenged and enriched.'

So, *Fly blind or not all* was the message. 'Why not,' she said, sensing, for good or ill, a life-changing decision.

Vibes hastily handed over the bag as another customer approached. Speaking in triplicates, as he had to her, he started, 'Good morrow, sir. Thackeray, trifle or treat?'

Time to go. As Orelia walked from the churchyard to the opposite side of the High Street she recalled the books on Professor Bolitho's list – Kepler on heavenly movement, cocktails (no surprise) and plate 8 of Thorburn's *Mammals*; surely Archibald Thorburn, the Scottish nature artist. She had passed just the place.

Hoy's pet shop had been let to a dealer with a triple 'F' logo, for *Fish, Fowl and Fauna*. Books and coloured plates made uneasy neighbours, the latter born of the former's destruction. On enquiry, they had two copies. Thorburn's paintings and pen-and-ink drawings were sublime in line and colour, but plate 8 proved a disappointment: nothing but a commonplace mole feeding above ground. She could see the appeal to Bolitho: he and the mole were both explorers of the dark, coming up once in a while for air.

She needed a break from books. It was time to chase real ghosts – time for her alternative plan – and for that she needed Fanguin.

Fanguin, unsuccessful in his search for Rotherweird's electoral rules, arrived in the churchyard just in time to glimpse Orelia leaving with an unfamiliar canvas bag under her arm. A glance at the barrow behind her confirmed the source.

'How's business, Vibes?'

'Patchy.'

'Today?'

'Sunny spells.'

'What did the lady buy?'

'*Semper discretio* is our motto.'

'Five quid says there are exceptions.'

Vibes grinned.

'How about the *Popular Choice Regulations*?'

'You refer to Rotherweird?'

'Come on, Vibes, you know perfectly well I am.'

'Try *Nowt So Strange as Folk* – halfway down off the High Street on the left.'

The shop more than lived up to the name, being a shrine to the outer reaches of human behaviour, from Inca blood rituals to witch-ducking, burial rites to fetishisms of every kind.

The proprietor had a monkish air: pink-cheeked, bald on top and overweight. 'Your predilection, sir?'

Fanguin blushed. 'I'm interested in odd election practices, more particularly odd *local* election practices.' He removed his glasses and began to polish the glass. He felt foolish.

'You may be in luck. I acquired some ephemera from old Claud's attics.' The portly bookseller crossed himself and, not without difficulty, bent down and rummaged through a box at his feet.

'Claud – would he be anything to do with Ambrose Claud, the Vagrant Vicar?'

'Everything to do with him, Mr . . . ?'

'Fanguin, Godfery Fanguin, retired schoolteacher, Rotherweird

School.' He was hoping the blush he felt didn't show; after all, he could hardly say 'dismissed' teacher. 'I bought a copy of Claud's *Peregrinations* from Mr Vibes at your last Book Fair. There's a section on Rotherweird.'

'Ambrose Claud settled in Hoy in about 1800,' the bookseller said chattily, piling some books on one side. 'The last of the family popped his clogs the other week. Always liked a drink and a smoke, did old Algernon.'

'Any luck?' asked Fanguin, for the moment keener on the present than the past.

'The posh dealers always grab the best books, but they turn up their noses at boxes – you'd be amazed what turns up.'

He dragged out two more from under the table and started sifting, until with a cry of 'Ha ha!' he flourished a dog-eared pamphlet in a plastic envelope. He stared at it and added 'Slightly foxed' – a conspicuous understatement – but the title was legible despite the profusion of brown spots and water damage. 'It's yours for twenty quid.'

Snorkel had ended Fanguin's teaching career for no better reason than his friendship with Flask. For the potential nuisance value to Snorkel alone, the price was a steal. As he paid, a seductive voice whispered 'Frackle's cider', in Fanguin's view the only worthwhile brew in Hoy, to be found on tap at *The Blue Lion*. He banished a subliminal rebuke from his wife; a sharp bicycle climb merited a fleeting visit to the local oasis.

A familiar figure downed her coffee and rose to meet him. 'Busted,' said Orelia.

'Frackle's cider – join me for a quick one,' he blustered. 'You won't regret it.'

'Your last quick one made the headlines.'

Change of tack needed, thought Fanguin. 'Vibes gave you a book.'

'Vibes *lent* me a book. I'll show you when you've shown me Wynter's house.'

No point in resisting. Fanguin had often thought of that mysterious ruin, Wynter's home before he usurped Rotherweird Manor, later Calx Bole's chosen campsite. He had found the skull of Ferox the weaselman, another of Bole's victims, so what other clues might lurk there?

After buying a picnic unblessed by alcohol, at Orelia's insistence, they set off to Hirstoak. From the station Fanguin retraced his route to the insignificant turning with its dead-end sign and, a few miles on, the skull and crossbones warning off visitors with the message 'Polluted Ground'. The razor wire and the *leylandii* hedge remained impenetrable, save for the gap Bole had made, which Fanguin had used on his previous visit. After hiding their bikes away from the lane, they crawled through into the wreckage of Wynter's garden.

Fanguin could see little change beyond the seasonal since his last visit. The dominating tree had shed its contrasting leaves, both roundish and spear-shaped. Calx Bole's tent had half collapsed. The canvas, streaked with spiderwebs, exuded an overpowering smell of mildew. A daddy long-legs wobbled across the top like a novice tightrope walker.

'Bole must be in Lost Acre,' Fanguin suggested, 'whether as Ferox or Flask or himself.'

Orelia shared Shapeshifter's authorship of the *Rotherweird Chronicle*'s Winter Solstice Special.

'That doesn't mean much – they all use pseudonyms.' He added, 'He could have submitted it well in advance, or left it with allies. In truth, we haven't a clue.'

'We have too many clues,' muttered Orelia.

The biologist sat beneath the tree and pondered. How did Bole's shapeshifting work? What price did he pay? Were his reincarnations changeable at will? And what about the crosswords themselves – was he communicating with others, indulging a hobby or mocking them?

While Fanguin wrestled with Bole's motivation, Orelia explored the garden, which must once have been imposing. Although earth spilled through breaches in the retaining walls, there were terraces to south and west. Traces of statuary included an angel-faced waterspout suffocated in grass and ivy, fed at one time by a dried-out man-made watercourse. Such elegance did not fit her picture of Wynter and she wondered who had lived here after his move to the Manor – and indeed, after his execution? Someone more benign, she felt.

The house proved more challenging to reconstruct. The upper floor had collapsed and the internal panelling had been stripped out, leaving only a few shattered bookshelves. It was by no means a small house, but even so, Rotherweird Manor would have been a substantial advancement. She stretched her arms across the surviving doorways, searching for the spirit of the place. She sensed the presence of layers, a more complex history than at first appeared, good and evil vying for supremacy.

She returned to Fanguin and showed him *Straighten the Rope*.

'Vibes *gave* you this?'

'He wants me to make sense of it – which is quite a challenge.'

'First the *Recipe Book*, then this – isn't it Wynter's work? Caterpillar to chrysalis to butterfly suggest rebirth and resurrection to me.'

'It's not him.' She pointed out the publication date. 'It's eighteen years *after* his execution!'

'So, it's Bole then – but look, have you ever seen such magnificent binding!'

They thumbed through the opening pages.

'How bizarre,' commented Fanguin. 'What connects this to Rotherweird?' He moved on to the later pages, then stopped and pointed. 'Look – there, there . . . and *there*!' The ink drawings included several geological outlines of Rotherweird Island – no buildings had been marked, but the draughtsman had measured the Rother's depth at regular intervals.

Orelia returned to a question which had brought some comfort at Ferensen's dinner. 'Let's say, for argument's sake, that Wynter *can* return – why would he wait for centuries?'

'I've been wondering about that too. Suppose the mixing-point pollutes with every use – and suppose its joinder with the Midsummer flower cleaned it somehow, so suppose now is the safest time. Suppose . . .' Fanguin was working through his theory out loud. 'Suppose luring Sir Veronal here was not *only* about revenge – suppose Bole needed someone who had already been in the mixing-point for this particular exercise to work? Suppose Wynter planned this from the very beginning – and that's why he was harping on about revenge at his trial, to conceal his *true* purpose.' He looked grim as he concluded, 'I fear *anything* is possible with him.'

That was what Orelia liked about Fanguin: He might be unreliable, but he could be relied on to bring original perspectives to bear. She raised a familiar question mark on the viability of Wynter's ambitions. 'But that doesn't answer Salt's point. Wynter hasn't lived on like Ferensen, Bole and Slickstone – if he were resurrected, he'd be a spent anachronism from the Elizabethan Age.'

'Know your enemy,' replied Fanguin. 'Wynter isn't one to overlook such an obvious handicap. He'd only come back for a purpose – something *very* out of the ordinary.'

They ate their picnic in silence, subdued by the edgy spirit of the place. Orelia noted how Fanguin had aged: humour still twinkled in the eyes and in the lines around his mouth, but his skin had a dull tone and he had put on weight: the work of drink and depression. She felt oppressed by the spirit of autumn – dead leaves, rotting branches, fly-ridden berries and the tang of burned stubble from neighbouring fields.

The ruins yielded no other clue, so they turned briefly to the *Popular Choice Regulations*, which lightened the mood. The provisions were intricate and bizarrely quaint. A host of complex formalities confronted any would-be challenger to the incumbent Mayor, obstacles which they suspected Snorkel would be eager to exploit.

'Democracy may need our helping hand,' announced Fanguin grandly.

Bypassing Hoy, they ambled back as afternoon waned. On reaching the Rotherweird escarpment, Fanguin rediscovered his *brio*, crying, 'Can't catch me!'

In younger, slimmer days, he had been quite the sprinter, and vestiges remained – the breathing, the pump of the arms, the high knees.

Orelia swore and pursued – she would *not* be beaten by a man twenty-five years her senior – but Fanguin's manic energy made for a close finish.

After concealing their bicycles for retrieval later, they re-entered the town through Salt's hidden door and parted in sober mood. Sir Veronal's death, they agreed, had most likely been but the end of the beginning.

From a distant vantage point high on the edge of Rotherweird Westwood, Hayman Salt glimpsed their hectic descent without asking the whence, the whys or the wherefores. His mind focused rather on seasonal ambiguity, the senescence of leaves and the ripeness of fruit, how this gradual dying compared to the youthful explosion of spring.

As thoughts of this timbre came and went in his divided being, an uncomfortable comparison with an old friend assailed him. In Ferensen's ancient guise as Hieronymus Seer, he had always sought refuge in nature when evil threatened. Seer had paid a terrible price for his disengagement, and Salt felt stalked by a similar doom.

But it did not change him.

A failing sun burnished the ferns at his feet. He shrugged and loped back towards Rotherweird, gathering the best acorns as he went.

2

Bequests and Dead Ends

That evening a passer-by paused outside *Baubles & Relics*, struck by the image of its young owner at her shop desk with an open book in front of her, stockinged feet tucked back to the side of the chair and a finger coiling her dark hair as she noted each page. These were the mannerisms of homework, not business.

Orelia scrutinised the diagrams. The four pieces on the early printed pages presumably fitted together, but she could not connect them to the contour maps. In the rear section, other maps appeared, together with more doodled pieces squeezed in among dense calculations. Most pieces had at least one curved surface.

Try as she might, progress stalled. She lacked both spatial awareness and scientific understanding, although she did catch fragments of astronomy, calendars and meteorology among the mathematical equations. Even to her untutored eye, the sums became more complex and the notations more modern as the notes progressed. Latin gave way to English; new algebraic symbols appeared, all symptomatic of a restless mind. Only the hand and the quality of paper remained constant.

Surely Vibes must have known he had entrusted her with a task she was wholly ill-equipped to execute.

On returning the book to the bag she noticed a small card sewn into the canvas. Above the name *Broken Spines* appeared the neat pun '*In a bind?*' with a Hoy PO Box number. Another miniature mystery: had *Broken Spines* neither address nor telephone number?

And that question led to another: where did Vibes store his books? Who were his binders? Their workmanship was exquisite.

She indulged in a small act of sacrilege: a paper knife removed the card to reveal two words on the back: *The Agonies*, the name on the sign at the valley rim.

Excitement flickered – but was she being manipulated, blessed by luck or merely a tireless investigator reaping due rewards? She laughed to herself: three alternatives, just as Vibes would have put it.

The evening post brought a slim parcel from the Delayed Action Service. 'Courtesy of the late Professor Bolitho,' intoned the postman deferentially, handing over the box.

Once alone, she carefully unwrapped the package to find a card in Bolitho's ornate hand:

To Miss Orelia Roc I leave my isolarion.

She held up a piece of beige linen, two feet square and frayed at the edges, that felt paradoxically both fine and granular. 'Isolarion' was a word unknown to her dictionary. Baffled by such an eccentric message and bequest from someone she barely knew, she wound it round her neck. She was short of scarves.

That was quite enough mystery for one day. *Time for a drink*, she decided.

That same evening the Delayed Action Service delivered a more explicable bequest to Gregorius Jones: a battered clothbound book entitled *The Rotherweird Runner – A Biped's Year* by Ambrose Claud. Runs in the valley were classified from 'Dawdle' to 'Heroic'. Maps and directions abounded, annotated with occasional nature notes. The bookplate featured crossed telescopes. Gregorius Jones beamed like a schoolboy, shed a tear and immersed himself instantly.

*

'Success?' asked Bomber, Fanguin's long-suffering wife, on his return from an unexplained all-day bicycle trip. She was pleasantly surprised to note an absence of alcohol on the breath.

Fanguin fumbled with his tie. 'I'd say fruitful – but whether it's ripe or rotten, I couldn't tell you,' he said mysteriously.

'You're in demand – you've had *two* deliveries today.' She handed Fanguin a parcel addressed in Bolitho's distinctive hand and a test tube, labelled with a pithy message:

1 *Do not open in company.*
2 *What is it?*
V V

Bomber smiled. He was crippled by the tedium of his enforced retirement so any challenge for her husband amounted to medicine. 'Supper at nine.'

The Fanguins' tower housed his study – part laboratory, part science library, and part amateur distillery – on the third floor. The test tube took priority: Valourhand would never seek help unless baffled and troubled.

He eased the cork open – only to close it instantly, so malodorous were the contents. He placed a mask over his nose and opened the windows.

Chemical evaluation and a microscope identified the shattered metatarsals of a badger, and peptin, the principal enzyme in bird digestion, but the smell suggested human faeces. A bird of prey might take badger flesh as carrion, but not the bones.

Bomber arrived bearing a glass of Vlad's best low-alcohol wine.

Fanguin recorked the test tube and placed it back in its stand before taking the glass as if handling a phial of nuclear waste. 'What's that?' he asked, knowing full well what it was.

'Wine for a tipsard.' She did not regard her husband as a drunkard, at least not quite. She judged tipsard a fair label for his current state of decline.

He raised the test tube. 'I've found a bird enzyme.'

'Good for you.'

Encouragingly, Fanguin looked dissatisfied. A deeper challenge would keep the stronger bottles at bay.

Only later did Fanguin open Bolitho's bequest: *De Observatione Naturae*, an Elizabethan copy of an early eleventh-century work by an English monk called Hilarion. His passable biologist's Latin revealed Hilarion to be an intrepid pioneer in his own time, but with an understanding of the natural orders which bordered on the basic now.

He managed only twenty pages.

Valourhand's bequest arrived the following day in her lunch break, accompanied by a provocative note:

To Miss Valourhand, North Tower rival and friend, I leave a speck of darK matter.

She took the box, unopened, through the Southern Gate to the Island Field. A large willow had split and bore a curt warning on its divided trunk: HAZARD: DO NOT CLIMB. Valourhand took the notice to be a dare and promptly shinned up to the highest branch of size, where she made herself comfortable in a fork.

Her scientific discussions with Bolitho had focused on antimatter, not dark matter, which was an entirely different animal, out there in quantity but invisible to even the most powerful telescopes. A speck of dark matter? What could Bolitho mean?

The tasteful box from the stationers *Rorschach & Blot* featured telescopes and stars in cream on a magenta background, but expectation turned to numb disappointment, for the box held nothing. She slipped to the ground, grazing her legs, and briefly raged – Bolitho had snubbed her from the grave.

She speedily reconsidered; Bolitho's mischief had always had *purpose*. He liked to tease, not abuse.

Then she smiled.

Think outside the box, he was saying, and, *Think dark matter*.

3

Sunday Night, Visiting Night

Thanks to Snorkel's meanness and his own Puritan nature, Gorham-bury lived close to Aggs, Oblong's general person, at the eastern end of town in the quarter inhabited mostly by the hardworking poor. It was known as The Understairs – although whether a reference to the menial roles of its inhabitants or the wooden walkways that wound between the crabbed houses at all levels, a less elegant version of Aether's Way, nobody knew for sure.

This dismal location shielded him from interruption, until the Assistant Head Librarian entered – or rather, *inveigled* – her way into his life.

He fought to keep Madge Brown's visits to a minimum, but she somehow contrived to establish a routine of visiting on Sunday evenings at six. By seven Gorhambury invariably turned fretful about his state of preparation for the week ahead and at ten minutes past seven Miss Brown would insist on administering a head massage – on the first occasion, almost by force, although in time he admitted to finding the experience curiously soothing.

Sensitive to Gorhambury's industrious take on the traditional day of rest, she would depart at seven twenty-five precisely, leaving him a pre-cooked meal far beyond his own culinary talent and ambition.

On this particular Sunday, a knock disturbed the fretful stage.

'Godfery Fanguin and Orelia Roc, on business of state,' declared his door grandly, before swinging open.

'What do you two know about business of state?'

'Rather a lot,' replied Fanguin, striding in and waving a pamphlet in front of Gorhambury's face.

The title, *Popular Choice Regulations*, rang alarm bells.

'Hello,' said Madge Brown, voice as mousy as her looks.

'Miss Brown and I were discussing library matters,' said Gorhambury, a little too hastily.

The librarian smiled. 'He only has two glasses – you'll have to make do with cups.'

'Any port in a storm,' boomed Fanguin.

Gorhambury's living space betrayed both his craving for order and straitened circumstances. Four chairs, two metallic and two wooden, rescued by Aggs from employers on the up, hugged a square table. There were no rugs, no pictures and no lampshades. A noticeboard listed Gorhambury's appointments in the coming fortnight, with outstanding clerical tasks marked in multi-coloured footnotes.

'You've been out and about – on your *bicycles*,' said Gorhambury huffily.

'We were exploring. We found a charming estate on the valley rim called *The Agonies*, as in the state of my calves,' replied Fanguin cheerily.

'No, you did not. You went to Hoy in clear breach of the *History Regulations*.'

Fanguin and Orelia exchanged glances. Nothing escaped Snorkel's eyes and ears.

'We went in search of our rights,' explained Fanguin.

'He's being pompous, but it's true,' added Orelia.

The word 'rights' discomforted Gorhambury. 'Rights' meant challenges, disputes, rulings, trouble. But the ancient paper confirmed that this was law from the founding fathers: first fruit, 1650, when hereditary Heralds ceded political rule to elected Mayors. Gorhambury had never examined the *Popular Choice Regulations* – nobody had ever stood against Snorkel in his time – and he felt a twinge of guilt. He should have shown more interest as the quinquennial anniversaries came and went. His practised eye discarded the marginal and focused on essentials. From the lawyerly text, startling provisions emerged.

'Well,' muttered Gorhambury, 'well, well, well. You declare your candidacy by slapping the Mayor's bust with a particular velvet glove on a particular day.' He hunted through the sea of text for the timing. 'Which will be Saturday week, between nine and two, in the Parliament Chamber,' he added.

'Let me guess – the bust isn't there.' Fanguin grinned at the two women.

'It's been removed for cleaning,' conceded Gorhambury. At the time, the decision had struck him as unusually domestic for the Mayor.

'On you go,' said Fanguin with a smirk.

Gorhambury stammered, 'Er . . . *Regulation* 32. "The Mayor must be present in the Chamber with his bust, and likewise a copy of these *Regulations*."' He shuffled across to his noticeboard. 'It appears the Sewage Sub-Committee meeting has been moved to that Saturday . . .' His voice faltered. 'Unusually, the Mayor will be there, and equally unusually, it's to be held in the Parliament Chamber – it says due to piling works, but . . .'

'There are no piling works,' boomed Fanguin, grinning. He was enjoying himself hugely: twenty pounds well spent.

'He has to have the bust there,' said Orelia, 'and if he doesn't, he has to resign and can never stand for election again. He wouldn't risk that, now would he?'

'Park that one with me,' beamed Fanguin.

'It's an open meeting?' asked Orelia.

'Technically,' the clerk acknowledged, 'but sewage and plumbing aren't much of a draw.'

'Why he chose it, no doubt.' Fanguin's tone changed. 'Gorhambury, advertise the meeting for what it is: our quinquennial chance to stand and vote – nobody else will.'

'Where does it say I do that?' Gorhambury was feeling the pull of contradictory currents. The *Regulations* implied notifying the electorate, but candidates, factions and extravagant promises would surely follow.

'There's the spirit, and the letter,' replied Fanguin.

'I will do what the law requires. You, of course, are freer spirits.' He winked clumsily.

'Very true,' chipped in Madge Brown.

Orelia felt a surge of sympathy for the much-put-upon town clerk, who had served them so well in their struggle with Sir Veronal. 'Poor Gorhambury – this is hardly his fault, and it's his only day off. Let's leave him in peace.'

'His massage will cheer him up,' said Madge, rolling up her sleeves like a surgeon.

Gorhambury turned puce. 'She only does the head,' he stammered, 'just the top of the head.'

Orelia's arm swept the room. 'I'm going to liven this place up, Gorhambury, from my unsold reserves – rug, tablecloth and a shiny brass standard lamp *with a shade*. It'll be on the shop.'

'Going rates,' insisted Mr Incorruptible.

'Going rates are what I choose to charge,' she said as they turned to leave.

Fanguin gave his verdict on Snorkel's electoral strategy as the staircase groaned beneath their feet. 'Slippery as a box of monkeys, that one.' Then he added pensively, 'Bomber says I'd make a lousy Mayor.'

Orelia said nothing, but she did not demur when he added, 'I fear she's right.'

On Sunday evening the chimes of eight initiated a weekly ritual, practised for centuries: the rewinding of Doom's Tocsin, the gargantuan clock housed in the hexagonal wood-tiled bell-tower in Market Square. As the Keeper of the Clock hauled open the oak door studded with nail heads the size of large buttons, the shadows delivered a sacrilegious proposition.

'May I join you?'

'You may not!'

'In this particular week, in this particular year, I am entitled to, being over eighteen and of sound mind.' The features of a town unreliable emerged, wearing an uncharacteristically serious expression. 'Allow me to explain.'

Fanguin's outlandish theory had the allure of elevating Doom's Tocsin, and therefore its custodian, to a prominent role in affairs of state.

Upon being shown the supporting *Regulations*, the Keeper relented. 'Five minutes,' he cautioned, 'no more.'

Fanguin scampered up into the gloom of the top storey, where the great bell hung in a forest of beams, a brooding presence. A feeble light from a single shielded gaslight danced across the rafters. The Keeper cried 'time!' just as Fanguin found what he was looking for: five small bells secured high in the roof, their ropes coiled and tied beneath them.

'I never noticed them,' exclaimed the Keeper apologetically.

'Because you've never heard them – because there's never been cause,' Fanguin reassured him. He unhooked a ladder, shinned up and, wobbling precariously, felt inside the lowest bell. His hand emerged to wave an old velvet glove. Protected from grime by the brass cloche surrounding it, the glove boasted an elaborate golden R embroidered at the wrist. 'The clappers are deadened by these! There'll be one in each of the others, sure as eggs are eggs.'

The Keeper of the Clocks grew an inch. 'An ancient indenture lists my duties – one I never before understood: *To admit aspiring rulers at due time.*' The Keeper smiled. 'The genie's out of the bottle now!'

4

Of Nightmares and Agonies

That night Orelia endured a vivid nightmare. Midget-sized, she pushed through engulfing grass whose blades were *actual* blades which cut and infected, her skin wounds turning into malformities. Fingers hooked into claws; feet curled to hooves; hair thickened to mane; arms dangled, jointless. A trunk of wood with rough steps offered escape and she climbed, only to fall over a crossbar, crucified. She could not move, but a sawing wind buffeted her face. The upright held a sign at its pinnacle: *The Agonies*. Untenanted bicycles flew past, just out of reach.

Below, a cart passed by, drawn by grotesques and piled high with books. A spectral coachman peered up at her: Bevis Vibes. He laughed and the grotesques laughed too, crying, 'In a bind?' as they passed.

Orelia wrestled herself awake to find herself soaked in perspiration. She knew now where she must go, no matter what awaited her.

On Monday afternoon, she shut the shop and set off again by bicycle. Light grey clouds deepened to slate and mushroomed, their edges sharpening as the intervening blue turned milky: a storm was brewing and she had only a flimsy waterproof without a hood. 'Wet to go back and wet to go on,' she muttered, and opted for the latter.

She hid her bicycle near the roadside sign to *The Agonies*. Wider than a track and narrower than a lane, the path twisted and turned as if itself in pain. A sudden wind, as oppressively humid as in her dream, flailed the bushes on either side. She slipped on her waterproof and began to jog towards the dark screen of trees crowning the perimeter of the Rotherweird Valley.

The rain started heavy, quickly turning the ground slick, and she slowed to a crouching walk until blocked by an iron gate festooned with chains and padlocks. She followed a low wall topped with high spear-headed railings towards the escarpment. Beyond, through the bars, sporadic lightning illuminated cultivated vegetable beds, stone paths and espaliered fruit trees fastened tight against the walls. In the corners, funnels fed by gutters spilled the rainwater into brick wells – but there was still no sight of a dwelling.

At the wall's end, the drop looked daunting. Clusters of spikes like sea urchins prevented her from swinging round. Below she could see intertwined evergreen trees growing horizontally out into space before rearing skywards. In the rain and failing light, their upper reaches lost definition, dissolving into slabs of darkness.

Below, a long bare tree trunk lay across the drop, extending just beyond the walled-off area. An explosive clap of thunder decided her. She slithered down on her front until her feet reached the trunk. It had not fallen naturally; she could see heavy oak piles, driven into the bank, supporting each end. Along the topside, footholds had been planed into the wood. It was galling to discover that her grazed knees had been unnecessary: a rope lay coiled under the lip of the bank above.

As dusk slipped into night, it turned chill. She could not reach the rope, but nor could she climb back, so steep was the incline. *Be rational*, she chided herself, and when she crouched down and felt along the underside of the trunk, her fingers touched metal: hooks had been hammered in to hold a long pole. She raised it – and a thick rope with knots at intervals plummeted down, missing her head by inches. She replaced the pole, rubbed her hands dry and climbed.

A trap door at the top slid across. She was entering through a floor, disguised by strips of bark, into a huge treehouse. Candlelight from a hanging lantern flooded through. She slid the trapdoor back across and took in a low-ceilinged lobby with benches, a set of lanterns attached to short staves, hooks hung with coats, small leather boots tucked underneath. Everything was child-sized, but *not* child-like. Living wood, trunk and branches merged in the walls, but the boarded floor was even. A ladder ascended to another trapdoor, this time locked from above.

She tiptoed into the neighbouring room, which was lit by the glow of a dying fire. Her torch picked out rows of workbenches set with vices and covered with presses, string, rags and pots of gold paint. Unfamiliar tools lay in neat lines and sheets of different leathers hung from the walls: she had found the bookbinders' workshop. But the sophisticated childishness unsettled her, as did yet another ladder ascending to yet another trapdoor, again locked. Strange pipes twisted like tree roots across the ceiling.

She retrieved a lantern from the lobby and lit it from the fire.

While this room held work, the next held recreation: board games on an array of tables, and hopscotch squares carved elegantly into the floor. Models, some complete and some in progress, hung from the ceiling and wooden sculptures, all finely rendered, often grotesques, crowded the mantelpiece.

But where were the inhabitants? And why had the outside door been left unlocked?

The last room on this level was a windowless larder with ducts pumping in cold air, filled with shelves of produce from the walled garden. *Lives in balance*, she thought. *Work, play, husbandry and art.*

A long table against the far wall had been covered with white sacking. Through the scents of vegetables and fruit she caught the tang of camphor.

The contour of the sacking took shape, and then she saw a white finger, peeking out, clenched and very dead. She lifted the shroud.

Bevis Vibes exuded peace. Death had ironed out the twists in torso and face. Only the discoloration round the neck spoke of violence. Orelia recoiled. She had liked Vibes, thought him a character. She forced herself to reason: surely the unseen residents had not killed him. Not only did he sell their work, his body had been lovingly cleaned and embalmed. Somebody else must be responsible and they had chanced on the body – hence the retreat behind locked doors.

Why had he been killed? For the book he had given her? If so, *Straighten the Rope* was a cruelly ironic title.

She lifted the shroud higher, revealing a hand clawed like a crab. No wonder he wore gloves. Vibes was a child of the mixing-point.

Had Orelia stumbled on a body in town, she would have reported it at once, but this death came from the twilight world where Rotherweird and Lost Acre connected: a world of man-made monsters, shapeshifters and immortals exempt from conventional rules. She was wondering what to do next when, beneath the patter of the rain, a muffled double thump, as of light feet landing, drew her back to the workroom.

A man stood below the ladder. The fair hair, freckled skin and the absence of any stubble shadowing the face made him look young, but he had the poise of maturity, ambiguous as so much in this place. He wore trousers and a loose-fitting shirt, but his feet were bare.

'Who are you?' he asked gently. The mild country burr sounded local.

'I'm from the valley,' she replied politely. 'And you?'

'I'm from the valley too, more than most places. Why are you here?'

'I saw your sign when I was cycling to Hoy – then I dreamed of it.' Something about the boy demanded candour.

He looked at her. 'You have held the stones.'

'I don't any more,' she said apologetically. 'I sold them, not knowing what they were.'

'Ah yes, *Baubles & Relics.*'

How could he know so much? She offered a hand. 'Orelia Roc. And you are?'

He accepted it, his hand as warm to the touch as any skin, the grip neither firm nor limp. 'Tyke,' he replied, 'will do.' He gestured above his head and added, 'The others will not show themselves.'

He leaned down, stoked the fire and fed it. In the sharper light, he looked uncommonly beautiful, yet sexless too: an announcing angel. His voice quickened as if in a confessional, as if glad to get the darkness off his back. 'I'm a pure, you see. I stepped out of my cage untouched.'

She understood. The others were not 'pures' but failed experiments; Vibes must have been the least deformed and therefore able to visit the wider world to mix with normal people. Where else could they live but somewhere both inaccessible and within reach of the Rotherweird Valley?

'Mr Vibes gave me a book,' she volunteered.

'*Gave* you – did he indeed? What colour was the binding?'

'A deep maroon.'

'We don't bind in maroon.'

'It has a very odd tile: *Straighten the Rope.*'

'Ah yes, Vibes looked after that volume for a friend. If he judged this one safer with you, who am I to disagree? But take care, Miss Roc: poor Bevis is dead.'

A friend? That implied someone else knew of the existence of this strange community. Instinct told her not to probe too closely. The boy would tell her whatever he wanted her to know.

'I saw. You take care too.' When Tyke raised an eyebrow, she added urgently, 'Wynter's servant is alive, and he can change shape. Maybe he wanted the book?'

Tyke appeared to be weighing the implications. 'How does he

change shape? At what cost? Can he be anyone whenever he wants?'

Orelia shrugged. 'I don't know.' Then she asked, 'Forgive me for asking, but where did you find the body?'

'At the foot of the escarpment.'

'Strangled?'

The boy nodded. 'He was my one true friend in the world.'

She touched his hand, wordless.

'Could I pass for a man?' he asked.

This time she did answer. 'Yes, but you would be noticed.'

'You should leave, Miss Roc. The rain has stopped. I'll return the rope for you.'

Back on the path, the moon ducked in and out of the clouds and the puddles shone like slivers from a broken mirror, a reminder that she had fragments of the truth only, and still so many questions.

Vibes had mixed easily with Rotherweird folk, including Fanguin. Had Fanguin been indiscreet on a grand scale? She doubted that, so Tyke must have other sources – Ferensen, perhaps.

She turned her mind to the bookbinding. Why bind Wynter's books after Wynter's death? Wynter was their tormentor, after all. Perhaps what had been done to them in the mixing-point might be *un*done by the mixing-point? So they lived in hope of an unravelling, restoration to their old selves, so they kept in touch with their origins. After all, she had seen Morval Seer restored by Bole-alias-Ferox to human form. Bole dangled clues wherever he went, a form of cryptic vanity. And Tyke had shown no surprise when she mentioned Wynter's henchman, enhancing her fears that the master's return had indeed been prearranged before his arrest and execution.

And what of the boy himself? He exuded a desolate loneliness, and his beauty touched her. No doubt the others had the bond of shared oppression, but how did they regard *him* – with envy or worship? He struck her as an embodiment of Virtue, semi-divine, almost.

With the wind in her face on the downhill ride, she thought nothing of politics, only of Calx Bole, Wynter and the Eleusians, and their stubborn refusal to stay in the past.

5

Election Fever

'It had better be important,' snarled Snorkel, despite knowing that Gorhambury only consulted on matters of moment.

'I see you're attending Saturday's meeting of the Sewage Sub-Committee.'

'What about it?'

'Your Worship's bust must be on display.'

The Mayor's face betrayed not a flicker of surprise.

'The bust must be *present*, and it will be.'

'But—'

'Advise me, Gorhambury, on the letter of the law. Does "present" mean "present"?'

'It means "present and correct", which—'

'My bust is correct in *every* particular: a bust of me, life-sized, in marble, Roman style, sculpted on my accession, and a pleasing likeness. As you've evidently tracked down the *Regulations*, you will know *you* have to be there too. I want a debate about effluent – *and no dirty words*.'

Dirty words – the Mayor must mean such disturbing nouns as 'vote', 'candidate' and 'election'. Gorhambury withdrew backwards in deference to mayoral authority. He ascended to the reception for Archives, a poky room on the landing between the basement and the ground floor, and asked for the outer ring key. A sub-clause in the *History Regulations* permitted the Town Hall to consult precedent.

A warren of rooms stored every minute of every Committee,

immaculately indexed. Recent decades were held in the central chamber. Twentieth-century records, bound by year and committee, resided in generous, well-lit rooms adjacent to the modern. The basement's outlying provinces provided a stark contrast: dingy rooms off ill-lit corridors where ancient loose-leaf records were, to Gorhambury's distress, strewn rather than stacked. The ink had faded, the text was obscured by dust. Here indistinct mottos adorned the lintels: *Of buildings*, *Of bridges*, *Of taxes and duties*, *Of extreme weather* . . .

Gorhambury walked the periphery, opening doors and checking documents, until his hands and shirt-cuffs were stained black as a chimney sweep's. An unprecedented shine on one brass door handle suggested recent visitors. The motto: *Of matters psephological*.

Inside, copies of the *Popular Choice Regulations* in all editions rose high to the ceiling, both bound and in pamphlet form. An elaborate hook beside the doorway held a chain of office with the words *In loco parentis* entwined through a pattern of oak leaves. The coloured enamel was dulled by dust.

Regulation 14 articulated his worst fears:

14.1 During the election period the Town Clerk shall at all times wear the temporary chain of office 'In loco parentis' and will exercise all Mayoral powers insofar, and only insofar, as is necessary to preserve efficient administration. He shall neither exceed these powers nor neglect them.

14.2 All contested matters solely pertaining to candidates' manifestos and the hustings shall be exercised by the Secretary to the Municipal Liaison Committee.

He sighed. Would the gods ever leave him in peace? Reading on, his apprehension grew.

6

Cracking a Code

Bolitho was not alone in using the Delayed Action Service for posthumous deliveries.

The packaging indicated an enclosure worthy of protection. Strimmer retreated to his study on the highest floor of the North Tower and carefully cut through layers of cardboard, paper and bubblewrap.

Sir Veronal had kept his promise. Despite vanishing without trace, he had returned *The Roman Recipe Book*, the ancient volume with incomprehensible diagrams Strimmer had found in the hidden observatory above his head and then lent to Sir Veronal.

Sir Veronal's ornate manuscript delivered a gothic message:

Dear Mr Strimmer,

If this book returns, I am dead or damaged beyond repair. To be worthy, find the means to understand it and revive the Eleusians. Here lies limitless power and immortality.

Yours in spirit,

Sir Veronal Slickstone

Strimmer had never heard of the Eleusians and would have dismissed the high-flown language as delusional, but for Sir Veronal's pragmatism and disappearance, which corroborated the suggestion of a deadly occurrence in the letter's opening sentence. As to 'immortality', he remembered the one question Sir Veronal had ducked at their first meeting in old Ley Lane: his age.

He flicked through the book without improving on his first speculative interpretations – an ancient musical notation, primitive genetic codes? Neither seemed weighty enough to justify Sir Veronal's paean of praise. Strimmer needed assistance – someone unwary but informed. Most passed the first criterion, but failed the second; Valourhand passed the second, but failed the first. A snapshot scene came to him: Sir Veronal in earnest conversation with two unlikely companions at the opening of *The Slickstone Arms*. Orelia Roc he judged to be alert, but the *other* . . .

Barbiturates: such an enchanting family, and his own North Tower variant was an angel, achieving a level the wider world lacked the ingenuity – or ruthlessness – to reach. In theory, relaxing the higher functions of the cerebral cortex induced candour, lying being far more complex a task than truth-telling. But sodium thiopental and amobarbital lacked subtlety; his version stimulated a desire to boast rather than suppressing the wish to lie.

He pressed the needle of the syringe through the cork and watched the seven drops coil through the cordial before disappearing.

He wrapped the single antidote pill in his handkerchief and hurried across the Quad, muttering, '*In vino veritas*.'

Oblong had chosen 'Victorian explorers' to open his second year. His pupils treated outsider history as fictional, which irked him; the pursuit of the North Pole and the source of the White Nile should make them admit reality. While rehearsing in front of the mirror his dramatisation of Speke's argument with Burton about the source of the Nile, he heard footsteps outside: too light for Fanguin, too heavy for Orelia or Valourhand and too quick for Aggs. He had an unexpected visitor: Hengest Strimmer.

'Mr Oblong!' Strimmer placed on the table a bottle of pear brandy, Vlad's price label still attached to the neck; he had been generous.

'Peace offering,' continued Strimmer, holding out a hand, 'on the first anniversary of your arrival.'

Oblong accepted Strimmer's extended hand. Despite a disquieting lack of engagement in his clasp, Oblong, ever the optimist, took the speech at face value. He produced two glasses.

'Excuse my early distaste,' said the unusually talkative Strimmer. 'Outsiders jeopardise our independence, and I distrusted your predecessor, Flask. But a friend to Roc is good enough for me.'

Oblong could not remember ever seeing Strimmer in conversation with Orelia, but his ebullience appeared genuine.

'To us!' cried Strimmer.

It would have been rude not to drink. The cordial had an odd metallic taste beneath the fruit, but keen to please, Oblong drained his glass and allowed Strimmer to refill it. Inconsequential questions followed, and Oblong felt a burgeoning urge to be expansive. He must welcome this *rapprochement* – indeed, he must *validate* it.

'I mean,' he started, a little incoherently, 'you're right to accept . . . me . . . I mean, us . . . for we have done Rotherweird proud.'

'Oh . . . how is that, exactly?' asked Strimmer with a sugary grin.

Deep down, a sliver of resistance surfaced. 'Can't say, really can't say . . .' A desire to boast surged through, overwhelming Oblong's natural modesty. 'Posterity will know one day . . . thanks to me . . .'

'Well, of course – you are a historian.'

'Not *any* old one, Mr Strimmer! I have the sweep of Bede, the colour of Gibbon . . .'

Don't let him find it, counselled Oblong's befuddled brain, and he backed into his desk, his right hand grasping the central drawer and holding it shut.

'. . . the majesty of Macaulay. And understand, Mr Strimmer, I don't only *record* history, I *make* it.'

'Bully for you,' replied Strimmer admiringly.

Oblong babbled on briefly before toppling into an armchair and an instant, snore-ridden sleep.

The desk drawer was unlocked, and Strimmer quickly located a leather-bound notebook. Having taken the precaution of bringing a miniature camera, he photographed every page of text. Ever thorough, he flipped through the blank pages and discovered at the end a sea of superficially nonsensical letters, numbers and dots. Intrigued, he photographed them too.

He washed the glasses, returned them to the kitchen cupboard, retrieved the bottle and left on tiptoe.

Strimmer projected Oblong's diary entries, page by page, on to the bare white wall of his study. The historian's fussy, common handwriting was easy to read.

Swirling a glass of brandy, Strimmer sniggered at his unflattering reviews –

> Mr Strimmer, the creepy North Tower scientist, cold-shouldered me in The Journeyman's Gist as in the staffroom. Why is he so churlish?

And at the end of the Great Race:

> It was galling to lose to the appalling Strimmer, suitably dressed as a wasp, but I do not feel I let Fanguin down. He did run out of puff rather, and I had never been in a coracle before, let alone up a church tower.

The next sentence prompted Strimmer to take a lengthy swig, such was its oddity.

> But the event did provide an unexpected benefit – I learned something which nobody else knows except perhaps Father.

Strimmer hurried on to find another tantalising entry.

Sir Veronal took me to his library, a veritable museum. He pressed me for information, so I played the 'modern historian' card and gave nothing away, especially not the church frescoes.

Thereafter harmless entry followed harmless entry, some hilarious, especially Oblong's account of his infatuation with Cecily Sheridan (*So elegant and well read – I think I am in love*) who, as the whole town now knew, had been Vixen Valourhand in disguise.

He moved to the two pages of code. Strimmer owned a slim book on the statistics of letters in language. He had no idea what lay beneath the code – more embarrassing sexual adventures, hopefully. He enlarged the heading and set to work.

jv3z.5un5vp42xy.h4b.4uvNi.e53tz

He reached two quick conclusions: dots divided the words, and each number (only 1 to 5 appeared) represented one of the five vowels. He knew E was king of the vowels. His borrowed book told him that U was the rarest, and A, I and O were all of a par. On a frequency count of Oblong's text, that left E as 3 and U as 1, with 2, 4 and 5 as the rest.

Every word had either one capital letter or none, never more, so any capital letter must therefore be the first letter of the word. In the absence of a capital letter, a vowel must be the first letter. If that was correct, it followed that Oblong must have jumbled the letters, since numbers and capitals appeared in random positions.

Strimmer paced the room, grinning. He would enjoy dismantling Oblong's defences, pitting a Rotherweird mind against an outsider's.

Further study of his book revealed 'the' to be the most common word; 'be', 'to' and 'of' as the second, third and fourth; 'a' and 'I' as sixth and tenth. Six more two-letter words appeared in the top twenty.

And yet Oblong's two-page text appeared to have few two-letter words and no single-letter words at all.

For some minutes Strimmer wrestled with this conundrum, before letting out a yelp of self-congratulation: on discarding every last letter as a red herring, you not only achieved the right proportion of two-letter words and always kept one capital, but also uncovered two different single-vowel words – 'a' and 'I', presumably.

Now he had five ground rules: ignore entirely the last letter; a capital letter is the opening letter; a full stop marks the end of a word; the letters are jumbled, or at least not always in the right order; 'I' or 'a' = 5; e = 3 and U = 1. O was probably 4. Strimmer decided to test 'the' as the first word of the title. It worked if you took the letters in the code vowel or not) to represent the letter two spaces before them in the alphabet. However, he soon found this produced nonsensical results unless – cue for a further swig – the letter in the code represented either a letter two places before it in the alphabet or two places after. You had to experiment.

Within the hour Strimmer had laboriously worked out a surprisingly intriguing title: *The Salvation of Lost Acre*.

The town had a Lost Acre Lane, but he could think of no meaningful connection. He hurried through the text, accelerating as he became familiar with Oblong's techniques. The opening sentence had such a pompous air, he read it aloud: '*As a poet I have been inspired by this peculiar valley to set down a romantic legend that was born and nurtured here . . .*'

Thereafter, the text yielded its secrets grudgingly. Awkward combinations of words held him up – 'mixing-point', 'Midsummer flower', 'Chronicle' – and his disappointment grew. He had never read such nauseating whimsy, with its parallel universe, communicating tiles, flowers with magical properties and a restorative force known as the Green Man. Oblong, an outsider whose profession existed to record true facts, had had the effrontery to foist upon his hosts a myth of his own devising. He had even added a feeble close to tantalise the reader:

1Zrq.q2f.r28.Rrf5y.nj2Q3k4?

'*But is it that simple?*' it read.

One detail did trouble him. *The Roman Recipe Book* was liberally decorated with monsters.

He kept his transcription of Oblong's inane legend, just in case. He also resolved, when time allowed, to check the church for frescoes. His parents had taken him there long ago and he recalled no wall paintings – another self-indulgent fantasy, most likely.

7

A Reunion

Only the squelch of feet betrayed Ferensen's presence on a night
without moon or stars. His transformation in the mere pool in Lost
Acre on Midsummer Day had upset the balance in his divided being
and he could no longer resist the lure of the river.

Once out of the water he kept to the hedgerows, head low,
offering no profile. He hated his feet, ankles, knees – all those
clumsy joints – when in the river he corkscrewed like a dancer. In
water he felt warm; in the open air he froze. True, being half-eel,
half-man, he had to dive deep and put himself in peril to transform,
but it was worth it.

Today he had visited the underwater island of Rotherweird
and reacquainted himself with its rare, even unique, striations of
coloured rock.

Bill Ferdy, taking the dogs out, watched the half-naked figure
disappear back into his tower. Even the dogs, who loved Ferensen,
held back, disliking the scent of stagnant water. Ferensen uncharacteristically ignored Ferdy's wave of welcome and the publican
closed his door with a heavy heart.

In the darkness of his refuge, among tanks of water and trailing
weed, Ferensen felt better – but for the unexpected burning candle
on the central table. He did not like candles these days. His eyes
narrowed. Someone had also laid the fire.

The boy moved from the shadow and even in his befuddled state,
Ferensen recognised the urchin from the mudflats of Shoreditch,

snared by Slickstone and delivered to Wynter: the impossibly beautiful boy, the first and only pure, untouched by time and his immersion in the mixing-point.

'Stop this,' said the boy.

'I would if I could,' Ferensen protested, the words bubbling out with difficulty.

'It is a question of will.' The boy stooped and lit the fire before handing Ferensen a locket containing a loop of golden hair secured with a pin. Ferensen's eyes welled with tears and his body started shaking. The boy opened the door and carried out the tanks one by one. He bedded the plants in the stream below the house and emptied the water. He did not hurry; the memento from Ferensen's sister needed time to do its work.

'She is alive then?' he said at last as the boy sat in front of the fire.

'As she was.'

'Entire?'

'Ferox unpicked the spider in the mixing-point. He had the stones. Why he did that, I don't know.'

Ferensen felt an unaccustomed thaw in intellect and body. The boy's name came to him, a Wynter word, punning myth and reality: Tyke or Tyche, an urchin boy or a Greek goddess of luck. Tyke had always had a gift for soothing away anxiety.

'It wasn't Ferox,' he murmured. 'Wynter used Calx Bole for his last experiment and created a shapeshifter. Bole murdered Ferox and took his shape.' Ferensen had no sense of how much Tyke knew – he had been inscrutable even before his immersion – but the boy merely nodded at the revelation. 'Why does Morval not come herself?' added Ferensen, his deep hurt evident.

'You can guess the reasons,' he said calmly. 'She will come in time.'

On reflection Ferensen did understand. She feared seeing him, centuries on: he had aged, but she, he suspected, locked in the spider's body, had not – *As she was*, Tyke had said. She might have read books in her underground lair in Lost Acre, but she had no idea of the modern world. She was not ready; she was still in recovery. Or had Tyke told her to keep her distance? Ferensen thought not – the boy never commanded anyone, preferring passive benevolence, as now.

Ferensen went to his sideboard, cut several slabs of cheese and poured two glasses of Ferdy's beer before changing his trousers and pulling on a heavy jersey. The locket had shocked him into revival – he had suffered nothing compared to his twin and yet *she* had guarded her humanity.

His manners also returned. 'It's good to see you, Tyke. How do you live?'

Tyke accepted the food and drink before replying, 'We bind books.'

'*We?*'

'Fortemain taught us.'

Fortemain: the name Ferensen had suppressed the longest. Fortemain, who had not only rescued the afflicted but who had brought Oxenbridge back – while he, Ferensen, had preferred his nature studies to confrontation . . .

'Fortemain survived?'

'We took over Wynter's old house for a time,' Tyke stood up. 'But . . . I must go.'

Ferensen shook Tyke's hand. 'Remember, I don't exist in Rotherweird Town – and out here the name is Ferensen, plain Ferensen.'

'I'd advise your friends to keep an eye on Orelia Roc – and whoever guards Escutcheon Place.'

In his losing struggle with the lure of water, Ferensen had quite forgotten his friends, and now he felt ashamed. Tyke would not elaborate, and Ferensen could not blame him; the story of the Eleusians had been riddled with betrayal and in recent weeks he had hardly been a model of reliability.

As Tyke slipped into the woodland by Ferensen's tower, moving with remarkable stealth, Ferensen had a disturbing thought. Had Wynter placed others in the mixing-point to ensure their longevity in the expectation that they too would be there on Wynter's return?

And, if so, had any survived?

He decided that coffee would best consolidate his return to the human world. He lit the fire and reached for his most potent tin: the *Black Bodrum Nightraiser Special*. A serious think was called for.

8

Any Other Business?

Scry's electric performance before the Guild's assembled Court secured her immediate election as an honorary Apothecary, and influence – but there was so much to do in so little time. She explained to Thomes the need to deploy the Guild's scientific supremacy if power were to be won and held.

Levamus.

Within days, the Apothecaries had suspended all work for the outside world. Energised by the promise of power, they laboured over devices of surveillance and repression, with Thomes at the helm and Scry as their *eminence grise*.

Mrs Fanguin caught this change in pulse and, almost as quickly, its cause.

Thomes made a rare visit to her kitchen and announced curtly, 'We're all busy. So from now on, deliver direct to my study.' He placed directions on the table. 'Nowhere else, mind.'

On her first delivery to the Master, the proprietor of *The Clairvoyancy* unexpectedly rose to greet her.

'Estella Scry,' said Thomes, seizing a white chocolate confection.

Scry's face contorted with suspicion. 'She's not an Apothecarian, so why is she here?'

By way of reply, Thomes offered Scry a marzipan mouse from the tray. 'She tickles the taste buds.'

Scry smelled, licked, nibbled and gave judgement. 'To judge any

Court's quality, look first at the cook and the jester. Courtiers are easy to come by.'

Thomes blinked. For all her undoubted gifts, Scry could be *very* odd.

She quickly turned to business, as if Bomber were not there. 'I understand you have regular meetings with the North Tower. I'd like to attend the next.'

Bomber left the room in a divided frame of mind. She had not warmed to Thomes or the Apothecaries, nor to Scry, but set beside the inertia of her home life, she found the Guild's palpable energy and sense of purpose stimulating. She liked a compliment, too.

Meetings between the Apothecaries and the scientists of the North Tower alternated between their two widely contrasting homes. The North Tower might be older, but it could not compete in budget, décor, laboratory resources, manpower or architectural grandeur. The Apothecaries had *always* had money.

Valourhand had often accompanied Strimmer to these high-level discussions, but no longer since their acrimonious split. The meeting agenda held promise: a well-funded joint project on theoretical underwater nuclear devices. Strimmer liked the subject: water's high inertia enhanced the potential for shockwaves and the radiation science was challenging.

His antennae twitched on entering the Hall; the Apothecaries boasted several nuclear physicists, but none were currently visible. Instead, he was greeted by the Master and a matronly woman whom he recognised as the owner of *The Clairvoyancy*.

'Don't frown, Strimmer,' said the Master. 'Miss Scry is a valued honorary member.'

'Miss Scry sells New Age mumbo-jumbo.' He spoke as if Scry were not there.

She responded by sitting down as if he were not there. She picked a rogue hair off her skirt before flicking a drop of cream into Thomes' coffee before her own, again as if Strimmer were not there.

'Allow me to explain,' continued Thomes, ushering Strimmer to the Founder's portrait. He started with the golden letters woven into the sleeves.

Strimmer distrusted Gurney Thomes. His predecessor had been a *serious* scientist who had immersed himself in the work in hand. Thomes, though undoubtedly clever, appeared to be a *dilettante* with an undeclared personal agenda. Now he was indulging in weird inscriptions and fortune-tellers. He wondered what Scry charged for massaging the Master's ego.

'A painter prophesies an unspecified act of levitation more than three hundred and fifty years later. Leave Miss Scry to her ley lines and let's get on with proper business, shall we?' Strimmer said flippantly.

Thomes looked apologetically at his latest honorary member. He had warned her, predicting Strimmer's rudery.

Scry had a very different perspective: Strimmer's paper had shown insight, and a refreshing lack of scruple. She put down her cup with a dainty flourish. 'The past has talons in the present, Mr Strimmer.'

'Assertion, assertion, assertion,' replied Strimmer, unable to look her in the face.

Thomes explained the figures. 'It's clever: the numbers represent the difference in daylight between the longest and shortest days of the year, and more importantly, they fit *this* latitude *this* year at the Winter Solstice.'

'If you'd care to listen,' added Scry, 'there is more. Study the *Popular Choice Regulations* and you'll find that this election, uniquely – *if there is one* – falls on the Winter Solstice.' She stood up and faced the portrait as if conversing with the Founder before continuing, 'The date was determined by a calculation fixed the very year this was painted. And you will note the letters on the sleeve, which I combine to read *levamus*: a coming to power.'

Thomes' nose twitched; Scry had withheld the detail about the election until now. However, excitement overcame his disquiet. 'The election falls on the Solstice? We rise then?' *Mayor Thomes*: he saw himself swathed in finery and enveloped by cheering crowds.

This time Strimmer did look at her. 'How could you know?' he asked, impressed by the extraordinary coincidence between the painting and the law, notably a matter for calculation, not clairvoyance.

'It is my job to know. That's what I do.'

'Like *Let the cards speak*?' he mocked.

'Yes, more or less like them ...' Scry had her opening; as if from nowhere, a Tarot pack materialised. 'And as you ask – flick any six, Mr Strimmer.'

Her oddly limpid eyes looked him straight in the face. *Dare you.*

Strimmer obliged and she flipped each of the chosen cards proud of the rest, collapsed the pack and dealt two rows of three: the Devil, the Chariot and Death over the Hierophant, the Magician and the Wheel of Fortune.

Scry ran a finger along the top row. 'Someone you knew ended badly and may have deserved it, but his past bears on the future.' The finger descended. 'The lower row is more interesting. The Emperor shapes the world, but the Magician is superior, changing reality through illusion. Enemies are tricked into acting as friends. The Wheel of Fortune is quite a last card. Destiny, Mr Strimmer, or as some say, Fate, beckons you.'

'What about the Hierophant?' He gritted his teeth as soon as the question slipped out. How could he be so foolish as to be drawn in?

'He or she is a medium for contact with these other powers,' replied Scry.

Hokum, thought Strimmer, *but* ... The first three could well be Slickstone – taking the chariot as the Rolls Royce. As for the Devil, Sir Veronal was no saint. The second trio intrigued him more. Before

'Someone you knew ended badly . . .'

dealing, Scry had gathered the pack with a distracting whip of the wrist – so had he chosen the cards, or had she?

Thomes intervened egotistically. 'Miss Scry, might I suggest that you dealt *my* cards, as you were looking at me. The first row clearly concerns our late Master, an inconsequential so-and-so. The Magician represents science, and myself as leader of the Apothecaries. *You* are the Hierophant, bringing me to my destiny, our rise, the Wheel of Fortune – *levamus!*'

Scry cocked her head but said nothing as Thomes surged on, persuaded by his own eloquence. 'Look at the card: the Hierophant may wear a pope's hat, but the face is decidedly feminine.'

Scry rose decorously, smoothed her pleated woollen skirt with her palms and threaded her handbag into the crook of her arm. Ever the matron, she buttoned her cardigan, before offering a parting shot. 'In your radiation calculations, Mr Strimmer, Caesium-137 merits more attention. And, gentlemen, do remember the Wheel of Fortune indicates an *opportunity*, neither more, nor less. *You* must engage to make her spin.'

The meeting did not survive her departure for long. Thomes had not even troubled to read Strimmer's paper.

Old History

Hieronymus Seer cherishes this season: spring on the cusp of summer, with many distractions from the horrors of the other place, although he never goes there now: out of sight, out of mind.

His sister Morval does, however, perverting her gifts in the Eleusians' service, recording their manufactured creatures in her exquisite style. He knows she works under duress, but he has not yet realised it is to save his skin, not hers.

Today it is damselflies, which abound in the freshwater pools south of the Island Field. Unlike dragonflies, they hold their wings flat to their bodies. The wings are equal; the eyes separated. He judges the word 'fly' inapposite. These creatures stop, look, shoot forward, stop again. They are true predators; like hawks they hover and strike, taking mosquitoes on the wing. *Dart* is the word, he decides.

He squats on his haunches, the better to admire the slim tubular bodies blue as cobalt or ruby-red. If only Morval were there to record them . . .

A noise in the water behind him is too vigorous for a rising trout. As he walks to the bank, a pipe appears, then a head in a most peculiar mask, with glass for eyes. The hands are lifted and the creature removes its artificial head.

It is Fortemain.

He removes his strange outer skin, settles down and feverishly draws from memory Rotherweird Island's rock strata as accessed from the underwater caves. Without looking up, he says, 'I have to disguise my work or they'll use it for their own ends. And not a word about my river-suit, Hieronymus, not to *anyone*.'

'Why play a fish to find the heavens?' Seer wonders.

'To find the wherewithal to find the heavens,' replies Fortemain mysteriously.

Half an hour later, he lays down the pen, bundles his papers and returns to a familiar subject. 'You and Morval should escape while you can.'

'I can't desert this valley. It's my place of study.'

'You're both in real danger.'

He shook his head. 'No, Wynter needs Morval – nobody can record for him as she does. Anyway, he has ears and eyes *everywhere*. At least this way she stays alive.'

Fortemain cannot shift Hieronymus' mix of obstinacy and inertia. He folds his suit, gathers his papers and leaves silently with a short wave. His disappointment in his friend grows with every failed attempt. Why is he so blind to the fragility of their existence?

1571. Rotherweird.

In Lost Acre, Fortemain has found the winking man. The sphere the priest showed him would fit exactly. He checks the underlying strata beneath the henge in Lost Acre and the church in Rother-weird and they match exactly.

He begins to think his private ambition may be realisable, but frets over what Wynter might achieve if he acquired this knowl-edge. He hopes that as science advances, he will be able to explore these complexities in greater detail.

Morval Seer knows her time is nearing its close, for *The Roman Recipe Book* and *The Dark Devices* approach completion. Slickstone habitually wears a gloating smile; she knows he will have her pulled to pieces in the mixing-point – how dare a swineherd's daughter refuse him! What kind of creature he will meld her with, she dares not imagine. Her nerves fail; scarlet deltas stain the eyes and she fears for the stillness of her hands, her ability to hold a line. Her complexion loses its bloom, her body its shape. Her brother is no comfort, apparently insensitive to the fact that his disengagement looks like acquiescence.

She sits in her room in the Manor surrounded by pens, brushes and the wherewithal for making paint. Wynter has not restocked the more expensive materials like ultramarine and azurite, another portent of her approaching fate.

Fortemain comes to her, but before he can speak, she says calmly, 'You can't stop him.'

'Oxenbridge will,' he replies, but how can he get a message across wider England to a man they have not seen in years? 'I have to leave – but Morval, I'll find you, *whatever* they do. And remember, all can be reversed.'

'*All?*'

'Whatever he does can be undone,' he says firmly.

She shrugs as if to say, little hope of that, but she is reconciled to her loss. With so little to lose she is a husk of her former self. She thinks only of him. 'You're dressed for a journey.'

'I have to go to ground. We *will* stop him, but he may return, and someone must be here if he does.'

'To be there then, you must have—' Eyes wide, she whispers, '*What* have you done?'

'A wicked experiment to do long-term good,' he replies. 'I can only ask you to trust me.'

He looks himself and he sounds himself. So, *what* has he done? 'Until whenever, then,' she says.

They kiss each other on the cheek, neither wishing their parting to be so chaste.

*

Fortemain turns away, unable to tell her of his self-inflicted wound, and still less of the reason. He makes his way to the outhouse where the familiars are kept. He expects a guard, but there is none. He quickly finds the pidgeboy, fastens the tiny capsule to one leg, gives instructions and releases him.

That task done, he goes to the old barrow behind the church, part excavated by Bole in search of Saxon gold. Wooden staves hold up the earthen ceiling. His visit to the mixing-point all those years ago will now be put to the test. The old priest's words chime in his head: *Live on, to resist when they return.*

In his anxiety, he has made one mistake: he has left behind his working papers and, worse, his copy of *De Observatione Naturae*.

But it's too late now. There is no going back.

1571. *Rotherweird Manor.*

The disappearance of Fortemain and the pidgeboy drain the Eleusians of vitality, creating a vacuum which fills with rage against Fortemain's perceived allies. The Seers' terrible punishment follows within the week: an eelman torn to pieces by carnivorous fish and a lovely woman imprisoned in the body of a giant spider.

Their absence creates another vacuum, but Wynter has prepared for the creeping tide of doubt – indeed, he exploits it, spinning a new narrative around his death and rebirth. There will be a second age of the Eleusians.

He plots their remaining time with Bole. 'It is a question of journeys, Calx – four, to be precise: the pidgeboy's flight to London, the message's onward route to Oxenbridge, the gathering of a company – that means men, horses, weapons and provisions – and the return to Rotherweird. We will see out the year at least, which is a mercy, with so much to do.'

Bole loves Wynter, his rescuer and mentor, but he has his own pride too and he watches, listens, notes, absorbs, cross-refers and, above all, *learns*. That he must slave to master complexities his charges consider simple drives him all the harder. 'Charges' is how he sees them, but to them he is nothing more than a *servant*. His corpulence, waddling gait and grey complexion have always attracted mockery; now they call him the Potamus.

He would change his appearance in the mixing-point: *Hercules* Bole, *Achilles* Bole. He and Wynter have been working privately with the mixing-point for months now, spending hours moving the stones to ever more extreme positions. In their last experiment, an owl and a mouse shared the cage, only for it to swing out of the mixing-point with no owl but two mice. One was dead, but the other could see in the dark and had turned hunter.

The stones can do *anything*. He and Wynter have decided: he will soon be Potamus the shapeshifter.

One of the young women stands apart from the snideness of the others. '*Potamus* means "we drink", Mr Bole, and I'd take it as a compliment. You *imbibe* knowledge, which is the wherewithal for everything.'

She says *Potamus* with a roly-poly playfulness, and pats him in unexpected places. He nurses a stunted, unexpressed love for her.

One night he is working late on Fortemain's papers when Wynter joins him. 'Fortemain was studying landscape and rock, here and in the other place – but why?' he asks.

Wynter taps *De Observatione Naturae*. 'Read this. Study Lost Acre and our valley. I have unlocked their mystery, Calx. There *is* a way.'

1572. *The Manor House garden.*

Summer's lease has not quite expired; it is the calm before the storm. Two young women are reclining, their backs against the trunk of a spreading beech, basking in dappled shade. Euclid is open in one lap, Robert Recorde's *The Whetstone of Witte* in the other. Bees amble among the early ivy flowers smothering a nearby wall, their nectar in demand now triter blooms have come and gone.

Neither woman has conventional good looks; the one is plain and slim, the other's heavy features do not quite cohere – but look again. In both, the eyes and set of the mouth declare intelligence and determination in abundance.

The slighter breaks the silence, asking, 'Have you decided what name you will choose?'

'Estella, Estella Scry.' She savours the word.

'A scry and not a seer?' giggles her companion. *Estella: out of the star.* Perhaps she intends a reminder of her rejection by Fortemain; once loved, now loathed. Wordplay is always popular with the Eleusians.

'And you?'

'Nona – plain Nona.'

Scry does not like the name. It is slippery: anon backwards, short for 'no name'. She seeks reassurance. 'You will be loyal to me, won't you? Always? Whatever awaits us?'

'All ways,' replies Nona with a smile.

'Where is Mel?' Scry asks suddenly, and Nona smiles again.

'In the other place with the Master,' she purrs, as good as saying that she is better informed.

'How do you know?'

Nona shrugs.

'You've been talking to the Potamus, haven't you? You really shouldn't. He's vile, fleshy . . .' She suppresses her true reason for loathing Bole. He is closer to Wynter than any of them.

'Clever Potamus,' replies Nona provocatively, 'part-of-the-plan Potamus.'

Scry declines the bait but cannot suppress her curiosity. 'What are they doing to Mel? Why take her alone to the other place?' she asks.

Nona dodges the question, saying only, 'We go tomorrow – our turn in the other place. How exciting is that!'

Silence descends. Tomorrow the mixing-point will give them

immortality – but what else? Does Nona know more about the future than she? What does 'part-of-the-plan Potamus' signify? Scry snaps off a daisy and plucks the petals as she thinks of Wynter and his ordeal to come. She wants to be the agent of his resurrection. In her mind she calls each white tear.

He loves me the most, he loves her the most, he loves the Potamus the most . . .

1572. *The Island Field.*

The dawn sky holds promise, the clouds high and thin, as Wynter, Bole and Mel make their way to the other place. Wynter calls a halt at the southern edge of the Island Field.

'You are the last of my men and the first of my women,' says Wynter, laying a hand on Mel's neck. 'You are my builder and architect. We will have a city of light and a city of dark, Olympus and Hades, and you will open the way to both.'

'I've never placed one brick upon another,' she replies.

'Would I be so primitive?'

'And when you return?'

'You'll be there, in the full bloom of youth.' His intonation scares her; it implies a price to be paid. His right hand still rests on the nape of her neck. 'To live on,' he continues, 'you must die a little – although not as much as me.'

She does not step from the cage but falls and rolls. It is the very moment of death, less a breath than a rattle of stones in a jar. She cannot stand or crawl: every cell is disfigured, all memory lost, her mind utter darkness. She cannot muster a scream, just manages a mew of pain. The slope tumbles her down to the stream, limbs too knotted and stiff to slow or grip, but as her ragdoll head lolls from side to side, one image is retained: two men, one tall, one squat, above her beside a spreading tree.

Water flows over wrinkled cheeks and into her ears, but the stream's abstraction – neither kind nor cruel, it would flow no differently for a stone – kick-starts a will to survive. Her heart flutters into a beat, and she is racked by another agonising breath, but this time the rattle is inaudibly gentler, one step removed from the moment of death.

Fight, fight, fight.

She summons a name: Mel, beautiful Mel, the woman of honey, and a first memory. The men had *smiled* at her agonised descent, *satisfaction* at a job well done.

They are her torturers.

Fight, yes, but fight *and* avenge . . .

Wynter pats Bole on the shoulder. After tomorrow's work, all will be done: the labours of the mixing-point complete in the first Age of the Eleusians; the Seers punished; the women transformed – and Bole no longer what he appears to be.

The vigil for the second and last Age will shortly begin. There only remains a suitable parting.

1572. Rotherweird Manor. A Last Supper.

Twelve disciples would have been orthodox for this last meeting of his Order of Chivalry, but four are missing: the Seers, dear Mel sacrificed for the greater good and Fortemain vanished as intended. Yet to have four each side of him at the refectory table in the Great Hall of Rotherweird Manor bestows a pleasing symmetry. They face the door, backs to the fireplace, as if the Green Knight of Arthurian legend were poised to enter.

Wynter rejects a proposal that marionettes should fill the empty spaces. 'Our own events define us,' he says firmly. 'We *rework* – we do *not* imitate.'

He eyes his disciples and servant. Of the nine, only four have the gift of near-immortality: Slickstone, Bole and the two women. He, Wynter, must take a different, darker road. The others are disposable in the greater cause of building his legend, not that they know it. He holds their lives in the palm of the hand, a true trait of divinity, the making of martyrs.

The familiars, when not secured in their dark outhouse, are tethered to the wrist like falcons, for all are winged, but tonight they are free to roam. They peer down from the hammer-beam roof like living gargoyles.

Cellars and larders have been scoured for the best. Swan and peacock, seasoned with pepper and ginger, follow pike stuffed with oysters; to end, blaunderelles swimming in honey and damson marmalade. They drink weak ale; Wynter is holding back the luxury of wine till last.

The plates are cleared, and the servants with them; most head upstairs to care for the children roaming the corridors. Whether the Eleusians' offspring remain in Rotherweird after the fall, whether they inherit the gifts of their parents – indeed, whether they survive at all – is in Fortune's gift, not his.

He rises and waits for true silence. Even the half-humans in the rafters catch the expectancy.

'You have all admired my astrolabe,' he begins, 'which can fix planetary positions yet to come.'

Sir Henry's astrolabe, in fact, notes Calx Bole, *but to the winner the spoils*.

The candles at the ends of the table have been extinguished. Wynter's gaunt face monopolises the light. 'But it is a mere toy compared to the clock we have fashioned for our return: an invisible clock which sets events in motion far into the future.'

We have fashioned? We? Scry's eyes dart around the table. She reads puzzlement of various shades; only Nona and the Potamus are inscrutable. That afternoon she and Nona had entered the mixing-point, one after the other, emerging ostensibly unscathed despite their strange companions, as Wynter assured them they would. She trusts him more than ever – but does Wynter trust her? And if not, whom?

Wynter continues, 'Yes, my children, now we leave the stage to ordinary men for a century or four, but my clock will continue to turn. A new Rotherweird will rise and *we* shall be there to claim it.'

He slips into myth, talking of afterlife and the underworld, of Theseus trapped in the chair of oblivion and his release by Hercules, of Aeneas founding Rome after surviving the world of the dead. He mentions the road to Emmaus – the stranger recognised, the divine returned to walk among the ordinary. And he prophesies his own death in the mixing-point, soon and unavoidable, and his resurrection.

When Wynter talks this way, science yields to a mystical belief in *him*.

He ends with a sacramental theme. 'We shall preserve a memento: a phial of each Eleusian's blood, that most distinctive of liquids.'

As arranged, Bole circulates with a tray of tiny phials and a sharp knife.

That night Wynter visits Nona and Scry in Scry's bedroom. They look, as expected, quite unchanged.

He fills in details. 'Oxenbridge will return, and I will be disappeared in the mixing-point,' he explains. Both women touch his gown, trying not to show their distress. 'It is such a pretty form of justice that Oxenbridge will not be able to resist it,' he tells them, adding, 'but you must use your ingenuity and buy clemency.'

'Master—' whimpers Scry, but Nona hushes her.

'We will,' Nona says.

'Here is the month and year of my return.' He hands them a scrap of parchment: it is *centuries* ahead.

'What else can we do?' asks Scry, trying to be practical and *necessary*.

'Prepare me willing servants.'

'There must be more to do than that.' She is desperate to serve.

'A particular enemy should be killed on the day of my return, otherwise his presence might sully it.'

'*Fortemain lives?*' they cry together; no other enemy could so exercise their master.

'I trust so,' he says enigmatically. 'Much turns on it.'

Scry has caught the Potamus studying Fortemain's old papers, to which he has added a most peculiar title, and she has seen Wynter with them too, so they must hold a great secret.

He kisses them each on the cheek, but Scry is troubled, for he has given Nona no task and she has not asked for one. Is Wynter's return her privileged assignment? A seed of resentment germinates.

'Sleep well,' says Nona, before leaving for her own room.

Much later, in the early hours, she hears that familiar double tread, the heavy and the soft: Wynter and Bole, and then a single whisper, Wynter's whisper.

'Tell her about the fastness near the time.'

Tell whom, what, and when, and why—

The whispers rise and fall, dropping other catchwords she can barely hear.

'He is buried deep . . .'

'. . . will open the way . . .'

'. . . be brave, join me . . .'

Wynter likes to test them – so must she join these fragments to understand the whole? Is Nona at her own door opposite thinking likewise?

The double tread descends the stairs and, lifting the hem of her nightshift, she follows, to find Bole and Wynter bent over two maps, one of the Rotherweird Valley and one of the other place. She steps back as Bole's familiar pads around the balcony towards her, teeth clenched and ribs aglow. She retreats, but now she knows: the Potamus loathes her as she does him. She must guard her back in the centuries to come.

1572. London.

Dawn, and birds small and large mob him – it is to be expected with his freakishness – but it does not last. He rolls, swerves, dives and stalls, switching from talons hidden to talons up. His quicksilver mind makes a virtue of his lopsidedness: a learning curve in every sense.

Below him, the snaking Thames widens and boats multiply; the surrounding green and brown retreats before a sprawling city. These alluvial mudflats were once his home, where he scuttled and probed for meagre pickings. Smoke plumes rise, stiff as vertical strings in the tranquil summer air.

Keep to the river, Fortemain had said, *and you cannot miss it*. He had drawn the configuration of the towers and the rivergate, even marking the window of the message's recommended recipient: the Tower's Master of Ravens. Fortemain's sketch has the exactness of a childhood memory.

The pidgeboy begins his downwards glide.

'Keep to the river, Fortemain had said, and you cannot miss it . . .'

NOVEMBER:
FIRST WEEK

I

Of Sewage and Psephology

Rotherweird's Parliament Chamber conveyed mixed messages. Rows of opposed benches set either side of a wide aisle implied robust debate between rival parties. A long table with modern chairs on a raised dais implied government by committee. A single throne, festooned in lions and birds, at one end of the table told the current truth: Snorkel controlled government, and any committee which mattered.

Meetings of the Sewage Sub-Committee – sewage disposal being a *scientific* subject – always attracted a sprinkling of observers. Each motion was open to the floor with public debate guillotined at ten minutes.

The Sewage Sub-Committee processed in with Snorkel at the head, and in his wake the Committee chairman, then Gorhambury, clasping the *General Committee Regulations* as an altar boy would the Bible, followed by the six ordinary members. Last in trotted Madge Brown, the Assistant Head Librarian and Committee Secretary.

Snorkel scanned the benches, noting with dismay the presence of lowlifes from the disgraceful Bolitho funeral – Boris Polk, the absurd Oblong and the impudent Valourhand (her 'Snorky Porky' retort at Sir Veronal Slickstone's party still rankled). None of them had previously shown interest in waste disposal. Roc had been seen sniffing around the Hoy Book Fair with that perennial troublemaker Godfery Fanguin, but at least he had not shown up.

More inexplicably, the Keeper of the Clock was in attendance, and the Master of the Apothecaries, with a young minion on either side. Apothecaries *never* attended municipal meetings. And most disturbing of all, Estella Scry sat at the back. His forecasted sunny day was clouding over.

'Our nineteenth-century pipework is ailing,' droned the chairman. 'Saltware drains are turning porous; cast-iron pipes are corroding, and the recent subsidence by the churchyard wall confirms the need for urgent action—'

The chairman stumbled as every head turned, transfixed by an apparition, which, on closer inspection, turned out to be . . .

Snorkel sighed.

Swamped in an oversized coat, one shoulder higher than the other, neck swathed in a scarf and bent forward like a duck, Fanguin shuffled in, supporting himself on a tall silver stick. From under the scarf emerged a vacuum hose and with his coat whirring like an electric egg-timer, Fanguin sprayed a plume of orange dust along the ledge between wall and ceiling.

'Security!' bellowed Snorkel.

'Seconded!' Fanguin bellowed back. 'I've a theft to report!'

The dust exposed a ghostly shape on a high ledge, the fragments of contour not yet recognisable. Fanguin's stick extended, sprouting rungs and feet; a device fashioned by Boris in his teenage years.

Committee members gaped and the caucus of unreliables, Apothecaries excepted, applauded.

Fanguin unloaded his spraying equipment onto a chair before clambering up the makeshift ladder, wobbling like a circus clown. 'Exhibit A,' he shouted at the mystified Sewage Sub-Committee, 'one sheet of invisibility film, stolen from the premises of Mr Boris Polk.'

A sharp yank revealed Snorkel's bust, eyes and mouth dripping with sly intelligence. Fanguin heaved the head off the ledge, secured it under an arm and descended. He positioned it on the committee's table so that the audience now faced two Mayors, one in flesh and one in stone.

Fanguin thrust back his shoulders; he was on a roll against his bitter enemy. 'Would the Town Clerk read *Regulation* 1, sub-paragraphs 2 and 3, of the *Popular Choice Regulations*,' he requested politely, while grimacing like a magician promising rabbits.

Gorhambury now knew the *Regulations* by heart, and in view of the public's right to know, he could only comply.

He stood up and recited, 'To inaugurate an election, a candidate, other than the incumbent, must slap the bust (see *Regulation* 5) during the challenge period (see *Regulation* 2) with the velvet glove (see *Regulations* 2 and 7).'

And next: 'The bust must be displayed in the Council's Parliament Chamber throughout the challenge period and the present Mayor must be present throughout the aforesaid period.'

Small words registered in the collective consciousness – *election, bust, glove, challenge period* – quaint details teasing at Rotherweird's love of ritual. A hint of chicanery registered too.

'Whose bust?' asked a committee member.

'His Worship's,' Gorhambury supplied, 'as you see here.'

'When does the challenge period begin?' asked Valourhand.

'In two minutes.'

'And end?' asked another committee member.

'Noon.'

'Whose glove?'

'That's history, where we cannot go,' replied Gorhambury, 'but they sit on the six clappers on the electoral carillon on the top floor of Doom's Tocsin: six gloves, for a maximum of seven candidates. The incumbent Mayor can stand as of right.'

Snorkel responded by rising imperiously from his seat and opening his arms in a gesture of welcome. 'After decades – *decades!* – of loyal service, I am not a little put out that Mr Fanguin has sabotaged my cheeky little surprise: unveiling myself to launch the challenge period. But sensitivity never was his strong point.'

'Challenge period?' asked a member of the Sewage Sub-Committee.

Snorkel kept to his principles: never use the e-word. 'It theoretically initiates a quinquennial ritual, which is best ignored,' he said.

Nobody spoke; the taproot of long unchallenged power ran deep.

'Business as usual, then,' Snorkel added smugly.

The Keeper of the Clock stood up, a respected figure. 'I do wonder how anyone could acquire a glove if I'm not told to open up Doom's Tocsin.'

'Nobody asked me to ask you,' replied Snorkel glibly.

Orelia stood up, cheeks flushed, voice wavering. 'Nobody could – because you can't get a copy of the *Popular Choice Regulations* for love or money. Why are we all in the dark, Mr Snorkel?'

The Mayor slipped adroitly from past to present. 'The *Regulations* should be in the Rotherweird Library for all to read.'

Orelia noted the *should be*. He knew they weren't, but whatever happened, it would not be his fault. She shook her head and the audience did likewise, shifting to and fro as if watching a tennis match. 'The Town Hall recalled them for rebinding months ago,' she said accusingly.

'Poor timing,' agreed Snorkel, 'but is anyone interested?'

'*I'm* interested,' chimed several voices in unison, their owners having belatedly grasped the import of 'quinquennial'.

'There are plenty of copies,' replied Snorkel casually. 'Take them when you go.'

'It's after nine already,' boomed Fanguin, running a rhetorical arm around the chamber. 'Are only those with an interest in sewage allowed to stand? We need the *Regulations now!*'

After a token whisper in Gorhambury's left ear, Snorkel shifted to a 'more in sorrow than in anger' strategy. 'It appears there has been a *most* regrettable lapse by Archives. The *Regulations* are under lock and key. I promise a full investigation, chaired by a magistrate.'

Gorhambury intervened with Roman impartiality. '*Regulation* 11 permits an extension of the challenge period until sunset in the event of fire, storm, act of God or other disabling circumstance. And His Worship has been misled: Archives have been working hard, gathering copies of the *Regulations* for all.'

'When's sunset?' asked a committee member.

'Four-thirteen,' replied Gorhambury.

'I move an extension to four-thirteen,' said the Keeper of the Clock.

'Seconded,' chipped in Valourhand.

A forest of hands jerked upwards.

'Carried,' said Gorhambury solemnly.

Snorkel would happily have strangled his clerk for his addiction to small print.

The Keeper of the Clock, an arch-conservative, but liberal in the defence of ancient freedoms, was warming to his role. 'Doom's Tocsin will summon the town to Market Square,' he announced portentously. 'Gloves can be retrieved by anyone who wants them.'

'Why, pray, are these matters for the Sewage Sub-Committee?' stammered Snorkel.

'They're entrusted with clearing up mess!' retorted Fanguin.

The audience murmured approval of their new champion. Only the Apothecaries and Scry remained inscrutable.

Finger ever to the wind, Snorkel changed tack again.

'We reconvene at two-thirty. I am most grateful to the Clerk for belatedly galvanising Archives – a most challenging task, believe me.'

The councillors withdrew as the audience, exhilarated by all this talk of rights, votes and elections, headed for Market Square.

Once into the labyrinth of rooms behind the Chamber, Snorkel ushered Gorhambury aside and hissed, 'What the hell are you up to?'

'Your office is at stake, your Worship.'

'It is now!' the Mayor snarled, before summoning his lead eavesman, a lean, sallow man with a name to fit, Bendigo Sly, and murmuring, 'You know what to do.'

'Two were missing.'

'They can't be – Doom's Tocsin is locked day and night.'

'Like father, like son?' suggested Sly.

Snorkel understood Sly's veiled suggestion – two aspiring candidates had slapped his father's bust before being bought off – so he embraced it while cursing Fanguin and Roc for stirring up a hornets' nest.

'Do the needful then, Sly, and quick about it.' Sly managed two steps before Snorkel hauled him back. 'And don't lose that stuff you nicked from Polk. It could be useful.'

Sly nodded, judging it a bad moment to admit that in the scrum around the Committee desk, the invisibilty film – secure, he thought, under a paperweight – had mysteriously 'vanished'.

On reflection, Snorkel saw no cause for concern, and some cause for optimism.

If he had to face the vagaries of election, he would surely win. Nobody played the system or the people it served better than him – and with a mandate, he could expand his fiefdom. Rotherweird Prison had been underused in recent times, for starters.

2

The Velvet Gloves

In the basement, on Gorhambury's orders, Archives had boxed hundreds of copies of the most recent edition (1688) of the *Popular Choice Regulations*, ready for distribution from the Town Hall steps.

The Keeper went straight to Doom's Tocsin to find someone had been in and out before him. Fanguin had removed one glove the previous Sunday night, but to his dismay, the other five had vanished. An inspection revealed disturbed dust on the floor and loose tiles near the bell-tower's upper window. *Act normally and await events*, he decided. The great bell struck and struck again, as its tiny relation, the Crier's hand-bell, tinkled through the streets.

'Challenge period expires at sundown,' declared the Crier, adding his own call to the hustings as he followed an ancestral route, which never covered ground already trod.

> '*Who'll slap the bust in Parliament Hall?*
> *Who will stand and who will fall?*'

The progress to Market Square began, and more Apothecaries, with dark stove-pipe hats added to their black-and-white garb, made a rare public appearance. Ordinary Rotherweirders in coloured clothing made way for them: *corvidae* loose among peacocks.

Otherwise, normality prevailed, with countrysiders plying their weekend trade. Boris spotted Megan Ferdy on her stall behind a pyramid of cheeses and warned her, 'Tell Bill to open early. There's going to be a communal chinwag.'

She nodded at a knot of Apothecaries. 'I don't like them.' He handed her a copy of the *Popular Choice Regulations*, but the worry in her face did not ease. 'Never shake a settled barrel,' she added.

'Even if the dregs are on top?' countered Boris.

'If the whole is drinkable, yes, even then,' she replied. 'I'll tell him.'

Boris respected Megan Ferdy for her earthy good sense. He had expected enthusiastic support for the democratic cause and her cautionary note gave him pause as townsfolk poured into Market Square from all sides to collect their copies of the *Regulations*.

A studious hush descended. Boris, Orelia and Fanguin felt like sidesmen distributing hymnals.

Only Hayman Salt and Finch ignored the Town Crier's summons. Human business no longer interested Salt, and constitutionally, Finch could not stand – and in any case, he had other concerns.

Estella Scry mingled with the crowds, listening and watching, rich pickings in all directions.

The dense text of the *Popular Choice Regulations* gradually yielded the basic rules: no more than seven candidates, the need to slap the sitting Mayor's bust with a velvet glove to declare candidacy, the Summoning – a calling-in of Rotherweird's expatriate voters in the event of a contested election – and the fixing of Voting Day by a complex sidereal formula. The Summoning generated particular interest; many Rotherweirders worked outside or over-seas, infiltrating boardrooms, universities and governments to sell the town's science (good and bad) and to monitor outsider progress.

'Get me a glove!' Thomes issued the order to the two youthful acolytes, the favourites who usually attended him.

Scry, in an all-encompassing blue shawl fastened by a jewelled phoenix brooch at the throat, extended a restraining arm. 'It would be wasted, Master Thomes.'

The implicit insult rendered Thomes briefly speechless. 'Wasted? *Wasted* on *me*?'

She put a calming hand on his arm. 'You're not eligible.'

'Who says?' he snapped, flourishing his copy from the Guild's library.

'You're working from the 1645 edition. The *Regulations* were amended in 1688, when wisdom or experience decided that mayoral office should be denied to the Headmaster, the Herald, the Crier, the Keeper of the Clock, the senior Judge and the Master of the Apothecaries. I believe they call it "separation of powers".'

She held out the relevant provision as corroboration, but Thomes barely looked at it, such was Scry's newfound authoritative status.

'What about the other bastards?' And when she raised an eyebrow, he corrected himself, 'I mean the other sodding Guild-masters?'

'They were not considered "powers", presumably.'

'Nothing but low-level manufacturers,' he hissed in agreement.

'Think of it as a puppet show, with the Apothecaries holding the strings.'

Thomes did not fully grasp Scry's message, but the gist felt good. 'So, who's the puppet?' he asked.

'Patience,' she replied.

The Keeper of the Clock emerged from Doom's Tocsin and took Boris and Orelia to one side. 'The other gloves have vanished, apart from the one Fanguin took on Sunday night.'

They assumed a pre-emptive strike by Snorkel. 'To the pub,' said Orelia firmly, and led the way.

She had never seen *The Journeyman's Gist* so full. She distrusted pub conversation, holders-forth preaching remedies for life's ills or repeating old stories as new to listeners too bored to dissent, but today the banter had edge as the holders-forth dithered and the listening classes pressed for explanations.

'With great regret I've decided not to offer myself.'

'Why, for God's sake, when you've spent years telling us what you'd do when you got the chance?'

All around her Orelia heard tactical retreat paved with feeble excuses.

'The office would grind to a halt.'

'My other half wouldn't take the pressure.'

And the best: 'We couldn't cope with the *grandeur*.'

The prevalent emotion pervading the inn like stale incense was *fear*: fear of losing, fear of Snorkel and his tentacular reach, fear of criticism, fear of the limelight.

Boris located Fanguin, Oblong, Gregorius Jones and Bert Polk at a corner table. Fanguin's glove lay in the middle, unclaimed.

'Increase the public health budget,' pronounced Jones. 'Compulsory yoga at seven, Pilates at noon and a five-mile run before tea.'

'You'd kill half the population,' protested Bert.

Orelia strove to raise the standard of debate. 'Rights wither if they're not exercised.'

'As does everything else,' smirked Jones.

Orelia shook her head, feeling deeply depressed.

Valourhand elbowed her way through the press, squeezed in beside Fanguin and came straight to the point. 'It's time for facts, not blather: Jones lacks brains and Fanguin application. Boris has inventions, Bert his family and Roc her shop. Finch is disqualified and Gorhambury induces coma.'

'He spoke well in the Chamber,' said Bert, digging Fanguin in the ribs.

'*Him?*' responded Valourhand incredulously. 'Who'd vote for a dismissed school teacher?'

'Mrs Fanguin,' replied Fanguin.

'And you?' Orelia asked Valourhand, put out by her rudeness. 'No shortcomings?'

'I alone protested against Slickstone. If the town wants a radical, you have one.'

'A radical from the North Tower as Mayor?' queried Oblong.

'Listen to the outsider with no vote.'

For once Oblong had a riposte. 'In fact, the resident historian does have the vote. Read the *Regulations* if you're going to stand.' He spoke with edge to his voice, the legacy of his suffering at the hands of Cecily Sheridan.

Orelia felt a flutter of affection for the hapless historian. At last he was standing up for himself – and he was right, the North Tower brought much money to the Town, but to give them the Town Hall too? Of course, the more fundamental objection, which nobody dared articulate, was Valourhand's essential *oddness*.

Rhombus Smith passed by, pint of beer in hand, musing on fictional elections. He placed a thumb on the glove. 'Ah, the heavy hand of power!'

Boris appealed to the headmaster. 'Your vote, Headmaster: which of my friends should stand?'

Rhombus Smith liked to answer difficult direct questions indirectly. 'Nobody *must* and maybe nobody *should*. If anyone does, consult the English novel, where lurks the winning slogan, *Ancient Institutions and Modern Improvements*.' The headmaster, a radical conservative, took a swig of *Ferdy's Feisty Peculiar*, smiled and moved on.

Valourhand seized the glove and stormed out.

Outside the leaded windows, mist began to form, indicative of gathering uncertainties.

Strimmer surveyed the crowded pub with disdain: narrow-minded teachers, scientists without political nous, common labourers, Oblong and his ghastly friends. The youngest head of the North Tower in living memory, he considered himself intellectually

Rotherweird's first minister, but the time-consuming grind and grime of politics had repelled him, until Scry's cards nettled his curiosity. He felt the tide of change lapping at Rotherweird's foundations: Sir Veronal's letter had held out the promise of power, and the prevailing mood of dissatisfaction and indecision meant a vacuum to be filled. *Levamus*.

'Hengest?' A tug at his jacket caused him to turn as the new Linguistics teacher sidled up. She was pretty and shapely, a pleasing short-term diversion. She waved her pamphlet. 'Have you read this?'

'Poor man's theatre,' replied Strimmer dismissively.

She giggled. 'Like what's in your jacket pocket?'

Strimmer glanced down to see two velvet fingers peeping out. He removed the velvet glove with its embroidered 'R' and checked the other pocket – a Tarot card. The Emperor.

He was being used, but did he mind?

At last, he had a thread of colour in his life.

By three o'clock every bench in the Parliament Chamber was occupied, with standing room equally congested. Mindful of the *Fire Regulations*, Gorhambury had managed, with difficulty, to keep the aisles free.

Being still technically the adjourned meeting of the Sewage Sub-Committee, the same members processed in, in the same order, and sat in the same places. All eyes were on Snorkel, but the old fox let them wait.

The chairman hurried through the Annual Report before the Mayor rose.

'Welcome to – if I may deploy a naughty word – this *historic* occasion, and apologies for the abruptness of today's events. The Town Clerk regrettably overlooked his quinquennial duties.'

Even Gorhambury, that inscrutable mandarin, gasped like a newt on a riverbank at this outrageous accusation. Snorkel, unabashed, surged on, slipping into his 'man-in-the-job' mode. 'Observe one of many committees at work – restoration after the fire, the reopening of *The Journeyman's Gist*, the Midsummer Fair; all down to them. Do they continue? Or would you prefer weeks of paralysis? And postponement of my tax cuts and extended public holidays?'

Tax cuts, extended public holidays – news to all. A sepulchral quiet descended as Snorkel's appeal to self-interest wove its spell.

Orelia felt a reality check. Who could trump the wiles of this master tactician?

'Any takers?' asked Snorkel to the sound of falling cards.

An ambitious Sewage Sub-Committee member folded first. 'Rotherweirders, we should heed the Mayor's wise words.' With an unctuous smile, he placed a glove on the table.

A second glove-holder followed suit. A man with a disappointing beard, gifted at algorithms and driven by his wife to seek social prominence, muttered, 'I know my place,' as he laid his glove beside the first.

Last but not least, the managing partner of Rotherweird's most expensive solicitors, *Finewad & Parchling*, glided down the central aisle. A tall man, head like an apple on a stick, he spoke with rehearsed *gravitas*. 'The law may rule, but she must also serve.'

In translation, another glove had been surrendered: this time for an increased share in the Town Hall's conveyancing business. Sly had succeeded in his task, delivering the right message to the right targets: remunerative sinecures in the next appointment round. *Such a pretty system*, thought Snorkel. *Control the gloves and you control the would-be candidates.* After a nod from Sly, council staff appeared at the doors with trays holding glasses of red and white wine. He had done his sums: all gloves accounted for, save for the two lost in his father's era, and that meant celebration time.

Fanguin was up for the fight, but he had neither glove nor support. Orelia felt numbed by the poisonous mix of apathy and anti-climax. She sat beside Valourhand, whose right hand clenched and unclenched as her head turned from the clock to the chamber and back again. She started to rise, subsided, half-rose again. *She wants maximum impact and no time for another candidate*, Orelia deduced; a straight fight with Snorkel would appeal.

Snorkel lifted his own glass. 'That's that, then – I propose to thank you all with a glass of Vlad's finest—'

A different voice rang through the chamber, cold, and commanding instant attention. 'Hold your horses, Mr Snorkel. Why go to all this effort for so little? Surely we deserve a contest to lighten up our winter? Your tax cuts and holidays sound like a sop to me. Are we to be bought for a glass of wine – which we're no doubt paying for anyway? I shall conjure a far more *interesting* change of direction.'

Strimmer sauntered down the aisle, velvet glove dangling from his right hand.

Valourhand swore as she worked through the implications. Two candidates from the North Tower would never win the day, but Strimmer would be *far* worse than Snorkel. She knew the darker reaches of his personality. She watched the clock hand slip another notch as Strimmer slapped the bust.

She thrust her glove in Orelia's lap, hissing, 'It has to be you.'

Snorkel eyed his opponent. He had dirt on Strimmer, and while the town welcomed the revenue from the North Tower, they distrusted its scientists. Moreover, Strimmer had the wrong kind of charisma, as confirmed by the muted response to his declaration.

'An excellent contest,' declared Snorkel cordially, ushering in the wine. 'May the best man win!' This would be easy.

The word 'man' enraged Orelia; since the meeting's reopening not a single woman had spoken. She strode down the aisle and Snorkel sensed a change in the atmosphere.

'I'm standing,' she said simply.

'Is this *possible*?' whispered Snorkel to Gorhambury. 'Can women stand? *Mrs* Anyone?'

'*In these Regulations "man" means "man" or "woman" in all contexts,*' quoted Gorhambury, staring straight ahead.

Snorkel turned back to Orelia with a twinge of genuine horror. If Mrs Snorkel behaved like this – if wives generally did – where would they be? He pulled himself together and asked, 'And what are you standing for, Miss Roc?'

Rhombus Smith's slogan tripped into her head. 'Ancient institutions and modern improvements!' She seized a passing glass and improvised. 'With busts you can see and *Regulations* you can read: transparency!'

'But you need a glove,' he said.

A smile of mock concern died on his lips as, her blood up, Orelia wrenched the glove from her pocket and slapped the bust with a violent backhand that made the real Snorkel recoil. Receptive to defiance, the Chamber *oohed* and *aahed*.

Snorkel played his last ace. 'Gallant try, Miss Roc, but you're too late, I'm afraid – it's four-fifteen, and, as Mr Gorhambury forever reminds us, rules are rules.' He pointed at the Parliament Chamber clock. It was 4.15, undeniably.

'Indeed they are, Mr Snorkel, indeed they are.' The reedy dryness of Gorhambury's voice and his perfect diction, born of a phobia of misunderstanding, had a surprising resonance. 'The clock is four minutes fast in accordance with paragraph 5(4)(a) of the *Municipal Timekeeping Regulations*,' he chimed.

An isolated clap swelled to a cheer to an outburst of applause.

Gorhambury rose to his feet. 'I declare this meeting of the Sewage Sub-Committee closed.' He turned to the Mayor. 'I require your chain of office, Mr Snorkel, as per *Regulation* 16.'

Snorkel seethed – *Mr Snorkel? How quickly* Your Worship *vanishes!* – but he graciously inclined his head. Gorhambury removed the chain and laid it lovingly on the table in a perfect oval, as for a neck in waiting. From his pocket, Gorhambury produced a second chain, less ornate but still imposing, which he handed to Snorkel.

Inclining his own head, so reversing the process, he intoned the ancient oath:

'*I undertake to protect Rotherweird's citizens during the election period. I undertake not to compromise the policies of the future or undo the policies of the past, unless strict necessity demands it. I undertake to treat the candidates with due neutrality. I accept the role my chain of office declares*: in loco parentis. *I declare myself clear of any illness of body or mind.*'

Snorkel, given a free hand, would have prosecuted the last sentence as perjury. Instead, he attempted a humble expression, so unfamiliar an exercise that he looked both oleaginous and insincere.

Strimmer did not 'do' pretence. He wore his natural haughtiness, a natural Mayor-in-waiting. Orelia sipped her wine and queried her sanity.

'I declare three candidates,' Gorhambury intoned. 'The incumbent, Mr Sidney Snorkel; Mr Hengest Strimmer, the Head of the North Tower Science faculty; and Miss Orelia Roc, the proprietor of *Baubles & Relics*. A speech-day will be held on the first of November in the Parliament Chamber. There is otherwise to be no canvassing. Candidates will answer questions from four to six on weekday afternoons at their home or place of work. The candidate with the largest number of votes wins. The *Regulations* have fixed this election for the Winter Solstice. The result will be announced in the Island Field at three in the afternoon. All citizens, including babes in arms, must be there. The Summoning starts tomorrow. Welcome our own when they return.'

The lugubrious cast of Gorhambury's face, sculpted by public toil and private grief, lit up with the semblance of a smile. He had journeyed the thorny path from abject disgrace to restitution.

Outside the Crier, a born thespian, strove to do justice to the unfolding drama behind him:

'In strides Strimmer, velvet-handed,
To flay the Mayor's marbled face.
As Fragrance too outwits the clock:
Ms Bric-a-Brac – Orelia Roc.

A three-way contest, no holds barred,
The choice is yours, to stick or twist,
One must win from our racing card –
Mayor, trader or scientist?'

In an anteroom off the Parliament Chamber Snorkel debriefed Bendigo Sly, whose moon-face twitched like a dog expecting a blow.

'Where did those bloody gloves come from?'

'Dirty pool, dirty pool,' mumbled Sly, his phrase of choice for any hostile moves he had failed to anticipate.

'Turn the Roc woman over – family weaknesses, dodgy genes, youthful indiscretions – and get me the lowdown on her men, women or whatever else she likes. I need ten-carat dirt.'

'I shall trawl the subterranean streams.'

'Cut the verbal posies, Sly. I'm not in the mood.'

'Your Worship—'

'Nor am I "your Worship"! I'm plain Sidney Snorkel.'

'The imminent people's choice,' replied Sly, with an unctuous bow.

'Who's behind Strimmer?'

'Some pale imitation of Sir Veronal?' suggested the eavesman to cheer his master, for unlike these amateurs, Slickstone had been a real threat, and Slickstone was no more.

'They'll pay,' he said, more to himself than Sly, 'in spades.'

Old History

With Wynter and the eight surviving Eleusians secured, Oxenbridge's men scour the Manor's grounds for evidence. A windowless
hexagonal outhouse boasts fresh brick the colour of ripe peaches.
A chute embedded in one wall is stained with offal and behind it
they can hear a gibbering chatter, a noise unknown even to these
well-travelled veterans. A torch is lit and swords are drawn.

Oxenbridge, drawn by the noise of conflict, arrives too late.
Corpses litter the ground and when he crouches, he sees they
are child victims, not the abominations they first appeared to be.
Murdered, or put out of their misery? He does not care to ask. A
soldier never dwells on the forgivable mistakes.

'Bury them with a prayer,' he says.

The pidgeboy is not so far away. For all his suffering, the valley
remains his home. He keeps to the hinterland, roosting in the dense
slopes of Rotherweird Westwood, until, years on, Hieronymus Seer,
now called Ferensen, finds him there.

'Fortemain always said you deserved a better name,' Ferensen
told him. 'His choice was Panjan – don't ask me what it means. I
think he just liked the sound of it.'

The pidgeboy plumps his feathers; he agrees. A man and a bird
in discussion on a grassy bank: such is the strangeness of Rotherweird. Of his sister, Ferensen does not speak.

January 1572. Rotherweird Manor.

Sir Robert Oxenbridge hunches over a small oak desk mean enough for a schoolboy. The leaded windows fracture the hook of the moon. A moth sputters up and down the glass – is it contented or trapped?

His goose quill scratches a single word on a sheet of parchment already rich in deletions and amendments: *godforsaken*, not an epithet to use lightly. God must be everywhere to see everything – how else could He judge fairly? Yet in this valley, even with order restored, horror stalks Oxenbridge's every turn.

Take the attack on Geryon Wynter by his gaoler, truly *unnatural* in its ritualistic savagery. The violence was inexplicable – until they found the gaoler's strangled body in a reedbed south of the town. Oxenbridge knows how to measure bodily decay after death – rigor in the limbs, temperature, the settling of the blood, which insects have arrived and which not. The gaoler was dead before his mysterious twin stripped the flesh from Wynter's back. *A scourging*, Oxenbridge concluded.

Old magick; only in a godforsaken place could such devilry flourish.

His recommendations as to sentence and the valley's future have been approved by the Privy Council. Isolated by enveloping hills, Rotherweird will be kept from the rest of England but at a price. Here the study of history will be forbidden.

Tomorrow he passes sentence on the men. One problem remains: two of Wynter's three women have survived and come to him as penitents. They wring their hands, and will not look him in the face. Unconvinced by this actorly show of contrition, he has imprisoned them at opposite ends of the Manor's warren-like top floor.

He blinks. Has the moon fleetingly vanished in a clear sky? He catches a scuffling on the landing and a squeak as from a swinging window, but he sees the guards below, motionless and in position either side of the outer gate. Nonetheless, he edges towards his sword.

The latch clicks and rises, a bare foot nudges the door open and one of the women, Nona, glides rather than walks into the chamber. Her eyes are shining. 'I have a proposal,' she says. Her shift is ruffled by a breeze – the window must indeed be open.

'How did you get here?'

She closes the door and answers a different question. 'I assumed you would have the room with the most commanding view and the best fireplace.' She extends her hands to the blaze, palms up.

'I meant, how did you elude the guards?'

'The Manor has hidden ways.'

Her voice rings false, but Oxenbridge lets her continue. 'We would stay, to record our story as a penance. We will preserve you and Sir Henry, and we will not spare Mr Wynter.' She places on the bed a piece of fine-woven linen, which depicts children standing beside a wagon. Yes, he is there, and his horse, a grey, just as was. They have talent, these young women, and remembering minds. 'When we are done, we would go to the nunnery near Hoy . . . to atone . . .'

Oxenbridge has seen tapestries before – heroes in plumed helmets, trees and plants too blue to convince, endless cornucopia, exotic animals – but this woodland scene has the vitality of truth. Still, he is torn: he knows he must not multiply records of Wynter's evil activities – but the wagon in wool entrances him, as does his personal appearance.

She reads his anxiety. 'We will not be literal – we would not want to be.'

'Continue for the moment,' he says at last. 'Mr Finch will decide.'

She moves closer. She has the gait of a panther.

Feeling an urge to assert himself, he asks, 'What happened to the third woman?'

'An accident – in the other place.'

'You were there?'

'Mercifully not.'

There is a quick, emotional glance; he thinks this is true.

She steps into that space which mere acquaintances leave unoccupied. 'Does the man who did this yet live?' She traces the zigzag scar above his right clavicle. The question holds an unsettling intimacy.

'He does not,' replies Oxenbridge truthfully.

'It still needs healing.'

She holds back her hair and bends her mouth to the old wound.

30 January 1572.

January, Mr Wynter's chosen month for execution day, and everyone dances their steps as he intends: Janus, the two-faced god of endings and beginnings. From their pinched attic windows, Estella and Nona watch the procession, with the Eleusians shuffling like obedient children in a line, hands clasped behind their backs. Wynter leads the condemned, followed by Slickstone. It is dry and cold, but there is no birdsong. The stones are there too; Nona felt them in Oxenbridge's room and she feels them now.

What is to come? Of the men, only Slickstone has previously entered the mixing-point, and he might even conquer *tabula rasa*. Time will dispose of the others, if the punishment does not.

Scry's mind settles on the absentees: Calx Bole – *where is the Potamus?* She dislikes the easy confidence in her companion's manner, as if everything were pre-ordained. She curls a lip. Centuries may pass before she knows the truth.

Nona takes a new skein and threads it with wool the scarlet of blood. Her needle dives, surfaces, dives. Their relationship is changing; Nona has the upper hand and now she declares it. 'I am Penelope; waiting, waiting, waiting.'

NOVEMBER:
SECOND WEEK

I

The Summoned

Looking more like refugees than Rotherweird's well-heeled *emigrés*, the Summoned huddled in the lee of the great oak as rain and wind swirled around Rotherweird Valley. There were no more than thirty men and women, less than the Town Hall had catered for. Up the hill, toiling towards them and the Twelve-Mile Post, came the charabanc and a convoy of bicycle rickshaws, hoods up, lamps glowing, multi-coloured umbrellas protecting the drivers. They had made the self-same journey the previous evening, but a train had been delayed somewhere in the mountains of mainland Europe and the connection had been missed.

Boris raised his goggles to consult the lodgings list compiled by Madge Brown, now acting secretary to Gorhambury in his new role. She had divided the visitors into two groups, North Gate and South Gate access, to prevent bottlenecks.

In the crowd, two figures drew the eye: a striking and intense-looking young woman, hair tied back, the face a near-perfect oval, ushered the shambling arrivals into line; while the other, a man, stood apart, ignoring the shelter of the tree. He carried a suitcase in one hand and a wooden paint-box in the other; under his right arm was a large easel. Although richly endowed with musical talent, Rotherweird lacked weight in the visual arts. Portraits were doomed to destruction on the subject's death under the *History Regulations* and suspicion of countrysiders had long sapped enthusiasm for landscapes. The town had a single art gallery, close to the North

Gate, home only to local work, where one painter stood out. Castor Everthorne's work, confined to the 1920s, was neither naturalistic nor wholly abstract, but had the gift of *suggestion*: spirits of wood, stone and ritual.

Everthorne's life had been troubled with periods in prison followed by an early death hastened by drink. His only son had gone abroad to promote South Tower optical products in Europe, but he too had died young, in his fifties. This man, Tancred Everthorne, must be the grandson. A stocky man with powerful shoulders, a fine if pugilistic face and dark hair worn quite long, his lone defiance of the rain would have fitted his appearance, save for a contradictory air of insecurity.

Attractive to women, Boris guessed.

Everthorne uttered only three words as Boris shook his hand. 'Observe,' he said, pointing to the mosaic of yellow-brown leaves glued to the road by the rain, 'water colours.' He broke away to help load the luggage.

A welcoming band attempting a medley of popular Rotherweird songs gave up as the elements prevailed. Gorhambury, chain of office round his neck, hustled from charabanc to rickshaw, shaking hands and providing contact details should any problem arise. A few he recognised; most not.

At a stately pace, the convoy wound its way back to town. Rotherweird was reconnecting with her own.

2

Matters Astronomical

Bert Polk's eldest, Ronan, had a bedroom high in the roof, where the eaves branched in crazy directions: a cabin where a crow's nest should be. His siblings enjoyed more generous rooms, but sharing deprived them of secrets – like the kaleidoscope, a bequest from Professor Bolitho to his old friend Uncle Boris. Kaleidoscope, according to the Greek dictionary, was for 'the observation of beautiful forms' – but this one offered only a blank screen. Uncle Boris had tried, his father had tried, and his mother, just as technically gifted, had dismissed it as broken.

'It's not broken,' Boris had told them. 'We're just not asking it the right questions. It needs a child's ingenuity.' By happenstance, Ronan had returned from school at that very moment, and Boris handed the instrument over. 'Menders, keepers,' he added by way of incentive; not that Ronan needed any.

The instrument had been lovingly assembled. The two interconnecting tubes, the smaller one circular and the larger hexagonal, had both been made with long matchsticks, glued together with meticulous care and held in place by metal bands with tiny screws. The larger tube turned a full circle, but the view through the eyehole remained a bare hexagonal light. The kaleidoscope didn't rattle, which, in Ronan's judgement, supported his uncle's diagnosis that nothing was broken.

Now he lay in bed and observed the small table under the skylight, where the kaleidoscope's silhouette caught the moonlight. *Talk to me*, he prayed, *talk to me, please*. A slender logical chain came in response: a gift from one man of machines to another – machines which *did* things, like telescopes and charabancs – so of course it must work.

Inspiration struck and he *knew* he was right before his feet touched the floor. This kaleidoscope needed *darkness* to shine, just like the Professor's telescope at school.

He aimed at the far corner of the room. Chips of light gleamed from the back of the tube. He knew the arrangement and the contrasting colours of the brightest: cold silver and a smouldering red, Rigel and Betelgeuse, 'stars' of Orion the hunter, the grandest winter constellation. He turned the larger, hexagonal tube and another light moved slowly though: this one multi-coloured, with the hint of a blur behind it. Rigel and Betelgeuse twinkled; the interloper did not.

Scrabbling into a jersey, he hurtled down the oak staircase two steps at a time in search of Uncle Boris.

Rhombus Smith had ordained that, as a mark of respect, the Rotherweird School Observatory should remain locked as Bolitho had left it until the New Year: in effect, a preservation order for a scene of monumental untidiness. The astronomer had preferred the floor to table and chairs, so reducing his chosen work surface to a collage of confetti.

Beneath this paper sea lurked the jetsam of Bolitho picnics: half-eaten crusts, dried-out bacon, rock-hard fragments of cheese and cake – staple forage for the incumbent house mouse, *mus musculus*. Operating a grid system, the mouse cleared several pages a night, a sufficient yield for himself and his family. He respected the vanished human occupier who, unlike his fellows, had ascended the evolutionary tree to movement on all fours. Tonight, he reached the centre of the room; no different to any other night until—

Click. Whirr.

The mouse's head rose through the paper like a surfacing submarine. A crumb fell to the floor, but he saw nobody and nothing alarming: no change to the door and, more importantly, no way in for the School cat.

Click. Whirr. Whirr.

The long cylinder above the human's only seat moved fractionally, and a ceiling panel retracted. Faint bars thrown by starlight spangled the floor. A steel arm lifted in a rectangular case on the opposite wall, dipped its point into a bottle of ink and moved to a spool of graph paper wound round a drum.

The mouse, not a believer in ghosts, seized the nearest rind and scurried back behind the wainscot.

At the narrow end of the tube a crystalline green lens slid into place and film on the longest of long exposures began to run.

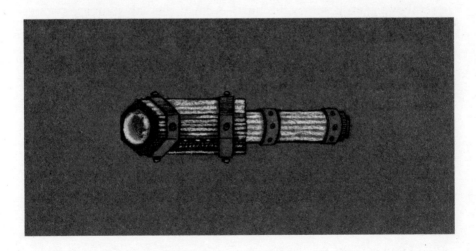

3
A Competition Won

Snorkel studied his list of the Summoned with apprehension. These were unfamiliar men and women, unexposed to his benign rule. They might turn vocal, or, far worse, be amateur investigators. He acted promptly. The Snorkel Foundation doubled their subsistence allowance for the electoral period. Who does not lick the hand that feeds?

His secretary handed him a brown envelope. 'It's the only one this week,' she murmured.

The Snorkel Essay Prize had run its course, yielding nothing better than subservient platitudes, but this manuscript looked different. The letters were oddly square, but also ornate: a hint of idiosyncratic boldness. Snorkel's knees jiggled like pistons as the opening struck home.

The two political imperatives, power and permanence, are best secured by the judicious use of three tools – policy, patronage and pressure. These fine instruments require sound intelligence for, and in, their user . . .

The treatise fell short of the prescribed maximum length, but had not a wasted word. Snorkel judged it a perfect pitch. Untouched by self-admiration, a quality for rulers, not subjects, in Snorkel's judgement, the entry ended with the signature *Pomeny Tighe*. She was one of the Summoned from an old Rotherweird family, who reported from abroad on breakthroughs in outsider science and, as important, on its areas of continuing ignorance.

He waved the envelope at his long-suffering secretary. 'Interview, tomorrow, soonest.'

Snorkel read aloud his favourite sentence. '*These fine instruments require sound intelligence for, and in, their user . . .*' He looked up at the young woman. 'What do you mean by intelligence?'

'I mean, sufficient data to identify the opposition and sufficient brainpower to read their moves before they make them.'

A compressed answer: she spoke as she wrote. The voice fitted the oval face, demure for so sharp a message. Pomeny Tighe's rich, tow-coloured hair bobbed just above her shoulders. The freckles on her nose added a Bohemian touch, but she was trim to a 't', as good government should be, and young for such an old head – early thirties, perhaps, even late twenties?

'Where do you work out there?' he asked.

'I assist Heidelberg University's mathematics department. I keep an eye out too.'

'You might stay on here after the election?'

'That depends.'

That's enough small talk, time for business, decided Snorkel. 'How am I to better practise what you preach?' he asked.

She hitched her skirt and pursed her lips. The eyes had a feline quality. 'You have seventeen committees and one Town Clerk.' She paused.

Snorkel encouraged her. 'Come on, Miss Tighe, candour is easy on paper. Tell me true.'

'Your Clerk has no time.'

'For what?'

'The political arts.'

'The Town Hall has a multitude of moving parts. Gorhambury oils, checks and calibrates, and in his absence, the mechanism grinds to a halt. I know this for a fact. We tried without him once.'

'But who *owns* this marvellous clock? Who is to preserve it from fire or theft?' Her change of tone, expansive if not poetical, took Snorkel by surprise.

'*Moi*,' replied Snorkel immodestly, before adding a painful qual-ification, 'assuming the people see sense.'

She re-crossed her legs, left over right – *shapely legs*, Snorkel noticed. 'Who else is in the frame – for the prize, I mean?'

Snorkel stood up and opened his arms. 'Nobody – you win the Snorkel Essay Prize!'

'Which is ... ?' Her lips parted, pink tongue darting through.

'Beyond my secretary is a small office. It's yours for the asking, with pay, pension and holiday to be notified, terminable on two weeks' notice by either party. On my re-election, Mr Gorhambury will be ... *relieved*.'

To judge from her smile, she caught the intended ambiguity. 'Mr Snorkel, you won't forget this.'

Snorkel tacitly agreed that was indeed most unlikely.

4

A Party Derailed

'Party?' croaked Aggs. '*Party!*'

Oblong looked sheepish. He had his faults, but he did give credit where it was due. 'Madge Brown suggested it.'

Aggs' face worked like a glove puppet. 'About bloody time, Mr Oblong, if you'll pardon my Austrian. You've had a year to bed in, the cold's a coming and we're all getting older. But there be parties and *parties*: The Fizz, The Droop and The Plain Sailing.'

'The Fizz sounds good,' stammered Oblong, cowering beneath his general person's onslaught.

'No wife, no children, no paramour – you can afford it. Bravo! Fizz means fizz; down with the plain sailors!' Aggs flung open the outside door of Oblong's flat and pointed at the loft space above and the landing below. 'Furniture up, accordion and fiddle down. Party mood! It's all about swing.' She swayed in a mildly suggestive manner. 'And once they're 'ere, give 'em a burner!'

'A burner?'

'Bubbles, brandy and sugar lump.'

'Er . . . *bubbles?*'

Expensive bottles, price tags attached, flicked through Oblong's head in multiples of twelve, to the tinkle of an old-fashioned cash till.

Aggs ignored the query. 'And don't get all doomed and gloomed by refusals. Outsiders ain't everyone's cup of cocoa.'

'If you say so, Aggs.'

'I *know* so.'

Finch, working by candlelight, found the Elizabethan mind more accessible in the early hours. The cat had prompted this bout of research: the animal who had tried to befriend him when Bole was pursuing Slickstone. He now knew it to be Bole's familiar from the mixing-point: a cat with fiery feet, an arsonist-cum-assassin with the gift of English. Finch had glimpsed the creature several nights in a row, peering through the glass roof-lights into the *archivoire*. Orelia Roc, not a witness to exaggerate, had accused the cat of trying to kill her during the fire in Deirdre Banter's house after a negative response to the question, *Do you have the book?* The book could not have been Wynter's *Recipe Book*, as Bole already knew the whereabouts of that volume – after all, he as Flask had left it in the North Tower as a trap for Strimmer to find.

Escutcheon Place held the contrasting libraries of Sir Henry Grassal and Geryon Wynter, the Manor's first two owners. Somewhere here, he suspected, must be the book Bole and his familiar were pursuing; hence his decision to return to the Elizabethan documents in their secret cavities. The more he read, the more concerned he became.

At his trial, Wynter had actively encouraged his obliteration in the mixing-point, calling it 'a suitable Passion'. Twice he had referred to resurrection. No less disturbing, Wynter had been viciously attacked in prison, but then his gaoler's strangled body had been found in a ditch at the edge of the Island Field. His unspecified injuries were described as 'unnatural'. The prime suspect had to be Bole, shapeshifting – but why would *Bole* attack his own master? To spare him obliteration in the mixing-point?

When giving evidence, Wynter had played down the incident, referring to it only as 'his scourging', as if collecting tokens of divinity.

He found one reference to books in Wynter's closing speech: *'Childless and stripped of my disciples – I bequeath my library to this Manor and, therefore I trust, to posterity. Man lives on through his learning.'*

Finch glanced at the two competing collections, rival armies of thought in the same bay, Sir Henry's bound in beige calf above Wynter's arcane jet-black volumes. He rubbed his eyes: three-thirty in the morning, the dead hour when even monks and condemned men sleep. He returned the trial record to its secret compartment and took out *The Dark Devices*, the record of Wynter's heraldry for the Eleusians. As he examined the strange coats of arms, replete with hidden references to the work of the mixing-point, he tested an alarming thought against recent events.

They had overlooked a yawning gap in the narrative.

As he fretted over the implications, he heard a telltale scratching above his head.

That wretched cat must be back.

Through the banisters of Oblong's dingy staircase twined tiny lights that changed hue from silver to red to gold at every visiting step, a typically benign South Tower entertainment. Below Oblong's outer door an accordion-fiddle duet delivered *boulevard* fare while Aggs handed out champagne cocktails.

Fizz meant fizz.

Orelia arrived first in order to leave early. She found the celebrity status so relished by the likes of Snorkel discomforting, being shunted to the front of shop queues and accosted in the street. She was already yearning for her former life, the richness of its casual dialogue and the freedom to choose her own company. Now she had to think before she spoke, a self-censorship alien to her nature. Even among friends the election fostered a stultifying respect ... the two musicians nodded in deference as she passed.

She had a subsidiary motive for arriving early: a question for Oblong with the smell of old history.

Aggs thrust a glass in Orelia's hand with a knowing wink. 'Early bird catches the worm.'

'Vote for me, Aggs – nobody else will.'

'The words of the lowly never won nuffink, Miss Roc, but the votes of the lowly might. More to Rotherweird than you might think.' Aggs adopted a conspiratorial pose. 'No party fizzes with a droopy host. Cheer 'im up, 'e's ever so nervous.'

On cue Oblong emerged from the kitchen and Aggs thrust a glass into his hand. 'Host shows the way,' she said.

'They were asked for seven – it's twenty past.'

'Lesson one: greet your guests.'

Orelia pecked Oblong on the cheek, relieved that the sofa, scene of their one intimate encounter, was not on view, before launching her question. 'Puzzles pass the time. Try this one – *Shown badly behaved flirt, Royal rages in empty house* – seventeen letters – three, five, four, five.' She had launched too soon; it sounded forced.

'Why me?' replied Oblong stiffly.

'We have no Royals; you do. We have no history; you do.'

'Whose clue?' he asked suspiciously.

'Shapeshifter's.'

Now Oblong understood. This *mattered*. He peered out of the doorway – still no more guests – while Orelia wrote the clue down. *Badly behaved* and *Royal rages* were anagram territory. *Empty house* must be the key. Empty house, empty house, empty *House* – he juggled the letters in his head until it felt right – it had to be. He rocked to and fro on his gangly legs and Orelia felt a flicker of affection; she had found his naïve enthusiasm attractive once.

'Well?'

'Anagram,' he declared, a stoop nearing a full bow, 'of "shown", "behaved" and "flirt" as signalled to the reader by the word "badly". The empty house is wider England's Parliament. The Royal is Charles: he's raging because the rebels have scarpered. The answer is—'

The doorway flashed with the reflected light from the string twisted around the banisters: he had a second guest, if not a third.

'The answer is. . . "*The birds have flown*",' he announced, flapping his arms and prompting an intervention by Aggs.

'Hold it, Mr Oblong. One moment, you're old droopy drawers, the next you go loco. Try settling between the two.'

'Did you say "birds"?' said Valourhand, skipping into the room. She wore a waistcoat, boots and, like Orelia, trousers. She even looked pleased to be there. Her unexpected sartorial effort cheered Oblong.

Orelia guided Valourhand away as an influx of arrivals detained Oblong by the doorway.

'*Shapeshifter* set a Winter Solstice crossword for the *Chronicle*,' she reported. 'One clue broke the *History Regulations* – and, guess what? It's an anagram.' She relayed Oblong's analysis.

Valourhand retreated to a corner, her turn to whisper. 'I found this foul shit in the marsh – Fanguin says it's hybrid shit – half-bird, half-human.'

At the head of the surge was Fanguin in a familiar battered tweed suit, waving a magnum ('be sure you keep the best to last'). Orelia coaxed him over and explained.

Fanguin enjoyed donning his biologist's hat. 'Such a creature must be nocturnal to escape attention – and that means a daytime roost.'

'Rotherweird Westwood has places where nobody goes,' Orelia pointed out.

'Most birds are territorial, and Westwood is miles from the marsh,' countered Fanguin. 'Also, Ferensen knows Westwood like the back of his hand. He'd know – he'd have said.'

Except he's disappeared from view, thought Orelia, before turning her attention to Valourhand. The physicist had a finger hooked in her waistcoat pocket, an oddly self-conscious gesture, but symptomatic of a general change; she was less spiky than usual.

'There's Salt, let's ask him – he walks the riverbank.'

Salt had made no such sartorial effort. Mud scarfed his boots and lower trouser legs, and he now shared with Ferensen an other-worldly presence.

'A bird – or birds – may have escaped from Lost Acre,' Orelia said, adding the context.

Salt's face darkened. He now found the very name 'Lost Acre' unwelcome. 'In the turmoil of Midsummer Day, I saw flocks of them,' he replied quietly, 'desperate for calmer air. They rapped the bubble's windows – the stuff of dreams or nightmares, depending on your point of view. Many had oversize eyes, suggesting they're nocturnal.'

'Nothing half-human?'

'None of them wished me a good evening, if that's what you mean.' Salt gave Orelia a grin, which she gladly returned. Her favourite curmudgeon had not lost his humour. 'You did say *this* year's Winter Solstice Crossword?' When Orelia nodded, he said, 'He's still among us then, this Calx Bole.'

The group divided and Salt joined Jones to discuss the replanting of Grove Gardens. In recent weeks, he had felt a kinship with the athlete, although for no apparent reason.

Gorhambury arrived late, as ever in suit and tie, wearing his chain of temporary office. His contribution to the rebirth of their democratic rights had, like his other contributions to Rotherweird, passed largely unnoticed. 'Glass of water, please.'

'Even bishops, what we don't have, drink on Fridays,' replied Aggs, thrusting the largest available cocktail into Gorhambury's hand.

'Oh, go on then.' He skimmed off a bubble with a delicate sip.

Madge Brown followed with a healthy swig. She too had dressed up.

Oblong sensed a winding-down – the odd glance at a watch, refills refused, the departure of fringe guests, only for Boris Polk to make a dramatic entrance.

Anxiety rarely featured in his repertoire of facial expressions. Even when the fire in Deirdre Banter's tower had threatened destruction, he had maintained a studied optimism – but not tonight. The jaw sagged; fingers raked his flame-coloured hair. Oblong recalled the anonymous finger at Belshazzar's Feast, dispelling cheer with a doom-laden message. The analogy proved apt.

'I've had a visit from Mors Valett,' announced Boris.

Orelia recalled Valett's visit to *Baubles & Relics* on the morning of her aunt's death. Undertakers do not deal in good news.

Boris sounded reluctant to spoil the party, so Valourhand reverted to type, slapping her thighs with impatience. 'And – *and?*'

'Finch is missing – *incomprehensibly* missing.'

Unease rippled through the party. More guests left, some in shock, so central was Finch's office to Rotherweird's constitution, others eager to pass on such dramatic news. With them went Mrs Fanguin, Bert Polk and his wife, the Smiths, Madge Brown and, to Orelia's disappointment, Hayman Salt. He had lost his appetite for adventure; the Green Man had stolen a chip of his soul.

Members of the company felt guilty, having barely thought of Finch, despite his position as mainstay of the stand against Sir Veronal Slickstone. His formal office and commanding intellect, his age and eccentric manner of speech all combined to give him a daunting quality; he was more admired than missed.

Put out by Finch's tart response to his request to review the documents in Escutcheon Place, Oblong had not even asked him to the party.

Orelia stood down the musicians and was about to close Oblong's front door when the stranger appeared, looking up from a lower step: dark hair, strong in face and build, with blue-grey eyes, vivacious but wary. Details of the moment lodged deep, as images can in childhood – the landing's contours, the pitch of the roof, the empty wine glass perched on the banister, all props in a portrait of *him*. Colours registered more than materials – dark grey jacket,

faded green trousers, heavy brown shoes and a frayed checked shirt.
Who on earth was he? And was that look quizzical or mocking?

'Yes?' she stammered.

'I'm sorry – moth to a flame.'

He had a mellow voice, and Orelia understood the simile: the
loner drawn to the party, the passer-by caught by the music.

Before she could reply, Oblong intervened. 'Everthorne,' he said,
'how rude of me – do come in.'

'Best wine at the end,' chirruped Aggs, not immune to good looks
despite her age. She pressed a glass into his hand as Boris joined
the welcoming committee, recalling Everthorne's unprompted help
in loading his fellow travellers' luggage onto the charabanc. Boris
judged people by their small kindnesses, or the lack of them.

'I like a man who doesn't mind rain – good to see you again.'

Boris completed the introductions. The distinctive name and
the flecks of oil paint spattering his shirt cuffs confirmed his
ancestry.

After shaking various hands, Everthorne walked straight to the
large oak beam above Oblong's fireplace. 'Art beetles,' he said
with a smile, tracing the furrows in the wood with his fingers.
'See? Crocodile, camel, a dog's head turning back.' He added a
skilful flourish with the tip of a pen-knife and they saw what
they would otherwise never have noticed. The likenesses were
uncanny.

Boris, feeling a need for urgent action, intervened. 'Forgive us,
Everthorne, but we have a minor crisis. Our Herald has disappeared.'

The remark conjured a portrait in Everthorne's head – *The Vanished
Herald* – full-length, swathes of black and burned umber framing
an abstract explosion of creams and greys with, at the centre, a
knot of armorial fragments and brilliant colours. The gypsy girl –
Everthorne's instant impression of Orelia – flicked a lock of hair over
her right shoulder. Everthorne had known beautiful women – the
painter's privilege – but here he perceived another quality: spirit.

Orelia felt obliged by her new candidate status to show initiative. 'Why "incomprehensibly" missing?'

'According to Mrs Finch he worked late in the *archivoire* with the doors locked. This morning there's no sign of him and the doors are still locked.'

'Who investigates?' Orelia asked.

'I do,' replied Gorhambury, nervously fingering his temporary chain of office. *Why on my watch?* he thought. *Why on mine?*

'I have Mrs Finch's spare keys as a start,' added Boris.

'Should we be discussing this in front of *him*?' muttered Valourhand, nodding towards Everthorne. She was distrustful of handsome men – indeed, anyone other than scientists – and dismissed the artist as no more than a salesman of South Tower fripperies in the wider world.

His riposte surprised even her. 'Your Herald might be in the tunnels. He'd have locked up before leaving and may have got lost.'

'How do you know about the tunnels?' asked Valourhand fiercely.

'My grandfather walked them – he drew them, and mapped them for his own amusement. I was planning a visit.'

Orelia recalled a painting in Rotherweird's Art Gallery, in the room devoted to Everthorne Senior's studies of arches, set in pools of shadow, exquisite in an understated way. 'It's true,' she said.

'Out there' – Boris waved gently in the direction of wider England – 'police use artists. Why shouldn't we?'

Valourhand withdrew her objection on no more than a hunch that Everthorne might contribute despite the unpromising exterior.

'We take the tunnels, then,' declared Gorhambury.

Finch's disappearance had unsettled everyone. Little was said in Everthorne's presence, but in their minds theories abounded – abduction, murder, a retreat into hiding or even a visit to Lost Acre – each raising its own subset of questions: why, how and where.

At least Gorhambury had sounded decisive.

'Mercifully,' Boris added, 'Mrs Finch and that dire son of hers have moved out.' Orelia remembered Mrs Finch from Sir Veronal's party, a snobbish member of the Snorkel set and visibly disapproving of her husband's unconventional ways.

Aggs added impetus. After a burst of water from Oblong's kitchen she announced, 'The general person clears for greater brains to do the needful.'

5

Escutcheon Place Revisited

Outside, Gorhambury reminded everyone of the location of *The Journeyman's Gist Underground*, Ferdy's replacement tavern during Slickstone's brief tenure as landlord; it had been their departure point for Escutcheon Place on the night of the fire. As Orelia waited for Everthorne, a threatening sky fleetingly broke to reveal a half-moon riding high. The artist emerged from his lodgings with two faded sketchbooks bound together with string.

Rotherweird's circulatory system allowed many routes to the same destination. 'Highways or byways?' she asked.

'Veins or arteries? You choose.'

She decided on the more picturesque side streets. Everthorne lolloped along beside her, peering at the pavement. 'Moon shadows,' he said, 'less sharp than their daylight cousins, and the devil to paint. I'm for the dark cobbles!'

Now Everthorne took the lead in a crazy hopscotch through the winding alleys. He had a casual energy – not, Orelia felt, generated to impress, but rather his way of interacting with the world. He pointed at any architectural features tha caught his fancy, even as cloud occluded the moon and rain and wind swept in.

Gorhambury was standing guard by the basement door. They entered to find Oblong, Boris, Jones and Valourhand debating who should carry the two available tube-lights and in what position. Of the former tavern, only one empty barrel survived.

Boris led the way into the tunnels, tube-light in one hand, compass in the other, with Jones bringing up the rear with the second tube-light. The journey lacked the excitement of the expedition on the night of the fire. They felt leaderless without Finch and Ferensen and, as the effects of Oblong's champagne wore off, the cold began to bite.

'Follow the carved flowers,' advised Valourhand, but without Finch the tiny little incised markers merely confused. After half an hour they were undeniably lost, and the compass was proving useless in the face of so many loops and switchbacks.

'We've been here before,' suggested Boris.

Valourhand shook her head. 'That was last time.'

'This time too,' corrected Orelia.

Gregorius Jones, freaked by the constriction and darkness, had a rush of blood. 'Finch is out there somewhere – starving, abandoned—'

'No!' cried Orelia, but, waving his coral-coloured tube, Jones had already rushed down the nearest tunnel. Cries of 'Finch!' and 'Marmion!' grew ever fainter.

'One down,' said Fanguin unhelpfully. 'Who's next?'

'We're down to one tube-light too, thanks to that moron,' hissed Valourhand, back to her usual peppery self.

'Where, I wonder,' said Boris in an attempt at light relief, 'in the pantheon of splendid failures, do we place the brave but mindless rescuer?'

'This has been the most shambolic expedition ever,' added Valourhand.

Everthorne struck a match and moved up from the rear. 'Left, right, left, if I'm not mistaken,' he said, holding out one of the sketchbooks. 'Grandfather's,' he added.

Boris held up the tube-light and everyone craned their necks over the complex map, meticulously drawn, with each arch marked and numbered. It stretched over several pages, the passages inter-spersed with random sketches of the druid-carved flowers, bird heads and skulls.

'All right,' said Gorhambury, 'you lead.' He walked behind the artist, tube-light raised over Everthorne's right shoulder. The procession gathered pace as the map, and Everthorne's decisive interpretation of it, restored morale.

They reached the chamber below the cellar of Escutcheon Place without further detour. After lifting the stone slab with ease, Everthorne said, 'I'd best go find Mr Jones.'

Gorhambury agreed; they could speak more freely without him. Boris exchanged his tube-light for Everthorne's matches.

Orelia liked the way Everthorne blended with people he did not know. That Boris liked him was a further endorsement. When the darkness swallowed him up, she felt deprived.

They made their way up several staircases to the *archivoire*, lighting candles as they went.

'We assume this is as Finch left it,' intoned Boris gravely, unlocking the double oak doors. A great candle flickered on the wooden candlestick as tall as a man. Escutcheon Place worked on natural light, despite the wealth of parchment, dry leather and wood; gaslights presented the greater hazard in Finch's opinion.

Boris distributed tapers from a tankard on the central table and other candles quickly flared into life. Shadows danced; the spines of gilded books gleamed; carved heads peered down. They were back in Rotherweird's forbidden garden, surrounded by their own history. Like an adolescent's second encounter with alcohol, the impact struck deeper. They drifted from bay to bay, half tourists, half aspiring detectives.

'I see no sign of a struggle,' said Oblong, but Boris shook his head.

'There,' he said, pointing at the table in the first alcove.

At first glance, Boris' comment baffled them. Finch's work in progress lay undisturbed on the table, two books open with paper markers at the ready.

Then the devil crept out of the detail.

The lid of Finch's inkpot hung open, and a slick of dried ink ran to the table edge, flecking a magnifying glass on the way – but with no sign of a pen. Finch wrote with drawing pens, slim wooden sticks with exposed changeable steel nibs.

'He was studying *The Dark Devices*,' announced Boris, turning the spine for all to see.

Gorhambury saw the significance instantly. 'Finch would never leave that lying around.'

Orelia read aloud from the frontispiece to underline Gorhambury's point, "This book contains the dark devices, coats of arms designed by Geryon Wynter and his disciples. It was fashioned at Rotherweird and found at the Manor there. Its use or distribution is prohibited by law, and preserved only to ensure that this law is observed and its justification understood." Sir Robert Oxenbridge.'

She moved to the first page of shields. The images were insidious, now they knew that every face or monstrous detail was potentially real. The names had been erased, save for those below the three blank shields: Hieronymus Seer, Morval Seer and Fortemain, all refused arms for opposing Wynter. The largest shield at the top, surtitled Magister, had to be Wynter's. One quarter held a tiny floating head of a fine-looking man with hair curled like a Greek hero. Orelia, peering over Gorhambury's shoulder, recognised Tyke's face, immaculately rendered, no bigger than a fingernail. What was he doing there?

Fanguin, who had not seen the book before, brought his biologist's eye to bear. Heraldic creatures flourished all over town, on beams, panels, mantelpieces, doorways and balustrades, but the creatures in *The Dark Devices* were true amalgams: patches of animal hair on human skin, fish-eyes with brows above. The artwork was truly exquisite.

'Painted by Morval Seer,' whispered Orelia to Fanguin, 'under duress, before Wynter and Slickstone wrecked her in the mixing-point.'

From the opposite alcove, Boris waved a thin wooden stick.

The nib had been bent back, its tip stained a rusty red. 'This is no way to treat a pen,' he said. 'Finch must have fought with the only weapon to hand.'

Gorhambury spotted the Herald's keys, still hanging from their hook. 'But where did the attacker go? Where did Finch go?' He took out a notebook and jotted down: *Table: Dark Devices, ink trail. Floor: damaged pen. Room: locked from the inside.*

'I did say "incomprehensibly missing",' added Boris, prompting Valourhand to lose her temper.

'There's no such thing as "incomprehensibly missing"! A man does not vanish into thin air. We look for the data, we analyse, we deduce. What's the point of twelve eyes if we don't look?'

Oblong picked up the second book on the table; the distinctive black binding marked it as another from Wynter's collection. 'Dante's *Divina Commedia*,' he read.

Gorhambury made another note.

'And what does that tell us?' asked Valourhand curtly.

'Something in *The Dark Devices* took Finch to this Dante fellow,' suggested Boris, before hastily adding, 'or vice versa.'

'Who's Dante?' asked Gorhambury.

Before Oblong could answer, Gregorius Jones jogged in, breaking the spirit of enquiry. 'No sign of him,' he announced breezily.

'You got bloody lost – idiot!' hissed Valourhand, flexing her fingers in irritation.

'The best way to find someone who's lost is to get lost yourself.' Jones' riposte did not improve her mood.

'Can I be of service?' added Jones.

'Disappear,' she replied, snapping *The Dark Devices* shut as she spoke. 'It's the best way of finding others who have.'

'Thank you, Everthorne,' said Gorhambury wearily as the artist walked in. 'We're looking for clues.'

Boris summarised, avoiding mention of Wynter in front of Everthorne. 'The doors were locked from the inside and the keys are still here. Finch was working at this table. We found his pen, which he used to defend himself.'

'Or the intruder used it to attack him,' interrupted Valourhand.

Boris continued, 'The candle was left alight, which is not Finch's practice.'

Everyone followed Everthorne's gaze to the skylights above every alcove. The library steps would not reach them.

'There must be a hidden way out,' he said. They tramped the room, tapping the floor, but found no hint of a cavity.

For Oblong, his party seemed months away. Nobody had spoken of it – nobody, he felt sure, had even thought of it and certainly nobody had thanked him, such had been the dampening effect of Finch's disappearance.

Orelia opened *Divina Commedia*, dislodging a small strip of paper. 'Finch marked this page,' she announced.

Oblong came over and delivered a schoolmasterly summary of Dante's great work. 'The *Divina Commedia* is Dante's masterpiece,' he started, 'written in the fourteenth century, in three parts: *Inferno*, *Purgatorio* and *Paradiso* – *Hell*, *Purgatory* and *Heaven*. This page is from *Hell*.' He pointed to the word *Inferno*. 'The verse mixes Latin and primitive Italian – but don't be deceived by the title: it isn't a comedy at all.'

Boris indicated a single ornate manuscript annotation on Finch's selected page and read, '*O amicae meae*.'

'That isn't Finch's writing,' said Oblong.

'It's old, most likely Wynter's,' added Orelia.

'Why would this book be of interest to Wynter?' asked Boris.

'Who's Wynter?' asked Everthorne.

Valourhand fumed at their stupidity. 'He lived here once, long ago. That's all you need to know.'

'He was interested in science and mystical stuff,' added Oblong politely, but Everthorne had taken no offence.

'Look – I'm from this town and I know the rules. You wouldn't be here if something wasn't badly wrong. Tell me only what you want to. I should however point out that two books are missing.'

Everthorne was right: the shelves holding Wynter's library had another empty space. The ever-efficient Finch had a card index for every alcove and Valourhand quickly identified the missing volume. 'Bizarre title,' she said. '*Straighten the Rope.*'

Orelia turned away: Vibes had given her that same book at the Hoy Book Fair, only it had not been bound in black. She sensed unseen connections.

O amicae meae. That single phrase nagged away at Boris. 'Who are these *amicae*?'

'We really must stop,' Valourhand interrupted, gesturing in Everthorne's direction.

'This is ridiculous,' countered Boris. 'Oblong is an outsider and he knows everything. Everthorne is one of us – and he found a way in the tunnels and he spotted the second missing book. I vote we tell him.'

They agreed, Valourhand reluctantly, and Orelia delivered the barest of narratives. The others thought it discretion, but in truth, she wanted to tantalise him. She wanted him to ask her for more – her, nobody else.

Everthorne inhaled the story, its richness, the scope for illustration. 'And I thought life here would be suffocatingly dull,' he said. 'My grandfather certainly found it so.'

Valourhand returned to Boris' question. 'As to these *amicae*, Wynter was "disappeared" – or, as I prefer to put it, "atomised" – in the mixing-point. Others had their minds wiped and were shipped to the Indies, where only Sir Veronal survived. But how many were there in all?'

'Six,' replied Orelia. 'I'm sure Ferensen said six.'

'Add Fortemain, and that accounts for seven of the ten children.'

'You're forgetting the Seers,' interrupted Jones.

'They were locals – they didn't come from London, and they're not among the ten. Duh . . .' Valourhand turned her back on Jones. 'We've forgotten the women! There were three who came at the very beginning: *amicae meae* – they're his lady-friends.'

Orelia offered another angle. 'Sir Veronal and Calx Bole lived on because they entered the mixing-point. The others had familiars – so maybe those creatures lived on too?'

Fanguin doubted it. 'Oxenbridge was a soldier, not one for half-measures – he'd have destroyed all traces of Lost Acre, including any familiars. Why leave the living proof of the past you're trying to hide?'

'He missed Bole's cat,' Valourhand pointed out, 'so he might have missed others.'

Everthorne had drifted away as if aware of the sensitivity of the conversation around him, but Gorhambury called him back.

'Show Everthorne the shields,' he said.

Everthorne picked up Finch's magnifying glass and gazed intently. They were sublime examples of the miniaturist's art, not a hair out of place and every feature rendered with a dispassionate, lifelike quality. 'I'd say aids to recognition, they're that detailed.'

He turned his attention to the women. There were three. One appeared of great age, with a mallet in one hand and a key in the other. The other two, while much younger, were cowled.

'Nuns, maybe?' whispered Fanguin.

'Cloth does not fall this way, and our painter is too good for such a mistake.' Everthorne spoke gently to nobody in particular, as if answering questions of his own.

'What, then?'

'They're winged; one pair is feathered, the other leathery.'

Oblong intervened. The thought of three women had prompted another possible connection. 'The *Commedia* – that page from *Inferno*, the one Finch marked, *Canto IX*? There was a name. Erinyes – aren't they . . . the Furies?'

Hands fumbled for the book and Finch's marker.

'*O amicae meae*,' repeated Fanguin. 'O my lady-friends.'

A shocked hush descended.

'Poor Finchy has been taken by hellish women,' declared Gregorius Jones melodramatically.

Valourhand ignored him, still weighing probabilities, the key to all solutions. 'It strains credulity,' she announced. 'Finch looks at *The Dark Devices* and sees what we missed. He then miraculously remembers an obscure note made by Wynter in the *Commedia* and leaves a marker at that very page, only to be interrupted . . . by them! It's far too neat.'

Fanguin seized the baton, to devastating effect. 'Finch consulted *The Dark Devices*, but he didn't leave out the *Commedia* and he didn't place the marker. It's a calling card from his abductors – *O amicae meae* – they're mocking us, just as Bole did with his trail of clues.' Fanguin added a qualifying, 'I think,' but nobody challenged his analysis.

'Winged Furies would hardly use the door,' observed Gorhambury, prompting another glance at the skylights.

Orelia had a domestic insight. 'They're crystal-clear – Finch must clean them.'

Boris, the inventor, got there first: the two library ladders fixed together to make a single ladder long enough to reach.

'Oblong, you're the lightest,' suggested Gorhambury, only for Valourhand to intervene.

'Of course he's not, I am.'

Jones carried the ladder from bay to bay with Valourhand perched at the top like a circus acrobat. Two alcoves yielded nothing suspicious but in the third, she cried out, 'There's a pane loose!' She manoeuvred the glass rectangle onto the roof. Cold, moist air swept the room as the wind roared over their heads. Fanguin caught a fleeting tang of decay, the same rancid smell of the excrement Valourhand had found in the marsh.

'The birds have flown,' Orelia whispered to Fanguin. 'It all connects.'

Valourhand lifted herself through the opening as Jones rested the ladder on the frame.

Gorhambury knew she would not wait, impatience being both her strength and her weakness: a maverick explorer with no sense of teamwork.

The roof of Escutcheon Place had captivated Valourhand ever since she first glimpsed its forest of ornate spires from Aether's Way. Close up, bizarre creatures in stone with gargoyle heads twisted their torsos around the spikes. She trod gingerly. Cross-winds gusted down the intersecting gullies, which mirrored the divisions in the alcoves below. She found a smear of excrement whose surface had congealed; a good day old, she decided, and surely from the same source as her previous find.

She crouched, feeling exposed: a mouse in a meadow quartered by owls. If these creatures had claws, they must be remarkably dexterous, lifting and then replacing a glass pane with such finesse.

She edged along the parapet to discover a low oak door, tucked into a corner in an arch bearing the carved motto *Ceryx audiet*. She had no idea who or what Ceryx might be. The outer stone architrave was sculpted with shell-like motifs – human ears; a place for Ceryx to listen? Beyond, a stairway descended into the dark, offering shelter from the storm and an escape route from her increasingly tiresome companions.

She counted sixteen steps before the passage levelled and widened. At intervals tiny diamond-shaped apertures had been cut into the walls, high enough for a grown man to reach. On tiptoe, she could make out a vertiginous view: the ghostly silhouettes of Rotherweird's towers against ribbons of lighter sky on the valley rim.

Where was she?

*

Everthorne followed Valourhand, but quickly reappeared to report, 'Be careful. It's blowing a gale, and your friend has vanished.' He offered a helping hand to those below.

Gorhambury surfaced last like the captain of a stricken ship. He felt apprehensive: an irascible wind, Furies on the loose and a perilously low parapet – the *High Structure Regulations* would never permit trained workmen on an exposed roof in these conditions, let alone well-oiled laymen gadding about. He issued directions as if marshalling a children's treasure hunt: 'Five minutes to look, then back – if Miss Valourhand doesn't show, she must take care of herself. And keep away from the edge.'

'Fury droppings!' cried Fanguin, but his words were lost to the wind.

Orelia quickly found the mysterious door and one by one they joined her.

Gorhambury blocked the doorway. 'We cover our tracks first. Jones and Boris, with me – the rest of you, wait.' At his direction, Jones manoeuvred the ladder to a resting place between two book-shelves, less of a giveaway than leaving it against the roof. They restored the pane and returned to find Oblong delivering another lesson, this time in mythology.

'Ceryx was the son of Hermes, the messenger of the gods. At a guess, it's ancient Greek for Herald. It looks like a passage for eavesdropping – maybe how a Finch ancestor kept his ear to the ground.'

To Oblong's chagrin his revelation received not a word of congratulation.

'That sort of knowledge suggests a troubled childhood,' muttered Fanguin.

Orelia privately agreed with Oblong's theory. The passage must run behind the social section of Aether's Way, home to coffee shops and gossip. A lesson from history: the dark arts do not change.

As Gorhambury led the way, Everthorne re-imagined The Vanished

Herald as a scene from Dante's *Inferno*: a troop of grotesques frog-marching a tabarded man down a tunnel to hell.

Valourhand moved on as soon as the scratching above her head ceased. Roc and Salt had been the cutting edge of the last adventure; this must be her odyssey. The descent levelled out to a dead end facing a wooden wall. She pressed and probed to no avail. Distant voices confirmed that her companions had found the passageway. She jumped up and down in irritation – only to release a disguised panel in the floor which revolved and tipped her towards the aerial bridge below.

Though not a long fall, a violent gust of wind caught her in mid-air. She twisted, flinging both arms at the parapet – and her grasp held. Years of nocturnal exercise, honing strength and flexibility, saved her. There were shops along this section of the Way, and the open space between them where idlers loitered to enjoy the view were unsurprisingly deserted. She hurried on towards the nearest downward stairwell, still hoping to escape her pursuing colleagues, but a cry of panic made her turn.

Valourhand's jump had obligingly opened the wall beyond and jammed the panel open, alerting those behind to the trap. They stepped across to a conventional descent on to Aether's Way, emerging through a concealed doorway in between two shops. Boris pointed out Valourhand, retreating on the other side.

Everthorne, hitherto a reassuring presence, broke away, running along the parapet, eyes down and arms outstretched like a child playing aeroplanes.

Nobody moved, but Orelia cried 'No!' loud enough to alert Valourhand.

'Quiet!' shouted Gorhambury.

One distraction, one false step . . .

Then it happened: an avian form with wings for arms and the

face of a hag, human-sized, swooped out of the void at Everthorne. Erinyes. Real time crawled, seconds dragging into minutes . . .

The artist eluded the first attack, stooping as his attacker stooped, his arms embracing the low flanking wall, but the creature wheeled about for another pass.

As Valourhand searched for a loose cobble, Fanguin the biologist saved the day. With an ear-splitting screech, he ran towards Everthorne, crouching and rising, his arms flapping wildly up and down: bird against bird. The creature opened its wings to the wind and pulled away into the night.

Everthorne skipped down from the parapet. Valourhand vacillated between rage at his idiocy and admiration of his *sang froid*, but decided to leave him to the others. She found a stairwell roped off for repair, lit by a single gaslight, and ran down to the first corner, only to recoil in horror.

The body was lying twisted near the foot of the stairwell, head jerked back, teeth locked, legs unnaturally splayed, eyes flared. She stepped forward again, muttering, 'It's only a corpse!' to herself. The lips and eyes had a human quality. The teeth were too big for a cat. The frozen expression mixed agony with release.

As the others joined her, she said, 'He's in *The Dark Devices*.'

'Calx Bole's fire-spitting familiar,' added Orelia, arriving with Boris, who placed a consoling arm on her shoulder. This creature had threatened to kill Orelia and set fire to her aunt's tower. She had cause to say much more.

Everthorne nimbly passed Valourhand and stepped over the body. They let him: he had seen animals in the beams in Oblong's flat and the wings of the Furies in *The Dark Devices*. He had the artist's eye.

Everthorne felt riven, both drawn to the face, a grisly jigsaw of cat and boy, and repelled by it. His brushes had never shirked the harsher subjects: maggots in meat, birds snared in mist nets, mad

'. . . a grizzly jigsaw of cat and boy . . .'

faces in the asylum where his father had spent his final months. He worked through the scene in his head.

'A fire-spitting cat, you say – and you're right! He descends the stairwell and is surprised from above. The wound to the head comes first. The attacker recoils. He or she anticipates the fire.' By way of explanation Everthorne traced a finger along the brickwork. 'Soot. Seconds later, there's a fatal strike from below.' His finger followed a raking wound from haunch to shoulder.

Fanguin stooped and picked a small jet-black feather from the congealed blood. 'Feather did for him.'

'Everthorne's attacker had leathery wings,' added Valourhand. 'When was Finch's absence discovered?'

'Yesterday evening,' replied Boris.

Fanguin resumed his diagnosis. 'There are early signs of decomposition. My money says whoever kidnapped Finch killed the cat-boy the same night.'

Gorhambury added another note to his burgeoning list: two Furies, feather and leather – different agendas, maybe.

Everthorne revealed a practical side.

'We can't leave the body here. There will be questions.'

Half-boy – does that make it murder, mercy-killing or pest control? Valourhand privately debated the philosophical issues while Everthorne removed his coat and bundled up the corpse.

'He deserves a decent burial – remind me where the gardens are?'

Nobody demurred, although Fanguin did briefly consider dissection, only to dismiss the idea as inappropriate.

Gorhambury handed Everthorne his key to Grove Gardens. 'Due east you'll find the gate. Salt is horribly untidy, so there's bound to be a spade. The rest of us need to talk. We might catch Ferdy if we're quick.'

The thought of the pub wrenched them back to reality. They were drenched and freezing.

'I've never known such an autumn,' grumbled Boris.

'Chin up,' retorted Jones.

Rotherweird had sucked in the storm. Cobbles and walls glistened with rain; down pipes gurgled and whistled.

Orelia came alongside Gorhambury. 'Everthorne needs watching – you saw him on the parapet.'

'Be quick, then, Miss Roc, and do nothing foolish.'

The storm diminished to a sulking passivity. The wind and temperature dropped, and the rain gave way to a fine mist.

6

Post-Mortem

The gate to Grove Gardens stood ajar. Orelia closed it behind her and retrieved the key from the lock. She advanced through the mist, her feet crackling on the gravelled paths. Her aunt had died here for no better reason than a surname shared with one of Wynter's executioners. Now she feared that vicious chapter had been a mere overture.

Walking the escarpment, she heard familiar words spoken by him, hauntingly beautiful: 'Man that is born of a woman hath but a short time to live, and is full of misery. He cometh up, and is cut down, like a flower; he fleeth as it were a shadow, and never continueth in one stay. In the midst of life we are in death: of whom may we seek for succour, but of thee . . .'

Beside the dark druid, Rotherweird's oldest statue, Everthorne leaned on a spade. He had worked fast; the turned earth was already level.

She linked an arm through his and led him away, as the mist thickened into fog.

'It's like burying a stillborn,' he said.

Nothing further passed between them until they reached *The Journeyman's Gist*. They found the windows shuttered and front door locked, but through the keyhole firelight flickered on the flagstones.

'I should go home,' whispered Everthorne.

'This is home,' replied Orelia, deliberately misunderstanding.

After tapping on the window shutter nearest the fire, she heard muted voices, then footfalls, and a side door opened.

Ferdy hurried them inside. He had not lit many candles, for the blazing fire gave light enough. The company sat in a semicircle, coats and jackets draped over chairs and tables. Boris stirred a large saucepan on a gas ring behind the bar. The aroma of lemon, cinnamon and cloves mitigated the clammy odour of a drying-room.

'Low voices,' whispered Ferdy with a wink, 'or Gorhambury will have our guts for garters. I understand Mr Finch is missing – no body, I trust?' He felt safe in asking: his visitors wore expressions of anxiety, not grief.

'There were signs of a struggle,' whispered Valourhand. 'They took him through the skylight. They wanted him alive.'

'Who did, and why?'

Gorhambury described the scene in the *archivoire*, the evidence that Wynter's women or their familiars still lived, the discovery of the mysterious rooftop passageway and the gruesome remains on the staircase below Aether's Way. He introduced Everthorne, who nodded politely to the landlord before helping Boris in the distribution of the mulled wine.

'There remains the "why",' observed Ferdy politely.

'Three possibilities,' suggested Valourhand, pacing between chairs and fire. 'They think he has something, or they think he knows something – or he's bait.'

The last hypothesis had precedent, for Sir Veronal had been lured to his death by a sequence of traps that they had unwittingly activated.

'Or any combination of those three,' added Orelia. 'Let's concentrate on what Finch might know or have. *The Dark Devices* was left on the table: we're all aware what an extraordinary book that is, so I deduce it told Finch's kidnappers nothing they didn't know already. The missing volume from Wynter's library was catalogued, so it can't always have been missing. Assume they were after that, and that Finch—'

Everthorne, sitting cross-legged on the floor, staring into the blaze, glass clasped like a chalice, announced, 'They took it.' He sat stock-still, no movement of hand or head.

'How can you know that?' asked Gorhambury gently.

All heads turned towards the artist, who delved into a coat pocket. 'Here,' he said, flourishing the remains of an old book. 'It was wedged in the storm drain on Aether's Way.'

The black-bound spine had been violently broken and the pages torn out or shredded. The sodden remnants suggested a book of diagrams. Although the golden letters were fractured, the title was clear. *Straighten the Rope.*

Orelia caught Fanguin's eye: Vibes dead, Finch kidnapped, Everthorne attacked – and all to do with this book? At least Everthorne's actions on the parapet now looked less eccentric.

A refreshed Fanguin voiced what others were thinking. 'You saw it sticking out – and that's why you crouched down on the parapet . . .'

Silence descended. Random thoughts and speculation came and went.

Valourhand vented her frustration. 'Calx Bole sets a crossword clue with the answer "The birds have flown" – and they fly. I find their excrement in the marsh on the night of Bolitho's funeral. They abduct Finch and leave a calling card. They pursue a particular book of diagrams. For reasons unknown, they kill Bole's familiar. That's not enough to form a strategy, let alone discover what the enemy is about.'

Fanguin glared at Orelia. *You know there's another copy. Tell them.*

Orelia glared back. *The shapeshifter could be among us now. What about Everthorne – is he all he appears to be?*

Bill Ferdy had a nose for a change in atmosphere. The urgency of the debate was ebbing; incipient torpor would turn to despair unless he could conjure a new note. 'I received a most peculiar bequest from our late lamented friend, Professor Bolitho.' He held up a tiny garden trowel with five shiny protruding teeth. A label in Bolitho's distinctive script said 'use in extremis'.

'You're not alone, Bill,' Boris broke in. 'I got a kaleidoscope that responds to dark, not light, and shows an unknown star careering through Orion.'

'It's not a star,' Valourhand responded. 'Stars are fixed. It's a comet if it's anything.' She paused. Why give Boris a toy? In the professor's last lecture, his pupils had played the solar system and Oblong, the outsider, had been cast as a comet – coincidence?

'Comets have an elliptical orbit that can take centuries to complete,' added Oblong sagely, mindful of Bolitho's commentary, and how he had moved far from the sun and the planets to the far corner of School Hall, metaphorically deep space.

'But we'd see it,' countered Boris. 'My nephew and I have peered through binoculars for a week – there's not a smudge or a smidgen of anything.'

'I saw it,' muttered Valourhand. 'I saw it in Lost Acre. I nicknamed it Orion's Lantern.'

Fanguin, his voice faintly slurred by the mulled wine, intervened. 'You mean its make-up masks it here and reveals it there? That's pretty rum.'

Valourhand felt a trail opening up. Bolitho had made a bizarre remark, which she had taken as jest at the time, but recent events suggested otherwise. 'Bolitho left me an empty box labelled dark matter – at the time I thought it a joke in poor taste, but at the end of that last lecture he asked a most peculiar question: Suppose Oblong – meaning the comet – was made of dark matter?'

'What's dark matter?' asked Jones.

'Use your grey matter,' giggled Fanguin.

'Think of your shadow,' replied Boris quickly, to pre-empt a crushing response from Valourhand, but the scientist's mind was elsewhere; she added a trite explanation, while thinking deeper.

'Dark matter cannot be seen by the best telescope, yet it makes up most of the universe – and it's not to be confused with dark energy or antimatter.' Her mind was racing in multiple directions – surely not – but why not? Relativity, gravity, radiation – she could barely keep pace with the potential consequences. But it felt right. It could be . . .

She spoke more forcibly now, centre stage, her back to the fire. 'I'd hazard a guess . . .'

They listened closely: Valourhand would resort to guesswork only if it alone could explain the otherwise inexplicable.

'I believe there is a comet, and it's our comet. A primordial impact made the bowl in which Rotherweird sits, Lost Acre, and the gateways. The debris made the comet, and Lost Acre's millennial cycle is the comet's millennial cycle. There had to be an explanation – now we have it!'

The image held them: coitus between rock and rock, unspeakable violence, fracturing dimensions playing tricks with matter itself.

'Cripes,' said Jones.

Ferdy loved big-picture science and the talk of creation and elemental forces, but leavened by the farmer's practical eye: keep your feet on the ground. Whatever the cosmology, Wynter and his acolytes presented the danger in the here and now. He nudged the debate back to its starting point.

'Closing time approaches, ladies and gentlemen, and we need something to mull over. When you lack answers, it is best to formulate questions. Let everyone provide one unanswered question which they think matters . . .'

Nobody challenged the proposal, so he started at the back and worked round. The first contributor predictably stated the obvious.

Jones: 'If the cat-thing works for Wynter's servant, and the flying things work for Wynter's disciples, why are they fighting each other?'

Oblong ventilated the question that had been exercising him since the funeral: 'Why did Bolitho rocket me skywards with the town on my chest?'

Gorhambury, ever political, asked, 'Where did Strimmer get his glove?' The question held a menacing innuendo: might the election be part of the enemy's grand strategy? In the matter of Sir Veronal Slickstone, disparate threads had joined to make the whole – the Fair, the church frescoes, the *Anglo-Saxon Chronicle*, the Midsummer flower, *The Roman Recipe Book*, to name but a few – and now the mysterious comet had joined the cast.

Boris, thumbing through the remains of the ruined book, said, 'What is *Straighten the Rope* about? Bell-ropes, anchor ropes, a hangman's rope? We only have fragments – but from the little I can see, there's nothing to do with ropes.'

Was the title yet another anagram? Oblong took out a pen and, affecting an absent-minded doodle, experimented on the back of a beer mat.

Orelia didn't intervene. She had a whole copy but she was none the wiser, despite hours of study. She felt exhausted. All these questions were doing nothing to illuminate; they only obscured.

Fanguin tried a new tack. 'We're right to focus on Wynter's women and their familiars, but we mustn't forget Fortemain. The trial record is silent, if I remember right – so what became of him?'

Valourhand blushed, a rarity. The name suggested an ancestor and yet she had given him little thought. She ran with Fanguin's question. 'If Fortemain escapes the mixing-point, old age takes him. If he doesn't, he's punished like the Seers.' She paused. 'Only with what in his cage?'

And Ferdy, last to speak, held up his gift. 'Why on earth give me a trowel?'

It was an inconsequential question, but talk of trowels and earth prompted Boris into spontaneous recitation:

'Earth to sky and sky to earth
Matter matters in rebirth,
Sky to earth and earth to sky,
Life's mutations do not die—

'Bolitho's self-written epitaph,' he explained.

Orelia sat bolt-upright in a moment of revelation: Wynter's first house had been taken over by a more benign presence; his victims had been reborn as bookbinders; and someone had brought Morval Seer library books and paints to comfort her in Lost Acre – but it hadn't been Ferensen – so who else but Fortemain?

'"Life's mutations do not die ..." Fortemain lived on!' she pronounced.

'As who?' asked Valourhand, her scepticism evident in the tone of her voice and set of her shoulders.

Orelia tossed a log on the fire before replying. Sparks flew. 'Bolitho.'

Disbelief and laughter greeted her suggestion, but Orelia held her ground. 'Think about it: both have an exceptional gift for astronomy. Bolitho was brought up abroad, so masking his origins. Throughout the summer he hides away in his observatory, only to emerge to give a midnight lecture in the countryside which revealed to Oblong the location of the celestial entrance to Lost Acre.'

Oblong offered support for her theory. 'He gave me a personal demonstration in his planetarium that showed the sky in England, centuries ago, at the time the Eleusians were conceived. He portrayed their genius as a freak of cosmic timing – but how could he know their birthdays, unless he was one?'

Fanguin, flushed by the fire and more than his fair share of mulled wine, followed suit. 'Bolitho arrived back here years before

Slickstone – he knew about Lost Acre's millennial cycle; he knew Bole was alive and active, but he didn't dare come out in the open.'

'Why not?' asked Boris.

'Because . . . because he wasn't privy to Bole's plans. He didn't know what form Bole was currently taking so he had to work under-cover. That's why—' He stopped and smiled. 'That's why he grew that beard for the Slickstone party – so as not to be recognised.'

Ferdy spoke quietly. 'If he did live on, he was put through the mixing-point.'

Valourhand, hitherto strangely subdued, joined in. 'Someone came to me in Lost Acre and delivered Bolitho's obituary, so that clearly wasn't Bolitho. Who else is out there?'

Orelia looked at the five silver teeth of the miniature trowel and remembered a coloured illustration . . . and a larger brick slid into place. It was a bizarre idea, even horrific, but it fitted all they knew. 'Bolitho's not dead; he's out there now.'

As others gasped, Valourhand hunted for reasons. 'How exactly?' she exclaimed.

Gorhambury had as yet said nothing, but this flight of fancy had to be grounded. He could not have Town Hall staff burying citizens alive, let alone the esteemed former Professor of Astronomy. 'Miss Roc, you cannot fool the undertaker, the doctor, the grave diggers . . .'

Orelia shook her head. 'In the summer Bolitho gave me a wish-list of books he hoped I might come across. They included *Mammals* by Archibald Thorburn, the nature artist. He wanted one particular plate, of a creature with feet like Bill's clawed trowel. Bolitho is a moleman!'

Valourhand returned to Bolitho's epitaph, sounding uncharac-teristically distraught.

'Earth to sky and sky to earth
Matter matters in rebirth . . .

'Orelia is right: the astronomer and the mole, sky to earth and earth to sky. He had himself buried alive so he could escape. Remember the Sewage Sub-Committee meeting? That discussion about subsidence by the churchyard wall?'

Orelia followed up. 'He went into hibernation, as moles do. He closed himself down – that's how he fooled everyone. Then he burrowed—'

'Wicker coffin,' Boris added, 'breakable open.'

'Time,' Bill Ferdy called, speaking both as the publican and more generally; they needed to absorb and reflect.

As he cleared away the glasses, Boris patted him on the back. 'Thanks, Bill. You got us moving.'

'A final glass for a final question,' said Fanguin, scooping out the dregs of the mulled wine, flecked with fruit peel and sediment. 'Or really, a question about your questions: which are the ones Bolitho wants us to answer, which are the ones the enemy has planted and which are the ones of our own devising?' He shrugged his shoulders. 'Best sleep on it.'

Coats, boots and scarves were gathered from chairs, tables and the floor. Shock and sadness pervaded *The Journeyman's Gist* and nothing further of moment was said.

Valourhand still couldn't work out who had delivered her mysterious letter in Lost Acre – Bolitho had not then been buried. And she sensed that Orelia was holding something back. Only one way forward beckoned: a perilous journey for which she needed a companion, someone malleable – and now.

Outside, fog and gas-lamps had dissolved the town into disconnected smudges of light. Partings in whispers provided the backdrop as she made her move.

'Oblong?'

Images of Cecily Sheridan surfaced whenever Valourhand addressed him directly, and he nearly answered 'Cecily'. He swallowed. 'V . . . Valourhand?'

'You're needed. No ifs, no buts; just follow.'

She stalked off, knowing he would obey, which he did with an apologetic wave to the rest. Anything was better than returning to the scene of his forgotten party, even with Aggs' restored tidiness. Still nobody had thanked him.

Orelia felt disappointment of a different kind when Everthorne declined her offer to walk him home.

'I welcome the challenge,' he said, flourishing the map distributed by the Town Hall to the Summoned. Though drawn to her, for the moment he needed to paint and settle the inner turmoil which had afflicted him since his return.

'We're here,' replied Orelia, laying a finger on the map, 'and you're there.' She kissed him on the cheek and disappeared into the fog without looking back. She felt both bereaved and concerned that his run along the parapet had been a reckless flirtation with death.

Boris watched Everthorne plod into the gloom, reflecting on the common demands of their respective trades, painter and inventor: intensity, imagination, technical know-how, bloody-minded perseverance and self-discipline. Yet artists attract women and inventors do not. The artist's subjects share the artist's vision in an intimate way, he reasoned, often the process as well as the product, whereas the beneficiaries of inventions just use them. The thought of women brought a twinge of guilt: Miss Trimble had made a bid for his attention outside Oblong's party, but he had barely acknowledged her. He trudged home feeling despondent, his thoughts turning on Bolitho's appalling secret.

Fog usually depressed Everthorne, obscuring line and draining colour; he thought of it as how an artist's vision might fail on the threshold of death. Yet tonight he welcomed the enveloping dankness: it was as if the town were exhaling its own uncertainty. The gypsy-looking girl, Orelia Roc, had spirit, but naïveté too. Her political rivals would be entertaining to paint: one wily and corrupt, the other cruel and hubristic. He suspected she would have little chance against either of them.

Focusing on others relaxed him. Back in 3 Artery Lane, he resisted his sketchbook and went straight to bed, wondering if the source of his unease had been lying dormant in his genes only to be awakened by the town of his forbears, this peculiar jigsaw of stone and wood, lost history and new inventions.

Topsyturvyland.

At dawn he set out north up the Rother to check on a family heirloom recorded in his grandfather's sketchbooks.

Fanguin had a miserable homecoming. His wife was in the kitchen in slippers and dressing gown.

'You shouldn't wait up,' he started; Bomber had her hands on her hips, which was never a good sign. On the other hand, his place at the table was laid and a pan simmered on the hob.

'Just a drink with Oblong, you said.'

'There was a crisis—'

'He's an outsider, Fanguin. Keep your distance.'

'He came to supper – you liked him,' he protested.

'He has an outsider's agenda.'

'For God's sake, Bomber, Oblong couldn't run a bath!'

'Then what's so gripping about his company?'

In search of diversion, Fanguin lifted the lid off the casserole, releasing a wave of flavour – kidneys, mushrooms and thyme. No cook himself, he still respected the art form. She deserved a peace overture. 'Bomber, you're a star.'

'Yes, I bloody am.'

The way she said it sounded peculiar. She wasn't a conceited woman, so she must be asking him to observe – but what? He was fairly confident that she hadn't had a haircut; and her clothes were undeniably familiar. 'Delicious!' was the best he could muster.

'I suggest you sleep in your study.'

He would have preferred her to shout or to storm out and slam the door, as anger meant engagement and engagement promised reconciliation. The main fault was, after all, his.

Bomber's Parthian shot finally lifted the veil. 'Food costs money, Fanguin.'

Of course: kidneys and rare mushrooms – on their non-existent income? He sheepishly made the long-awaited enquiry. 'You've been working?'

'Who else does in this benighted household?' she asked. 'How could you not notice, Fanguin? You take out cash every week.'

'But . . . why not tell me?'

'It was a little test,' she said curtly. 'You failed.'

Fanguin placed an apologetic hand on his wife's shoulder. 'Who for? What do you do?'

She shrugged him off. 'I do the one thing I'm good at, for the one organisation in this town that knows how to work. It's a hive, Fanguin: each to his or her own task, and no drones.'

'Not – not the Apothecaries?'

Fanguin loathed the Guild for its aloof arrogance; he had thought Bomber felt likewise.

'If Strimmer wins, you might get a job – ever thought of that?' And now Bomber did storm out.

After a supper marred by the workings of conscience, he retreated to his study with *De Observatione Naturae*. The Latin had an elegant simplicity, but after a long day of alcohol, adventure, mystery and spousal rebuke, he flipped to the end. The closing passages described the construction of a church beneath the brow of a modest hill on an island in a valley. A pagan henge had vanished in a storm of apocalyptic intensity, so marking the site for a house of God. Local legends had been added to the church walls.

Oblong had talked of frescoes in the church belfry, and the arch over the church entrance bore the words *sub hanc petram*,

under this rock. For valley, read Rotherweird surely; there could be
no sensible alternative. With a scientist's distrust of miracles and
relics, he shelved the book, more amused by his accidental breach
of the *History Regulations* and touched by Bolitho's generosity than
impressed by the content – although the thought of two monks
braving the elements to found a church put his feeble endeavours
in perspective.

A bottle of Vlad's finest, wedged in a Bomber-proof cavity beneath
the floorboards, screamed for attention. He poured pencil shavings
into a glass of fruit juice, drank, spat it out and repeated the process, but to no avail. He sank to his knees and scrabbled at the
loose board – but stopped suddenly.

He, Godfery Fanguin, had discovered Wynter's former residence
and the weaselman's skull, major pieces in resolving the summertime puzzle.

Repeat, repeat . . .

The window swung off its latch and a plan took root, irrespon-
sible, but adventurous. Was his tower high enough? No . . . but
there was another way . . .

From an understairs cupboard he retrieved a scarecrow-looking
apparatus, scanners on a tripod, designed for him by Boris to
monitor bats in the shallow caves on the valley escarpment. He
squeezed himself through the window, tearing a pocket and grazing
an arm, while thanking the Almighty that Bomber was tucked up
in bed. He clung to the window, swaying forward and back, his
shoes slipping on the damp sill.

The base of the neighbouring tower abutted the corner of his
windowsill before rising to a wooden crow's nest, a commanding
viewpoint topped with a weathervane. One good step would carry
him across. Wooden rungs ran up to the crow's nest and looked
secure despite the peeling paint. He shouldered the apparatus.

Now for the difficult bit . . .

7

Into the Deeps

Valourhand made no concessions, never stopping, not even at corners. Oblong felt undignified, struggling to keep up with a woman who, as Cecily Sheridan, had rendered him a laughing stock throughout the town.

East-northeast was the general direction, although the plethora of junctions and turnings were the more disorientating for the fog. Predictably, he lost her, but maintaining her line led him to a low stone wall and then an arched entrance festooned in ivy. An eerie coloured light glimmered through patches of intense darkness: stained glass behind yew trees. He was in the churchyard.

Rotherweird could not readily accommodate its dead; some opted for cremation, but many did not. Underneath the privileged few with gravestones above ground lay a maze of catacombs, Rotherweird's second circulatory system, whose intricacies were known only to Mors Valett and his staff.

At the entrance stood a freshly painted sign: DANGER – SUBSIDENCE – KEEP OUT. Beyond, the twin barred gates hung ajar; the lock appeared to have been expertly picked. No need to debate the culprit's identity; only Valourhand would relish a late-night ramble in a catacomb. At the entrance he found a rack of workers' overalls with a tube-light obligingly left in one of the pockets. Oblong shook it, revealing a circular chamber with many arched exits and abundant signage. Arrows in stone, with destinations carved or painted, showed the way to the dead, divided not into sheep and goats but by calling: Scholastic, Sciences Practical, Sciences Theoretical, Doctors of the Mind, Doctors of the Body, Municipal Staff, down to human *vin ordinaire* marked merely by Others.

Finding no mention of astronomers, he followed Scholastic down a meandering tunnel to another hallway and another outbreak of signs, the last resting place for School staff. Predictably, he found no historians. In the far corner the ceiling had been propped up by Valett's workmen after a collapse that had sundered the nearest inscription, splitting Physi from cists. An odour of stale earth pervaded the room.

Oblong jumped over the subsidence and wormed his way through into another chamber, where a candle guttered on the ground. Valourhand must have helped herself at *The Journeyman's Gist*. Tablets inscribed with the bare statistics of birth and death, occasionally alleviated by an epigram, adorned the walls.

'What took you so bloody long?'

The voice came from an opening in the floor towards the rear of the room. A hoist was lying beside it and a ladder protruded near the flickering light of another candle.

The quaint signs and archways had induced a sense of security; here, in the crypt, Death made a shocking entry.

Surrounded by bones and rotted coffins, Valourhand tossed a skull from hand to hand. 'Bolitho's,' she said.

Oblong followed the skull, hypnotised.

'Not this – there!' She pointed at Bolitho's coffin, which had exploded like a chrysalis. 'He went that way,' she added unnecessarily, her finger moving to a gaping hole in the ground. It had a pleasing circularity. An adult would fit, but only just.

'You're not going—'

'We are.' The tunnel had smooth walls, fastidious workmanship. 'He's down there somewhere.'

Oblong failed to curb the panic in his voice. 'We'd have no room to turn if it collapses . . . which it probably will . . .' He suppressed any reference to his party best; he already looked like a jobbing gardener.

'I have a trowel and a pick,' replied Valourhand, resuming her game of toss-the-skull. 'He wants us to follow – why else direct Roc to that illustration? Why give Fanguin a trowel and an instruction to use it in extremis? And why choose that epitaph – "life's mutations do not die" . . . ? Ferensen never took on Wynter and nor did his sister, but Fortemain did and he still does. He knows what Bole is planning, he needs allies and he wants us to follow.'

She knelt by the mouth of the tunnel and peered in. 'I'll take the light. You take your pick.' She delivered the pun with a faint smile before shaking the tube-light on. 'Cheer up, you'll face backwards and I'll face forwards so we can dig ourselves out if there's a collapse.'

Valourhand's slight frame allowed her space to move, but Oblong's gangly build required contortion to keep his back clear of the tunnel roof; and she had the light. He found the constriction and darkness terrifying. 'Controlled breathing,' he muttered to himself, adopting Fanguin's advice before the Great Race. 'Inhale, one, two; exhale; one, two . . .'

The path levelled and, after twenty minutes of slow progress, they met the cave-in. The tunnel roof flickered over Oblong's shoulder as Valourhand waved the light. She moved on a few feet, then disappeared sharp right round a solid blockage of stone, earth and split boards.

Valourhand turned her head to face Oblong, cheeks and forehead streaked like a miner's. 'The path curves back into the original tunnel – which means I'm right,' she whispered, as if ordinary speech might bring the tunnel down. 'Look at how the two paths join: it collapsed behind him, but he went back to clear a way round. I repeat – he wanted us to follow.'

Or to be sure of a quick retreat, mused Oblong silently.

Oblong found the gradient challenging when the gentle descent became steeper and the claustrophobia more intense. The mustiness became intrusive too, as the air grew warmer. An age passed before they reached a small chamber with enough space to sit and face each other. Shelves of rock glowed red and brown.

Valourhand held the tube-light to the ceiling. 'Good God,' she said.

Incised in the stone was a Roman numeral – MDLXXII/I.

'Number one in 1572?' suggested Oblong.

'The second number may be a milestone.'

'You walk a mile in twenty minutes. We're going way slower – surely not long enough for a mile.'

'How about – we've a mile to go.' Valourhand spoke wearily, as if to a slow child.

'To what?'

'Get there, and we'll find out.'

Oblong ran a finger around the inscription, raising a puff of dust which, defying gravity, reattached itself to the rock.

Valourhand grimaced. The idiot historian had a maddening gift for stumbling on significance without realising it. 'Magnetism,' she said.

Her thoughts turned to Bolitho the moleman – how he transformed, how he might look – and to Geryon Wynter, the torturer. She vented her frustration on her companion. 'Oblong, Calx Bole would never choose you as his next host. But has it not occurred to you he might choose me?'

'He'd soon regret it if he did!' responded Oblong.

'Onwards,' she added gruffly.

Runs of rock became frequent, blue and spectral white now joining the red and brown streaks. Discomfort in Oblong's lower back turned to soreness and then to pain. Valourhand allowed an occasional break so he could stretch out flat, chin in the earth.

How deep we must be, below roots and any ordinary animal burrow, Oblong thought. This is truly the moleman's kingdom. Claustrophobia came in waves as he imagined his mouth filling with earth, breathing earth, tasting earth, eyelids closed by earth.

When the tunnel briefly bulged like an oesophagus, he made a bid for change. 'Vixen, it's pretty grim being a rear gunner with no taillight. How about a swap?'

Revulsion at the thought of his body squirming past hers dictated an instant response. 'You're the historian: you look backwards.'

Oblong tried a new tack. 'What are you expecting to find?'

'Can't you guess?'

Oblong's imagination ran riot: perhaps giant maggots, dull white, blind and carnivorous, were wriggling up the tunnel towards them. His position at the rear acquired fresh appeal.

They resumed their journey. To keep fear at bay, Oblong exchanged his breathing regime for a countdown from four thousand, his estimate of the number of knee-paces to the mile.

'Do you blow up at zero?' whispered Valourhand, but she made no direct complaint. The gangloid was doing better than expected.

At 2,087, Oblong-distance, she stopped. 'Smell it?' she murmured, but Oblong's finer senses had succumbed to his sciatic nerve.

He rolled onto his back and caught the fragrance – bittersweet, incense almost, soothing and familiar. He had encountered it before in Rotherweird – in someone's home – but he could not think whose.

At 1,098 Valourhand stopped again. A slender green stem ran along the roof of the tunnel towards them. More stems appeared, then tiny buds and flowers, deep carmine with golden anthers.

Now Oblong remembered. 'Hayman Salt has one of these in his hallway. He calls it the *Darkness Rose*.'

'It's from Lost Acre then,' replied Valourhand. 'Just as I thought.'

Obligingly, the rose had few thorns. It clung to the walls and roof of the tunnel, as if aware that adorning the floor would be precarious. The plant had a mysterious presence beyond its beauty, which eased Oblong's panic.

'You're the historian: you look backwards.'

His calculation of distance proved pessimistic: at 692 the tunnel ended in a circular space with no exit. The *Darkness Rose* had rooted at the far end. Even at its base the stems remained slender. Oblong gently ran a thumb along the strongest cane. Neighbouring leaves trembled as if sentient.

'It's very alive.'

'Everything in Lost Acre is very alive,' replied Valourhand. 'Which is why, no doubt, someone left these.'

Two spears of contrasting length were lying against the chamber wall. The shorter looked primitive, but the flinthead had a sharp edge and the shaft was straight and strong. The other, a more sophisticated weapon, had been forged. Both shared an unusual adaptation: a small spiked iron collar encircling the shaft near the head, where the wood had the stained appearance of charcoal.

'Pilum,' observed Oblong of the longer weapon. 'Two metres, iron shank, wooden shaft and pyramid-shaped head.' Valourhand looked baffled and Oblong, so often at the receiving end of her scientific know-how, enjoyed the moment. 'A Roman javelin,' he explained. 'For throwing, they used soft iron for the shank to bend on impact, so it could not be returned with interest. The other shank is hard – that's for close-quarter work.'

Valourhand took the cruder spear, which, unlike the other, did not dwarf her. 'It must be somewhere here,' she said, re-seizing the initiative.

'What must?'

'Oh, do engage, Oblong! A Roman spear, a Lost Acre plant – what do you think?' She paused, sarcastically scratching her head, before announcing, 'A tile, Oblong: a tile!'

'Ah, yes, well naturally, of course, goes without saying ... see what you mean.' And again he was back on the bloody defensive.

'Get looking, then!'

She found the earth-coloured tile. Despite the camouflage, the telltale incised flower left no doubt.

'How do you know everything is so alive in Lost Acre?' Oblong asked.

Valourhand's instinctive secrecy succumbed to a desire to put Oblong's fancy historical knowledge back in its box.

'I devoted several weeks in the spiderwoman's lair to field-work. Weapons are no use if you don't know what your enemy does.'

Touché. Oblong did not doubt her; Ferensen had been at ease with her absence at his celebratory dinner; he had even used the same explanation: fieldwork.

'Imagine being sucked down a plug-hole,' she added with a gentle grin.

'So where do we end up? In whose lair?'

An imbecilic question, she thought; how could she know?

She grudgingly shared a few facts. 'Lost Acre and Rotherweird share calendar and clock. Dawn and dusk are the main mealtimes, so we've a good three hours of relative safety.'

Oblong doubted that Valourhand's notion of 'relative safety' accorded with his own.

She appeared to agree. 'I question your resolve, Oblong. I'd follow you in – but vice versa?' She looked sickeningly at ease, lounging spear in hand as if to say she did adventure.

Stung, Oblong stepped forward – only to meet a restraining arm.

'Do nothing foolish before I get there – or better, do nothing at all! The tile may take time to recharge.'

She withdrew her arm and Oblong, looking thunderous, disappeared.

Disembodied, then miraculously reconstructed, Oblong staggered from the tile, his vision seriously impaired. Or was it? The balls of light at his feet neither flickered nor moved. He blinked. Glow-worms? Carnivorous glow-worms? He strained his ears for breathing or movement, but heard only his own. Clouds scudded above.

Fingery shadows at the rim of the bowl suggested vegetation, but they too were still.

He touched the nearest light source, which mercifully turned out to be an inanimate stone, the circumference smooth and rounded, save for a flattening on one side and a chip on the other. He tried others, all of a similar size, all imperfect, all mildly luminous. Near the tile lay strands of dead vegetation, half-burned, plaited like hair. Fallen from the plants above, he assumed.

Climbing proved a challenge, his feet forever sliding back as if on loose shingle. Encouraged by the prospect of urging Valourhand to hurry up, he persevered, planting his spear and kicking his toes into the slope: climb, slip; climb, slip. He had made fifteen laborious feet when a familiar voice gave a familiar command in a familiar tone.

'Stop!'

Oblong turned, the shift in weight costing half his painful progress. 'Bloody woman,' he muttered, then, louder, 'I'm doing well, thank you.'

'Don't move, not an inch. Don't even breathe.' Valourhand's nostrils flared and her eyes darted this way and that. She looked feral.

Unlike Oblong, she climbed with power and nimbleness, quickly reaching him. She stooped and sniffed the charred vegetation.

'Give me your javelin,' she whispered. She picked up some of the plaited straw and wound it round the spiked iron collar at the top of Oblong's longer spear shaft before muttering, 'And this time, don't bloody move!'

Oblong seethed as Valourhand climbed above him with ease. When she produced a box of matches, he violently waved his arms. 'You'll attract predators—' The gesture sent him slipping back towards his starting point.

She lit the dead straw, turned into the slope and held up the spear.

With a thunderous explosion the air above them ignited and a sheet of purplish flame ran out from the spear's tip: Valourhand the magician, flourishing a wand of awesome power.

'Riddle for an idiot,' she shouted down. 'What's odourless, invisible, lives in rocks and kills?'

Oblong shrugged.

'Methane! Why do you think there are spikes on the spears? Why are the shafts blackened? Why were there lengths of plaited straw on the ground?' After this volley of rhetorical questions, she resumed her climb to the rim, pocketing a selection of stones on the way. Oblong attempted the same, but his progress resembled a game of snakes and ladders, with the ladders painstakingly slow and the snakes depressingly fast, until at last an accommodating tree root provided an impromptu rail up to firm ground.

'There's a river below and forest on the rising ground behind us,' said Valourhand. 'We need to go upstream, I think – but it's a gamble.'

Oblong pulled out his handkerchief to mop his brow, dislodging a Ferdy beer mat.

Valourhand retrieved it. A maze of letters covered the cork. 'Yours?' she asked.

'I thought *Straighten the Rope* might be an anagram.'

'Perhaps it is. The diagrams were bugger-all to do with rope.'

'But they are shapes, yes?'

They took turns, Oblong first. 'No c for a circle.'

'No l for a triangle.'

'No m for a pentagram, or any other-gram.'

'No d for a tetrahedron or any other-hedron.'

'No q for a square.'

So what was left?

The stone in Valourhand's cupped hands inspired the breakthrough. 'Hold on, hold on . . .' Oblong cried.

'Ssssh! They have ears round here, even the plants.'

'Sphere,' whispered Oblong.

Valourhand pondered. 'Yes – yes, it could be.'

'How about The Something Sphere? There's an -ing left.' Oblong jumped with excitement. 'Eureka! The Rotating Sphere!' He ticked off the letters with his finger.

Concern flooded Valourhand's face and he stopped. 'What's the matter now?'

'Nothing,' she said.

'Come on; I share, you share.'

'A hunch without evidence is nothing more than a hunch.' She shook the tube-light gently. 'Follow!'

The descent had its own hazards, including stems with thorns which moved and a deep circular pit. On the valley floor a stream flowed through alluvial mudflats littered with detritus from Midsummer's apocalyptic storm. Dead branches, some suckered, some dotted with multi-coloured shells, choked the stream at intervals. A flock of fungal faces with shark-like teeth roamed the fringe of the forest, prospecting.

'We're too close to the trees – we have to cross the stream,' Valourhand said.

'Right-o,' replied Oblong with false bravado.

'Jump high and away from the water,' she advised. As she leaped, a flurry of tiny emerald fish broke the surface, all swivelling eyes and long-quilled backs. She twisted her torso in mid-air to avoid the poisonous spines.

Oblong almost toppled on take-off, but his larger stride saw him over. The flying discs lost interest, veering back to their roosts in the trees.

'We'll keep to the bank,' she ordered. 'The grassland isn't safe, only safer than the forest.' She led the way upstream, her shoulders hunched, her steps regular.

Predator avoidance, thought Oblong, following suit.

After an hour the stream, now much larger, divided, looping round to rejoin itself before flowing on. A towering rock with a perfect circular hole at its apex dominated the centre of the island.

'Do we risk the island?' she wondered.

'Not with those bloody fish,' replied Oblong. 'Second time unlucky.'

Valourhand weighed the options. 'All right,' she said, 'we go round,' not admitting to Oblong that she too could do with a break. She had been toying with a detour to the mixing-point to check for recent activity, but resisted the temptation. Oblong would do something foolish and time was short. She took the direct route over to the island.

'I know that skyline,' she whispered. 'It's not far now.'

'Why aren't the plains teeming with life?' Oblong asked. 'We've not seen or heard anything. I thought night-time was danger-time – and why did the discs withdraw? We're easy prey.'

'It's an unpredictable place,' replied Valourhand, unwilling to acknowledge that he might have a point.

A ribbon of chilly air floated by, disconcertingly cold, stinging the cheeks.

'Feel that?' asked Oblong. Behind them the level plain stretched away to a distant upland rim and he could see nothing untoward . . . except—

'There – there!' he shouted, gesturing straight ahead. Pockets of grass lay flat, the trampled stalks glistening with frost.

She glanced upstream and stared: some two metres of the river had frozen hard, bank-to-bank.

'Run!' she screamed, sprinting from the exposed riverbank into the tall grass, Oblong hard on her heels.

They heard it first: a bellowing roar and a crackle like breaking sticks. The temperature plummeted and a swathe of nearby mead-owland turned white under a blast of snow and frozen shards. A huge scaled shape rose, wings outstretched, mouth dripping sky-blue. Unlike the Fury, this monstrous creature had no vestige of humanity. Oblong threshed at the rigid stems with his spear.

Confuse it, Valourhand decided, that's all we can do.

'. . . *a bellowing roar and a crackle like breaking sticks* . . .'

But Oblong's frenetic behaviour had given them away. The head levelled at its target; the creature's ribs glowed. Drops of cerulean blue spilled from the creature's mouth, raising clouds of vapour in the warmer air.

She threw the spear, followed by the rock fragments from her pocket, as high as she could. If perfect stones manipulated the mixing-point, and this creature had been fashioned there, maybe, just maybe . . .

The beast's head jerked back, disorientated, and it banked away.

'Now!' yelled Valourhand, but Oblong had temporarily lost her.

Head covered in frost, trousers solid as metallic breeches, he plunged into a Midwinter nightmare, yelling, 'Where, where?'

Respite was short: the creature settled into a glide, bearing down on them in a low slow arc. Valourhand wondered how death would be – blood frozen, lungs rigid, heart turned to stone, flesh cauterised – and regretted throwing the spear. The grass obstructed them like straws of iron. She had to kick and punch her way through, but Oblong plunged past her, only yards to the left, still flailing with his spear.

'This way,' she screamed at him, and a swathe of ice, snow and hail curled towards them. 'Hug me!' she screamed.

'What?'

'Hug me!'

With seconds to spare, he did; Valourhand held him close and stepped back.

Rotherweird's beeches looked down from above; ferns and brambles clutched at their ankles. *Landfall*. Soft ground betrayed the earlier storm, but the mist had gone.

'What now?' asked Oblong.

'Now, we sleep,' replied Valourhand.

'Surely not here?' He squelched his feet to underline the point.

Not for the first time in their journey, Oblong had shown a smidgen of initiative, a development to be carefully watched, Valourhand decided.

They barged through the undergrowth into the meadow beyond, where Oblong pointed to a stand of trees. 'Jones recommends pines.'

'Does he indeed!'

'Needles dry fast, make a yielding mattress and have fragrance.'

'You sound like an advertisement.'

'That's what Jones said!'

She strode ahead. 'You take this tree, I'll take that one.'

Valourhand's allotted billets were at opposite ends of the spinney, clearly not an invitation to share bodily warmth.

'Right-o,' he replied, his new phrase for agreeing with Valourhand; it felt less compliant than 'yes' or a nod.

The pinkish tinge to the elegant trunks reflected a lightening sky. Sleep engulfed them in moments.

Such variety in the waking process: Oblong surfaced, sank and resurfaced; Valourhand switched on, eyelids snapping open like a vampire at the moment of sundown.

Sitting with her back against her tree trunk, hands on her knees, she watched with mild distaste as Oblong subsided once more, mouth open, snoring.

She walked over and dropped in a pine needle. 'We're being manoeuvred,' she said as Oblong spluttered into life. 'Fortemain collapsed that tunnel where the subsidence would be noticed. Fortemain left the spears and the straw and the milestone in the ceiling.' She ignored the groan as Oblong achieved the vertical. 'He wanted us to find the quarry – but why? All the stones we saw were imperfect.'

'Maybe he wanted us to meet the ice-dragon.'

Oblong had spoken facetiously, but Valourhand did not dismiss the idea. 'Maybe he did.'

'*Straighten the Rope* had diagrams for the construction of a sphere. Maybe the pieces came from the quarry?'

'The rock which makes the pieces,' corrected Valourhand wearily.

'Do atoms spin?'

'For God's sake, Oblong! *All* elementary particles spin – is there anyone in this town whom you don't irritate?'

'You'd be surprised.'

'Like whom?'

Oblong smiled at Valourhand's exactitude, *whom*, not *who*, dealt his ace nonchalantly. 'Hengest Strimmer.'

The name struck home, for Valourhand started jumping up and down like a spoiled child. 'Where? Why? How?'

Oblong pressed home his advantage. He came to me, uninvited, and a nasty wet evening it was too. He brought a bottle – and not just any old bottle – and he proposed a toast to us ...' Oblong struggled to summon any more detail of Strimmer's visit – it had been that surprising. 'The rest is a bit of a blur,' he admitted.

Valourhand marched up and down the meadow as if changing guard. Bizarrely, she looked more agitated than impressed.

He felt pang of discomfort, and not from the absence of breakfast.

'Talk me through it,' shrilled Valourhand, 'and start with that bottle!'

'He'd really splashed out – Vlad's best ... it was pears ... pear brandy.'

Valourhand's step accelerated. 'It tasted of pears?'

Oblong giggled slightly as he deployed the wine-taster's phrasebook. 'It had a fruity taste with a metallic tang to the finish.'

There was no let-up in Valourhand's aggression; if anything, it upped a notch. 'And how did this unexpected encounter end?'

Good question – how did it? 'He ... left.'

'And you?'

Oblong, honest to a fault, strove to replay the evening. 'I woke up, eventually.'

Valourhand's cheeks pinkened. Cecily Sheridan had never looked like this.

'Strimmer, who *loathes* outsiders, buys you an expensive bottle from Vlad's. Chemicals swim in the fruit. He tramps across town on a foul evening as if in love. The moron outsider wolfs it down and sinks into slumber.' A horrible thought struck Valourhand. Strimmer, an exceptional chemist, could mask the taste of a sleeping draught with ease, so this demon phial must have had other properties. She added a savage prompt. 'Did you say *anything* about Lost Acre?'

'Nothing like that,' replied Oblong, but a worm of doubt instantly wriggled.

Valourhand quickly wheedled it out of him: Oblong had recorded in his diary the rescue of Lost Acre, the mixing-point and the existence of the tiles. He had excluded Sir Veronal's destruction and real names – enraging Valourhand further when he said, 'I'm not that dim, you know!'

His 'safe place' turned out to be an unlocked drawer.

'It's still there,' he protested.

'Of course, it is – why would he let you know that he knows?'

A camera . . . Oblong felt sick. 'But it's in code – with false trails and—'

'You seriously think your puny puzzles would outfox *Strimmer*?'

Valourhand strode off towards town. Every twenty steps, she shook her head and waved her hands in despair.

Oblong had been proud of his contribution to their journey, and now he felt unfairly chastised. Was accepting a flag of truce so reprehensible? Should not a historian set down living history? He was a victim, not a perpetrator – and yet he had to acknowledge a familiar naïveté. He would have to confess this disaster to the company. He idled over to the river for solace.

Standing on a natural promontory, Oblong gazed at the amber foam clinging to driftwood and rocks, not breaking as ordinary bubbles would. He indulged the hope that a naked Miss Trimble might break the surface, come ashore and invite him to warm her toes, an invitation he had foolishly declined in high summer out of misplaced loyalty to 'Cecily Sheridan'.

But instead of a nubile Miss Trimble, an earless, bullet-headed creature with a black sheen to the skin clambered ashore.

It spoke. 'My sitting place!'

The shape resolved into an old man who slumped onto the bank, where he started pulling on his clothes. The black lustre seeped away, his features settling into the recognisable.

Ferensen.

A dreadful urge to unburden himself seized Oblong. 'Thank God you're here! So much has happened—'

'All in good time, all in good time.' Ferensen offered a handshake, a gesture so calming that Oblong descended to mundane small talk.

'You come here often?'

'I did, but I shouldn't now. I find swimming a divisive experience.' The old man extended legs and arms as if rediscovering how they worked, while fumbling past and present. 'I am here, where you are, watching insects. He rises from the water. He wears glass eyes and breathes through a tube – Fortemain, Mr Oblong. What was he looking for all those years ago?' Ferensen tilted his head as if catching a scent. 'I dislike sunshine after a swim.'

He rose to his feet and stumbled along the edge of the Island Field, hands flapping at his sides, feet dragging. Oblong followed. His body loosened as pastureland gave way to sloping woods of beech and oak. He was soon picking his way through the undergrowth with the aplomb of a wader in mud.

In the shadow of an oak he retrieved a basket and shared its contents: round slices of bread spread with fish paste and a flask of greenish liquid. They shared the single cup.

'Part of the drying process,' he said.

Whatever the cause – food, the relief of new company, or the kick in Ferensen's strange brew, which tasted of cucumber and mustard – Oblong's brain freed up. He had witnessed a transformation – eel, newt, water-snake, whatever. Ferensen was another of Wynter's victims, and now he spoke like one.

'Has someone appeared?' he asked urgently. 'Has someone beautiful appeared? Has someone appeared who paints like an Old Master?' Ferensen fingered a locket round his neck and spoke with hope in his voice. The movements might have eased, but the eyes remained glassy, the skin stained with wheals of black. Ferensen's recourse to an anonymous 'someone' nettled Oblong; the incisive leader in the Midsummer crisis had turned neurotic mumbler.

'No, I'm afraid not – but two town notables have disappeared.'

'That's hardly news, hardly exciting news – people forever go missing.'

Oblong surprised himself – he grabbed the locket and snapped it open. The golden hair, wound round a circle of pins, gave him the opening.

He seized Ferensen and let rip. 'Wake up! This will not do, Mr Ferensen, this moping, it will not! We need you, and your sister deserves better. You're a disgrace – really!'

Ferensen's grimace eased to a smile and the livid grey patches on his skin lightened. 'My wits restored by an outsider – that is good. Tell me then, who has gone missing?'

'Mr Finch, the Herald.' Oblong recounted the scene at Escutcheon Place, the fleeting appearance of the Fury, the death of Bole's cat and the abandoned copy of *Straighten the Rope*. He slipped in his decipherment of the title's anagram, but 'the rotating sphere' meant nothing to Ferensen.

'*Two* disappearances, you said?'

'The School astronomer – well, we thought he was the School astronomer, and we also thought him dead.'

'Name?'

'Professor Bolitho.' When Ferensen looked blank he explained, 'Alias Fortemain.'

Ferensen staggered back. 'No! No, that cannot be . . . They would have shown no mercy. Explain, Mr Oblong, slowly, square by square.'

Oblong recounted his odyssey to Lost Acre with Valourhand, the man-made tunnel, the *Darkness Rose*, the quarry, the spears and the methane. Ferensen asked searching questions to which Oblong had few answers – how long Bolitho had been abroad, how often he ventured out of the School, whether he pursued any particular projects. He listened intently, his old self.

'I proffer my thanks, Mr Historian, most cogently presented,' he said at last, and Oblong glowed. 'But why did they let him escape? Why did they let him live on? Wynter does nothing without purpose.' Ferensen changed the subject as he packed up the picnic. 'Bill mentioned an election.'

Oblong had quite forgotten. Speech Day in the Parliament Chamber started at noon that very day. He explained the mystery of the velvet gloves, how Roc and Strimmer had emerged to challenge Snorkel.

'You mean the Strimmer who cosied up to Slickstone? That's concerning. How much might he know?'

Oblong gulped, his glow fading fast. 'Not my finest hour,' he said, head drooping.

'But this could be.' Ferensen winked. 'Square by square, Mr Oblong.'

Oblong recounted the whole sorry story as best he could remember it.

'How did Strimmer know to visit you?'

'It must be the company I keep and . . .' He paused. 'Strimmer thinks I'm easy prey.'

'That's how Wynter regarded me, and not without reason. Accept the truth, Mr Oblong, and let it settle – accumulated failure can be a potent catalyst for change.' Ferensen rose to his feet and shook Oblong's hand. 'You have an appointment, I can tell. So off you go. Dry all day, and the mist will not return.'

He left a pensive Ferensen marooned in the shade as the sun climbed free of the trees.

8

Miss Trimble's Bequest

Another expedition took place on the night of Oblong's party. Miss Trimble had lost her nerve on reaching Artery Lane. In under a year the callow outsider had evolved into form master and party-giver, while she remained the School Porter, a lowly, if essential, cog in Rotherweird School's administrative machine.

The label devalued her: she bent the rules in deserving cases, she kept secrets, she worked all hours and she ministered to teaching staff, pupils, parents, cleaners and cooks alike. Even Rhombus Smith relied on her for early intelligence on staff disputes, bullying and maladministration. She concealed her social insecurity beneath a brusque exterior, save in the company of Gregorius Jones, which whom she enjoyed a warm but platonic friendship: hot chocolate rather than brandy, as Bolitho might have put it.

She had been hesitating at the foot of Oblong's staircase when Boris Polk appeared. She barely knew the Polks; indeed she barely knew anyone outside the universe of Rotherweird School. 'Mr Polk . . . ?' she started, unsure how to introduce herself.

He gave her a warm smile and held out a hand. 'Boris – Boris to everyone.'

Thrown by the warmth of his reaction, she turned businesslike. 'I trust you got your bequest?'

'Indeed I did, and very odd it was too.'

He appeared not to own a hairbrush, his flame hair spiking in all directions as if electrified, and he was hopping from foot to foot. She detected a subtext: a naturally jovial face looked strained.

Boris described the kaleidoscope and how his nephew had used it to discover a celestial intruder in Orion, his words coming abnormally fast, before ending so abruptly that she had no opportunity to mention her equally odd bequest. 'Miss Trimble, I'm sorry, I've bad news to deliver. You go first. Enjoy a few minutes – I'll wait.'

'No worry, Mr Polk. I should get back to the lodge.' A lie – but was it black or white? The School rules barred her from the staffroom and she felt as much an interloper here.

Boris caught her shyness. 'I can walk you up.'

Miss Trimble's cheeks burned. 'No really – how kind – sorry—'

She fled, and Boris hurried upstairs alone.

Safely back in her rooms, and encouraged by what the Polks' kaleidoscope had revealed, she sought distraction in exploring her own bequest: a virgin sheet of astronomer's black paper for marking celestial bodies with a long-nibbed pen and a pot of silver ink. She dipped the pen and dotted the paper. The ink spot sat for a moment – before sliding like a bead of mercury to the centre, only to disappear and re-emerge as three smaller dots in a rough straight line. A phantom draughtsman. She recognised the configuration from her schooldays: the belt of Orion with its diamond-bright studs – and she remembered the names of the stars too, Alnitak, Alnilam and Mintaka.

Bolitho had a penchant for veiled messages, even when ordering lunch. She sensed an invitation to visit his observatory.

Outside, the storm raged, providing excuses aplenty: a dislodged slate or a window left open. Lights burned in the Quad, but all behind curtains, blinds or shutters.

Professor Bolitho's name still adorned the whiteboard at the foot of the stairway, and the engraved brass plaque on the door had yet to be replaced. She and the professor had enjoyed an easy, joshing relationship: she would bring Bolitho food from High

Table, memorable during Mrs Fanguin's time as staff cook, and, in vacation, her own humbler efforts.

On entry, the set of a one-man play came to mind. A presence lingered, more than a memory, less than a ghost. Nobody could have been in since she had locked the oak door on the Headmaster's orders, and yet the observatory felt active. The hinged cap of the telescope's eyepiece hung open and a lens had slotted into place, when she felt sure she had closed it. An instrument in a glass case attached to the wall recorded moving objects captured by the telescope. An indigo line like a patient's heartbeat crawled across the graph paper, which had been blank on her last visit.

Suspicious, she sprinkled chalk dust from Bolitho's blackboard onto the telescope tube. It soon began to slide, gently but perceptibly. The telescope was on the move. Bolitho must have set a programme before he died.

Intrigued, she broke an unwritten rule and wriggled into the astronomer's chair. Through the sight, a luminous smudge held centre field between Orion's belt and Betelgeuse, the red star at the hunter's shoulder, as in her self-drawing star map. Running beside and attached to the main tube was a slimmer twin, the finderscope; its fixed eyepiece had a much broader field and low magnification. Here she could see the entire constellation, but with no sign of the intruder.

The unfamiliar lens opens to view the otherwise concealed, she concluded. She had never heard of such a phenomenon, which gave her an excuse to visit Boris Polk.

Dare you, she said to herself, before an austere voice intervened: *You're only a porter, he co-owns Rotherweird's only travel company. Be real.* For the moment the second voice won.

9

The Smart Outsmarted

Strimmer's pen darted through essay after essay on sub-atomic particles. All were highly competent, none betrayed a scintilla of originality. His mind wandered instead to Oblong's diary. Boredom, a familiar demon, had given way to its more irksome relative, frustration: he had found his way into the belfry to find that the frescoes in Oblong's narrative truly existed. He had also found a swirl of footprints, which included the tiny soles of Valourhand's distinctive boots.

The idiot history teacher had not been writing fiction – at least, not entirely.

However, he had made no further progress. The tile eluded him; likewise the mysterious countrysider whom Oblong called X. It enraged him that countrysiders should dabble in the past while the town languished in self-imposed ignorance.

Engrossed by these mysteries, he neglected not only his hapless students, but his political commitments too. The forbidding mastiff at the North Tower entrance kept would-be enquirers at bay, while anyone discourteous enough to approach him in the street was bluntly dismissed with, 'Wait for my speech.' In truth he had no policies, and no interest in policy beyond the abstract notion that the North Tower, Rotherweird's heartbeat, should hold sway over all.

Estella Scry, however, *did* intrigue him. At the next meeting with the Apothecaries, she had intervened to correct a minor detail about mass and binding energy in different nucleons – a detail well beyond the most gifted sixth-former.

He would not demean himself by visiting *The Clairvoyancy*, but he would have to declare his hand soon.

A knock disturbed his reverie. Strimmer resented any disturbance, as his fellow teachers knew. He shouted an obscenity, but to no effect. A young woman stepped through the door towards him as if she owned the place. Grey-green eyes flecked with amber and set in a pleasing oval face darted from walls to ceiling to floor before settling on him: eyes which narrowed when she focused. Late twenties, he guessed, but with the poise of someone much older.

'Pomeny Tighe,' she said.

'Come in.'

She smiled. *I'm in already, in case you hadn't noticed.* 'I'm from the Mayor's Office.'

Strimmer's heart sank: he had miscalculated. She must be a minor functionary working for the nauseating Snorkel.

'I wrote an essay,' she added.

'I see,' replied Strimmer coldly. Snorkel's Essay Prize had caused high mirth in the North Tower. They had spent hours penning sickening eulogies which they had submitted under the names of various unsuspecting townsfolk. She must have stooped even lower to get the job.

Pomeny Tighe perched on his desk, an intimate move – and elegant legs, too. She recited her opening paragraph: '"The two political imperatives, power and permanence, are best secured by the judicious use of three tools – policy, patronage and pressure. These fine instruments require sound intelligence for, and in, their user . . ."' She paused. 'So, not the sycophantic ode to Snorkel you expected?'

Unused to being a move behind, and intrigued by both her looks and the lack of respect in her use of the bare 'Snorkel', Strimmer decided that Miss Tighe merited a closer look. 'Coffee?'

'Black and strong.'

He probed as his coffee machine hissed and gurgled, 'Are you one of the Summoned?' An implicit compliment: if not, he would have noticed her already.

She picked up the *Popular Choice Regulations* and flexed her right foot as if examining her toes. 'It's time for change. The Roc woman is an amateur. The Mayor likes his wallow as it is.' She arched her back and turned her head. Freckles stippled the sides of her nose. 'You're standing for change, presumably?'

Uncharacteristically, Strimmer found himself drawn to confessional speaking. 'It was a rush of blood to the head, frankly. I've no policies, and the electorate can live or die for all I care.'

'You'd waste this opportunity?' She gave him a look of ferocious disappointment.

Strimmer could not fully articulate her attraction, but she made him feel alive, and he sensed fragility beneath the steel.

She did not wait for his reply. 'I've persuaded Snorkel that on Speech Day Roc goes first, then him, then you. You see, Snorkel has a policy that is sound in principle, but his application of it is feeble.'

Strimmer translated this criticism of Snorkel as *you can do better*. 'You said he likes his wallow as it is,' he pointed out. 'What is this new policy?'

'He does, but to keep it that way, he needs votes – but let us imagine that he floats the idea, but then you, speaking last, embellish it and seize the glory.'

'This policy wasn't your idea, by any chance?'

'I like to be creative.'

'Has it a victim or a beneficiary?' asked Strimmer.

'It has both: greed is the driver.'

'So, whom does it feed, at whose expense?' he wondered aloud.

'Guess,' asked Tighe, leaning closer.

Her skin had a fresh, translucent quality.

'Well, it sounds risky: you make new friends in the winners but enemies in the losers.'

'They aren't enemies who matter,' she said dismissively. 'Come on, guess!'

'It's someone out of town?'

'Clever boy,' she said, 'but more than just some*one*.'

'Countrysiders!' he announced.

'They take your money, they give nothing back, but they're rich, rich, rich.'

'Are they?' For the second time in his life (the first had been Slickstone), Strimmer felt outsmarted.

'They're rich in property, land and what the land yields.' She paused. 'In my world, Mr Strimmer, shared likes are a boon, but common hatreds make a bond.'

Within half an hour they had a strategy, even though Strimmer was feeling like a privileged pawn, promised elevation to royalty if he followed the ordered moves.

Within an hour Tighe had drawn the curtains and with busy, slender fingers was pulling his shirt open.

'Let's celebrate,' she said.

Later, as she lay naked on her back, head propped on a cushion, he showed her *The Roman Recipe Book*.

'It must be what it says it is,' she said.

'Being?' said Strimmer, applying a long match to the fire.

'A recipe book.'

'For what?'

She did not know, but felt vindicated in her choice of Strimmer as the man most likely to find a cure for her terrible predicament.

10

Figures of Speech

At noon, an old scene was replayed: same set, the Parliament Chamber, and packed with the same cast, including the Town Crier, tasked with delivering a running commentary to the milling crowd in Market Square. Only the Costume Department had upped its act, for democracy had turned fashionable. For Rotherweirders, the hustings felt like party-time.

Snorkel had awarded his cause colours (yellow with brown stripes), which his minions freely distributed as scarves and flags. Snorkel wore a blazer, decorated likewise: a Mayor elect, at one with his people.

After washing off the grime of his adventure and changing, Oblong arrived early to secure a seat. Despite Orelia's infatuation with Everthorne, he felt proud to be one of her core supporters. He waved in her direction, but elicited no response.

At five minutes before ten o'clock, the candidates took their seats in order of speaking – Tighe had sold this arrangement to Snorkel because it placed him where he liked to be: centre stage. Each sat behind a small desk, with a single lectern standing centrally between them and the audience. Every gas-lamp in the Chamber had been turned high.

Orelia was struggling to engage. She had not written her opening words and was armed only with a sequence of bullet-points, one page of statistics and a sheaf of supporting documents. Her confidence waned; her argument might be compelling, but it threatened to sag under the supporting detail.

If Snorkel felt any self-doubt, he did not betray it. His podgy fingers drummed the tabletop while his eyes darted from row to row; he looked like a man convinced his message would startle.

Strimmer, by contrast, affected mild boredom. Orelia wondered how such *froideur* could garner votes.

Gorhambury, the words *in loco parentis* still fast about his neck, made a ponderous entry, followed by a pedestrian introduction which he had carefully written out in full. 'Welcome to Speech Day,' he started, 'as defined in *Popular Choice Regulation*, 42(3). "Speech" means "speech" – and that means no questions. Our candidates may not exceed the allotted fifteen minutes. I shall tinkle the bell with a minute to go. They will speak from your left to right. Miss Roc, the floor is yours.'

Gorhambury sat to the side, bell in one hand, stopwatch in the other.

Orelia acted on instinct, leaving all her papers on her chair save for her one-page bullet-point summary.

'Evidence,' she said, pointing back at her chair as she reached the lectern, 'for you to read if you wish.'

Evidence against whom, evidence of what? Necks craned. She had won their attention. 'I run a shop—'

Not the way to go, thought Snorkel.

Strimmer barely heard; she was a woman with no science, end of story.

Orelia built her attack: how Snorkel gifted the Committee chairmanships in exchange for policies to his commercial advantage; how those in his coterie received scholarships from the Snorkel Foundation; how the Committees outsourced contracts to businesses in which the Snorkel Foundation held shares.

Gorhambury gaped in horror and elsewhere a few cheeks puffed; a loud 'Disgraceful!' from Fanguin momentarily turned heads – but otherwise polite attentiveness reigned. A dismaying truth dawned on Orelia: they would turn a blind eye to corruption so long as Rotherweird worked.

Riled, she raised her voice and changed gear. 'This is your money, your trust betrayed! It's time for a change – that is what elections are for.'

A surprising figure rose – surprising even to Snorkel. Estella Scry projected her silky voice across the Chamber. 'Elections are for policies, Miss Roc, and in you I hear and foresee a lack of them.'

The word 'foresee' had resonance from her, whatever her place on the spectrum between 'prophetess' and 'charlatan'.

Orelia floundered. 'I . . . I was making the case for change . . . I—'

A volley of well-directed questions from Snorkel's placemen followed. They had been briefed to ignore Gorhambury's prohibition. Orelia fought to keep control, saying gamely, 'I'll take them one by one—'

But it was too late; she had lost her audience – and in what felt to Orelia a matter of moments, Gorhambury's bell guillotined any worthwhile reply.

Snorkel peered heavenwards in rhetorical disgust: If she can't time a speech, how on earth can she be trusted to run a town?

Orelia slunk back to her seat, as disappointed in herself as her audience.

Snorkel waddled past, his unhurried gait counter-intuitively more suggestive of political acumen than Orelia's striding approach. He adopted a tone of apologetic disappointment. 'I don't run a shop of dead antiques. I run a town of living people. Dealers in old chairs have no grasp of company law, the complexities of charitable giving or the dedication of our Committees. Has Miss Roc ever sat on a Committee? Has she ever tried to? No, of course not – she has a shop, and profits to make.'

Oblong sprung to his feet, and Orelia closed her eyes. *Please no!* 'That's very unfair,' he said, 'really, very unfair.'

Snorkel sneered, 'Listen to her pet outsider, the historian.'

Oblong turned crimson and subsided to a chorus of hissing.

A lamb among wolves, Orelia felt horribly exposed. Several women glared as if she had betrayed her gender.

Snorkel moved seamlessly to self-accolade and then proffered the killer blow. 'But I am fallible,' he conceded, his voice lower, 'and I declare a single regret.' He paused. 'We indulge the countrysiders. Rotherweird Town has the vote and they do not – and yet in they sneak, with their carts and high prices. Why should we pay through the nose for our own produce? I offer a new covenant: we pay a fixed fee – no more than workers of the land deserve – and if they do not maintain the yield, we will take back our land and farm it scientifically. Have we not the wit to double the yield and halve the price?'

'You try digging potatoes,' shouted Boris Polk.

'He's too busy muck-spreading,' added Fanguin.

But they were lone voices in the crowd; many townsfolk were enthusiastically engaging with Snorkel's new dispensation. He stopped seconds before time, raising a hand aloft to acknowledge the wash of applause.

However, Orelia's message did linger and, with it, unspoken questions. Wouldn't Snorkel and his friends control distribution? How much of the benefit would truly reach them?

Into this breach sidled Strimmer, who clapped his hand above his head, twice, slowly, without enthusiasm, on his approach to the lectern. 'I applaud Mr Snorkel's idea,' he said. 'But I deplore its execution. The antique dealer has no policies, but she does know a shoplifter when she sees one.' He nodded backwards at Snorkel, without the courtesy of turning. 'He and his mates always clean up – after all, truffle pigs don't change their spots.'

The image raised a ripple of mirth. Snorkel had been forced by a legal ruling to abandon his attempt to wrest control of the town's ancient herd of truffle pigs, which, with spotted hams and flanks, looked uncommonly like him.

Snorkel spluttered, 'Preposterous!' but Strimmer sailed blithely on.

'I give you a policy: this valley boasts more than a hundred barns, which can serve as luxury homes for countrysiders. Their present houses and gardens are above their station. We will do a census – the *Regulations* allow me an inspection to put flesh on the bones of my policy – then we will evict and re-allocate. Every town family will have a week's timeshare in a countrysider's home – apologies; *former* home. There will be auctions, negotiation and a right to exchange.'

Strimmer had pressed all the right buttons: Rotherweirders liked a market and they liked a gamble. Gorhambury did not open his copy of the *Regulations*; he knew them by heart. The Secretary of the Liaison Committee, an otherwise insignificant clerical office entrusted to the Assistant Head Librarian, would oversee Strimmer's inspection. At least he knew he could rely on Madge Brown to keep a weather eye out for improprieties.

As Strimmer extolled the virtues of the town (the electorate) and decried the vices of the countrysiders (the disenfranchised), Orelia felt physically sick. A missing volume had lured her and Fanguin into hunting down the *Popular Choice Regulations*; now she cursed their moral rectitude.

Strimmer, exuding the arrogant chutzpah of a born ruler, strutted back to his chair, swamped in applause.

Gorhambury closed with an announcement: 'Within the next fortnight, the Guilds may invite candidates to their respective Halls for a private conclave.' His tone became stern. 'But should they invite one candidate, they must invite all.'

Bill Ferdy watched Snorkel and Strimmer spin their ugliness from a side street off Market Square. He had long viewed himself as the countrysiders' ambassador and *The Journeyman's Gist* as cementing the join between the rural and urban communities. Snorkel's cynical sale of the pub to Slickstone had been a warning, but this onslaught felt different.

Strimmer worried him more than Snorkel. He was cruel to women, but had a knack for attracting them. He also had an unreasoning dislike of countrysiders, and Ferdy had little doubt he would execute his policy with relish. Yet he had always judged Strimmer too aloof for political ambition. He recalled *The Journeyman's Gist* on Challenge Day, and Strimmer's baffled face when his jacket pocket had yielded a velvet glove. Darker forces were at play. He locked the pub, drew the shutters, loaded the empty barrels on the beer-cart and hastened home to brief Ferensen.

They would not go quietly.

'We need to watch this Strimmer,' said Pomeny Tighe to the Mayor. 'Commandeering your policy on the hoof was really quite disgraceful.'

'He's a physics teacher,' replied Snorkel, now in recovery, 'and physics teachers lack the common touch.'

'You're right,' reassured Tighe. 'He has no chance.'

11

Licking of Wounds

Gorhambury slunk back to his rooms. He took out a small tower made of three open circular trays, each indented with shallow scoops, and placed it on the desk in front of him before lifting an old, deep-grained, gleaming mahogany box from the drawer. This was his only heirloom after his parents' debts had been paid, but an invaluable one. Nobody in Rotherweird owned marbles comparable to these. His father, a glassblower, had excelled at his craft, but sadly, not at the management of money.

The resulting bankruptcy had spawned Gorhambury's obsession with fine print, detail and good order.

He placed the marbles in their allotted depressions. The objective, leaving a single marble remaining dead-centre in the middle tray, had to date eluded him, but he played three-dimensional solitaire for its therapeutic value.

The board was looking promising when Madge Brown arrived.

'Well!' she said.

'No,' Gorhambury disagreed, 'not well, not well at all.'

Madge's benign face flickered with anxiety. 'I thought Secretary to the Liaison Committee was a clerical role.'

'It is,' he reassured her. 'You record time of departure, whose homes you visit and time of return. You ensure due process and the common courtesies. Mr Strimmer's right of survey is limited to one working day. Be strict. I'm afraid it is your job, not mine, and you cannot delegate.'

He felt exhausted by pressure and controversy on every front, and there was still no sign of Finch.

'Snorkel wants to join,' she said.

'It's not his policy,' Gorhambury said firmly. He leaned back in his chair as she kneaded his scalp from behind the ears to the crown, her touch first firm, now gentle. His angst slowly ebbed away.

The return home compounded Fanguin's depression. He and his long-suffering wife had always shared a spiritual bond born of a common loathing of Snorkel – but now, to Fanguin's deep surprise, it sundered.

'Outrageous!' he yelled, but she was shaking her head.

'You don't buy the vegetables. They charge the earth.' Bomber had a distinct flush about the cheeks.

'They're the ones who work the earth.'

Her thoughts tumbled out, unrefined, but buying in to Strimmer's twisted vision. 'But why should they own all the space? All the views, all the stand-alone houses? They use our roads, our School, our square ... and our earth.' Bomber saw the utterly appalled expression in her husband's face – at that word 'own' in particular – and half-relenting, she searched for middle ground. 'I'm sure he meant outbuildings – and if he did mean their houses, he must have been talking exchange.'

'That's not what Strimmer said.' Fanguin located a bottle and wrenched out the cork. 'And if they are moved from their farms, who tends the livestock, the crops, the hens, the hops, the fruit trees?'

'You only care about hops.'

'No, I care for their children.' He had unwittingly strayed into painful territory, which they'd always avoided until now.

Bomber winced as if physically struck and left the room.

Old History

1590. *London.*

Mist dislocates London, blurring contours and dulling her street music; the sun's sharp disc is but a distant lantern in smoke.

Such special effects mimic the haziness of early recollection (so much has happened since) and his present desire for secrecy. He has come full circle: from youthful book thief to a grown man on legitimate bookish business.

He is fretting over his choice of bookbinder – Mr Pinnart of Oxford, or Mr John Gibson of Edinburgh, now fleetingly in London? Nothing separates them in skill; both bind books to last the centuries he needs. The issue is security, for everything will turn on this book-to-be. Bole fears Oxford's studious minds – imagine Mr Pinnart showing the diagrams to a student of letters? No secret is beyond teasing out, even his own identity.

Mr Gibson of Edinburgh wins, hence his visit to London.

A slat in the door flicks open. The young girl peeking through has pinched cheeks and squirrel-coloured hair. He reads in her look and clothes straitened circumstances, and a fear that he is creditor or bailiff.

'Mr Mason of Cheapside,' lies Bole grandly, 'with a commission.' He brandishes the fur on his sleeve; *good for money*, the gesture says. In this quarter, a rich man's cuffs open all locked doors.

He is ushered into a back room with a workbench against one wall and a table for business in the middle. Gibson's ornate ledger sits in the centre, a fine advertisement for his work, with its gilded spine and semi-precious stones studding the covers. It promotes the craft and records its rewards.

Gibson sidles in: he is short in the body but long in the fingers. He has a clever, wary face.

They sit opposite each other, like chess-players, and Bole unwraps his velvet parcel. 'The job is simplicity itself,' he explains. 'These pages are to be bound in this leather. There are to be two books: both have the diagrams at the front. In the first they are followed by these worked pages and then a goodly section of blank pages. The second has exactly the same number of pages – but with the second section blank without the workings.'

Gibson eyes the printed diagrams, the manuscript calculations and the blank pages, all of a size. He has never encountered such a request before, binding virgin paper. He notes the provoking title, *Straighten the Rope*. The leather is maroon and of rare quality.

'It is work in progress, like your ledger,' adds Bole.

'Is this registered with Stationers' Hall?'

'It will be, when it matures.'

Gibson drums his fingers on the tabletop. 'Printers lose their hands for forbidden books – we binders may be next.'

'These are for my eyes only. The duplicate in blank is for over-flow,' Bole reassures him.

Gibson senses that there is more to come, and he is right.

'And I would like these in gold, on both spines.'

He places the ink drawings on the table. Gibson cannot suppress a gasp of appreciation: the draughtsmanship is exquisite. Bole orders them, with the caterpillar at the base to crawl the shelf, the chrysalis in the middle on its blade of grass and at the top, the butterfly, free to fly away.

'The author's name?' asks Gibson.

'None.'

'Dedication?'

'None.'

No patron then, thinks Gibson; it is truly for his use only. 'What is the subject matter?'

'The study of solids,' replies Bole.

Gibson's Scottish royal master has Euclid in his library – an unusual subject, but respectable.

'Would you wish a "I" on the first spine with a "II" on the second?'

'Neither; just the butterfly symbols on both. From the outside they are to be identical twins.'

As Gibson states his price, Bole taps the ledger. 'And there is to be no record here. For your oath of secrecy, Mr Gibson, I offer a generous advance.' Bole picks up a beautifully bound Bible; and Gibson, one hand on the cover, swears.

Gold coins spin on the tabletop, hands clasp and the contract is made.

On Bole's return, London is very different, all gleam and bustle under a cloudless sky. There are trunks in Mr Gibson's hallway and the squirrel girl has new shoes. Mr Gibson, he is told, is shortly to return to Scotland; he is back in royal favour and has a contract for a Psalter.

The bookbinder hands over *Straighten the Rope* as if it were nothing more than a common prayerbook. On the spines, Morval Seer's drawings have turned from ink to gold.

'Should your draughtsman ever want work, I pay well,' Gibson says.

'My draughtsman is otherwise engaged,' replies Bole curtly.

Gibson senses a story he would be unwise to explore. Bole hands over the balance and leaves.

He walks past St Paul's and up the Strand. Young and old, the tall and the short, the dumpy and the lean, the gifted and the dumb, articulate lawyers, all pass by, and Bole smirks. *I can be you, any of you.*

A hawk plummets into a cloud of sparrows, prompting him to

restrain his exuberance. It will not be easy. He has barely tried the shapeshifting power yet, but he will have to use it again and again in the centuries to come. *With what consequences?* he wonders; *how many garments can you hang on the same frame?*

But for now, he must return the book to Rotherweird, putting in motion the intricate machinery of Mr Wynter's resurrection.

1592. Rotherweird.

Twenty years pass before Fortemain returns to Rotherweird. It's a spring day and the light is soft, a time for new beginnings.

Already Sir Henry's island estate taxes the distinction between a hamlet and a town. A forest of wooden scaffolding surrounds the built and half-built; piles of materials and pegged ropes criss-cross the ground. Finch's house is as imposing as the Manor, and the foundations of a perimeter wall break the earth like new teeth.

The Herald welcomes the only man to face up to Wynter and presents him with a beautifully bound volume headed *Straighten the Rope*. Fortemain flips the pages to see his own calculations staring back.

Finch explains, 'Workmen found it in the North Tower – it had a slip of paper in it, recording your authorship.'

Fortemain examines it carefully. 'It's not my binding, nor my title either, but they are my notes,' he says, mystified.

'Take it as an invitation to keep up the good work.'

'But who bound it? And why?'

'An admirer, no doubt – you had many here, and there are several excellent bookbinders near Hoy, so consider yourself thanked.'

The flaw in the argument – the cryptic title – slips past him as an old ambition rekindles. The many blank pages invite further research. The symbols of resurrection on the spine also encourage: someone knew he would be back to revive his research. Science is ever on the move. Even now, twenty years on, his initial workings are primitive.

Deftly, he changes the subject. 'Am I the last? Where are the women?'

For the first time, Finch looks uneasy. 'Both served their penance,' he says. 'Five years' incarceration in the Manor. They wove a confessional tapestry; then undertook never to return. To be honest, I'm glad to be rid of them.'

'*Both* – weren't there three?'

'One died before Oxenbridge arrived.' He lowers his voice. 'An accident in the other place – even Wynter accepted that at his trial.'

'He showed regret?'

'Oh no, he seemed proud of it.'

Pleasantries take over, and after a guided tour of the works, they shake hands and Finch watches Fortemain go. The man has held his youth uncommonly well.

NOVEMBER:
THIRD WEEK

I

A Commission

Dusk in Ember Vine's studio. The sculptress had chosen the neutral light of a northern aspect, not that any light could penetrate this fog. A trestle table held her instruments – mallet, gouge, chisel, rasps and files. Sleeves rolled like a surgeon, she was polishing the beak of a large griffin when the wooden owl on the wall waggled its ears, hooted and rotated brightly coloured eyes.

Despite the inclement weather, she had a visitor.

'Do come in,' she said politely, moving to one side, but the cowled figure stayed outside, stock-still in the greyness. The gas-lamp above her door had failed, or her visitor had extinguished it.

'I'm told you work in stone.' The voice had a neutral, sexless timbre. A muffler and wide-brimmed hat starved the face of detail. The figure held a sack in one hand, a thick envelope in the other. The mouth looked curious, as if waxed with black lipstick.

'I'm also told you have a gift for exactness.'

Ember opened the proffered envelope to find a rarity: a maroon thousand-guinea note and a complex plan. She retreated a pace to read it and found a scrupulous sketch of different-shaped pieces, each colour-coded.

'You fashion, I assemble,' continued the figure, opening the sack and holding it out towards her.

Inside, a jumble of multi-hued rocks peered back at her.

'My stone is rare, flawless and never splinters.'

If the rock is so rare, how did he – or she – come by so much? she wondered.

'My terms are exactness to match your reputation, delivery within the fortnight and absolute secrecy. You will receive a further two thousand guineas on completion.'

Ember Vine had never lacked boldness. 'What does the object do?'

'It's for an anniversary.'

'Whose?'

'The town's.' The figure opened its gloved hands and asked, 'Do we have an understanding?'

Troubled by both the size of the payment and the purpose of the pieces once assembled, she nonetheless nodded. Love of a challenge and the novel beauty of the rock had decided her.

The figure walked backwards, as if to deny her even a profile, and disappeared into the fog.

2

Dreamland

Ferensen had long lost the art of dreaming. In sleep, he sank into unrelieved darkness – a rebuke, he felt, for the loss of love and ambition in his life. He felt a need for solace after hearing of the election speeches: countrysiders had assisted in the destruction of Wynter and the Eleusians; countrysiders would be marked men if Wynter did return.

On this particular night he sought refuge in his most potent brandy, only to wake in the early hours to a nightmare scene: monstrous creatures were processing around his bed – clawed, dragging a wing, armoured or maned – bearing slivers of glowing bark which exhaled a pungent incense. Hearing, movement and speech failed, depriving him of the faculties to protest, as all his possessions – books, shelves, carpets, scientific and travellers' paraphernalia – disappeared through the front door.

His heart leaped as, the clearance done, his sister entered, on her toes, like a dancer, in a loose shift with golden hair held back: Morval Seer in her prime. She looked at him from the foot of the bed and the anguish in her face eased into a smile. Ferensen felt ravaged by time, even while warming to her recognition: the unbreakable bond of the twin. His amphibian curse slipped away and old scenes replayed – their rescue as children by Sir Henry Grassal; the blossoming of their remarkable gifts.

Then horror overwhelmed him as from every aperture, crack and crevice, spiders of all shapes and sizes – pinheads on stilts, bulbous bodies on stubby props – skittered in. These weavers worked their skills on walls, sills, beams and windows until the interior was festooned in greyness.

Morval stooped and gently closed his eyes. The incense engulfed him and childhood dreams returned: he flew over the hayricks and conversed with animals, a reverie born of long-forgotten happiness.

A dream, but not a dream: at first light he woke to a bare interior hung with cobwebs and wearing the neglect of centuries, even his bed. They had anonymised a residence which had previously been unmistakably his. If Morval had been here, her monstrous companions must be no less real – survivors from the mixing-point. And if she judged him in danger, the threat of Wynter's return must be real indeed.

He staggered outside to find the *Darkness Rose* and his rucksack, packed with necessaries for a journey. Everything else, diving suits and parachutes, snowshoes to butterfly nets, had vanished.

Rational thought gave way to emotion as Ferensen realised his sister had been inches away from him for the first time in centuries – and yet she had stultified their reunion with soporific incense. She had said not a single syllable. He felt hurt, jilted even.

Was the gulf in their appearance holding her back? Or did the idea of Ferensen the eelman repel her? Or had she never forgiven his inertia when Wynter wrested control of the Manor . . .

He felt displaced, a man without hearth and home – until the *Darkness Rose* caressed his wrist and somehow prompted a more positive construction. Morval believed that a new age of the Eleusians threatened and was offering him a chance to lead the resistance and atone.

Plant in hand, he shook hands with Bill Ferdy and ascended the hill towards the recesses of Rotherweird Westwood.

His time would come.

3
A Warning

Making love was not the *phrase juste*; it was more a bout of shared exercise with a rousing finalé, which suited Strimmer: he liked to be admired, not clung to. Yet Pomeny Tighe did have two disturbing traits. She insisted on putting her hair up first, checking all angles in the nearest mirror to ensure it was perfect. Once, in his excitement, he had interrupted the ritual – and she had dragged a steel comb across his arm, drawing blood.

And she never talked during the act, barely before – and after, almost incessantly.

She had a warm side: she brought him a bottle of wine from Vlad's and two glasses with 'S' engraved on one side and 'T' on the other. She sent him cards with pithy epigrams – he would have instantly ended the relationship, however gratifying the sex, had this meant a saccharine touch, but it did not. She had phenomenal general knowledge, an exceptional grasp of mathematics and a peculiar but fascinating hobby, constructing automata with clockwork innards. When not wheedling from Snorkel his electoral strategy, she spent time with the Toymakers' Guild.

A bizarre interest in medical matters also surfaced. 'Does Rotherweird have any peculiar illnesses?' she asked on more than one occasion.

'Only peculiar people,' he would respond, more intent on her naked form. 'We have fresh water and clean air.'

On this particular night, she targeted Strimmer's political

weaknesses. 'You don't reach out – you don't engage with anyone,' she started.

He raised an eyebrow. 'I'm offering them land – what more do they want?'

'But so will Snorkel – and there are others – The Understairs is packed with—'

'—retards,' he interrupted.

Unexpectedly, she slapped him hard on the arm as a child might. 'Voters.'

'I've got everything in hand,' he said grandly.

She was lying on the rug before the fire, her skin glowing like soft wax. The remark came quietly, offhand, delivered with a half-smile. 'Betray me, Hengest Strimmer, and I'll cut you to pieces.'

4
Special Offer

In his latest consultation-cum-séance Snorkel mentioned one of the Summoned, a young lady by the name of Pomeny Tighe.

'Is she loyal?' Snorkel asked as he crossed Scry's palm with the usual ten-guinea note.

'Does it matter?' she replied, intrigued. Snorkel rarely asked unpredictable questions.

'Her mind is sharp as a knife, and she's certainly more engaged with the election than anyone else. She identified the countrysiders as a target – only for Strimmer to steal my idea!'

That evening Pomeny Tighe eyed the resulting manuscript invitation with suspicion.

INVITATION TO THE SUMMONED
(A select few)

From Estella Scry

A free panorama of your past and possible futures

Terms: Absolute discretion
Place: 5 Gordian Knot, behind The Clairvoyancy,
           after hours, rear door (my private residence)

I do not do readings or predictions. I do panoramas, where the past is settled landscape and the future an outline in mist.

Scry had pencilled in a date (the coming Saturday) and a time after dark, sensitive to Tighe's working hours and an assumed desire for privacy.

Tighe clasped and unclasped her delicate hands. Nobody living could know the horror awaiting her, but might this promised 'panorama' offer some unexpected hope? The studious if decorative handwriting lacked the flamboyance of the charlatan.

Why not give it a chance?

She found her way to *The Clairvoyancy* and the twisting alley behind. The door to Number 5 had been left on the latch.

As she entered, a door above her on the third-floor landing swung open, an arrival perfectly predicted.

'Confident tread,' said Estella Scry, 'with neither rush nor hesitation.' She was wearing a gold-coloured blouse over a charcoal pleated skirt, with discreet pearl earrings and her gold Pi medallion on a chain.

'3.141592653589793238,' observed Pomeny Tighe, 'and so on. In my prime, I could reel off a hundred points.'

'Memory failing?'

Was that jest or diagnosis? Tighe peered into Scry's eyes, limpid as ocean water. She had no inkling what might lie in those deeps.

The clairvoyant poured two glasses of something grey with a mild froth, a fruit juice with a sharp citrus taste, then twisted a china pot in the centre of the table, releasing an aroma of ginger and cinnamon. The white tablecloth had a silky, expensive sheen.

Tighe understood: taste, touch, smell: you have to chivvy the senses if you want the gods to speak. Only the savage sculpture with its pointed silver ribs on the side looked incongruous.

They sat down and Scry did not pussyfoot. 'Let's focus on what's wrong with you,' she suggested.

'Wrong?' Tighe repeated, taken aback.

Scry elaborated, 'You're different and you don't know why.'

'That could be said of most of us.'

'Only the ill and the mad,' she pointed out, 'and you're neither. You're in full bloom.'

An inappropriate remark if ever there was one, thought Tighe, but Scry could not know that. The big question, hitherto half-suppressed, slipped through her defences. 'When was I first here, and why?'

Scry leaned forward, clasping Tighe's hands. 'Is that a test or a genuine enquiry?'

'Both,' she admitted candidly. She knew she had been here before, but her failing memory denied her the details. She could vividly recount the last decade of her life, but little more.

Scry scowled, which Tighe thought odd; surely she, the client, should be the unsettled one?

'You're the victim of trauma,' Scry said after a moment, 'a cataclysmic event whose nature I cannot discern.'

'How can I have been here before, when nobody knows me?'

'You were a babe in arms perhaps. I cannot see what is lost.'

'Ah, but you do see more than you're saying,' said Tighe.

'I do,' replied Scry, still soft, still authoritative. So far, she had spoken in short, sharp sentences, fencing practice; now she suddenly turned poetical. 'We set out adrift – tides drive us, winds play the compass. The ordinary settle comfortably as soon as they can; they are much of a muchness. Only the special await reunion. Whoever you are, Miss Tighe, keep the vigil. It will be worth it.'

Tighe searched for Scry the person; despite her dwindling powers of analysis, she found a starting word, one she had always hated: *spinster*, with its connotations of desiccation and waste. Predictably, there was no equivalent word for men, although she knew plenty like that. Was Scry a spinster? Tighe had thought so at first, taking into account the prim, sexless way of dressing, the lack of warmth and the bare walls. No doubt celibacy suited her trade; passion would disturb foresight like a heat haze.

And yet ... her short speech had carried an emotional charge, and the unlikely sculpture had a disturbing fierceness.

What reunion with whom? Why invite her to join this vigil? Tighe nodded her thanks, shook hands and left.

Outside, the twisted shadows enveloped her. Touched by the soothsayer's ambiguous gift, she felt welcome and unwelcome, anchored and adrift, better informed but more ignorant.

Estella Scry paced her room. The young woman's hands had that telltale aura: Tighe had been in the mixing-point. But who had put her there, and when – and most importantly, *why*?

5

Just Checking

After her initial dynamic impression, Pomeny Tighe's performance disappointed Snorkel. She carried out her administrative tasks, but to his political plans she contributed only superficial compliments with a mischievous edge.

'A fine speech, Mr Snorkel,' was her response now, and when he thanked her, she followed up with, 'Give the Guilds more of the same.'

'They're a different audience,' he felt the need to point out. 'They have to be bought.'

'That sounds like more of the same to me.'

As worryingly, she was pursuing a mission of her own.

'Why the hospital records, Miss Tighe?' he asked.

'I'm looking for improvements for which you might claim credit.'

'Child mortality is neither a problem nor a vote-winner, take it from me.'

'I'm hunting for clusters.'

Snorkel, an inveterate liar himself, had a nose for lies in others. 'Well, you can stop right now – and do put that toy away.'

Tighe did so, but with a petulant look that unsettled him, as did the deterioration in her handwriting: initial angular clarity had changed to florid loops.

Bendigo Sly, Snorkel's lead eavesman, observed the dainty pock-marks in the dust on the top flight of stairs. Tighe must walk like a dancer.

No hard evidence, Mr Snorkel had said, just a need for reassurance. The refined political nous of their first meeting had meant an agenda, but she had recently been acting dumb and he wished to be sure.

The door was unlocked and Sly debated this curious fact. Most, given a key, would use it. 'Nothing to hide' was the obvious message – but maybe the intended one?

He slid the door open. He prided himself on sniffing out opposition to the interests he served.

On the bedside table lay a loose-leaf manuscript entitled *The Sieve of Eratosthenes Revisited*, which was little more than a sea of numbers. On the desk lay a screwdriver and automata parts, not a cause for concern. Many Rotherweirders, Sly included, designed and built mechanicals in their spare time.

Tidiness prevailed everywhere: clothes scrupulously folded, shoes perfectly aligned. The chest of drawers and the wardrobe yielded nothing untoward; the skipping rope explained her lithe figure, the ranks of cosmetics her immaculate appearance.

She had hung an ancient print of a foreign university beside her bed. His nose twitched at the potential breach of the *History Regulations*, but you could not judge the Summoned by local standards.

Sly's summary: the room of an adolescent sixth-former of unimpeachable character – until he turned to leave. A horizontal pencil line marked the bare white wall beside the door: her height, marked with her initials. On the bed lay a teddy bear with ears, nose and mouth heavily restored.

He did not linger. Nothing was visibly wrong, but something intangible was.

6

A Bicycle Made for Two

Bert Polk and his wife had their birthdays in the same week in November, and this year marked twenty years of marriage. A tandem struck Boris as the right present: a symbol of travel and togetherness, teamwork and pleasure. For bicycle rickshaws and the charabanc, his vacuum technology factored in weight distribution, likely load and pedal-power. The tandem would require additional calibration to cater for hard climbs to the valley rim. He needed a co-pilot for testing, and one came quickly to mind.

He decided, hesitated, decided, reconsidered – and then on Saturday evening had a rush of blood after a pint of Sturdy. He marched to the School gate, almost turned back and had a second rush of blood, which propelled him into the Porter's Lodge.

'I wondered . . . ?' Boris blushed.

Miss Trimble, severe in School uniform, blushed back.

'I need help.'

'With?' asked Miss Trimble, half perturbed, half enchanted. He looked so delightfully batty.

'A tandem.'

The Porter's Lodge had witnessed many ribald reports of Polk prototype failures.

'Naval, aeronautical or—'

'A two-wheeled traditional, wholly terrestrial,' replied Boris.

Now or never, thought Miss Trimble. 'Tomorrow at ten, outside the School gate?'

'Tomorrow at ten, how splendid!'

'The forecast is good, I'm told.'

'Is it? Double splendid!'

'Ten then.'

'Yes, ten! Bravo!' Boris beat a hasty treat as a bevy of sixth-formers approached.

Miss Trimble had dressed for cycling below the waist with running trousers tucked into coloured socks, and running shoes; she was less the bicyclist above in a fluffy purple jersey with her golden hair hidden beneath a jaunty beret.

Boris wore traditional testing kit: tweed trousers, tweed waist-coat over a collarless shirt, laced boots, and goggles pushed back on his brow.

Boris smiled. She looked magnificent.

She smiled. He looked barmy but benevolent.

'If you feel uncomfortable, holler,' he advised. 'We'll drop in on the Ferdys for a refill.'

The forecast had not played them false. Undiluted sunlight made for a magical morning of unusual warmth for the season of mists.

They passed over the South Bridge and made sprightly progress along the valley. Boris quickly decided that the seats were too close. Every time Miss Trimble leaned forward to speak to him, her ample bosom kissed his shoulder blades, oddly soft and firm at the same time. Was this intended intimacy or just small talk on a tandem? His steering was becoming distinctly erratic.

'What do the pipes do?' she asked with another teasing nudge in the back.

'They give a whoosh.'

'How much of a whoosh?' she whispered in his ear.

The morning chill receded, but Boris' body temperature was rising faster.

Miss Trimble imagined herself in a chariot with a red-haired woaded Saxon. She pedalled faster and Boris accelerated to keep up, until the gentle slope steepened.

'Here goes then,' she shouted, as in the spirit of the moment, she yanked off the beret and shook her hair free.

'Right-o!' cried Boris.

Instead of edging the vacuum switch forward, he gave it a flamboyant kick, as if starting a motorcycle from cold, the better to impress his passenger.

The tandem surged from dawdle to breakneck, and counterintuitively, uphill, dislodging their feet from the pedals – including the brake. Miss Trimble abandoned her handlebars and clung to Boris, further loosening his control. On the tandem sped, the riders leaning in and out as the bends demanded, until the curve ran out. More by luck than judgement, Boris steered the tandem through a fortuitous hole in the hedge into a field and a head-high heap of cut grass.

Boris came to seconds later to see the tandem on the ground, front wheel spinning like a sewing machine. The front handlebar had acquired a modernistic twist but otherwise the damage appeared superficial.

Miss Trimble surfaced beside him, hair everywhere, cheeks flushed. 'Whoosh!' she said, brushing grass off her chest.

'Minor adjustments needed,' replied Boris, still on his haunches.

Miss Trimble's eyes widened.

Their colour defeated him.

'Sod the minor adjustments,' she said, pulling her jersey over her head. 'Let's make hay.'

Boris could not remember an hour better spent. A few minor adjustments might be needed next time, but as test flights go, this had indubitably been a success.

Afterwards, they walked through the fields, finding a wood store with logs stacked in the shape of a dragon, and a bridge over a bubbling stream with a rail carved with recognisable inhabitants of tree, water and earth – nothing fantastical here. As they rambled, Miss Trimble unburdened herself, listing the unsung duties of a committed School Porter.

'You've nothing to prove to me,' said Boris.

But nothing lasts; what is sunlight without shadow? Through the hedge they glimpsed a convoy of rickshaws flitting in and out of view. Several passengers held clipboards.

'Bloody Strimmer!' cried Boris.

'Look,' Miss Trimble added. 'Apothecaries too.'

They ran back to the tandem. The vacuum technology had expired, but pedal-power remained.

'Measure and mark,' barked Strimmer. 'Count windows, habitable rooms and staircases; record the aspect. Find a barn to move them to. Preferably not too close; they're bound to smell.'

The Ferdys stood on their front lawn. Bill considered protest, even violence, but decided against it. Madge Brown kept a semblance of order: no doors were kicked down, nothing was broken, no plants were trampled; although it remained a shocking intrusion aggravated by a misplaced sense of entitlement.

'I'm booking in,' crowed a Town Hall employee. 'Their kitchen's twice the size of mine. Not bloody fair, is it?'

'What's in there?' Strimmer pointed at Ferensen's tower.

'Dust,' replied Ferdy.

Bill had served Hengest Strimmer many times in *The Journeyman's Gist*, but now he behaved like a stranger. Strimmer seized a tape measure, but Madge Brown blocked him.

'I said: I do the inside measuring, Mr Strimmer, and that's all you're entitled to, statistics.' Strimmer protested, but to no avail. 'I supervise you,' she said forcibly, 'not you me. That's the law. I don't want any unpleasantness.'

True to her word, Madge Brown measured the tower and the

house, inside and out. The Apothecaries showed no interest in either. They split up, noting the lie of the land, the placement of hedgerows and larger trees. They took plant, rock and soil samples, looking to Bill like a swarm of mad examining doctors for whom health meant infection.

The Ferdy children stood stock-still and silent, traumatised. They huddled around their father as if facing instant eviction.

Strimmer and the Town Hall contingent, including Sly, Snorkel's eyes and ears, peered in through the ground-floor windows. They had not expected such furniture, the carvings, the toys, the crockery and carpets. The fireback had a finely cast sun and moon overlooking a field of corn stooks.

'They sure have been ripping us off!' cried someone, eliciting a chorus of agreement, which overlooked the outhouses holding the loom, the kiln, the workbench, the foundry and the carving tools. Nothing had been bought; all had been fashioned by hard work and skills acquired from centuries of application and tradition.

Having reduced the Ferdys' home to a page of statistics, Strimmer's party trudged back to their rickshaws.

Strimmer consulted a long list. 'On to the Guleys next!' he cried.

Boris and Miss Trimble arrived too late to intervene – whether for good or ill, Bill could not decide. A roused Boris was not the usual gentle, shy Boris. He would probably have laid Strimmer out.

Instead, Miss Trimble calmed the children by treating them as adults.

'Why was Mr Strimmer here?' asked Gwen. 'Why were they measuring our house?'

'He's standing for Mayor,' she replied. 'You're part of his plans for the valley – and they are not good plans, so we are opposing them.'

'We don't like Mr Strimmer,' added Ben, Gwen's brother.

'Nor do I,' Miss Trimble agreed.

'And why were the Apothecaries here? Why is our home their business?' asked Gwen.

'They envy you. They don't understand the work that goes into everything here.'

'So they'll just take our home and let it go to seed?' asked Gwen.

'We're fighting to be sure they don't – and we've every chance of seeing them off.'

Bill Ferdy adding a sobering thought. 'I'm afraid they have a point of sorts: some of us do overcharge, especially those with a monopoly. We've been lax as a community.'

Megan Ferdy made a wise call, banning political talk during lunch.

The journey home was mostly downhill and little handicapped by the failure of the vacuum technology. For no obvious reason, which made it doubly pleasurable, Miss Trimble kissed Boris on the nape of the neck as they came in sight of the town.

He responded by offering to extend her co-pilot's brief. 'Would you care to assist me on an even more unusual project?' Sensing a rare seriousness, she waited until he added, 'I refer to The Thing-amajig.'

'Boris, do explain.'

'It's the world's most unconventional ballot box,' he replied.

7

Solitary Confinement

Had Finch not been destined by birth to be Rotherweird's Herald, the biological sciences would have appealed. He treated his incarceration as an opportunity to analyse the effects of prolonged exposure to solitude, darkness and starvation, although the latter lost point after two days when food arrived – a balanced diet of water, fruit, bread and dried meat – and at irregular intervals thereafter. With the delivery of the food, pitch-black briefly turned grey and he glimpsed the ceiling, as well as the entrance and steps cut into the rock, but they were all well out of reach.

But food ensured only physical survival. Finch reasoned that the brain handled a vast volume of data, both auditory and visual, and that deprivation of both would quickly disorientate, so he used his chiming pocket watch to keep a hold on time and reality.

He still suffered from occasional hallucinations: flashing lights at the periphery of his vision, and grotesque apparitions. To keep them at bay, he devised an exercise regime, set himself mathematical problems and pursued his penchant for nonsensical word-chains.

Life ... force ... way ... point ... blank ... page ... boy ... soldier ... ant ...

A square hole in the floor catered for bodily functions with a mercifully long drop. The cell was cold and windowless, the walls thick.

One of his grotesque visions turned out to be real: a luminous stag beetle, a species unknown to him, which would scuttle across

'. . . a luminous stag beetle, a species unknown to him . . .'

the ceiling before parachuting down on an extended umbrella-like membrane. Finch kept crumbs for the insect, which quickly adapted to his regime, appearing whenever the food did and waving its antlers in apparent gratitude. The friendship sustained him as much as his watch.

He slept fitfully at best, sleep bringing back the horror of his abduction. Shock had disconnected the scene into fragments which replayed at random: the hag's feathered face, her claws, her vile breath.

Days passed and silence became the new enemy. His own voice felt alien and intrusive, and even the tick and chime of the watch he now found as irritating as an unresponsive companion with a monotonous voice and only one figure of speech. He resorted to party games: ripping a button off his jacket, he would throw it along the cell floor, then kneel and search in the darkness until he found it. He repeated the process again and again to the point of madness.

The interrogation came as a relief.

A sliver of moonlight caught the steps above. A long tube snaked its way into his cell, although staying far out of reach. Through the tube came a gravelly voice that gave no hint of sex or age; he suspected a masking device for the Fury. Nobody on foot could cross the marsh.

'You are Mr Marmion Finch,' the voice stated.

'I am he.'

'And the Herald of Rotherweird?'

Pause.

'A shake or nod of the head is no use in darkness, Mr Finch.'

'I am he.'

There followed questions about his childhood, his godparents, the remoter corners of his residence, all of which Finch answered truthfully. He wanted to build a relationship. The Fury had taken him from Escutcheon Place; she had known about the black books. Whoever sent her knew the layout of his home, and his role in the town, which raised an uncomfortable but plausible explanation for these otherwise pointless questions: he might look like Finch, he might inhabit Finch's quarters – but neither of those proved he *was* Finch. Maybe his interrogator feared he was Calx Bole, shapeshifting – hence the identity test. If that was the case, Bole had not sent this Fury, and a new power had arisen.

The questioning ended to a chime of his watch.

'An heirloom, Mr Finch?'

The personal touch took the Herald by surprise. 'Yes, from way back.'

'Rotherweird workmanship?'

'Certainly.'

'It never stops?'

'Not in my lifetime.'

'Nor in mine.' Finch felt a tremor of wry amusement in the voice. 'Goodnight, Mr Finch.'

So businesslike, and a far cry from the Fury.

A sack of food and jug of water followed, together with a return to the darkness, save for the luminous stag beetle.

Two nights later the tube returned. This time the focus shifted to eminent residents: Snorkel, Gorhambury, Rhombus Smith and other prominent teachers, the priest, the town's judge, the editor of the *Chronicle*, the Head Librarian. Had they been their usual selves, the voice in the tube asked; had he seen any of them with a slouching cat?

Finch fleshed out his thesis. The enemy were divided. His captor knew Bole was a shapeshifter and suspected him of taking over one of the town's prominent characters. The cat, as pictured in *The Dark Devices*, had been Bole's familiar – and, of course, find Bole, and you find the stones. He remembered the old rule: examine what's missing, find the dog that does not bark. Bolitho, Rotherweird's most original scientist, had arranged a funeral heavy with obscure clues, and the cause of his death had baffled the doctors. Why not ask about him? The Fury must know Bole was not Bolitho. Finch found this tangle of half-clues more restorative than his mathematical puzzles, but he made little progress unravelling them.

Finch found the wait for his third session excruciating, as if a pleasing flirtation had been abruptly broken off.

'On the question of books . . .' said the tube.

If the Fury has found what she sought, why waste time on this topic? he wondered, but again he answered truthfully. Perhaps in the questions he might uncover the answer.

'Who rebinds the books in Escutcheon Place?'

'I do.'

Asked to name the bookbinder's tools – another credibility check? – he rummaged in his muddled mind, struggling to reconnect its damaged circuits. The questioner showed patience, and slowly the words returned with their specialist uses: pallets, gouges, brass rolls, finishing wheels, needles, the clicker's awl and the bone folder.

'Do you hold any other copies of *Straighten the Rope*?'

Finch detected a smidgen of unease at the end of this question, as if the voice feared the hand had been overplayed. He remembered the hag seizing that very book from the *archivoire* as it rose towards the ceiling. The enquiry suggested the Fury had pursued the right book, but found the wrong copy.

He said conversationally, 'Only the one from Mr Wynter's library.'

The voice acquired a judicial quality. 'You have not dissembled, Mr Finch. You may yet serve the new dispensation.'

Then silence; this was an envoi. Desperation seized him. 'Please . . . please . . . can we—'

The tube snaked back up the shaft and grey faded to black once more.

No more food came, which Finch could not reconcile with the

Fury's friendly last words, and this, with the loss of company, pushed him to the edge. Time's anchor drifted; senses tangled. He saw music and heard the walls. As his wits deserted him, he grew to loathe the know-all voice of his watch, until he dropped it through the hole in the floor, punishment for regaling him with such an ambiguous chime.

Noon or midnight, he no longer knew or cared.

Old History

Wider England is in turmoil; Hoy declares for Parliament, but Rotherweird maintains a studied neutrality – or rather, John Finch, her Herald and ruler, does. But sooner or later ideas slip through physical frontiers and Finch knows his power must be shared – but he will not force the pace. He prepares, and waits.

Rotherweird has burgeoned on the rich mulch of the Eleusians' scientific gifts and the practicality of Oxenbridge's men. Invention and craftsmanship: a sure-fire recipe for progress. Carts move faster here; cranes lift heavier weights, eased by gears developed from da Vinci's drawings; forges burn fiercer when fanned by hydraulic bellows siphoning the power of the river; the enhanced heat gifts superior metals; and students of the invisible isolate the flammable gas which seeps from the marshes on the Rother's eastern shore.

The Rotherweirders start to trade learning with the outside world in return for materials, while still guarding their deeper secrets. They acquire gold and silver, and their coins feature tools of science, not the Herald or his arms.

Sacheverell Vere is one such scientist. He is diligent, acquisitive, humourless, and in the matter of religion, very much of his time. A Puritan, he frowns on vestments, statues and all flamboyant distractions; the Good Book holds the Word. He is spared the troubling issue of bishops, for Rotherweird has none. He is unmarried, an unconcerned virgin at fifty. He finances municipal projects, of whose potential he is an astute judge, lending at rates just short of the sin of usury.

The town's Master Carver, a tall, cadaverous man of similar age, pays a visit.

'Mr Vere,' he begins after an exchange of pleasantries, 'I worry for your gold in these tumultuous times.'

Vere winces: his gold is nobody's business but his own.

'I have designed an under-floor cupboard I believe to be as good as a hidden vault. You open it with a remote device.' He describes the mechanism and Vere is hooked.

'At what price?' he asks.

The figure, even to Mr Vere's Spartan eye, is modest enough to border on the reasonable.

Within two weeks the promised coffer is installed, as secure and inconspicuous as promised. Its upper surface is indistinguishable from the floor which holds it, and the opening mechanism sits snug behind a wall panel.

As he takes his fee, the Master Carver has a new proposal. 'I wondered if I might decorate your panelled hall with a verse or two from the Holy Book?'

'This not a church, Mr Roc,' Mr Vere says severely.

'But why not let your piety inspire posterity?'

'Which verses?'

'These we all relate to – I had in mind a parable or two.'

Vere agrees to one, a test sample for the cost of the materials only, to be carved on a beam in the hallway roof, a reward for those who look heavenwards. The Good Samaritan, his roadside beneficiary and the insensitive 'others' passing by duly appear, moment frozen in oak. The scene has drama; the workmanship is vital and exquisite.

The Master Carver takes a second modest fee, then suggests, 'Might not a single parable languish for lack of company?'

Vere scowls, but undeterred, Mr Roc continues, 'You might even be thought a mean man, displaying one verse only, or narrow-minded with only the one virtue on view – unjustly, of course.' He pauses. 'I offer discounts for quantity.'

Vere accepts, on condition that the central beam should bear the legend *Veritas Non Vanitas*. He does not want an awkward conversation at Heaven's Gate. The Master Carver will leave the wall panels untouched.

For many months Vere's Great Hall is tenanted by ladders with precarious walkways running between, for Roc works on several tales at once. He eyes each beam from below and beside; he feels the wood, he even licks it – then his edged tools turn, incise, shape and contour, until the ceiling is transformed into living visual text.

Vere learns that the Master Carver is much consulted on the matter of Rotherweird's architectural development. Not unlike his home, the town increasingly reflects the carver's eye.

1650. *Rotherweird.*

In wider England, the king has lost not only his crown but his head. These are turbulent times.

The Master Carver works on, as parables spread to neighbouring ground-floor rooms. At times Vere is disturbed by their secular feel; there is often a sense of everyday events – but maybe that is the point.

While working on the prodigal son, the Master Carver broaches a new subject. 'My Guild, the Woodworkers, has elections and a written constitution to ensure accountability. I believe the town must follow if we're not to succumb to outside rule.'

This is a different carver from the one Vere thought he knew: this man is articulate, pragmatic and forceful. Yet the argument is appealing, and he certainly does not want his monopolies disturbed by Hoy's acquisitive traders.

Roc continues, 'We need a temporary Mayor before our first

election. I have taken soundings. Who else but you: *Veritas Non Vanitas*? We have drafted *Regulations* to preserve the Herald's true prerogatives.'

Prerogative – the Master Carver even knows the new vocabulary. 'Mr Finch is most amenable.'

Indeed Mr Finch is. The burdens of the Rotherweird statute are heavy enough, and he judges multiple minds better than one, and less likely to be corruptible. Above all, he must not jeopardise the valley's precious independence. He accepts the offer of dialogue because the Master Carver seeks no position for himself. The constitution has some peculiar obsessions with time and place, but it does the needful and he concurs.

When the colonel from Hoy clatters in with his troop of cavalry, Finch is prepared. A large table with practical chairs awaits him in the shadow of Doom's Tocsin, as do Mr Vere and other worthies. The colonel reflects the spring weather: bright and breezy, a true scion of the New Model Army.

'We respect the law, but also the rights of Man, Mr Finch,' he opens.

Finch smiles. 'The two are not incompatible.'

'You are a king in all but name—'

'A single hand was necessary, that's true, but not so now. I abdicate this month, retaining only my necessary duties.' He pushes the bound *Constitution* across the table.

As the colonel reads, he furrows his brow only twice. 'The timing of your elections is quaint, to say the least.'

'You cannot play with celestial fixtures,' replies Sacheverell Vere, parroting the Master Carver.

'Any man of majority and property has the vote?'

This time Mr Finch replies, 'Anyone educated, and all of age are educated here. Mr Vere will hold office pending the first election.'

The colonel knows of Mr Vere, a virtuous gentleman. He eyes

the clean streets, the work in progress and the architectural inno-
vation. 'Tell me about this statute?'

'I cannot,' replies Finch, 'but believe me, it is necessary.'

The colonel considers the point. There is a local whisper; this
valley is best left alone. Queen Bess did not give freedom lightly.

He accepts.

1663. Rotherweird.

Kings are back, but not in Rotherweird. Mr Vere is no longer Mayor,
though still a citizen of high standing. The Master Carver, well
armoured against Time's arrow, pays him a visit.

'I have been foraging for the best wood in wider England,' he
begins. 'Have you heard of Gresham College and the Royal Society?'

'Indeed, I have, Mr Roc. They do most serious work.'

'Should not Rotherweird follow suit? We have no truly scientific
Guild.'

Vere senses another invitation building. His post-mayoral life is
as dry as dust; it needs the water of new ambition.

'You mean we collect together men and women of a serious and
moral outlook.' Vere pauses. 'They might meet here in my Hall.'

'A characteristically generous notion, if I may be so bold, Mr Vere.'

So Mr Vere founds the Apothecaries' Guild. The flounce and bustle
of Restoration life is not for them; they dress to mirror their moral
universe: in black and white. They meet weekly in the front hall,
surrounded by carved parables, and talk new science.

NOVEMBER:
FOURTH WEEK

I

A Conclave of Guilds

The twelve Guilds issued invitations – the Carvers, Glassblowers, Bakers, Timekeepers, Tanners, Milliners, Metalworkers, Toymakers, Masons, Mixers, Fireworkers and Apothecaries – to interview their prospective Mayors. No Guild entertained more than one candidate on any given day, but all conclaves had to be completed within the fortnight.

Aether's Way dominated the addresses, for most Guild Halls comprised no more than the shop or workspace of that year's particular Master. Only the Apothecaries' and the Fireworkers' Guilds had fixed Halls, large, grim buildings hidden away in The Understairs.

Drelia's first conclave, with the Metalworkers, turned out to be typical.

The Master, a rotund man with an open personality, showed her round with professional pride. 'We supply all the other Guilds, Miss Roc: *we* are the hub of the town. And yet Mr Strimmer appeared to be bored by our preoccupations. I do so hope you'll be more attentive.'

She took out a notebook, presciently headed 'Guild Concerns', and with a smile said, 'That's why I'm here.'

'The planners ignore the clear space required by weathervanes and as a result they swing irrationally,' the Master started, 'which misleads the public and gives the Guild a bad name.'

Orelia scribbled a note, before adding a personal touch. 'At

Baubles & Relics I've seen more cut-price door-knobs in the last year . . .'

'Spot on, Miss Roc,' the Master interjected approvingly, 'and fancy hinges of poor quality.'

'We do have quality regulations,' she pointed out, 'and *I* will make sure they're enforced.'

Encouraged, the Master entered more delicate territory. 'Can we not be regulated, as the Carvers are, by Mr Finch? The Mayor expects favours in return.'

He winked; she winked back.

Another grievance surfaced. 'And why do the Metalworkers come behind the Timekeepers in the Mayday Procession – when we make half their parts? Why are the Apothecaries always first?'

'Perhaps we should rotate precedence annually?' she suggested.

Other meetings followed a similar template: a welcome, concerns particular to their trade, Snorkel's 'extras' and, invariably, quibbles about ranking. After the debacle of her opening speech, Orelia felt that now she had at least entered the race.

Membership of the Fireworkers' Guild was confidential, and the Guild required an advance undertaking that she would divulge nothing of her visit. To her astonishment, Boris Polk held the Mastership; he was a predictably welcoming and convivial guide.

Only the Apothecaries remained. Orelia resented the fact that Strimmer had been invited to their Hall, while she and Snorkel were expected to make do with the Parliament Chamber.

Master Thomes arrived with the now-familiar pair of fresh-faced acolytes. A burly man with an almost-square head, a self-regarding goatee beard and piggy eyes, he did not fit Orelia's stereotype of an accomplished scientist. The Apothecary's usual black-and-white was relieved by a scarlet sash attesting to his office. The piggy eyes went up and down in appraisal.

'I expected more of you,' said Orelia, sitting on the bench opposite. Clearly diplomacy would cut no ice with Master Thomes.

'I represent all members,' he said grandly. 'You have before you their ears and voice.' He had a flowery way with words, but coldness too, an unsettling mix of vanity and the austere.

'The largest Guild musters the smallest turnout? I find that disappointing.'

'The *busiest* Guild musters the smallest turnout,' he countered, 'which is wholly predictable. The opposite would be disappointing.'

'You asked Mr Strimmer to your Hall – I hear the whole Court turned out.'

'Mr Strimmer is an honorary member. He understands our aspirations.'

Orelia had anticipated this response and now took a leaf from Gorhambury's book. 'I can read, Mr Thomes. The *Regulations* stipulate: "*Candidates may be invited by any Guild to their Hall to address their Court or general membership, but the favour must be shared between all.*" Your Hall has had the pleasure of Mr Strimmer; now it's my turn. Say no, and I'll raise the matter in the Parliament Chamber.'

Thomes gathered his stovepipe hat. His tone hardened, steel beneath the velvet. 'We'll see you tomorrow then, as darkness falls.'

Orelia had had little cause to visit The Understairs, home to Rotherweird's working class: cleaners of houses more opulent than their own, sewage workers, bicycle rickshaw repair shops, Mors Valett's underlings, who toiled in the morgue: in short, workers too menial to have a Guild to represent them.

To avoid getting lost, she kept to Hamelin Way, where beams, balustrades and doors boasted carvings with more vigour than refinement, the unpaid work of apprentices keen to practise and showcase their burgeoning talents. Shattered slates at pavement level attested to neglected roofs and municipal inattention. Taking in the dingy, twisting side streets, she found a new cause: time to invest in this downtrodden enclave for the hardworking poor.

One skill did flourish in style: high-balcony gardening. Climbers launched from window boxes hung from the wooden walkways, running on high wires round chimneys and up towers to wherever sunlight could be caught.

The forbidding square that housed the Hall of the Apothecaries had no window boxes and minimal exterior decoration, as if to inform the public that their wealth was not to be shared. A lamplighter was working his way around a horseshoe of gas-lamps, linking one wing to the other. The starkness of the scene induced second thoughts. Why fritter her time away on the unpersuadable?

She was ushered into the Great Hall, where the Guild's Court, four men and three women, sat unsmiling and impassive in a horseshoe mimicking the gas-lamps outside. Their hats rested beside them.

A conclave of conjurors, thought Orelia, *but without the desire to charm and entertain.*

Thomes sat on an ornate throne at the centre, his back to a blazing fire. Nobody rose or acknowledged her presence.

The wall panels displayed emblems of knowledge: a microscope, a phial held to a flame, light splintering through a prism. Figures, theorems and atomic numbers jostled round a central panel of the periodic table.

Incongruously, oddly sensual scenes from Christian parables were plentiful elsewhere in the room. Orelia found them disturbing. *Carving is in my blood*, she thought. *My ancestor, Benedict Roc, was the town's first carver – before his murder by Calx Bole, twenty years after Wynter's execution. Has he a connection here?*

Over the fireplace hung a motto, also carved in wood: *The world is not thy friend, nor the world's law.* It was familiar in style, if not content, but she could not place it. Foliage surrounded the main door with the words *Me*, *This* and *Vine* intertwined in the leaves. To one side stood an empty easel.

Thomes coughed, a call to order, and she sat on a plain wooden chair set facing the Master: more a witness to be questioned than an electoral candidate. Each Court member had a small white card like a menu in front of them. She must be the *hors d'oeuvres*.

'What kind of Rotherweird do you offer, Miss Roc?' Thomes asked coldly.

This at least she could answer. 'I offer ancient institutions and modern improvements.'

A stern woman, hair wrenched into a bun and secured by a profusion of pins, spoke with prim exactness. 'The first is easy, being the very nature of Rotherweird, but the second is not, unless you have the right vision.'

'I'm here to listen,' Orelia replied.

A younger woman surprised her with a compliment. 'You exposed Mr Snorkel's petty thievery. That is commendable—'

'We have no interest in Snorkel, Sister,' interjected Thomes. '*He* is an irrelevance.'

Sister. The mode of address fitted this closed community.

'He should be,' the anonymous Sister agreed, 'but he has patronage. I would not be too dismissive, Brother Thomes.'

Orelia kept to her innocent agenda. 'Well, let's be frank, it's going to be Mr Snorkel or Mr Strimmer, isn't it? What chance does a female shopkeeper have? But I appreciate your warm welcome.' She spoke without a hint of sarcasm. 'I do have one proposal: that we rotate the Guilds' positions in the Mayday Procession.'

The Apothecaries mustered a ribald guffaw, a rarity within these hallowed walls. Hitherto unused cheek muscles pulled and stretched, then reset to granite.

'How about agriculture?' asked the stern face.

'We leave it to those who know,' she said.

'"Leave it to those who know"! I thought you stood for modern improvements, not leaving these primitive countrysiders to plough, sow and reap as they always have.'

Orelia squirmed; she had been exposed by her laziness. She had not prepared. Crude counter-attack and platitudes were all she could muster. *Next time—*

But of course, there would be no next time.

'We have other business,' said Thomes wearily.

While retrieving her coat, she pocketed the card on the table beside it. Nobody stood; nobody thanked her for her time. The great door opened and spat her into the dark.

She read the card by a streetlamp:

COURT MEETING

Order of Business

Mayoral Election, Conclave:	*Miss Roc*
Honorary Admission:	*Miss Estella Scry*

Orelia was baffled. *Why award a purveyor of superstition such a privilege?*

On her doorstep, she found a note from Boris. 'Drop in *chez moi* at ten for news welcome and unwelcome.'

The news drew her less than the promise of sympathetic company.

The office of *The Polk Land & Water Company*, with its orderly ledgers and neatly printed charabanc timetables, reflected Bert, not Boris. Bert allowed but one distraction: a photograph of his six children, with Boris sitting in the centre like an oversized seventh. A patched coracle hung on the wall.

'Tonight, I had a conclave with the Apothecaries. They're up to something, if you trust my feminine instinct.' She showed Boris the card.

'Estella Scry elected an honorary Apothecary? That *is* rum.'

'And what's your news?'

Boris made an unwelcome announcement. 'I know it's late, but I've called a meeting. You have to see Oblong.'

'Boris, please – it's been a long day and he – well, he irritates the hell out of me.'

'He has a confession to make and a discovery to share, and both should come from him.' He looked at her sternly. '*And* you have a book to collect from the shop.'

'What book?'

'*Your* copy of *Straighten the Rope* – you should have told us.'

Orelia, weary and not in the mood for rebuke, reacted fiercely. 'Who told you that – bloody Fanguin in his bloody cups? Anyway, why should I? Bole could be *anyone*.'

'So who's acting out of character?'

'Fanguin certainly isn't,' she fumed, knowing she had no choice. Her hand had been forced.

Irritation over the sharing of her secret pushed Everthorne from her thoughts – until they reached the hallway of 3 Artery Lane, where the dull white plaster overflowed with murals. Mischief prevailed: a satyr's head peered through a curtain of ivy; sea-snakes pursued a shoal of brightly coloured fish; two lovers, festooned in honeysuckle like a human gazebo, embraced. A ladder lay on its side, the rungs spattered with paint. He must have been working day and night.

Boris pointed out a flying charabanc with him and Jones in the front. In the back stood Fanguin, raising a glass, and Gorhambury, with a book, was seated beside Orelia. At the roadside Oblong raised a pedagogic hand, while Valourhand looked spiky. Orelia pointed at the opposite wall where two Furies, feather and leather, eyed the charabanc with malevolence.

Everthorne had absorbed character as well as appearance.

Boris and Orelia ascended slowly, dazed. Music and carving had always flourished in Rotherweird, but never painting. Behind Oblong's door, voices brayed in merriment.

'He can't!'

'He's going to!'

'Watch my carpet!'

Orelia flung open the door to see Everthorne kneeling, head tilted back, a double spoon balanced across the bridge of his nose with an egg in each bowl. In his right hand, a glass of apple brandy rose towards the artist's gaping mouth. A Rotherweird guinea by his knees testified to a bet in progress.

Fanguin and Oblong sprawled beside him, equally well refreshed. Fanguin gave a cheery wave. 'It's the tenth, the last, the grand *finalé!*' he boomed.

The schoolboy frivolity grated with Orelia, bringing weeks of simmering pressure to the boil. She grabbed the eggs and tossed them at Oblong, who caught one and dropped the other.

'Steady on,' moaned Fanguin. 'Friday night is party night—'

'I came here for a serious meeting' – she pointed at Oblong – 'having been told *he's* made a fool of himself, *again*, and *you*' – now pointing at Fanguin – 'don't know the bloody meaning of the word "in confidence".' Orelia rarely swore, but ordinary language was not having the desired effect. 'I mean, *fuck it*,' she added.

Fanguin looked at her. 'I understand why you're cross—'

'I'm not *cross*, I'm *livid.*'

The three miscreants rose unsteadily to their feet. Everthorne looked quizzical, Fanguin half-defiant, half-shifty, and Oblong pink with embarrassment.

Storm Orelia moderated, only for Hurricane Valourhand to sweep in. She pushed Boris aside and levelled an accusing finger at Everthorne. 'What the *fuck* are you doing, painting us for the world to see? *And* the Furies as they are?' Her face as white as flour, she quivered with rage.

'Haunting images,' replied Everthorne enigmatically, 'have to be painted. It's an exorcism.'

Orelia thought she understood: he could not tolerate the Furies flitting about in his head, polluting all they touched, so he painted them out. But Valourhand was right . . . 'Edit them,' Orelia suggested, and he shuffled out.

'Bloody fool!' Valourhand shouted after him.

Orelia felt foolish. She had lost her vigilance.

Valourhand gathered five chairs round Oblong's table.

'Five coffees,' Orelia murmured to Oblong, who obediently slunk into the kitchen. Twice in a matter of days, a party atmosphere in his rooms had been punctured, and worse was surely to come.

Fanguin advanced his defence first. 'I'm not apologising, Orelia. Secrets mean stumbling about in the dark. *You* don't understand the book, but Valourhand might. The risk of trust outweighs the risk of its absence: that's the case for the Defence.'

Orelia tossed her hair. *Straighten the Rope*, still wrapped up, was resting on her knees. She felt buffeted every which way.

Before she could respond, Valourhand launched a new diatribe. 'I trust everyone knows about Oblong's masterly performance?' Fanguin and Orelia shook their heads, and she continued, 'He told Strimmer about everything that matters – Lost Acre, Wynter, the mixing-point, the stones . . .'

In the kitchen, Oblong winced. Did nobody else make mistakes? He added another measure of coffee, as if doubling its strength might wipe out his error.

Orelia gaped at the enormity of the revelation: Hengest Strimmer, head of the North Tower, candidate for high office, friend of the Apothecaries, had been gifted the key to Lost Acre's deadly secret—

'How *could* he?' she burst out.

Boris did his best to mitigate. 'It was ill fortune, not intention. He kept a coded diary, and his drinks were spiked. He didn't mention Ferensen and he didn't give away the white tile's position.'

'He's good in a coracle,' whispered Fanguin.

'He's even better at anagrams,' added Boris, standing up. '*Straighten the Rope* – any takers? Come on! He's the fool; we're the clever ones.'

Silence descended, save for a shuffling of feet. *'The Rotating Sphere!'* declared Boris. 'Copyright, Jonah Oblong.'

Seizing these crumbs of support, Oblong sashayed in like an apprentice waiter. Five mugs from Ember Vine's emporium on Aether's Way slid precariously before Boris made a timely interception.

'Milk, anyone?' asked Oblong, brandishing the jug.

'Two sugars,' added Fanguin cheerily, but Boris launched the more effective diversion.

'It's time for the book, Orelia.'

Fanguin, as the oldest person there by almost two decades, felt responsible in the absence of Finch and Ferensen and in consequence was mildly irritated by Boris' initiative. *Boris* had called the meeting. *Boris* had persuaded Orelia to bring the book. *Boris* had heard Oblong's confession. *Boris* had not been sullied by Everthorne's party trick. And Boris was – well, decent and honourable, and dynamic with it. *It was always bloody Boris.*

Orelia placed the cloth-wrapped copy of *Straighten the Rope* dead centre on the table. With a communal intake of breath Oblong's misdemeanours flitted from centre stage.

'A bookseller called Vibes gave me this at the Hoy Book Fair – or rather, he *lent* it, hoping I'd winkle out its secrets.' Pages and pages of manuscript calculations flashed by as Orelia flicked through.

Valourhand stared, mesmerised.

Orelia awarded Oblong a conciliatory smile. 'The pieces in the diagrams, I *now* see, make a sphere.'

Valourhand's voice changed, businesslike now. 'We found a quarry in Lost Acre. Bolitho has been there, many times, I suspect.' She pointed at the diagrams. 'The four stones rearrange matter – if you fuse different rock types into a single sphere, what then?'

'In the mixing-point they'd surely rotate,' suggested Oblong, trying to imagine the effect of so many contrary forces. 'Just like the title says they'd do.'

'But to what end? Something must be changed, something that *matters* . . .' Orelia pushed the book across the table to Valourhand, who carefully flipped through the pages.

The history of physics paraded before her, not as a chronicle but as a developing exploration of a particular problem – but *what* problem? She traced the impact of Newton and Einstein. She glimpsed Benjamin Franklin's kite, the lead spheres used by Henry Cavendish, Joule's water container with its paddlewheel.

'Force fields, kinetic energy, magnetism, weather patterns. Early on – see there, 1600 – we have Gilbert's *De Magnete*, the discovery of the earth's magnetic field. Then . . .' Valourhand fumbled fifteen pages further forward, '. . . come the giants of the 1820s and 30s – Ohm, Ampere, Savart, Faraday. And lots of the nineteenth century's favourite subject.'

'Evolution,' suggested Oblong.

'Geology,' corrected Valourhand. 'It's all fiendishly complex, but it's Bolitho's writing, no question.'

'Or rather, Fortemain's,' added Fanguin. 'This is history as we've never seen it: the same eyes over four centuries, constantly looking, learning and revising.'

Orelia turned to the spine and examined the caterpillar to chrysalis to butterfly. 'Why these symbols?' she mused.

'Resurrection,' said Oblong.

'Obviously – but why *here*?'

Fanguin the lateral thinker had an uncomfortable thought. 'There's a prior question: who chose the binding? And whose title is it? Bole's anagrams always have a double life – remember the inscription in the *Recipe Book*? *Bearing mysterious recipes* was an anagram of *Geryon's Precise Bestiarium* and both titles turned out to be true. Is this another such title, where both are true?'

Straighten the Rope; *The Rotating Sphere*.

The literal title assumed a darker resonance: strangulation, the garrotte, the hanged man.

Valourhand spoke, more to herself than her companions. 'The comet is here – and he's calculating force fields, the effect of heat as it nears the sun. But it's only a part of the whole, and I can't . . . I need to borrow it.'

Orelia snapped the book shut, wrapped it up and placed it in her bag. 'Sorry, but this book is going nowhere near Strimmer.'

Valourhand did not dissent; she had memorised enough to work with.

Boris tactfully changed the subject. 'Orelia's visit yielded another oddity.'

'We have a new suspect,' she added, presenting the order card for the meeting of the Apothecaries' Court.

'Scry, the honorary Apothecary?' spluttered Fanguin. 'She can't possibly be what she seems.'

They all knew Scry by reputation: a charlatan who preyed on Rotherweird's superstitious fringe; chalk to the Apothecaries' cheese when set against the Guild's ruthless pursuit of hard science.

'She's started attending North Tower meetings with Thomes and Strimmer,' Valourhand added. She charged her coffee from Oblong's brandy bottle; no thought of asking first. 'That means she has more science than she lets on – Strimmer wouldn't wear it otherwise.' She paused. '*If* – and it's a huge *if* – Wynter were to return, he would need enforcers. Only the Apothecaries have that potential. Perhaps Scry gets Thomes to prepare the ground and persuades Strimmer to stand as Mayor.'

'Who is she then?' wondered Orelia aloud.

Fanguin snapped his fingers. 'Feather or leather – the Furies live in town, so says my bat detector, but in different quarters: one's definitely in Scry's vicinity while the other is close to The Understairs.'

Boris slapped his thighs. 'My old bat detector? Fancy that! Talking of detectors, did you return my invisibility film?'

Fanguin shook his head impatiently. 'You're missing the point. Think habitat, behaviour, roost, *guano* . . . The Furies are not *familiars*; they're *Eleusians*. They transform, just like Fortemain. They couldn't live in town otherwise.'

Nobody dissented, but for the moment, they concluded, they could only listen and watch as best they could.

The meeting broke up, leaving most unsettled, for different reasons: Boris over Rotherweird's political future; Valourhand over the elusive contents of *Straighten the Rope*; and Orelia over where her attraction to Everthorne might lead. Only Fanguin had enjoyed the chase and the company in the knowledge that he needed the opposite of a rest-cure to keep the demon drink at bay.

On the ground floor the ladder had moved and the mural had changed. A flight of terns with black caps and red-orange beaks had replaced the Furies; the charabanc had turned electoral bandwagon. Facial expressions declared the candidates' character: Orelia all girlish enthusiasm bordering on the naïve, Snorkel wearing a venal smile and Strimmer oozing glacial disdain. Orelia peered closer. A splash of guano stained her jacket – had it been there before? Was it a mark left from the vanished Furies, or a wish of good luck? If Everthorne had not been billeted so close to Oblong, she would have succumbed to the urge to knock on his door and find out.

2

An Aerial Scout

The following evening Boris made his way to the School. He admired academic excellence and Bolitho's fevered workings in *Straighten the Rope* had entranced him. The thought of his brilliant friend imprisoned underground in an alien body dismayed him.

A faint light glowed through the shutters of the ground-floor window in front of him and the presence of his quarry was confirmed when he put his ear to the door.

'*Vides* ... ho, ha ... *ut* ... ho, ha ... *alta* ... ho, ha ... *stet* ... ho, ha ... *nive* ... ho, ha ... *candidum* ...'

As he pressed closer, trying to make sense of the gibberish, the door fell open to reveal Gregorius Jones, seated cross-legged on a small mat. Naked from the waist up, feet bare and eyes shut, he was clasping his hands over his sternum like a man in prayer. A sickly-sweet scent emanated from a squat, coloured candle on the floor beside him. The 'ho, ha' represented an exaggerated form of fast but deep breathing.

'*Arma* ... ho, ha ... *virumque* ... ho, ha ... *cano* ... hi, Polk ... *Troiae* ...'

'Jones, what *are* you doing?'

'*Qui* ... ho, ha ... *primus ab oris* ... I am clearing the mind.'

Boris doubted the exercise would take long, but he played along. 'Excellent news, as I'd like to hire that very organ.'

Jones sprang to his feet, touched each ankle with the opposite hand and cried, 'Fire away, dear Polk, fire away.'

'That candle stinks.'

'Honeysuckle rose,' said Jones. 'There's a cordial goes with it.' He pointed to a glass filled with liquid of the same purple-orange colour beside his map.

'We remember the Hydra and your gallant rescue of Miss Roc from the blazing roof,' Boris started.

'In the words of the Brahmin, "I take what comes",' replied Jones modestly.

'I've a special task for Vulcan's Dance.'

Jones edged closer to reality. 'What have you to do with Vulcan's Dance?'

'I am, confidentially, the Master of the Fireworkers.'

'That was a bizarre appointment.'

'So is this.'

Boris explained Jones' proposed role, whose qualities Jones then summarised. 'Put shortly, you require nerve, skill, strength, presence before an audience, quick reactions and fearlessness in the face of the elements.'

'All six,' confirmed Boris.

'At your service.' Jones bowed, but the handshake with which the athlete sealed the deal did not match his outward aura of calm; the grip was as tense as strung wire.

Emptying the mind of what? Boris wondered. By an open fire, a pair of tracksuit bottoms hung over a clotheshorse, the legs grotesquely stiff and caked with mud from the thighs downwards. The scented candle had a secondary purpose.

'I should have taken *The Rotherweird Runner*'s advice,' said Jones, indicating his bequest from Bolitho. The red leather-bound book lay open on the floor at a page headed *One Walk NOT to Do* with the title *Mired in the Marsh* above a muddle of dots and tussocks.

'That's plain stupid! You're lucky to be alive.'

Jones abruptly changed the subject. 'Do I make the official programme?'

'Aerial Director,' suggested Boris.

'Aerial Scout would be better,' proposed Jones, an odd request, but it caused Boris no difficulty; after all, Jones would be on the lookout for misfiring fuses.

'Just keep it under the hat.'

'Mum's the word.' Jones resumed stretching and bending. 'I have a spare mat, dear Boris. Come and shed the twings and twangs of life.'

'It's been a long day—'

'My point exactly, dear Boris.'

'Another time, but thanks all the same.' He waved farewell and left Jones to his callisthenics, pausing on the outside step for long enough to hear the strange mantra resume.

'*Odi* . . . ho, ha . . . *et amo* . . . ho, ha . . .'

Boris foresaw another first in a year of increasingly bizarre events: a Latin poetry recital at a firework display.

Deeply inhaling the incense, Jones revelled in his new exercise regime. It held back the darker memories, whose closing footfalls were gathering in pace and volume.

In the absence of Finch, Oblong tried Madge Brown in the library, only to meet the usual stone wall.

'Well, obviously, Mr Oblong, there's no history of anything here, and that includes the Apothecaries and any other Guilds. Why are you so interested?'

'Their support of Mr Strimmer struck me as odd. I understand they've never shown any political interest before.'

'Always a first time,' replied Madge Brown.

'What did you expect?' Orelia said when he passed on the news.

3
Molecular Matters

A tinkle of hammers, scrabbling, a pummelling thud . . .

Finch instantly thought *mirage*, an illusory hope of escape. A stone brick shuddered, dust puffed from a widening gap, moss dislodged and fell. He rested a palm flat on the speaking part of the wall.

Shudder. Shudder. Shudder.

He thrust his fingers into the crack and nearly lost them to claws the colour of tortoiseshell ripping through the frangible mortar. He blinked and squinted, starved of light for so long, and blinked again, trying to focus his eyes on a candle fixed to a twisted wire whose flame danced in front of him.

Looking down, the Herald saw for the first time his coarse beard, all coal and frost, and his jagged fingernails. The candle, protected by a glass ampoule, was fixed to a crown-like contraption on his visitor's head.

A giant mole – and yet, *not quite*: he took in burned umber fur and bunched clawed hands, but the creature had enlarged eyes, extended arms and legs and the straight-backed bearing of human anatomy. And it stood a good five feet tall.

In a fruity bass the moleman said in flawless English, 'Get your skates on, Mr Finch, this tunnel ain't sound and we don't want an entombment.'

The moleman trotted back up the tunnel at a businesslike pace. Bending head and knees, Finch kept as close as he could, aghast that his bizarre rescuer knew his name. Walls and ceiling bled ill-

'A giant mole – and yet, not quite . . .'

smelling mud, glistening slicks which soiled Finch's already filthy clothes. Cracks zigzagged between the leaks, sandcastles assailed by the tide.

'Marsh,' cried the moleman over his shoulder, 'dead trees, dead plants, dead men, dead everything.'

'Have you a name?' cried Finch, flailing for an anchor in all this strangeness.

'*Talpidus sapiens*, but my other half calls me "tope" for short.' A dull thump ahead caused the moleman to pause and sniff the air. 'That's the trouble with tunnelling where your nose says "don't": the further you go, the longer your early work has to fall in!' Energised by the threat, the moleman worked through the malodorous debris, showering earth in all directions, rebuilding as he cleared, patting walls and ceiling firm with feet, paws and even the top of his head. Eventually, after an intersection, the earth became drier and the tunnel doubled in height.

The moleman turned to scrutinise Finch while combing his coat. 'Nothing scissors, soap and a cocktail won't cure,' he announced.

Their pace improved as first the air freshened and then duckboards appeared. This more salubrious tunnel soon brought them to an antechamber which resembled an organ loft: pipes of all shapes and sizes ran up the walls and into the roof while dials, levers and wheels protruded at different levels. Gas-lamps hissed along the walls.

The moleman offered a commentary, tapping each pipe or glass face as he passed: 'Heating, methane-lamps, ventilation fans, drinking water, waste disposal, humidifiers, security sensors, a seismograph, a barometer *and*' – he paused by a pipe thicker than the rest – 'that most essential trench-tool, the periscope. Don't ask me about the technicals; they're down to the other half.'

Familiar names were engraved on the brass and stencilled on the dial faces – *The Rotherweird Barometer Company*, *Turnpull & Sons* (plumbers on the Golden Mean, known for quality and prices to match) and *Cycloptics*, the telescope shop. The barometer bore the year 1881. The tope's haunt had been long in the making.

The moleman flicked the cover from the periscope. 'Have a gander while I fix us a sharpener,' he said, before disappearing through a circular oak door studded with a crescent moon and stars in black iron.

Finch lowered his face to the eyepiece and swivelled it, bringing into focus the bleakest of landscapes: Rotherweird Marsh at nightfall. The tussocks had an untethered look, the splashes of green too emerald for ordinary grass. The limbs of a dead tree protruded like a beggar's disappointed hand. No animal or human ventured here.

Faced by two rows of numbered levers with polished wooden handles alongside the telescope, Finch pulled the first and largest and the swamp spun away to a sweep of the Milky Way. Other numbers brought other objects – a planet, star groups, the face of the moon. Immersion in deep space felt vertiginous after his long confinement.

The last lever summoned Orion, the most brilliant winter constellation. An elongated smudge marked the deep blue-black of the sky northwest of Rigel – a smear on the lens? The ceiling whirred like the buzz of a trapped fly as the eye latched onto its target.

The circular door beyond swung open, and his host carried through a tray with two small decanters, one a tawny brown and the other barley-sugar orange, two cocktail glasses and an array of dry biscuits. Prosthetic fingers attached to the claws offered Finch a glass of orange cordial.

'Welcome, Mr Finch, to our humble "digs". It's Richter One for the convalescent and Richter Five for the hardworking miner. All in one go for best results.'

The moleman hurled back his glass like a Cossack, Finch following suit without the flamboyance. The liquid warmed from the inside out and the ill-effects of his incarceration receded.

'Come on in.'

The large rectangular chamber, illuminated by gas-lamps, held eating, living and sleeping quarters. Marquetry decorated the walls, but whether artwork or geological maps, Finch found it hard to tell. He took in a workbench, a sink and a cooking range, as well as Jacobean chairs of dark oak with barley-sugar twist legs.

One of the ten children from London had resisted Wynter, Finch recalled, a boy with a precocious talent for stargazing and optics. 'My other half,' the tope had said. Like Ferensen and the spiderwoman . . . ?

'Fortemain?' stammered Finch.

The moleman's voice changed, up an octave from the tope's bass to a half-familiar singsong tenor. 'I am he and he is me – for richer, for poorer; for better, for worse.'

Finch's cosy first impressions shifted as he imagined agoraphobia warring against claustrophobia in the moleman's divided being: tunnels winding this way and that set against starfields spilling into deep space.

They sat down at a circular table, and Fortemain turned serious. 'The mixing-point is versatile. She makes grotesques, but also "doubles" like us, where the human form rules until exposed to a particular element. Drown Ferensen in water or immerse me in earth, and hey presto!' He paused, then said softly, 'We got what we deserved.'

'Really?' queried Finch gallantly.

'*Really* – Wynter seduced us, promising us an indelible mark on human history. Once in Lost Acre, we quite forgot Sir Henry's murder. It was the ultimate playground: real, dangerous and utterly mesmerising. His decisive trick was the mayfly, which should live for a day but instead, week after week, it buzzed in its box. He said he would make us immortal, if we dared.'

Finch pointed out that he, Fortemain, had led the opposition; three shields in *The Dark Devices* had remained empty, Oxenbridge had been called back and the Eleusians had failed.

'They suffered a setback, no more – it may even have been a planned setback; later, I felt Wynter had manipulated everyone, including even Oxenbridge. Anyway, I had to live on to resist him if there were a second time round, and to achieve that I had to disappear. I used the mixing-point and went to earth. The tope is a most charming companion, but he borders on the garrulous.'

Valourhand had recounted a similar conversation between the two halves of the spiderwoman; for the time being the tope appeared to have left the stage.

Fortemain refilled the glasses. 'How was my memorial service?'

Finch gulped. *How was my memorial service? What was he talking about?*

Fortemain clacked his claws impatiently on the side of the decanter. 'Did the costumes work? How about the *stellarium*? Did Rhombus speak well?'

Finch felt a fool – here he was, surrounded by unconventional cocktails and optical equipment, precise fits for Professor Bolitho's interests. Bolitho was Fortemain and Fortemain was Bolitho – and half the moleman too.

He gathered his wits and described the scene from the roof of Escutcheon Place: the dance of the atoms, Oblong hurtling into space, the otherworldly music. 'It was a riot, Professor,' he concluded.

Fortemain changed tack. 'Your kidnapper is from Lost Acre, one of *their* creatures. I have a telescope trained on the marsh – one night I saw her leave. I came as quickly as I could – I'd never seen the like of it before.'

Nor had Fortemain seen Finch's cell before. The rock steps high in the ceiling troubled him; Man had built them long ago, a lot of work to create access to such an inhospitable place – *why*? And his enhanced hearing had detected another sealed chamber beyond. Like Morval in the spider's body, he was able to keep these inconclusive fragments to himself, so avoiding a barrage of questions from the tope.

'It dropped through my skylight, seized a book called *Straighten the Rope* from my shelves and then rejected it.'

Fortemain chuckled. 'How droll – take it from me, your copy is worthless.'

The moleman's voice deepened as the tope butted in, indiscreet as always. 'The Professor's work-in-progress is full of forceful meanderings,' said the gravelly bass.

Finch was bewildered. How could Fortemain's work assist Bole? He tried a different question. 'But this Fury can't be Bole's creature – she had no idea who Bole was.'

The moleman's eyes narrowed. '*Who* Bole *was* – what do you mean?'

'Bole is a shapeshifter. He acquires his victim's appearance – that's how he duped Slickstone – he was playing Ferox.'

The moleman thrust his face into Finch's. 'You mean he could be you?'

'Trust your senses,' Finch pointed out. 'You've been in the mixing-point. *I* haven't.'

Fortemain, not sounding wholly convinced, said, 'So you assure me you're Mr Finch through and through.'

A strange *tinging* sound halted the exchange as a young woman wearing a simple woollen shift entered the chamber and placed a bag and Finch's pocket watch on the table. She kissed the moleman on the brow of his head.

She had beauty's conventional attributes – rich copper-gold hair, high cheekbones, an aquiline nose, an unlined brow tapering to a delicate chin and a graceful neck. She was the tall side of average in height, and lissom – and yet her non-physical presence commanded more attention, being a melding of opposites. She was strong but frail, remote but direct, disengaged but alert, gentle, yet feral too. You did not need to know of her harrowing past to sense it.

The tope did the introductions. 'Morval, this is Mr Marmion

Finch, Rotherweird's Herald. He's on the right side, and he knows about Lost Acre. He was abducted by one of Wynter's creatures and brought to the marsh – it was after *Straighten the Rope*, but it got the wrong copy. Finch, this is Morval Seer. She has a gift that Wynter craved, the art of pictorial record. She protected us until the pages ran out. The gift lives on.'

Apprehension coloured these closing words: if Wynter returned, would he not come for her again, to illustrate another chronicle of horror? Morval anxiously flicked her fingers, in, out, in, out. Paper, ink and a nibbed pen lay on the table. As if in response, the moleman pushed them towards her.

She drew a man of dwarf-like appearance lying dead upon a slab, but instead of a hand, he had a lobster's claw. Finch had no idea who he was, but the moleman recognised him.

'Vibes?' cried Fortemain. '*Not* Vibes?'

Morval nodded, and a terrible truth struck Finch. Morval Seer had not spoken because she *could not* – no doubt the result of her unwinding. She added strangulation marks to the neck, then drew a bookshelf with an empty space among the volumes with fancy bindings.

The moleman shook his head, violently this time. 'Not *the* book? Not *my* book!'

The pen danced across the page, ever faster: a face, feral and long, with the eyes of a killer. Finch needed no introduction; it was Ferox; he had seen the skull beneath the skin at Ferensen's Midsummer party.

Fortemain lost his composure. He struck the table. 'What did you say, Finch? Bole assumed Ferox's shape to kill Slickstone? Well, now he's killed Vibes and he has the book – the *real* book, *my* copy.'

'Who's Vibes?' Finch asked.

'Who's Vibes? Vibes is the best – Vibes is their carer. Without Vibes . . .'

Despondency settled on the chamber. Finch fumbled for a change of subject. He turned to Morval. 'Your brother would send his love, I know he would.'

Physically he placed her in the twenties, her age when transformed by the vengeful Slickstone. Her eyes narrowed and glazed; the pen flicked out flawless concentric circles, the first little more than a dot, then growing wider and wider. Her face acquired a pinched, twisted look, which horrified Finch, and he noticed the moleman watching him: *Observe this lesson.*

She added lines, radiating out through the circles, equidistant from each other.

She stopped, eying the diagrams as if they were the work of a stranger.

Webs! She had been drawing webs, and in her head, spinning them.

'Well done, well done,' said Fortemain. 'The grip weakens by the day.' He placed a blank sheet in front of her. 'Let's do another circle,' he said gently, 'and let's make it a wheel this time.' She did so, with effort.

Finch felt privileged to watch: repair through patience and kindness.

A cart grew from the wheel, then horses, a pile of luggage and the front porch of Rotherweird Manor. Finch recognised the scene from the tapestry at Ferensen's party: the child prodigies arriving in the valley, and the beginning of the end of the Seers' idyllic upbringing.

The watch chimed again, bringing an end to the exercise, and Finch rediscovered his affection for the old timepiece. She must have cleaned and polished it herself, not a pleasant task. He thanked her, and won a smile.

From her bag Morval produced ham, eggs, potatoes, mushrooms and more. Valourhand had spoken of the spiderwoman's love of *haute cuisine*; the mixologist and the cook, a perfect match.

The moleman lit a fire before showing Finch the outlying

chambers – bedrooms and another workroom. The tope provided the commentary. 'The changelings stay, just a few at a time – they're a right handful and it can be a job to get them here. Vibes will be a terrible loss.'

'Who'll care for them now?'

'I hope you meet Tyke. He's a pure, Mr Finch: he went in and he came out, untouched.' The tope spoke with a respect bordering on reverence. 'I apologise for not forewarning you about Morval. She can't write words any more than speak them. The pen is her voice-box.'

The decanters of Richter were exchanged for water, which tasted fresh and delicious to Finch's straitened palate. Morval conjured a remarkable meal from such simple ingredients, the flavours all in perfect balance.

The tope's warm bass held the table. 'I expect, Mr Finch, you'd like to know about the art of tunnelling. Well, you start by scraping the earth from in front of the snout and pushing back past the body. It saps the energy, Mr Finch, and gives you an outrageous appetite.'

'How do you two divide the day?' asked Finch, gently broaching a delicate subject.

The tope did not answer directly, but said instead, 'We moles live a solitary life, with procreation the brief, loveless exception. My other half has brought a capacity to reflect and the ability to socialise.'

The table cleared, Fortemain's tenor resumed. 'I need a recruit.'

Finch buckled slightly. The real world was knocking at the door.

Fortemain quickly reassured him. 'Not you, Mr Finch, you're too prominent.' Fortemain produced four pieces of coloured stone from a drawer and explained, 'They make a sphere.'

With impressive dexterity Morval twisted and turned the pieces until they fitted perfectly. Fortemain placed the sphere in Finch's coat pocket.

'And once assembled?'

'Our recruit throws it in the mixing-point at dusk on the Winter Solstice. No other moment will do.'

Fortemain's tenor turned bass. 'What does it do?' asked the tope.

'It furthers a modest ambition of mine,' replied Fortemain to his other half.

'That's the day of the Mayoral election,' observed Finch. 'I don't like it,' he added. 'Too many event lines are converging at the same moment. It doesn't feel like coincidence.'

'It isn't coincidence: the whole town will be on the Island Field and therefore safe from any side effects,' said Fortemain. 'It's all to the good.'

'Do you have anyone in mind for this mission?' asked Finch.

'We need a bumbling innocent with hidden resolve.'

Finch thought of Jones and Oblong, until Fortemain added, 'And a brain of sorts.'

'Oblong, perhaps?'

'An excellent choice.'

Finch, still acclimatising to this fractured three-way conversation between two physical beings, glanced at Morval and saw another more elusive quality. Despite her extravagant gifts and her suffering, she remained *unspoiled*.

Fortemain turned to her and smiled. 'Morval and I have another errand, if you would be so kind.' He left the room and returned with a long slim package wrapped in brown paper. The attached label read *Apocalypse (Last Chord)*.

'Keep away from heat,' he warned Finch. 'It took weeks to construct.'

The shape and the warning were as good as a description. 'I deliver this to the Fireworkers? Be a pleasure.'

'By tomorrow's deadline, if you'd be so kind.'

A day and date at last, thought Finch, who knew the form. Every family could submit anonymously one named firework to the

Guild in the hope of selection for the Vulcan's Dance festivities. They had to be named and deposited in a large metal bin beside the Guild Hall's front door. Submissions were assessed for safety, impact and reliability before two, known as the First and Last Chords, were chosen, one to open Vulcan's Dance and the other to close it.

'Be a pleasure,' Finch repeated.

'Another thing,' said Fortemain. 'If Miss Valourhand has been to the other place, she may have some answers – I fear the enemy knows something we do not.'

The moleman's paw covered Morval's hand and Finch glimpsed the tragedy of a doomed relationship. Kept apart in Wynter's time to save themselves and Ferensen, then by her hideous transformation, now they were sundered again by his dual nature and the practical impossibility of her returning to town.

The conversation ended abruptly. 'Time to go, Mr Finch. You should sleep in your own bed tonight,' said Fortemain.

Hand shook paw, and the tope regained control, refitting the crown-like contraption to his forehead and relighting the candle as Finch said his farewells to Morval.

'On, on,' cried the tope impatiently.

At the intersection they took a downward tunnel, this time through smooth grey rock streaked with lichen where water gathered like perspiration on glass. At the end a wheeled platform rested on a narrow wooden rail. The tope tied Morval's package to a cradle at the front.

'Relax and drink in the view. Nature's forces will do the work.'

Finch tottered onto the platform. The tope embraced him like a Russian and released the brake. The trolley lurched and moved slowly off. The dark was not absolute; a glow from contrasting rock strata illuminated the way. Belatedly he understood the dampness: the rail was taking him under the Rother.

The cart veered into a slow, spiralling ascent before levelling off into a dead end. He untied Morval's package, stepped off and ascended the iron rungs on the wall in front of him.

The cart shivered and returned the way it had come. Finch glanced at his restored pocket watch: five past eleven. The outer gates would already be closed. He lifted a hinged metal lid marked Rotherweird Drainage Department No 1472 and clambered out.

Back in the moleman's lair, Fortemain reflected on the disturbing news about Bole's shapeshifting gifts and his repossession of *Straighten the Rope*. He thought of Flask, and of other, older figures in Rotherweird's history after Oxenbridge's final departure. Unsettling possibilities occurred to him and he worried that Oblong's mission might not be so straightforward. At least his underwater investigations had revealed a failsafe provided by Nature. If Bole tried to use the technology behind his modest ambition for anything extravagant, the seismic reaction would destroy Rotherweird, an outcome Bole would never risk. Perhaps it was no bad thing that Bole had acquired his copy of *Straighten the Rope*, for his calculations addressed the dangers in detail.

But he was still apprehensive: *Never underestimate Wynter or his acolytes*.

'We need to amend our display, Morval, and for that we'll need Tyke's help.'

Morval's pen dipped again, drawing the stars and streamers of a magnificent firework.

4

Back to Earth

It was a dry night and a chill, boisterous breeze slapped Finch's cheeks. Walls without windows reared into the night sky to a roofline with a sweeping curve. He was standing in the lee of the South Tower, Professor Bolitho's observatory and Rotherweird home.

He walked to the Golden Mean, returning a perfunctory wave from two young teachers rolling home from *The Journeyman's Gist*, easy as you like.

As he retrieved his spare keys from behind a brick in a flanking wall by Escutcheon Place, two men emerged from the shadows.

'We're glad to have found you,' said one.

'Welcome home,' said the other.

Finch recognised Snorkel's cronies: the insincere greeting was shorn of any enquiry about the whys or wherefores of his disappearance. They turned on their heels and trotted off into the dark.

A single gaslight on its lowest setting hissed in the hall of Escutcheon Place; otherwise it was silence and darkness. The pleasure of homecoming shifted to unease.

Red wax sealed the note to the staircase banister.

Blink, scratch. Lost mannerisms returned as he read Mrs Finch's square, humourless script and its brutal message:

Dear Finch,

   A man of your age disappears for only one reason. Be good enough to thank your grubby consort, whoever she is, for rescuing me from Pokey Place and Mr Gloom.

Cindy has arranged rooms appropriate to our station on the right side of Market Square (rent deductible from your salary). Divorce papers will be filed next week. Look in the mirror and you will know the grounds. When Master Finch reaches majority, I shall press for his immediate succession. You are not fit for purpose.

Yours formerly,

Fennel

Finch gasped.

Take two measures of guilt. He delved into his bruised ego. Mrs Finch had, he had once believed, married for love – and so she had: love of the pride of place that his hereditary office would bestow on her. The small words '*appropriate* to our station' and 'the *right* side of Market Square' testified to her values. He had not fought hard enough to change them.

Add one measure of relief. Life had been joyless for years, relieved only by the brief adventure with Slickstone. He had been gifted a chance to rebuild.

He retreated to the *archivoire*, where the scene of his abduction had been restored to normality, books returned, including *The Dark Devices* to its secret alcove, and the skylight windowpane resealed.

He sank to his knees, overcome by the onslaught of events, until his watch chimed. Gathering his wits and Morval's package, he returned to the open air.

The two men reported to Bendigo Sly, 'Finchy's back.'

'In one piece?'

'Bit beardy.'

Sly handed over a pre-prepared press release. 'Straight to the *Chronicle* editor.'

'Suppose he asks where Finchy-boy's been?'

'That's for Finch to divulge if he wishes – and he won't, 'cause if he does, Mr Snorkel will let his ghastly missus loose.'

The two men glanced at the headline: *Snorkel Foundation Rescues Herald*.

'Nice one, Mr Sly, nice one.'

Valourhand perched on Orelia's desk at the back of the shop and tucked one leg under the other.

'More coffee?'

Valourhand did not look up. Two hours' study of *Straighten the Rope* had generated chains of calculations mushrooming across *Baubles & Relics* notepaper.

'More brandy?'

Valourhand uncoiled and accepted the refill with a cursory thank-you before delivering a verdict of sorts. 'Right, we've got force, celestial calendars, barometric pressure, spheres, the geology of Rotherweird Island, the physics of dark matter, seismology, cloud studies – and they're all over the place. You get a scribbled note in the 1650s, then add-ons centuries later. But I can tell you this: something will happen – or *could* happen – on Election Day.'

'Strimmer or Snorkel will win.'

Valourhand ignored the levity and continued, 'One event he wants, the other he fears – but he considers the second one impossible. The feared event concerns the river somehow.'

'The moon draws a tide,' Orelia commented, 'so what might a dark matter comet do?'

Valourhand did not answer; towards the front of the shop a tall stooped figure was pressing his face against the glass.

'Finch!' she exclaimed, snatching up Orelia's keys and skipping to the door. She admitted Finch with a kiss on both cheeks.

Orelia blinked, both eyes, Finch-like: a first, Valourhand entranced by the sight of a fellow human being!

'Hail the Herald, back from the dead!' Valourhand cried.

Finch replied with a wan grin. Orelia pulled up an armchair, settled him in, poured everyone a brandy and rebuilt the fire.

Finch took a sip and summarised his adventures. 'I've been imprisoned, interrogated, rescued, entertained – oh, yes, and Mrs Finch has buggered off.'

His cheeks had hollowed, his natural gauntness now haggard; tiny bursts of red scarred the whites of his eyes and grey flecked his hair: a tawny owl turning snowy.

Orelia imagined his return to an empty Escutcheon Place, abandoned by wife and son after such an ordeal.

Without warning, Finch turned violently on his companions as he seized *Straighten the Rope*. 'You can't have this! Not unless you're in league—'

'Calm down, Finchy,' said Valourhand.

'I was given it,' Orelia explained, 'by a diminutive bookbinder called Vibes.'

Finch steadied himself. 'Vibes is dead.'

'I know, I've seen the body – lobster hand and all,' Orelia said.

The detail reassured Finch, and he crumpled back into the chair. 'Please do forgive me – I've been away, completely out of touch. Bole killed Vibes, masquerading as Ferox. He must have been after the book – it's Fortemain's – but somehow Vibes got it to you in time. I wish I'd known earlier. The moleman would have been most reassured. The Escutcheon Place copy just had the diagrams. This is the one that matters.'

Orelia felt a need for order. 'I think Finch's news will be better informed and more informing if he hears ours first. I'll start with Vibes.' In deference to his fragile state, she took her time, recounting the mission to the Hoy Book Fair, the visit to Wynter's ruined house, their attempt to reconstruct Finch's abduction, the attack on Aether's Way, the desecrated copy of *Straighten the Rope*, the corpse of Bole's cat, the grandiose plans of the Apothecaries, and their conclusion that Fortemain was Bolitho. She shared for the first time her visit to *The Agonies*, having extracted a concession that neither of them would attempt a visit themselves. She also raised their suspicions about Estella Scry.

'That old fraud?' commented Finch. He had once ordered Scry to desist from selling heraldic mottos as guardians against the evil eye; her look of disdain had unsettled him. 'The eyes have it ...'

Valourhand followed, describing the subterranean road to Lost Acre, the quarry and the ambush by the ice-dragon.

Finch's narrative came in fragments – his cell, his interrogation and the moment of rescue. Thereafter, his thespian gifts shone through. He brought the moleman's divided being and his subterranean realm to vivid life before turning to Morval Seer. Affectingly, he conveyed her voiceless, drawing her thoughts, achingly beautiful.

Valourhand, uncharacteristically, asked first about Bolitho's welfare. Finch preferred to treat him as Fortemain, being who he really was.

'The moleman is not like the spiderwoman,' Finch assured her. 'They make cocktails and chat in different voices – but Fortemain is paranoid about Bole.'

Valourhand filled a gap in Orelia's summary. '*Straighten the Rope* is an anagram of *The Rotating Sphere*. In Bolitho's calculations, the comet and various spheres interact.'

Finch decided not to mention the sphere in his coat pocket; Oblong should be the first to know.

Valourhand continued, 'So, I have a question. Our comet last appeared in 1017 – so how could Bolitho possibly know about it?'

Finch, the archivist, whispered Rotherweird's worst blasphemy: 'Someone recorded what happened. A *history* – the *Anglo-Saxon Chronicle*, maybe?'

'Oblong spoke to *the* expert on the *Chronicle* and he said *nothing* about comets.'

'Hardly surprising if it's invisible,' mumbled Finch.

'It's not invisible in Lost Acre,' Valourhand pointed out, before exploding in righteous indignation as she saw the answer. 'Bloody

Fanguin! What did he say Bolitho left him? A natural history by an eleventh-century monk—'

'*De Observatione Naturae*,' chipped in Orelia.

Valourhand drummed her feet against the floor in frustration. 'So *that* is where the truth is, if only that dypso had read it properly. We're surrounded by morons!'

Finch did not hear; his head had dipped and he looked hollow, a shell of a man, spent adrenalin demanding repayment. 'Mr Gloom of Pokey Place she called me,' he muttered, getting up and shuffling towards the door. 'Thank you for the kind words and warmth. I'll mend – I'm used to my own company.'

The Herald let himself out, prompting a litany of male failure from Valourhand. 'Finch broken, Ferensen fled, Fanguin perennially pissed, Oblong hapless, Bolitho in hiding . . . Anyone I've missed?'

'Jones?'

'Juvenile.'

'Boris?'

'Busy.'

'Everthorne?'

'Enigmatic.'

'It's up to us then.'

5

An Unexpected Gift

Pomeny Tighe liked her rooms for being high up. Her ordeal had started earthbound, crawling on all fours with a ditch for a bed until the almshouse in Hoy had taken her in. The following years had not diminished the horror of that opening decade or the fate she now faced.

Tonight, after a grinding day indulging Snorkel, she planned her next moves. Her handicap was worsening, her memory and libido fading fast.

As she cantered up the stairs, pointing her toes in the dust, she noticed another's clumsier prints. This had happened once before, when Bendigo Sly's distinctive feet had paid a visit, but this tread was heavier. She found no marks on the handle: so, a careful visitor.

She sensed the object before she saw it: a large multicoloured sphere, sitting dead centre on her single table, spinning unaided and unprovoked. A note beside it declared in neutral capitals:

TAKE ME WHENCE YOU CAME,
SUN SINKING ON THE SOLSTICE,
AND TIME WILL TURN AGAIN.

Caution deserted her: she had a cure, and instructions for its administration – why and from whom did not matter; that they knew her condition was enough. She had no wish to return to that accursed place, but then, vaccines are fashioned at the seat of infection.

She reached for her skipping rope.

6

Glass to Order

In the Glassmakers' shop on Aether's Way, the Master completed the last transaction of the day. 'Thirty, as ordered.' He awarded the customer a smile instead of a Madam or Miss, unsure which fitted best.

She counted them; women nearly always did, in his experience, while men rarely bothered. Nature or nurture? The ampoules had an unusual shape: long in the body with a weak neck sealed with a glass screw-top.

'The books praise the resistances of glass,' she said softly.

'Nothing can beat it – alkali, almost all acids, water, gases, electricity,' replied the Master, reassured that she was the mildest of customers.

She paid exactly, picked up the package and left.

Once home, she filled each ampoule, resealed the top and slid one into the readymade cavity in every shaft. She used razor blades for fletching to minimise air resistance, and broad heads to maximise bleeding. Impact would drive the spindle down the shaft into the ampoule's neck.

All she needed now was the town to empty in the hours of darkness, and an impending Rotherweird ritual would see to that.

7

A Selection Committee

The unrelieved dressed stone, small windows set in iron frames and studded steel door gave the Fireworkers' Hall the air of a prison. However, life within belied the morose outer shell: Fireworkers were enthusiasts, united by their love of harmless special effects.

The ground floor held both citizens' submissions and the Guild's own creations. Mounted on a huge wooden frame, a muscled figure with hammer in hand, moveable joints and fittings for various devices occupied an entire wall: Vulcan at his forge.

The basement held the Powder Room and the Ignition Chamber while the upper floors housed a warren of small rooms, each devoted to a particular expertise, loosely in order of assembly.

This year's better submissions stood in two Ferdy beer barrels beside the Master's desk; the current favourites, *Argent Sparkle* and *Borealis*, were lying on top. In truth, they were not the spectacular show-stoppers (or starters) their exotic names suggested.

'Where's the devil gone? They're nothing more than wee bangs and sparks!' Boris protested.

'Try these, boss,' brayed a bumptious apprentice, placing the weekend's closing submissions on the table. Two stood out for size and ambition, and also as polar opposites. *Apocalypse*, a double-sticked rocket over waist-high in elegant black paper, had been submitted for the Last Chord; the white-paper *Fatherly Wonder*, a squat, ugly aerial shell, for the First Chord.

Argent Sparkle and *Borealis* were returned to the barrels. Boris took out his patented instruments for probing without disturbance: the ocle, the swab-poke and the decrimper. Word spread as he summoned his Senior Technician, luring fuse-fitters, designers, powder monkeys, chamber-makers, packers and other esoteric specialists downstairs to the Master's study, mugs of morning coffee still in hand.

Each new finding raised a cheer.

'Multiple chambers . . .'

'Slow fuses, fast fuses . . .'

'Spolets . . .'

'Hummers . . .'

'Parachutes . . .'

'Strontium, barium, sodium, calcium . . .'

The ocle gave way to the swab-poke, which burrowed into the bowels of *Fatherly Wonder*.

'There's one colouring agent I don't recognise, but, boy, is she ambitious!'

On to *Apocalypse* and another running commentary:

'Different binders: dextrin and paron . . .'

'What artwork . . .' added an envious decorator.

The black paper boasted an array of motifs in gold paint – dragonflies, volcanoes, tiny insects identified by the Senior Technician as glow-worms. Never had any of them encountered such exquisite draughtsmanship on a firework casing.

'All in favour?' asked Boris.

A forest of hands went up: no dissenters.

'To print!' he declared, tossing the programme onto the table. *Argent Sparkle* and *Borealis* were erased in favour of *Fatherly Wonder* and *Apocalypse*, each inscribed in a flourish of crimson ink. Applause broke out. Their spectacle would neither start nor finish with a whimper.

The Fireworkers kept their membership secret and only one name adorned the credits at the foot of the programme, a promise kept: *Gregorius Jones, Aerial Scout.*

8

Old Haunts and New

Observing gas-lamps dimming at eight o'clock precisely, when they usually brightened, Oblong left his lodgings for the Golden Mean to find a *Marie Celeste* of a town. A deathly silence hung over the empty streets; every window was closed and shuttered.

A low whistle rose to an ululating crescendo before dying away. The shutters swung open and spectral, disembodied faces appeared – *Hallowe'en pumpkins at the end of November? Why did nobody warn me?*

His anxiety eased. Rotherweird's take on the Feast of Lost Souls would surely be entertaining. He anticipated children in outlandish costumes, toffee apples, candyfloss, trick or treat . . .

None of these happened. Instead, a floating gourd with spinning rotors, candlelit mouth agape, flitted down a side street.

'Welcome to Lazarus Night, Mr Historian. Your time has come.' The unknown voice had a grating quality.

Oblong spun round to face the devil himself, with cloven feet and a leathery tail, which twitched like a cat's. A tray of masks hung around his neck.

'This is yours: the outsider brings justice and death.' The devil handed over a crimson headsman's mask and a long-handled axe made of *papier mâché*.

The fabric of the mask had an unpleasant clinging quality.

The devil shook his head in exasperation. 'Hold it like Mr Flask: have *style!*'

How to carry an axe stylishly? he wondered. *Over my shoulder, head down by my side or across the chest on outstretched arms?* He opted for waist-level with the head pointing forwards.

The gas-lamps sputtered and went out; he checked his watch. Eight-thirty precisely. A prearranged programme must be playing out. By the time Oblong had matched his eyes to the mask's slits, the devil had vanished.

At the approach to Market Square, grey-ribbed sacs hung from the lamp posts. Oblong prodded one with the axe-handle. The skin twitched as a claw cut through the material, to be followed by feelers, then spindly legs. The emerging creature, a skull-faced purple butterfly, climbed to the top of the lamp post, freed its wings and skimmed up a wire to alight on a chimney stack. Others followed and in short order the roofscape was teeming with grotesques.

Was he not playing Oxenbridge, summoned from wider England to bring the Eleusians and their grotesque creations to heel? Oblong recalled the nursery rhymes of his childhood, their lyrics rooted in dark historical fact.

At eight forty-five a skeleton band marched into the north end of Market Square playing a stately *chaconne.* Behind them, bearers carried a life-sized clock, its pendulum a suspended man swinging a scythe. The physique and rictus grin were uniquely Gregorius Jones.

A second band marched in from the south in perfect time and tune with the first.

The Apothecaries joined from Hamelin Way, in pitch-black tunics and stovepipe hats, torchlight flickering on expressionless faces: judges to his executioner.

Street doors disgorged the remaining citizenry, a mix of witches, warlocks, werewolves and vampires, costumed to convince, all processing to Market Square and chanting:

'By the pricking of my thumbs . . .
The graves are open,
Winter comes . . .'

The press herded Oblong into the centre of Market Square, where an Apothecary placed a lifelike block at his feet while two more spread-eagled a straw guy on the block.

Estella Scry strode forward. 'Strike, you fool,' she hissed.

He did so, and with a conjuror's flourish, Scry held up the head to the crowd.

The two bands struck up a livelier dance as a coffin appeared. Scry commanded it to open as if calling Lazarus to life and a spectral prince – none other than Hengest Strimmer, crowned in a golden wreath – rose into view. As he did so, carnival erupted: a frenzied dance of the dead. From the highest towers machines belched man-made snow across Market Square and the aerial walkways of Aether's Way.

Winter comes. Wynter comes.

'How did Strimmer wangle that?' snarled Snorkel from the balcony of the Mayoral Suite. 'This is Lazarus Night, not a canvassing spectacular.'

To any neutral observer, Snorkel the vampire bat looked repulsive – but not to Mrs Finch, an imp with a daring *décolletage*.

'Disgraceful,' she cooed, as Mrs Snorkel, an elegant gorgon, scowled.

She loathed Mrs Finch and her pushiness in all its aspects, but found compensation in the clock's human pendulum – if only he were not a mere gym teacher. Still, window-shopping was better than nothing.

Snorkel's ire moved onto Scry. 'How *dare* that woman summon Strimmer like an anointed king! She wangled her way onto the Steering Committee – and the chairmanship, I'll have you know.'

By 'wangled', Snorkel meant that he had eased her way.

'Her shop sells the most frightful tat,' simpered Mrs Finch.

Why now? he fumed, ignoring his guest. He knew better than most that endorsement mattered – every handshake, every cheer, every baby tendered for appreciation – but *subliminal* endorsement mattered more. Her performance was a betrayal.

Oblong threaded his way through the Apothecaries to the empty eastern quarter, the music receding in the twists and turns of Hamelin Way. Houses stooped lower here, as if weighed down by the harshness of their inhabitants' lives. Stars glittered in the slivers of night sky between opposing roofs, symbols of unattainable wealth.

A familiar refrain floated by.

> '*By the pricking of my thumbs . . .*
> *The graves are open,*
> *Winter comes . . .*'

But who was singing? Nearing the end of Hamelin Way, he peered into the side alleys. Nobody – but the uncanny refrain came again. Oblong lengthened his stride into a wider space. He had stumbled on the Fireworkers' Hall. The feminine voice closed, but still nobody was visible.

Oblong the schoolmaster took control. 'Hey! Show yourselves! That's quite enough tomfoolery.'

A shove from behind sent him sprawling forward. '*By the pricking of my thumbs . . .*' whispered the voice.

Oblong felt a jab in his left arm, and clasping his sleeve, his fingers reddened: blood was seeping through. A dagger point appeared and Oblong kicked out, but too slowly. A second blade flicked down the cobbles, raising a trail of sparks. Panic-stricken, Oblong went berserk, swinging in all directions with his *papier-mâché* axe.

'He wants to play,' hissed the same female voice with another thrust, this time at Oblong's right leg, as a kick from his invisible assailant dislodged the axe from his hand. The unseen attacker chuckled and hissed, 'The eyes have it!'

Oblong looked about frantically for a loose cobblestone, a dustbin lid, any makeshift weapon or shield, but to no avail. With a cry for help, he started spinning round, arms outstretched – and he made contact, too solid for any ghost.

Touché!

But he could not sustain momentum; already breathless, he adopted a boxer's pose, flicking out his feet, but with decreasing frequency and power. In the heat of this one-sided battle, Oblong registered how absurd he must look, a lumbering bull goaded by an invisible picador. The steel tips grew slowly, one circling to the left, one to the right, level with his face, poking closer and closer.

'Eeeny . . . meeny . . . miney . . . mo . . .'

Oblong wanted to cover his eyes, but that would leave him defenceless.

'*En garde!*'

A second female cry announced the arrival of a dark purple moth, body painted and eyes goggled, swinging crazily down the plant wires trained between the houses and walkways; some held, some snapped, but the creature landed gracefully, shrugged off its wings and cartwheeled towards the blades.

The insect ducked a scything sweep by the second blade, smearing the owner with grime as it passed. Fragments of an attacker's body appeared: a bare shoulder and a lower wrist. Oblong followed suit, scouring his fingers along the lip of the pavement and hurling the accumulated dirt.

'Go for the face!' cried the demented insect, pirouetting while kicking like a can-can dancer.

The threat had an instant effect: the knives and disembodied limbs fled down an alleyway – fear of recognition had won the day.

'Who were they?'

'Don't flatter yourself,' said his rescuer. 'There was just one, a slim "her" with not a stitch on – have you been insulting your class?' The voice and its tone were as distinctive as Jones' physique. To his acute disappointment, he had been rescued by Valourhand.

'I thought Hallowe'en opened November—' he stuttered.

'This is not *Hallowe'en*, this *is* Rotherweird. We have our own festivals on our own dates – and you owe me a pair of wings.' Valourhand pushed up her goggles.

Oblong rubbed his leg, adrenalin having ousted the pain until now. More blood stained his fingers.

'Shirt up, trouser legs up,' she added. He dithered, so she did it for him.

'Ouch!'

'They're flesh wounds – grow up!' She tore strips off her discarded wings and bound the deeper cuts, including, lastly, one on her own arm. 'So, someone thinks *you're* a threat – how weird is that?'

'You don't understand,' he said. 'I'm Rotherweird's only historian – I am *the* threat.'

'Fine,' said Valourhand, 'as a pompous abstract proposition – but, pray, do tell me what you know about our past that I don't. And remove that absurd mask before I finish the job.'

'The only other person in town with historical lowdown has been kidnapped. The opposition clearly don't agree.'

'I repeat: what do you know that I do not?'

Oblong floundered. 'You're lucky I'm not a lepidopterist,' he countered feebly, before gracefully conceding, 'Let me buy you a drink.'

'Why?'

'You saved my life.'

She grinned. 'So I did.'

'I'll put a sign up,' whispered Ferdy as Valourhand redressed their wounds, '*No Invisibles*.'

His remark galvanised Valourhand. '*Somebody* had the skill to rework Boris' invisibility film as paint – let's hope it's all used up. He never bothers with where his inventions might lead.'

Rather rich, coming from the North Tower, thought Oblong.

'Question is, how did she get it?' continued Valourhand.

Front-of-house remained quiet, poised for a late surge from Market Square. Pumpkins glowed on tables and the bar; swathes of garlic hung over the lintels. Ferdy's assistants ministered to a sprinkling of the Summoned, among them Everthorne, sketching in a corner, and an attractive young woman, also with a pad on her knee.

'You are?' Valourhand asked her bluntly.

'Pomeny Tighe. And you?'

Valourhand, distracted for some reason, did not reply, so Oblong thrust his hand between them. 'Hi, name's Oblong. I'm the School historian.'

She dipped her eyelashes and Oblong, ever vulnerable to feminine interest, wobbled on his wounded legs.

'I have a historian on my staircase in Germany. Aren't you rather on the young side?'

'That's Euler's equation,' interrupted Valourhand, staring at her pad, which contained a simple equation, $V - E + F = 2$, above a tangle of figures.

Oblong felt out of his depth, but Tighe smiled. 'Let's help our historian, shall we? V equals vertices, E equals edges and F equals faces.'

'And below?' asked Valourhand.

'Musings,' replied Tighe. 'I do like to muse.' She turned back to Oblong. 'It talks of the beauty of spheres.'

An urge to change the subject seized Oblong, so unexpected was the answer. *Spheres*. Did anyone study anything else in this godforsaken town? 'Who's Mr Euler?' he asked.

'Herr Euler could recite the *Aeneid* by heart and pinpoint the first and last line on every page. Isn't that something, Mr Historian?'

'I trust he's not pre-1800,' said Oblong primly.

'He may well be, but his equation is eternal.'

Valourhand remained silent.

Oblong glimpsed an unexpected object in Tighe's bag. 'Oh, that looks fun.'

She dipped in and placed a toy mechanical on the table, a fisherman on a riverbank. '*Third Time Lucky*, it's called. Press the button, lift the tiny lever – and hey presto!' She demonstrated: the waves moved to and fro; the fisherman dipped his rod, and on the third cast a metal fish emerged hooked to the line. 'Eventually the magnet goes low enough to draw,' she explained.

Oblong thought it odd that a woman with such exceptional geometrical understanding should be mesmerised by a toy.

'I shall change it so the fish is bigger and the angler falls in,' added Tighe, with girlish enthusiasm.

'Where do you work out there?' asked Valourhand, indicating the great beyond with a flick of the wrist.

'Heidelberg University.'

Oblong restarted the mechanical, only to find his hand jabbed by Tighe's index finger. 'Mine!' she said firmly, returning the toy to her bag.

Valourhand and Oblong exchanged glances, a rare flash of agreement. There was something amiss with Pomeney Tighe.

9

Dance Moves

Vulcan's Dance and the Great Equinox Race shared with Lazarus Night themed costumes – but with more restraint. All wore black, enhanced by only one decorative *motif*, but with a wide variety in shape and movement. Rosettes, fixed to the coat like badges, changed colour as they rotated; cloth Catherine wheels spun; hats opened to release multi-coloured stars; rockets climbed from heel to shoulder before sinking and rising again, all powered by tiny clockwork mechanisms fashioned by the Metalworkers. Those who could not afford such luxuries wove fantastical patterns in luminous beads.

When Aggs enlightened Oblong about his latest sartorial duties, he protested, 'I'm not paying to dress up as a firework.' His humiliation as a self-propelled rocket at Bolitho's funeral still rankled. 'And, Aggs, you might have tipped me off about Lazarus Night! I bet you warned Flask.'

''e didn't need telling, did 'e? Anyway, next year you'll know.'

'If there is one,' he retorted grumpily.

Aggs stood, one hand on hip, the other grasping a feather duster. She spoke like a travel guide, ramming home the essential facts. 'If you're after lowdown on the Dance: bakers have programmes, free with any purchase. Town gates open at seven; they fires the Hag at seven-thirty; fireflies before the main course at eight, and every south-facing window – *including* those what belongs to outsiders – gotta be covered over from two in the afternoon. Get it?'

'I get it: no peeping in daylight – but where's the show?'

'The Island Field, Mr Oblong – where else in a town made of wood? High time I gave whatever lurks between them lug-holes a right old scrub and polish.'

'What's the Hag?'

'She's a beauty like me, only with wings!' She lunged at him with a hideous grin, top teeth clenched over her bottom lip, flapping her arms. Oblong had a fleeting vision of the Fury swooping on Aether's Way.

Aggs was now in full flow. 'All right, droopy drawers – save yer guineas for women and song. I'll find you a hand-me-down.'

A dark herringbone coat arrived the following morning. It had seen better days – the clockwork mechanism had rusted through, leaving the woollen rocket stranded halfway up his back – but Oblong made no complaint; he had no wish to stand out.

After perusing the programme and the list of innocuous display titles, he relaxed, a little.

That same evening Tyke addressed the inhabitants of *The Agonies* with understated eloquence. His audience, a miscellany of half-human creatures, sat at their benches in the main workroom. Morval Seer stood at the back, a reassuring presence after Vibes' murder.

'Tomorrow night, Morval and I must leave for a few hours,' he told them. 'We'll be back by midnight.' He offered no reason for their absence. The changelings made their own clothes and grew their own food, but in most the human part of their make-up had been frozen at the age of their abduction, hence the need for supervision. The changelings feared the prophesied return of their torturer, Geryon Wynter, and he had no wish to discomfort them further.

3 p.m. Boris' convoy rolled onto Hamelin Way. The fading sky glowed deep blue, but the Guild's instruments had shown fast tightening millibars from late evening. Forecasting in the valley was a fallible science, but the odds favoured an undisturbed display.

Gregorius Jones sauntered alongside. 'All set, Master Polk?'
Boris waved a hand. 'All set-*ish*.'

4 p.m. The Fireworkers had unpacked the carts in the Island
Field and spread out the contents. Every firework, iron peg, wire
and helium balloon had a number, the latter being tethered to a
heavy millstone anchor. The chosen ground looked like a rock-
face patterned with pitons. Between the pegs ran horizontal wires
with rings attached for the vertical wires to which the balloons
would attach. A heavy windlass, anchored to the ground, would
hold Vulcan and his forge in place. Jones, honorary member for
the day, eyed the small crow's nest, his station for the night, with
mild apprehension: it would be a tight fit, and the vertical wires
were dauntingly long.

5.30 p.m. The Forge had been set out ready for launch, with fireworks fixed in their allotted places, each set to draw the eye away
from its dying predecessor. Boris placed the First Chord, *Fatherly
Wonder*, nearest the audience, and the Last Chord, *Apocalypse*, fur-
thest away.

On a raft on the Rother stood a towering pyre of crisscrossed
branches and planks above a brushwood core. Attached to the raft
was a tall gibbet embedded in the riverbed, where in time the Hag
would be raised, by tradition the responsibility of the Apothecaries.

6.30 p.m. The most perilous moment had passed without upset:
twelve helium balloons, their skins coated in Polk-patented fire-
resistant paint, had raised the model forge with its fireworks high
into the sky.

6.50 p.m. Gregorius Jones clambered into his basket, where he
stood, back ramrod-straight like a guardsman, brass lighter-stick
held perpendicular. Boris explained the primitive rudder, only for

use if – a *most* unlikely if – the balloon should escape its moorings. The Fireworkers fixed a large balloon, fashioned for safety with three separate chambers, to the basket and launched.

Jones fastened the chinstrap of his aviator's cap and said not a word. *Orders are orders.* He peered at the constellation of Orion: no sign of any comet, no ill omens to trouble him. On Rotherweird Island the portcullis remained closed. To the south and west, the dark shadow of the great woods lined the valley rim. He looked across to the marsh.

A thought came, half-observation and half-insight, as extravagant as it was horrifying . . . surely that could not be Wynter's secret?

'Gregorius!' The voice broke the spell and Jones snapped back into military mode. 'We're moving you left.'

Boris looked miniscule waving his loudhailer. Wheels careened along the wires, sliding Jones within reach of the black and yellow master fuse by the fire god's right ankle. He sat on the retractable stool and emptied his mind – eyes shut, limbs still, only the ears active, tuned for the faintest sound – as if waiting in ambush.

7.00 p.m. The procession emerged from the South Gate. The Apothecaries led, bearing the Hag, bound by her wings to a gallows-like structure. The rest of the town milled behind in no particular order. The pyrotechnically minded – of whom there were many – assuaged the disappointment of rejection for the First or Last Chords by constructing miniature fireworks known as fireflies. The *Firework Regulations* dictated the quantity of gunpowder and the size, and the method of launch (metal runnels fixed to the eastern shore of the Island Field). There were five permitted classes: dragons for distance (sub-divided into red for height and green for horizontal travel), damsels (colours), bottles (sound), swallowtails (acrobatics) and bees (multiple displays).

Families declared for one school and usually stayed there. Competition flourished, judged by senior members of the Fireworkers'

Guild – and with what prizes! The Woodcarvers, dealers in permanence, supplied tiny carvings of the class emblem endorsed with the year in gold – trophies exempted from destruction under the *Inheritance Regulations*.

10

Rockets and More

Countrysiders clasping homemade optical aids of varying sophistication gathered on the prominence behind Ferensen's tower to watch another town ceremonial from which they were excluded.

A whisper took root and spread, that Ferensen was back – and there he was, emerging from the woodland in a long travelling coat. Like sheep to their shepherd, they flocked around him.

He opened with a subject on which he never erred. 'Weather is coming, *exceptional* weather, and danger with it. Take advantage: if we treasure home and livelihood, it's our collective duty to keep Snorkel and Strimmer from power. Be generous, and use your ingenuity. You won't see me for some time, but rest assured, I shall be watching with your interests at heart.'

They dispersed, no longer interested in the town's frivolities.

Nature would be their ally.

7.10 p.m. Bert Polk tried to explain the next act to his distracted fourth child, Imo. 'The Apothecaries walk down the Island Field to the pontoon bridge they built this morning. They cross it, hoist the Hag and light the pyre—'

'That looks like Uncle Boris!'

'It's the Master of the Fireworkers, and you're not listening.'

'I am, Dad, honest! They go to a bridge to light the pyre – only they haven't built it. Your pontoon-thingy isn't there.'

Bert stared at his daughter and then at the river surging around the platform. There was indeed no means of crossing, a serious breach of ritual.

Thomes felt all eyes fixed on him, *very* gratifying. As the Apothecaries reached the end of the South Bridge, he tugged the chain beneath the Hag, the crossbar snapped back, hooks released and beneath the skin motors whirred. Synchronised wings flapped and the Hag rose above the crowd before skimming over the Rother and the Island Field to a perfect landing on the gibbet above the pyre.

Uncomfortable silence yielded to tumultuous applause.

The Apothecaries walked on to the eastern shoreline. By now the onlookers had registered the absence of any bridge. Surely the immaculate Master would not *wade*?

Thomes readied the device Scry had designed and tested as his Guildsmen held back the crowd. He leaned backwards, opened his mouth wide, stabbed his head forward and spewed a gout of flame across the river into the lower reaches of the pyre. Flames leaped high. For a fleeting moment the Hag held its form like a phoenix, an image of renewal and rebirth.

Bomber watched with mixed feelings. Had the Guild's frenetic work been devoted to merely enhancing its role in Vulcan's Dance? She could see no sign of the strange silver sticks stored in the Master's study. It must be part of some wider game.

Orelia caught the similarity between Hag and Fury. Scry, honorary member of the Apothecaries and chair of the Lazarus Night Committee, had excelled herself in seeding omens for Wynter's return.

'Orelia?' She recognised the voice: Ember Vine, the town's outstanding sculptress and an occasional browser at *Baubles & Relics*. 'Talking shop in your own shop can't be much fun. Could you drop in – I've a problem to share?'

Orelia's politically inquisitive visitors had dwindled to a trickle and she needed energising. Ember Vine might be fifteen years older, but her Bohemian outlook made her a kindred spirit.

'Say, Monday at nine?' added the sculptress.

Orelia caught an unfamiliar thread of angst in Vine's voice. 'If it's politics, I wouldn't waste your time. I'm not going to win,' she said. 'You must know that.'

'I trust you, and so do others. It's a more important commodity than you realise.' She lowered her voice. 'But it's not about politics; at least I don't think it is.'

'Monday at nine, then,' Orelia agreed, as Vine melted away into the crowd, as if anxious not to be seen with her.

Nearby, Mrs Finch, having caught sight of her estranged husband, put an arm around their son and nestled closer to Snorkel, just to deepen the wound.

7.30 p.m. Families placed their fireflies on the launching runnels, watching the flight, awaiting with trepidation the scorers' marks. High above, Jones had the impression of a shattered stained-glass window doubled in the river's reflection.

Everthorne sat on a canvas stool with his sketchbook, well back. Everyone else sought proximity; he craved the open view.

7.59 p.m. In contrast to his private life, Boris was a model of exactitude on Guild business. He fleetingly registered a dislike of the First Chord's swollen body and narrow head, which resembled a well-fed tick, before applying the lighter-stick to the fuse.

No other firework in Rotherweird's experience had surged a hundred feet straight up, propelled by a jet of red flame, before pausing and repeating the movement, until, high above the crowd, it burst into a crimson crown, sparks flying as if forge-fresh.

The crown sundered, transforming into elegant silver letters:

Fatherly Wonder

Surely the mortar was spent? But no, the letters rearranged, silver turning gold:

Herald of Wynter

'Winter, winter!' cried Rotherweird's children, waving and clapping.

Estella Scry rubbed her hands in glee; if only *he* were here to admire. 'I do so love the old spelling,' she said to her neighbour.

Boris had no time to reflect on the *double entendre*; displays required quick-fire performance. He preferred multimedia 'gags' to mere 'colour and bang' as with his opening shot, *Pot Pourri*, whose slow streamers in lavender-blue and faded pink drenched the audience in fragrance. With similar surprises, the Guild's display proceeded to its climax, Vulcan's Forge.

Tiny lights from the Polk Christmas decoration box winked green in the weave of Jones' basket. *Time to go.* He leaned over the edge and held the lighter-stick against the main fuse, which sputtered brightly – and went dark as intended: within a protective sheath, a guard against the elements, flame raced along a network of tiny tunnels, sparking sub-fuses as it went.

Despite a detailed briefing from Boris, Jones had forgotten this feature. He saw only a dramatic opportunity for gallantry. Using his lighter-stick as a boathook, he hauled the forge towards him. Subsidiary fuses offered a wealth of alternative ignition points. Leaping like a salmon, he grabbed the rim above Vulcan's hammer – a mistake, as the plywood structure yawed under his weight and the divine blacksmith, anvil, hammer and furnace came to violent life.

Below, the attendant Fireworkers gaped in disbelieving horror as the forge swung to and fro, with Jones silhouetted in a miasma of explosive colour. By contrast, his adolescent charges from Form VIB went delirious.

'Greg-or-ius! *Greg-or-ius!*' they screamed in unison, until the Town Crier joined in with a swiftly composed tribute:

'Gregorius was a candle,
Gregorius was a spark,
Gregorius liked to dangle,
Enlightening the dark . . .'

Still clutching the lighter-stick, Jones contrived a prodigious flip back into his basket, landing head-first, legs flailing, clothes and eyebrows a-smoulder. The forge stabilised, Vulcan regained his dignity and the Guildsmen hastily moved the basket as far from the forge as the wire would allow.

No lasting damage had been done: the god in all his illuminated glory raised his hammer and struck the anvil, covering the sky in molten snow.

Boris hurried to the hillock behind the main display where the Last Chord stood. The First Chord and the aerial forge had raised expectations to unprecedented levels and he feared anti-climax.

He muttered a prayer and lit the fuse.

Boris need not have worried. *Apocalypse* rose without any whoosh, explosion or visible flame, silent as an ascending angel, here one moment, gone the next – until, higher than all its predecessors, a single effulgent light appeared and split into eight. Boris' imagination ran riot. *The eight grim signs of the Apocalypse? Have I launched a Doomsday device?*

Evidently not: the points of light resolved into letters and a mysterious summons.

FOLLOW ME

The crowd gaped in puzzlement. What was the Last Chord saying: *Watch me* or *fly yourselves* or *support the rocket's unknown creator?*

The first letter fell in a lazy arc to hold position some sixty feet up, lost shape and flared bright as a beacon. Slowly in a pre-ordained sequence, the other letters followed, the next at the edge of the Island Field, and the rest further and further away: the firework was pointing a path.

The crowd obeyed, first stumbling, then picking up pace, the children leading the chase. Nobody gave up or broke away, even the strong-minded; Orelia, Valourhand and Everthorne all succumbed. Only Gorhambury, wary of where the path might lead, tried vainly to stem the tide.

Jones watched the surge. He waved and yelled, but to no avail; he had been forgotten – out of sight, out of mind. After his recent out-of-basket experience he decided to wait. Perched on the tiny stool, he reverted to his new discipline.

Inhale. Exhale. '*Quid faceat* ... ho, ha ... *laetas segestes* ... ho, ha ...'

Several stanzas later the basket jiggled. 'Jones, you up there?'

The gymnast peered into the gloom. The silhouette suggested a young man in urgent need of deportment lessons. 'Obbers?'

'We'll get you down,' bellowed Oblong, but the horseshoe-shaped gadget holding the vertical chain to the lateral wires had no obvious catch that he could see; he'd have to disengage and fasten it to the windlass to haul the basket down. The rest of the populace were already crossing the footbridge over the tributary at the edge of the Island Field and heading further south.

He fumbled and fiddled, but the link held fast.

There was a *snap* in the air ...

'Get on with it, Obbers!' brayed Jones.

Another *snap* – wing-beats – and Panjan alighted beside him. Oblong had never seen the bird up close, but according to Boris and Ferensen, Panjan's misfit appearance belied a sharp intelligence. Panjan directed Oblong's attention to an S-shaped link above the horseshoe by pecking at it. Oblong released the catch with the aim of connecting to the windlass, but woefully misjudged the pull of the balloon. Desperate to anchor it, he snaked his right leg round the chain – only to join the ascent. A rising breeze swept Oblong, Jones and the basket in a westerly direction. Panjan, apparently satisfied at this unhappy turn of events, launched into the night.

'What the heck! *Obbers?*'

But Oblong wasn't listening: terror at the vertiginous drop revived his dismal memories of Bolitho's funeral, further aggravated by the painful chaffing of the glacial chain on his inner thigh. He groaned quietly to himself.

Above, Jones' concerns quickly shifted to his involuntary passenger. He heartily shouted instructions: 'Hold fast! Bear the weight! Lean in! Good man!' As they accelerated, he attempted reassurance. 'The altitude's settling, we're not bound for the moon.'

They might not have been bound for the moon, but the looming shadows of the escarpment and Rotherweird Westwood drew ever closer.

11

Planetarium al Fresco

An inbred desire for novelty drove the townsfolk on, their excitement intensifying as each of the eight letters – the eight *beacons* – spluttered and failed. The Winterbourne stream served as a hikers' path in the dry summer months, but, now a vigorous brook, it halted the march. Beyond, the final beacon had settled over an open meadow hemmed in on three sides by woodland. On the far bank a rope fastened to staves surmounted by carved heads – Comedy and Tragedy in various guises – cordoned off the meadow. They had reached their intended destination.

In the centre of the meadow stood a giant barrel with arms protruding like the branches of a tree. The first arrivals shouted encouragement to those behind.

As ever, rank determined position. 'Space for Mr Snorkel,' hissed Sly, pushing aside ordinary citizens to make way for the former Mayor and his retinue, including the ubiquitous Mrs Finch. The Apothecaries retaliated, pushing their Master into the front row, flagged on either side by Scry and Strimmer.

The crowd *liked* their Headmaster and made way for Rhombus Smith and his wife, and then Gorhambury and the other Guild Masters. Behind, parents lifted children onto their backs while the tallest onlookers obligingly kept to the rear. Boris removed his Master's robe in a patch of thick cover and joined the throng.

Orelia sat on a knoll some way back; her view unobscured. The structure's shape bore an uncomfortable resemblance to the tree by the mixing-point.

Everthorne joined her and whispered, 'Someone has taken a great deal of trouble.' She felt him inhale her hair as he withdrew. His fingers splayed across both knees, elegant, despite the strong forearms, and spattered with charcoal.

'Draw it,' she said, 'when it fires.'

'Fireworks are hell to paint. To catch the essence – I mean that fleeting existence from ignition to splendour to nothing – you have to go abstract.'

He showed her a sketch from his pad with the head of a lighter-stick, a whorl of stars and a spent casing, all fractured and merging with each other.

Valourhand had no interest in spectacle: the structure and rope meant a display, and a display required *operators*. She left the crowd and leaped across the stream into the woodland beside the meadow. Coiled roots and fallen trees made progress slow.

Gorhambury examined the structure through his telescope; it bristled with cones and other irregular shapes. Smelling a serious breach of the *Firework Regulations*, he summoned Boris.

'Well, Mr Polk?' he asked in his formal mayoral voice.

Boris borrowed Gorhambury's telescope. 'Call it a launching pad,' he said. 'It's expertly done, but nothing to do with us.'

'We should cross the stream and disarm it,' said Gorhambury. 'It's illegal.'

Boris pointed out two more structures, one on either edge of the meadow, the dim shapes half-merging with the trees beyond.

'It's more for enlightenment than entertainment, if you want my view.'

'We should not be sanctioning rogue events, however sophisti-cated, Master Polk. I'm surprised at you,' whispered Gorhambury.

Boris responded with equal formality. 'On occasion,

Mr Gorhambury, you have rightly recognised a public-interest exception to our *Regulations*. This is another. We should look and learn.'

Gorhambury was spared a decision as smoke started pouring from the central structure, followed by a numinous haze which gave the impression of cosmic dust. The crowd fell silent. A sphere took shape, blue with ribboned clouds: a planet emerging from Chaos as seen from space. A second smaller sphere, no bigger than a cricket ball, collided with the first in a loud explosion and another swirl of dust – from which a tailed body emerged.

'Comet!' cried several children.

Scry's face contorted, half astonished, half ecstatic. She had her confirmation: this display could only be Fortemain's, so her quarry was there to be despatched at the due time.

Valourhand, keeping to the edge of the wood where the under-growth was lighter, stopped. Through the trees stood a wooden model of a tall rock, fashioned from light canes and canvas, with an open circular hole at the peak. It resembled the rock she and Oblong had seen in Lost Acre. As she looked, fireworks flared along its contour, only to fade away as the structure collapsed. Simulta-neously, a replica of the same rock flared into life at the opposite edge of the meadow, but remained in place.

Fanguin blinked: the last page of the monk's narrative had been dramatised – only the henge had *moved*, not vanished. But he had no time to reflect, for Bolitho's tree launched a dark shape which moved from horizon to horizon, swallowing a series of coloured aerial shapes as it went. Then high-spinning Catherine wheels trans-formed to umbrellas as the sky wept to the sound of artificial rain.

Apocalypse had one last trick: the penultimate beacon reignited, followed by its companions, no letters this time, just blazing lights and an unequivocal message: time to go home. Overhead, as if on cue, dark clouds began to build.

*

Valourhand passed where the henge had been. The structure's joints had been blown by tiny charges. A figure rose from the nearby undergrowth and darted away.

She had never chased someone so fleet of foot. Her quarry ran, jumped and sidestepped in the unrelieved darkness. They climbed for a mile and the pace never slackened. With the advantage of her tube-light, she kept in contact until a stand of oaks halfway up the escarpment, where she abruptly found herself alone.

She tiptoed round the clearing, spent leaves crackling beneath her feet. She classified telepathy as a physiological fact, not a mystical gift: a tuning between minds, electricity discharged by one brain and picked up by another. So now: her quarry was watching her. She twisted round.

He made no attempt to hide. Sitting on a low bough, a study in nonchalance, he was more beautiful than handsome, a mix of knowingness and innocence, Adam after the Fall. As to his age, she had no idea.

He slipped down, landing as gracefully as a cat. He wore long shorts, almost to the ankle, and a loose shirt. The laced boots looked curiously old-fashioned.

'Hey – stop!' she cried as he bounded away, and this time not even Valourhand could keep up. Bramble brakes, thick pockets of fern and half-submerged rocks hampered her on these higher slopes, but he jinked effortlessly over, round or through them all.

She dropped to her haunches to get her breath back. *Where does he live? Where's he heading?* Belatedly she remembered Orelia's description of the treehouse on the Rotherweird escarpment and the young man who guarded it. That explained his speed. He knew the way.

Everthorne thanked Orelia for her company and trudged off homewards. He seemed sullen and unsettled, but she reluctantly concluded that only he could exorcise his demons. She felt adrift, a failure personally, politically and spiritually. Life had felt worthwhile with Slickstone as a resourceful *known* enemy, but Calx Bole's wiles were intangible. She felt disengaged from everyone and everything.

Tube-lights and lanterns were flickering prettily along the Island Field as she joined the Polks, who were bemoaning the absence of Ferensen when they most needed him. The final display must have been Bolitho's work, operated from underground, they agreed.

Fanguin joined them. 'That book Bolitho left me . . .' he said. 'Well, it ends with an account of the comet's last millennial visit. The author was an eleventh-century monk and he founded our church. He records the henge vanishing in foul weather – but what's its relevance now?'

Nobody had an answer, and Fanguin re-joined his wife.

Boris raised a different query. 'The last sequence, before the umbrellas – the dark cloud swallowing all the other effects – anyone have any ideas?'

'How about Calx Bole, killing and changing appearance as he goes?' suggested Orelia.

Finch murmured, 'I agree with our illustrious candidate. Bolitho is obsessive about Bole, but he wouldn't just tell us what we already know. The cloud absorbed the green light but did not extinguish it; it moved on, absorbing the red light – and again *keeping* it . . .'

Boris glimpsed Miss Trimble some way behind and beckoned her over, feeling a pang of guilt. Invisible in his Master's gown and absorbed in his work, he had not acknowledged her until now. She gave a small wave back – and disappeared into the crowd. 'Damn,' he muttered to himself.

Finch continued, 'If Bolitho was being literal, the dark cloud consumed four different colours – which gives us *four* murders. We know about Ferox and Flask, so – two more. Who were they?'

'Slickstone,' suggested Bert, but Orelia shook her head.

'No, his death was different,' Finch agreed.

Orelia recounted her visit to *The Agonies*: Vibes must be another.

'Who was that becoming young man with the sketch pad?' Finch asked Orelia, in his old-world roundabout way.

Bert answered for her. 'He's called Everthorne; he's an artist.'

'Why do artists always look like artists?' mused Finch.

'He's the grandson of Castor Everthorne,' said Orelia, trying not to sound defensive.

'He's out of sorts,' said Finch, adding, 'it takes one to know one.'

Nothing express had been said, but Orelia caught a hint of suspicion in the *politesse*. Boris provided a pithy defence. 'He's helped us, he's kind, he has his grandfather's talent, and he was attacked by a Fury on Aether's Way.'

Above them, the final beacon flickered and Boris jumped. '*Jehosephat!* I *completely* forgot Jones – he's still up there!' he bellowed, and took to his heels.

Only, he wasn't.

When they reached Vulcan's forge, stained with gunpowder and yawing in the rising wind, Jones, basket and balloon were gone.

Strimmer had watched Tighe watching the fireworks with her distinctive mix of knowingness and wonder. He sidled up and whispered in her ear, 'Fancy a nightcap?' She gazed at him as a stranger might, more bafflement than rejection in her face. 'Pomeny, I'm talking to you.'

'I'm working on my fisherman,' she said at last.

'Your *what*?'

'My mechanical – the fish pulls him in, it's that big.'

'I'm not in the mood for games. You coming or not?'

'Come and see when it's ready.'

But for the crowd, he might have struck her. Instead, he transferred his attention to the pretty linguist.

'First reserve?' she responded tartly.

'New favourite,' countered Strimmer, loud enough for Tighe to hear, and the linguist laughed.

'Enjoy your evening,' replied Tighe cheerily.

At that moment, even Strimmer, for all his insensitivity to others, wondered what had afflicted Pomeny Tighe. Had her loyalties switched back to Snorkel? Surely not – but why lose interest in him at the climax of their campaign? Her lack of engagement made no sense.

Miss Trimble trudged home. She was more observant than Boris gave her credit for. The physique beneath the Master's gown had unmistakably been Boris. Nor did she begrudge his commitment to his duties. She was cross with herself: she had failed a test of nerve on seeing him with the Herald, an electoral candidate, the former Head of Biology and the brother to whom she had yet to be introduced.

Minutes later, Gorhambury asked her to ensure no children strayed between the Island Field and home. She readily agreed, *that* was her proper station.

I 2

Fall of the First-Born

The changelings slept in hammocks, each marked with a name embossed in a leather tag, on the top floor of the treehouse. Portholes provided ventilation. There were bathrooms at each end, with pipes running into a sophisticated sewage system designed by Fortemain and improved over the centuries.

In Tyke's absence, the changelings had withdrawn, locking the trapdoor to the rooms below and extinguishing all lights save for slow candles above the bathroom doors.

The Mance remained the most mobile and dextrous: he could stand on his hind legs like a man and run on all fours like a dog. His claws might not grip, but they could drag, pull or turn, and he had a highly refined sense of smell. Only the set of jaw and eyes hinted at his more complex ancestry. Black curly hair covered his body, with straighter, finer hair on his face.

An unnatural acrid scent had woken him. He pulled the blanket off with his teeth, clambered onto the bedside chair and pressed his nostrils to the porthole. The scent was moving closer.

As he stepped down, the floor shook violently as a beam end swung free from the ceiling. The Mance hooked open the trapdoor and dropped through – just as the frame split. It felt like a shipwreck: the hull shattered by rocks as their workbenches, tables, bookbinding gear, all their cherished possessions, slid through a gaping hole in the planking of the floor below.

Around him, the dormitory disintegrated, a slow candle fell and fired the floor and the screaming started.

The Mance weighed his choices. He could not climb back through the shattered ceiling, so his friends would have to fend for themselves . . .

A winged changeling with an arrow through the throat fell into the workshop, howling in pain, its skin smoking and dissolving . . .

The Mance suppressed his human side and engaged the animal. *Think for yourself. Forget sentiment.* He leaped through the widening chasm to the ground below. A large bat-winged creature wheeled above him, bow in hand, unmistakably a child of the mixing-point: an Eleusian returned.

As the fire took hold, the massacre took on a garish glow.

Jones steered the basket towards the blazing tree as planks and beams cascaded down. He heard unnatural cries of panic and saw the Fury soaring and diving around the blaze.

'We're going in, Obbers!' he cried with martial *brio*, but Oblong did not hear.

His ankle, the back of his knees, his upper thighs and his arms throbbed from the chaffing of the chain and they were still too high to jump.

'Obbers!' screamed Jones again, and this time Oblong caught the sound and raised his head. He half thought it hallucination: a giant moth with a bow circling a guttering candle. Then he saw the falling planks and beams. How could arrows bring down such a structure?

The basket was moving at a stately pace and the primitive rudder made steering cumbersome. Despite their vulnerable position, Gregorius Jones – now Gorius of the XX *Valeria Victrix*, legion of Imperial Rome – elected for counter-attack. He braced his legs, thrust his left arm forward and grasped the lighter-stick – or rather, his *pilum* – in his right hand. *Javelin time.*

Oblong, below, felt powerless. He could not fight, alter course or defend himself.

The Fury wheeled away towards them, loosing an arrow as she did so. The elastic skin of the balloon had sufficient give to keep the glass phial in the shaft intact, even as the tip of the arrow pierced two of the balloon's three chambers. The basket started falling as a second arrow struck the chain securing Oblong. He caught a whiff of corroded iron as the links sundered and he plunged into the treetops, now just a few feet below. The branches of an ancient cedar cushioned his fall to the escarpment slope.

Oblong's departure levelled the basket, and, as it cleared the trees on the escarpment edge by inches, Jones took advantage. Achieving balance in this brief moment of relative stability, he hurled the lighter-stick. The Fury shrieked as a third arrow ruptured the balloon's surviving chamber, sending the battered basket into a topiary hedge in the walled vegetable garden.

Jones clambered out and ran towards the blazing remains of the treehouse. To his horror, Oblong's distinctive silhouette appeared, clambering up onto open, level ground. Above, the Fury wheeled about and closed on the dazed historian. It had exchanged bow and arrow for a stiletto in each hand.

Jones knew his own speed. He would not reach Oblong in time.

Panjan came from nowhere, a scissor-dive, claws extended, wings tucked in. Like a crow mobbing an eagle, the pidgeboy rolled and wheeled, giving his adversary no time to settle. The Fury shrieked again, an ear-splitting cry of primal rage, and flailed with her knives, but Panjan gracefully eluded them and harried the creature out beyond the valley rim. Soon, both were out of sight.

Jones cast an expert eye over Oblong. Grazes crisscrossed cheeks, forehead and hands, but he detected nothing deep and nothing broken. 'Clean yourself up, Obbers,' he said. 'Nothing like a slap of cold water!'

'The basket started falling, as a second arrow struck the chain . . .'

Oblong, still dazed, trailed his blistered fingers through the stone water trough in the garden wall.

'Splish, splash and no moping,' added Jones heartily.

The reprimand echoed Valourhand's rebuke after the attack on Lazarus Night – that attacker had favoured stilettos too. The connection shook him from his torpor. 'I have a light,' he said, struggling to extricate the tube from his pocket.

Jones grabbed it. 'Stay here while I check for survivors. Keep out of the firelight – and zigzag if the Fury shows up, not that I'm expecting her. Grand display by Panjan.'

'Yessir,' stammered Oblong, without irony.

Jones let the tube-light fade – better safe than sorry – and loped towards the wreckage at the optimum speed for acceleration or evasive action. Split-seconds divide the living from the dead.

The smoke puckered the nostrils, redolent of scorched timber and burned flesh. Nothing approaching a room remained. Jones listened for the quickened breath of survivors, but heard nothing. He shook the light. A spool of cotton dangled from a bough; a small iron vice protruded from the ash. The Fury had destroyed a workplace as well as a home. Remains scarred the wreckage: not people but *creatures* – here an outsized wing-bone, there a scaly foot. Even as he watched, flesh dissolved, leaving no torsos, only extremities. Spent arrows littered the ground.

At a rustle of bracken Jones spun around.

A young man with striking looks materialised. He looked desperate. 'Thank you for trying,' said the stranger.

'You are . . . ?'

'I live here. I left them unguarded.' He sifted through the ash. 'We must build a pyre.' He set about collecting the wooden remnants of his home. Jones had built a pyre to pay tribute to Ferox, better than mumbled words over cold ground. He joined in as

Oblong materialised and, to their astonishment, Valourhand. Jones, Valourhand and Oblong introduced themselves.

The young man's voice barely held. 'I am Tyke, and these were my charges. They lived here for centuries, blamelessly binding books.' He grimaced. 'Do not blame yourselves. Your presence would have made no difference.'

Valourhand stepped into the firelight and produced a bow from behind her back, ebonised wood carved with fantastical heads. In her other hand she held a single arrow, the glass phial in the shaft still intact.

'Yours,' she said, handing them to Jones, 'but watch the arrow, it's armed with acid.'

Oblong had seen Jones, standing stock-still in the falling basket, his arm outstretched, aiming the lighter-stick like a spear. His throw must have dislodged the Fury's bow and arrow, which explained the creature's recourse to knives. And Valourhand – whose presence he could not begin to explain – had found the weapons and awarded them to Jones as spoils of war.

Valourhand's analysis probed deeper. She discounted Jones' length of throw – he was a PE teacher, after all – but his accuracy had been *uncanny*. Her presentation was as much trap as tribute, and Jones fell for it, unstringing the heavy bow in a single expert movement.

Valourhand broke a difficult silence with familiar directness. '*How* did it know where to come and *why* did it come?'

Jones' stock had risen as a man of action, but not as an analyst; she put her questions to Tyke and Oblong, who half-answered the second.

'Wynter liked omens and prophecies, and his servants want to please. We've had "someone will come before me"; we've had Lazarus Night and that "pricking of my thumbs" business, we've had a star in the sky, and now ...' Oblong stopped, baulking at the tastelessness.

'No time to be squeamish,' said Valourhand.

'It's the Massacre of the Innocents,' he muttered, 'or the first-born.'

Valourhand saw more than Biblical connection in this mass-murder. Wynter's acolytes did not want the first – *failed* – experiments to sully their master's return. She continued her forensic enquiry. 'What does Wynter need to return?'

'A body and a mind,' replied Oblong.

'Tyke?' she asked, which made Oblong wince – the poor man had just lost his home and his friends, hardly the time.

Jones remained silent, working on the pyre.

'I'm a nothing from the mudflats of London – what do I know?'

Valourhand might be drawn to Tyke, but she did not tolerate evasion. 'You've met Wynter.'

'I exchanged words with him once.'

'Orelia told me you survived the mixing-point.'

'Survived? I did not say that.' *I'm a freak in my way*, he appeared to be saying.

Valourhand felt his calmness like a knife. *Why didn't he rail against Wynter? Why wouldn't he say more?* 'Where were you from originally?'

'I remember Old Father Thames and the mudflats of London,' Tyke replied softly. 'I remember Malise – he came in search of children. I remember Wynter. Mr Oblong is right: he needs a mind and a body,' he added.

And both were atomised, thought Valourhand. *We're getting nowhere . . .* 'How did Panjan track down the Fury?' she asked Tyke.

'Panjan is from the mixing-point, so he would have sensed her.' He paused. 'Fortemain rescued Panjan, as he rescued all of us.'

Valourhand developed Tyke's answer. 'Panjan lived with Bolitho in Rotherweird, so he knows Ferensen, Boris, Salt – everyone who matters. He carries their messages. So, Bolitho gives him to Boris for safekeeping because he, Bolitho, is going to be needed elsewhere – but who else is Panjan in contact with? Who else does he serve?'

'He serves only his friends,' Tyke replied.

The loyalties of the poor, thought Oblong, picturing a scene of six-teenth-century estuarial decay, muddy urchins scuttling for filthy scraps in the flotsam. These denizens of the foreshore would have had their own code, their own argot, their own leader. Tonight, Tyke had lost his family.

Tyke pointed down to the valley below, where scintillas of light jostled along the Island Field. 'Stragglers,' he said, 'but the gates won't stay open all night. You'd best hurry.'

'Ah yes, what happened? Where did that firework take you?' asked Oblong.

'Not now,' replied Valourhand. 'We'll explain on the way.'

'Up for a jog?' asked Jones, asinine heartiness restored, but Valourhand ignored him.

'What about you?' she asked Tyke.

'The Mance is not here.'

'The Mance?' parroted Oblong.

'More dog than man, a survivor, like Panjan,' he explained. 'I must find him.' He gave a shallow bow to the fire and was gone.

Valourhand took command. 'Set the pace, Jones, but remember, Oblong is pigeon-toed.'

'Just like Panjan,' countered Jones loyally, giving Oblong a sup-portive punch on the shoulder.

As Jones ran, memories of the *pilum*'s versatility flooded back: you needed four to frame a hide for a tent; three for a tripod; two for a stretcher and one for a walking staff. He thought of what he had gained and what he had lost, then turned to counting his steps to oust these echoes from another life: *Unus, duo, tres, quattuor, quinque* . . .

Or was he in fact striving to banish the thought prompted by his first aerial view of the valley or, more particularly, the view of the marshland east of the river? It had felt too grotesque to be believable, *but* . . . A *speculator* had to trust to instinct, and instinct said he was right. He shuddered at the thought of a terrible secret which *nobody* should know . . .

Behind him, Oblong reflected on the end of the changelings and the vicious cruelty of the Eleusians. Valourhand thought only of Tyke's remarkable dancing feet.

Jones called a rest at the foot of the escarpment. Valourhand updated them on Vulcan's Dance, its sequel and Finch's subterranean adventures. 'Don't go writing this down, Oblong!' she concluded.

The air felt uncomfortably close, an unseasonal humidity building as if the heat of so many exploded fireworks had been harvested by the heavens to be returned with interest. Valourhand mentioned the display's closing scene, a sky filled with spinning umbrellas, and they hurried on.

Recent History

2005. *Switzerland, winter.*

The clientele, women of a certain age and would-be class, come here in sleek, chauffeur-driven cars with smoked-glass windows. She takes the U-Bahn and a bus, then walks. The road runs straight, the view a layering of colours, dull green pasture giving way to grey rock and snow. The white porticoed house stands alone outside the village, incongruous in a landscape dotted with functional farm buildings. It has its own meadow, filled in early summer with blue-purple lupins the colour of veins; she knows because they crowd the brochure cover, below the cod shield and Latin motto.

The waiting room is pristine but soulless. Picasso lithographs adorn the walls: bullmen eyeing women half their age – rich bullmen, presumably. She flicks open a magazine: diamonds on a sable fur on one page, a tiny cut-glass phial on the other with a name from myth.

She is from a different universe. She wears neither jewellery nor scent. Her shoes are laced; her skirt a dull beige pleat. But she has an aura, sufficient for the receptionist not to question whether she has the right address or, if she has, the means. The expensive pen helps, as does the ornate, educated script. She writes *Nona Lihni*, an exotic name for such an unassuming woman.

The consulting room is in like style, save that Picasso gives way to Chagall, floating figures in a dreamy blue.

Dr Obern rises from his desk and proffers a hand, elegant and fastidious as you might expect for this work. His gaze unpicks her, feature by feature. In his long professional life, he has never encountered such *dowdiness* in a prospective client.

'You would be beautiful?' he asks, the smile sufficient to reveal perfect teeth – another service they offer.

'I would be unrecognisable and inconspicuous.'

Dr Obern blinks. A criminal on the run? It does not seem possible. 'That will require work,' he says.

In his mind, his silver-tinted instruments slice, pull and stitch. Skin stretches, eyes change colour, even bones reshape.

No one will know her in Rotherweird, not Estella, if she still lives, not even the Potamus.

Hide in plain sight, the only way.

DECEMBER

I

Avant Moi, le Deluge

At three in the morning the rain came, instant and hard, barging into the valley. The wind would not settle, spinning weathervanes, slamming windows, soughing through the streets. In the southwest corner the miller and his sons, roped waist to waist, valiantly dismantled the sails before the gale could shatter the brake and tear the mill to pieces.

Little penetrated the Snorkels' first-floor bedroom. At high cost to the public purse, drainpipes had been diverted to neighbouring walls and eaves extended to protect the Mayor from 'intrusive rain patter' – uninterrupted sleep meant sound decision-making, and therefore, municipal health.

Meanwhile, at 3 Artery Lane, the cacophony in Oblong's attic bedroom was deafening as the skylight juddered and pipes gurgled and spilled. Below, Everthorne woke to the more muted *slip-slap* of rain on cobbles and the dull drum roll from the rickshaw taxi roof beneath his window. *A job for charcoal*, he instantly thought.

At *The Polk Land & Water Company*, where Boris had installed a system of whistles to identify defective gutters and downpipes, a ghostly chorale added to the din of the storm.

Elsewhere in town, water hurtled through a labyrinthine network of drains to subterranean reservoirs and, within hours, to overflows on the eastern rock face below Grove Gardens. Gargoyle faces, long masked by ferns and ivy toadflax, cleared their stone mouths and belched water onto the shore below.

Only one citizen greeted the deluge with enthusiasm: Gorhambury's *magnum opus* on the town's exterior fittings would now be tested – though not above ground level, for the roofscape had exceeded his reach. 'Ladders and rods,' he muttered to himself like an excited schoolboy, 'ladders and rods.' In galoshes and a knee-length waterproof he summoned the Sewage and Drainage Departments for 10 a.m. sharp: a call to arms which met with modified rapture.

Wrapped in a black silk dressing gown embroidered with stars, Estella Scry sat at her bedroom table painting her fingernails a light mauve as the tempest rattled the windows. She mumbled portentous words with a common stem and shades of meaning:

Vigil, a period of purposeful sleeplessness, waiting for the moment of death, and the eve of a religious feast. Her wait had been all of these: the Vigil of Wynter. Seeds sown long ago would blossom and fruit in perfect sequence, that was the dream.

Vigilance, alertness to danger and absence of complacency.

Vigilante, a citizen who compensates for the inadequacy of current enforcers, always self-appointed. Moulding the Apothecaries for this role had given her deep satisfaction. Her own vigilante action had also prospered: within a day of exposing herself to the telescope in the marsh and allowing the cell to be found by Fortemain, she had seen Finch in the street. His rescue confirmed Fortemain's presence there, *buried deep*, exactly as Wynter had said.

So much for the present, but pieces of the past nagged at her still: Wynter, bent over her bed holding a sheaf of Fortemain's papers entitled in Bole's distinctive writing *Straighten the Rope*; and that overheard fragment of conversation between Bole and Wynter in the passage outside her bedroom and Nona's opposite. *Tell her about the fastness.* But tell *whom*? *She* had been told nothing. The Herald's copy of *Straighten the Rope* contained nothing more than arcane diagrams of a four-piece puzzle sphere. Was the 'fastness' Finch's cell? And if so, *why did it matter?*

Fastness or not, Fortemain, having seen the rock steps, would return to investigate – so she had work to do, and quickly.

The old resentment, that she had been kept from the 'where' and 'how' of Wynter's resurrection, flared again. She had enjoyed disposing of Bole's familiar, surprised on the roof of Escutcheon Place, yet she had seen no sign of Nona or the Potamus – had the Resurrection Project failed? Had the centuries sapped their will or found a way to strike them down?

If so, she knew her duty. She would rule in Wynter's likeness.

The Tower struck by lightning.

Judgement.

The Empress.

2

Of Waterworks and Rocks

The countrysiders did not come, even though they traditionally sold the week's best produce on Sundays. In such conditions, those braving Market Square forgave the aberration.

Mutterings on Monday turned to pithy curses when the gates opened as ever at six, but admitted nobody. Larders were developing visible gaps.

After thirty hours of relentless rain, the Rother broke her banks and Gorhambury diverted half his workforce to clear the driftwood damming the river.

'This weather is beyond coffee,' said Ember Vine in a warm *mezzo* voice. 'I'd rather be tucked up in a four-poster with a handsome man than legging the streets.'

Orelia envied her *joie de vivre*; from anyone else, this might have sounded coarse, but not from the sculptress.

Vine's daughter, Amber, arrived, still in her dressing gown, bearing mugs of steaming beef *consommé*, which Vine liberally laced with Vlad's best vodka.

'We'd vote for you, if we were allowed to,' said Amber. She had promising ugly-duckling looks and the lazy energy of the adolescent: Ember and Amber, quite a combination.

'She could do with a father around,' observed Rotherweird's only single mother as Amber slammed the door shut. 'As could I.'

'Strange fireworks,' murmured Orelia.

'And prescient in the matter of umbrellas,' Vine added, 'but what do we make of the rest?'

Orelia retreated into small talk. 'I hear Amber carves too.'

'The young are better at ambiguity. We get set with age, like it or not.' The conversation danced around an undeclared subject, but Orelia was happy to wait. 'Your friend Everthorne has a rich talent, although it's not yet as honed as his grandfather's – have a gander in the Gallery if you've never been. Castor Everthorne's spatial awareness was second to none.'

Unlike most Rotherweirders, Orelia had been to the Gallery, though only once. 'Good thought,' she said, and meant it; Castor's work might fill in the detail of Everthorne's troubled inheritance.

Vine put down her mug. 'Have you ever done a truly confidential sale?'

'Valentine's Day,' replied Orelia, 'but it's less the present than who it's for.'

Vine did not smile. The effervescence had vanished. 'But not to someone you can't see for the fog, who disables your front door lamp, who has money to burn and who pays *exactly*, who wears a contraption to disguise his or her voice, who warns "all is secret on pain of death" and who collects from an obscure drop-point at midnight?'

Orelia had an uncomfortable premonition, which Vine quickly confirmed. 'I've carved unknown rocks into strictly prescribed shapes. They're for a puzzle rather than decoration. The rock *tingles* in the fingers. I'm rubbish at science, but there's energy there – kinetic, magnetic, one of those. I'm worried about what the assembled whole might do.'

'How many pieces?' Orelia's question suggested she knew *something*, but it had to be asked.

'Sixteen. The pieces are multi-edged and quite small. Assembly was beyond me, and the interior is fiendishly complicated, but they clearly fit together to make a sphere. The curved surfaces were a giveaway. I didn't keep copies because I was afraid to.'

'Could you draw me one or two?'

Vine's sketches resembled doodles in the manuscript workings in *Straighten the Rope*.

'You've seen them before,' Vine added: an observation, not a question.

'I have, or similar, but only in drawings – and, yes, they do have a purpose, but what that is, I've no idea.'

Vine gave Orelia an appraising stare. 'I don't want to know what I shouldn't, but I don't want lies either.'

'It *is* a sphere,' Orelia confirmed, 'and it spins, and when spinning, it may alter the state of things.'

'What things?' asked Vine.

'Truly, I don't know – but you're right, it's not going to be for the better.'

'Those strange fireworks featured a cosmic impact – that's how new rock types are made. Were they mined from beneath our feet, I wonder?'

If only Vine were in the company; she had intuitively grasped the pieces' significance without knowing anything. She would contribute and enrich . . .

Vine picked up an alabaster piece from her workbench. 'I'll give you a memento to explain your visit – just in case I'm being watched.' She placed the small abstract, a ball with a whorled centre, in a box lined with wood shavings. She even scribbled a receipt. 'Carry it visibly, but not obviously,' she asked. 'You came to collect. "On pain of death," the client said, and I believe him – or her. You understand my caution. I have a daughter.'

3

A Morning at the Pictures

Rain still teemed from a sky dark as fresh slate; only the wind had eased.

Up to us, then, Orelia had said, but Valourhand taught classes and Orelia had no legitimate reason for visiting in school hours, so Vine's news must wait. By mid-afternoon, with the streets near-deserted and little prospect of business, she could at least act on the sculptress' advice.

Everthorne stood perched on a ladder in the hallway of 3 Artery Lane, a brush behind each ear, a third between his teeth and another in his right hand, with the paint-box balanced in his left. On opposite walls he had added the lettered messages from the First and Last Chords, exact in colouring and script, and was now painting the spinning umbrellas in the night sky above the Winterbourne stream. Everthorne had assumed the role of town chronicler.

He removed the brush in his mouth and asked, 'Who needs artistic licence when real events so tickle the eye?' He had lost the dourness of the previous evening.

'Are you up for a walk?'

He descended the ladder and methodically packed up. 'To where, pray?'

'Our art gallery: you to pay your respects, I to refresh my local knowledge.'

Everthorne dived into his room and emerged in an ancient dogtooth overcoat, collar turned up: the artist's crafted scruffiness.

'Grandfather's,' he said. 'Sad to sully it with an embossed compli-mentary umbrella.' He twirled the umbrella to display Snorkel's personal arms embossed in gold. 'Mayoral largesse never comes without strings.'

She laughed and pointed the way. The rain threading off the rims of their umbrellas proved too heavy for conversation.

Rotherweird's leading institutions – the School, Library, Town Hall and Escutcheon Place – boasted impressive exteriors, but not her only art gallery, which had been squeezed unceremoniously into the northwestern wall.

Ember Vine's work dominated the reception area, the charcoal natural history studies enhanced by the sculptress' three-dimensional physicality, but other artists did not sustain the early promise. 'No heart,' muttered Everthorne, as room after room offered chromatically clever but soulless abstracts, or townscapes more accurate than creative . . . until the topmost room.

The plaque above the doorway read: *Camera Castor Everthorne.*

Directly opposite, between two narrow windows, hung a large oil painting entitled *Theseus Lost.* True to its title, it illustrated a journey through a multitude of archways and fragmented passageways, not unlike Rotherweird's tunnels. A fractured candle heightened the impression of odyssey and disorientation: a hero lost.

Everthorne stood stock-still, eyes fixed on a second large painting on the adjacent wall: *Incarceration.* Finch had noted that the shapes were different from, but similar to, those in Escutcheon Place's damaged copy of *Straighten the Rope.*

Everthorne turned to *Theseus Lost*, eyes darting from one detail to another. 'It's a narrative – forget Theseus the hero; he's a man all at sea. It's a self-portrait.'

Orelia pointed to a faint line running through the brushwork. 'Look! Tiny Roman numerals by the doorways—'

'He used a pin.'

The numbers jumped from one archway to another with no

apparent rhyme or reason. 'From where to where is Theseus going?' asked Orelia.

'There is no place of arrival. We call it the vanishing point.' He described art's most celebrated example. '*The Hunt in the Forest* by Uccello shows hounds and hunters vainly scouring a dark forest, which recedes forever with the unsettling suggestion that their quarry is invisibly present in their midst.'

As he was speaking, the Curator, a retired schoolteacher wearing a shapeless smock and highly polished shoes, shuffled in. She had a refreshing directness. 'Few make it to the top – but then, you are the great man's grandson.' She shook his right hand with both of hers.

'You've hung them well,' Everthorne said with a charming smile.

'They're too strong for company, so they have this floor to themselves. As to why they're up here, we have the Town Hall to thank. They disliked him because he lampooned them.' She turned towards *Incarceration*. 'He spent two weeks in solitary for disorderly conduct – if you visit the prison, you'll find similar shapes still there. They must have inspired him.' She pointed at *Theseus Lost*. '*That*, however, is a mystery.'

Everthorne returned to *Incarceration*. 'Not quite solitary,' he said, producing a finely carved wooden mouse from his pocket. 'This is an heirloom. According to family legend, he and the mouse became inseparable and left prison together.'

Artistic banter continued between Everthorne and the Curator while Orelia moved between the two oils. She sensed a connection between them, but she could not articulate it.

They returned to the reception desk, where she bought cards of Everthorne senior's two oils. The Curator added a free bonus: a dim photograph of the cell carvings, from stock supplied by Denzil Prim.

'I'd avoid cards,' said Everthorne gently. 'The colour is never true and the *impasto* doesn't show.' He sat down in a chair by the desk and sketched the carved mouse without a misplaced line, distinctly his grandfather's mouse and no other.

He gave the drawing to a beaming Curator. 'He's yours and only yours,' said Everthorne. 'May he bring you good fortune.'

In the street Orelia patted him on the back. 'That was kind.'

'It's the least I can do – she's given my grandfather the afterlife he deserves.'

The artist's desire for permanence, she thought, *one pressure I don't have.*

The atmosphere tightened between them, both debating the taxing question of whether the mutually attracted should progress. Everthorne made the move, dousing her immediate hopes while promising a future. 'When this weather abates, I've a snippet of family history to show you – art history of a sort. It requires an excursion upriver.' He kissed her on both cheeks, his hands resting lightly on her hips, and playfully rubbed her nose with his as he withdrew. 'You're good at earthing the lightning,' he added, 'which is a rare gift. I'll come when the sky has colour again.'

Slow, quick; troubled, at ease; intense, playful; razor-sharp or disengaged; she could not read him – but at least he did not do 'conventional'.

Frustration prompted a desire to assert herself. 'Bring your sketchbooks!'

He raised a hand of acknowledgment as he strode into the gloom.

4

Bruma

Valourhand engaged her eidetic memory. After every night at *Baubles & Relics*, mulling over Bolitho's workings in *Straighten the Rope*, she returned and recreated two pages, pinning the results to the driftwood decorating the walls of her room, so she could flit from one to the other, just as the author had done whenever new learning emerged.

The puzzles had a multi-dimensional quality – by discipline (maths, physics, geology, astronomy), by detailed subject (dark matter, comets, unstable molecular activity, changing physical states, magnetism), and, most brutally, by time. The jottings followed the *Zeitgeist*: pages revisited as learning progressed. Topographical maps added another evolving layer. Many appeared to be of the same place, but the visible features did not fit any known part of the Rotherweird Valley. The ancients had delved into subterranean Rotherweird, so why not Bolitho? The shaded shelves looked like strata, and, according to Oblong, Ferensen had encountered Fortemain conducting underwater exploration in a self-designed diving suit.

One thought engendered another: small numbers preceded by an 'r' had been placed next to many of these geological maps, together with calculations of force and resistance: Richter scale measurements for seismic waves, Valourhand surmised.

With nothing but half-clues, Valourhand decided to pursue an unexplored avenue. The late hour and hideous weather offered a perfect opportunity for the visit. She pulled a wet-weather skin over her working clothes and climbed the roof outside her window. She made a difficult vault, a double, to the top of the North Tower perimeter railings and pulled herself onto the Quad buildings without mishap. Moisture swirled about her and the roof slates glistened; she felt at home.

Unwanted chattels littered Fanguin's study, including a full-length mirror, whose damaged frame leaned against the wall beside his desk. An inverted human face appeared there, part-obscured by the curtains of rain. Fanguin undid the catch, allowing Valourhand to slide in like a seal, drenching the carpet. Reacting with the unflappable tolerance which had so endeared him to Form IV, he tossed her a towel.

Valourhand did not procrastinate. 'Where's the book Bolitho gave you?'

Fanguin fished it out of a drawer. 'It's a lifetime's nature record, quite brilliant in its time, but mundane now. They traipsed all over England and ended up here. A pagan henge vanished in a storm of – I quote – "apocalyptic intensity" and they – these two monks – took it as a sign and founded our church. That's how it ends.' Fanguin paused before raising a troubling detail. 'It ends this book, and it ended Bolitho's display last night.'

Valourhand squinted at Fanguin suspiciously. How could he know, when he had never been to Lost Acre?

'Really? How?'

'See that word, *nictitans*? Sharks have a *membrana nictitans*, a third eyelid: it means winking. Our monk describes the henge as a winking man – and Bolitho's disappearing rock had an eye, remember?'

'I've seen the identical rock in Lost Acre. If Lost Acre and Rotherweird did emerge from the same impact, you'd expect similar rock formations. It's slender like a stack, so extreme cold – or an earthquake – could easily shatter it.'

'We have that word too when they describe this special storm.' Fanguin pointed. '*Tremor.* But he doesn't say "shattered", he says "vanished". And in Bolitho's display, the henge shape went from one side of the Winterbourne stream to the other.'

'Meaning from one *world* to another?' queried Valourhand, still defeated by the multi-faceted calculations in *Straighten the Rope*. 'But what would Bolitho want to transport from here to Lost Acre?'

Since his ignominious departure from the School, Fanguin had lived in permanent fear of being marginalised. 'Any recent events I should know about?' he asked.

Unreliable he might be, but unconventional thinking had value. She decided to share. 'You saw our Herald is back.'

'And shot of his ghastly missus—'

'*Pay attention*, Fanguin. A Fury took him to a cave in the marsh where he was quizzed about town bigwigs – and *Straighten the Rope*.'

'*Which* Fury – Leather or Feather?'

And Fanguin's back, she thought. 'Feather, he thinks. Anyway, he's rescued by Bolitho, who's a half-mole with an underground home: telescopes, kitchen-dining room, even his own private railway, driven by magnetic forces.' She omitted the attack on *The Agonies* as irrelevant to their present conundrum.

Fanguin, under pressure to perform, shuffled the facts and examined them from all sides. A troubling question came to him: why would Bolitho devote decades to building an observatory in the marshes when he had one in town?

'You say he has telescopes?'

'Finch says they're sophisticated, *Cycloptic*'s best. He even saw the hidden comet through a special lens.'

Fanguin waved his arms in excitement. 'Listen: from his early days Fortemain wants to explore Lost Acre's inverted sky – what astronomer wouldn't? But nobody could build an observatory in Lost Acre; quite apart from the practicalities, it's far too dangerous, and he's on his own. So, what does he do? He plans to transport the terrestrial one.' He patted *De Observatione Naturae*. 'This was his, remember.'

'My money's on 1017 as the year of the vanishing henge,' Valourhand added. 'It's the year in the frescoes, a millennium ago. The *Chronicle* entry concentrates on Midsummer, but didn't it also talk of a terrible winter in Rotherweird? Does your monk mention any other special effects?'

'Ice, hail and a battle of the clouds – he calls the clouds *incus maior*, a greater anvil.' His finger followed the Latin.

Valourhand pointed. 'And *bruma* – mist, maybe?'

'The grammar doesn't fit.' Fanguin had not previously read the text with such close attention, but fragments of childhood learning were returning. Virgil's *Georgics* allowed three months for planting winter barley from the Autumn Equinox to— 'It's a contraction,' he added, 'for *brevissima die*, the shortest day.' He exploded into life. '*Bzoom, bzaa!* Lost Acre had its cyclical crisis on the longest day – but *we* have ours on the shortest, *bruma*, the Winter Solstice – which is the day of the election, as fixed by *Regulations*, which appear *after* Wynter's death. I call that coincidence stretched to breaking point.'

'But why go to so much trouble?' Valourhand asked.

Fanguin was on a roll. 'The election clears the way. The *Regulations* say everyone – *everyone* – has to be on the Island Field for the result.'

'But how could they guarantee there *would* be an election?'

They looked at each other. They might have outsmarted Snorkel in securing the election, but had they been used in a grander design? 'That bastard Bole is always one step ahead,' muttered Fanguin.

Valourhand opened the window. 'I'll tell the others.'

Rain swirled into the room. 'You're barking, going out in this,' said Fanguin, 'and the wind's up again.'

'It doubles the fun.' She gave a cheery wave and disappeared into the night.

Fanguin checked his bat detector. Nothing yet, but a foul night often preceded activity from near *The Clairvoyancy*. Hitherto the signal had travelled eastwards towards the marsh, but on the night of Vulcan's Dance, the trace had headed southwest from a different part of town with no obvious suspect, unless you included Gorhambury.

Leather and feather: double the fun.

5
Paper Trail

'Pssst!'

Oblong dismissed the hiss from the shadows as a special effect induced by the rain.

'Psst – *Oblong!*'

He peered into a gloomy side street, fast-flowing rivulets breaking around his boots.

'To the *archivoire*, seth he, two by two, as the finch flies.' The cryptic, peremptory order was a giveaway.

'Finch!' But to Oblong's acute disappointment, the Herald strode straight past his welcoming hand and headed towards the Golden Mean. Oblong followed Finch's crablike route to Escutcheon Place at a distance, where, for once, the front door stood ajar. Oblong entered and closed it. The Herald's sodden outer clothes lay draped over the banisters; his boots had been kicked across the hall.

'*Frau Finch geflogen ist,*' explained Finch, ushering Oblong into the *archivoire*, as ever illuminated by the great slow candle. A pair of heavy gloves rested on the central table. He gestured for Oblong to sit and delivered a résumé of his adventures. 'Imagine a slimy prison, and a bulldozing moleman breaking through. Imagine his trench-life: boards, tunnels, telescopes, cocktails and mud.'

Oblong always found conversing with Finch taxing. 'You met a moleman?'

'Oblong! In *The Journeyman's Gist*, remember? Miss Roc rootling out the truth? Mr Thorburn's Plate: the mole.'

Oblong thought of his own claustrophobic journey. 'Keep going.'

'I met Morval Seer. They have stripped her of speech.' Pain furrowed Finch's face before he returned to the practical. 'Forte-main alias Bolitho alias the moleman has an errand for you and you alone.' He placed a particoloured sphere, little bigger than a cricket ball, on the table and nudged it with his forefinger. 'Turn again, Whittington.'

The ball spun lazily, master of its own momentum, the spots of colour elongated by the rotation.

'What does it do?'

'I haven't the rainiest.' Finch pulled on the gloves, held them to the candle until the palms steamed, gripped the sphere, top and bottom and twisted in opposite directions. Faint indented inter-locking lines scarred the surface like a three-dimensional jigsaw, only to vanish the instant Finch released the pressure.

'*Shut sesame*. You can mark them off, the four pieces from the opening pages of *Straighten the Rope*,' he explained.

'You said an errand?' asked Oblong apprehensively.

He was not alone; not knowing the errand's purpose had left Finch equally uncomfortable. 'Assume it's dangerous.'

Paradoxically, the mention of danger enthused Oblong, keen to impress after recent setbacks. 'I'm game,' he said.

Finch took an exaggerated breath. 'You're sure?'

'What do I do?'

'You toss it in the mixing-point at dusk on Election Day. He was most particular about the timing.' Finch placed the sphere in Oblong's pocket and conjured up a bottle, two glasses and his familiar biscuit tin: prelude to an apology of sorts. 'Rifle and rum-mage . . . you were right, Mr Oblong, the records do hold the key.'

Drinks poured, Finch moved to a lit alcove. Towers of books littered the table, some open, some shut, all marked with Finch's telltale paper strips. 'I swam with scarlet herrings,' he started, 'the Eleusians, Oxenbridge, the trial, Ferensen – *until* I encountered

Rotherweird Hall, now the Hall of the Apothecaries.' He flung out a melodramatic arm. 'Our tale is a two-hander: Sacheverell Vere, man of means and a desiccated Puritan, meets a master carver. My sources for this drama: carving permission requests, a transformed private home, a Guild's founding charter, the *Popular Choice Regulations* and my multiple-great-grandpater's record of a meeting with a colonel from Hoy . . .'

'Finch, just the story, please, in plain English, *once upon a time* . . .'

'In 1646 the introverted Mr Vere, owner of the Hall, secures permission for a hidden coffer to protect his coin. This is how the woodcarver gains his introduction – carving permission request, left-hand pile with the blue marker. Carving requests for the Hall multiply like rabbits – witness the yellow markers. Many are elaborate in the extreme and all are morality tales: wise virgins, the lost sheep, a barren fig tree; you get the drift. The carver becomes a long-term presence in the Vere household.'

Oblong opened the books to find pages and pages of applications, filed, dated and numbered; the ink now a yellowing sepia.

Finch continued, 'The carver sucks Vere from his shell and propels him to high office as Rotherweird's first Mayor. Vere publishes the *Popular Choice Regulations*, but they're drafted by our carver. Witness: the manuscript first draft as retained by Escutcheon Place – that's the freestanding document in the middle there. The childless Vere founds the Guild of Apothecaries, a society of scientists of Puritan disposition, and bequeaths the Hall to them: see his will, the black marker.' Finch deployed his supporting documentary exhibits with the manic *brio* of a conductor. 'And still the carvings multiply. They come in groups – witness the red markers – and always a generation apart: 1751–9, 1814–1820, 1867–1893, 1909–1914 and 1980–1991. Religion disappears and scientific subjects take over.' Finch slipped in the deadliest fact without emphasis. 'They're all by the same hand . . .'

'Finch, come on!'

'He leaves letters like footprints,' Finch explained, 'a florid capital R and an oddly tailed C, all the way through.' He showed Oblong the letters; they did match and were distinctive.

'This is Bole's house style. The Apothecaries gave him a base for centuries.'

'But Bole isn't a carver—'

Finch impatiently drummed the table top. '*Who* was found strangled twenty years after Wynter's execution?'

The detail had emerged at Ferensen's celebratory dinner. 'The carver who built this room,' he stammered, 'Benedict Roc, Orelia's distant relative.'

'Hours *after* his body was found, you may recall, our good friend Bole – now Roc's spitting image – gained admittance here to remove the stones. But, *question*: how would Bole know where to find their unfindable compartment? Horror of horrors, Bole steals *minds* as well as physical shape. He absorbs his victims' *knowledge* and their gifts. Bolitho's worked this out: that's why his dark firework consumed the others but kept their lights. That dark elusive shape was Bole.'

They sat and stared at each other.

'He's here now as a carver?' Oblong asked.

Finch shrugged. 'There's been neither hide nor hair of him since the 1990s.'

'What about Flask?'

'A later victim.'

'He changes shape at will, then.'

'Not necessarily. The sequence we know about goes: Roc, Flask, Ferox, Vibes – and none have appeared after their successor is first seen. So, I reserve judgement.' Finch looked careworn. 'Bole's cause-and-effect machine is unstoppable. We're doomed, Oblong. I wouldn't mind being a bat-finch. I could hang from the rafters – good for my gippy back.'

'Nothing is unstoppable.' Oblong's rallying call sounded feeble.

He had been infected by Finch's depression, two solitary men seeking solace in an exercise which only emphasised their adversary's resourcefulness.

He refilled Finch's glass, fitting in another small brick. 'So, the R and C stand for Roc?'

'R and C with nothing in between – classic Bole, cryptic as ever.'

'What about these?' He indicated the last unexamined pile, huge volumes, roughly bound, with unadorned numbers on the spine.

'The green strips mark Bole's leases: always basements, always in The Understairs. The names change, but the writing doesn't, and R and C are always the first initials.'

A mischievous wink illuminated Finch's face as a salving idea occurred. 'They're all now occupied, save one, which is condemned. Fancy a stroll?'

Action alleviated depression. Oblong leaped to his feet and embraced the Herald. 'Onwards!' he cried.

Arms and feet squeezed back into sodden sleeves and dank boots, they re-emerged to face the storm, its savagery more evident in the gutterless Understairs. Cascades from opposite roofs pummelled the centre of Hamelin Way. Flowerpots blown down from above spattered the cobbles with orange flashes. Finch leaned into the rain, head down, like a dog on the scent.

The place turned out to be part-condemned. Slivers of light broke through the twisted shutters on the higher floors. Narrow steps slick with moss led to a half-basement and a padlocked door, the surface blistered and colourless. Finch descended, Oblong on his heels.

'Standard municipal,' boomed Finch dismissively through the din of the rain, producing a skeleton key and a small tin labelled *Polk Multi-Purpose for Doors, Burglars and Cyclists.* 'Pick and squirt, pick and squirt,' sang Finch to himself, and within moments the padlock gave way. The door, jammed in the architrave, succumbed to a vigorous kick from Finch.

A deep chamber greeted them. Two rough-hewn stone pillars supported the ceiling. Expecting damp, they inhaled instead the dry fragrance of old timber. Finch shook his tube-light. 'Easy, we're walking on dead skin.'

Layers of wood shavings, grey and curled with age, overlaid a choppy sea of broken floorboards. Finch gingerly picked his way to the centre, wood shavings sticking to his damp boots or slipping through holes in the floorboards. He pulled from his pocket a pierced pebble attached to a length of string and lowered it through the largest hole. He waggled the line and dropped it deeper until the clink of stone on stone echoed back.

After retrieving the stone, he removed his boots, lay on his front, eased himself forward and cleared the broken boards. 'Ankles!' he commanded.

Oblong gripped a pair of stridently odd socks as Finch's torso twisted out of sight, a tube-light clutched in one hand. The ensuing commentary was not informative – 'Aha!', 'Hmm . . .', 'Look at that—', and 'My, my . . .' The bellowed, '*Up!*' came as a blessed relief.

Spangled in cobwebs and dust, Finch announced his findings. 'A path below joins the tunnels one way and is blocked the other. And, dear boy, a heavy masonry hammer sits on the ground right beneath us.' Finch's eyebrows danced. 'What a *very* busy bee our carver is!'

Finch crawled to the far corner where a rotten sack had spilled wooden pieces; on closer examination they found pieces of a tower and a sloped roof. Finch picked up a tiny carved bird on a rotating weathervane.

'Truly a master,' he said, spinning it. 'This is a gift for any century. You'd earn a living all over in the world, and you'd have access to the rich anywhere.'

'Joseph was a carpenter,' mumbled Oblong, now alert to mystical connections.

'We're done here,' Finch replied bluntly. Oblong had never

worked him out: he could be avuncular, but at other times he was distant and severe.

But back in Escutcheon Place after a silent journey, Finch, a lonely man who could recognise loneliness in others, opened up. 'I thought husband and wife were meant to say nicer things to each other than to anyone else,' he admitted. 'With us, it became the opposite, and that sits on my conscience like a crow.'

'I've not had much success myself,' replied Oblong. He gaped as Finch extracted – or appeared to extract – a coloured paperweight from his left ear.

The atmosphere lifted as he handed Oblong a slim book. 'Borrow this – it's better than it looks.'

Better – was Finch referring to content or morality?

The binding, black as coal, declared the slim volume, *Conjuration and the Ancient Art of Legerdemain*, to be from Wynter's collection. Finch added a bag of props – cups, balls, a wand and the like.

'Nothing's new in the world. Dr Faustus had a conjuring stick,' he added.

6

To Believe or Not to Believe

Strimmer saw himself as a victim of *déjà vu*. Sir Veronal had assigned him an unspecified role in a new Rotherweird. Now Estella Scry had done the same, but with this difference: Scry served another; Sir Veronal had served only himself. But *whom* did she serve, to what end? And when would he be told? To ask outright struck him as subservient, so he wrote, playing his one card with characteristic directness:

Dear Miss Scry,

I have a most unusual book on which I would welcome your expert opinion. But I would not be seen dead in your shop. Suggest time and venue, if interested.

He signed off his letter with the same words which Sir Veronal had used to him: 'Kind regards'.

The reply came by return.

Enter by house door, 5 Gordian Knot, midnight. If the book is Elizabethan or connects with Sir Veronal Slickstone, be sure to protect against this invasive damp. Estella Scry

Strimmer's hackles rose. Midnight! Was Scry propositioning him (God forbid) or planning some bizarre ritual? But the second sentence tantalised: why would she suppose he might have obtained the book from Sir Veronal? The 'Elizabethan' reference he considered equally bizarre – why be so selective about protective measures? Would not a first edition of the *Principia Mathematica* or a lost Leonardo *Codex* be as deserving?

He obeyed, and at midnight to the minute, with the book swaddled like a newborn baby, he arrived at 5 Gordian Knot to find the door unlocked. The Spartan interior had a timeless, pristine quality and none of the dispiriting knickknacks that so disfigured the shop window of *The Clairvoyancy*. Expensive monochrome rugs on the landings spoke of wealth, but nothing else.

The upper door stood ajar. 'Do come in, Mr Strimmer.'

The décor remained spare, the only light provided by the silver eight-sconced candelabra in the centre of the table, its twirled arms branching from a stem populated by Bacchic heads and serpent tails. Sir Veronal had also preferred candles, Strimmer recalled, clasping the book tight to his chest.

A bolt slid across and a ceiling trapdoor in the room's far corner swung down, admitting a halo of candlelight. A shoe appeared, tied with ribbons, followed by a lower leg in a white stocking, and the hem of a dress, deep scarlet velvet slashed to show off pink silk. The figure, her back to Strimmer, descended the stairs set into the wall to floor-level. A spangled fabric netted her hair above a white starched ruff.

Strimmer stood in shock at this flesh-and-blood visitation from the past. The woman turned. Her face was alabaster-white; jewels adorned ears, fingers and neck; cochineal flushed lips and cheeks. She gestured to Strimmer to sit beside her. A finger crooked and twitched. *Show me the book*, it said. Only then did he grasp that it was indeed Scry.

He unbound *The Roman Recipe Book*, declaring knowledge gleaned from Sir Veronal as his own. 'It was bound in 1572 or thereabouts by the Hoy Press.'

'Was it now?' said Scry.

He caught in her face a fleeting look of disappointment. Had she hoped for a different volume? 'Sir Veronal Slickstone judged it useful.'

'Did he now?' said Scry.

She flicked through the pages, her face suffused with nostalgia. Occasionally she rubbed the paper as if to seduce it into speaking. She looked decades younger, a trick of the light or the make-up, or both.

Her voice assumed a cold, no-nonsense tone. 'You will now listen without interruption, for this is a privilege with no equal in the world. Rotherweird hides a natural phenomenon, a mixing-point where matter mixes and merges. With special stones and cages you learn to control the process. This book holds the details of what can be done and how.'

Plausible, thought Strimmer, *familiar creatures on one side, amalgams on the other, with coloured circles – the stones? – and the bars.* 'Where is this place?'

She ignored the question. 'The process confers great longevity. Mr Wynter discovered the mixing-point and we mastered it with him – then pygmies interfered.'

Strimmer struggled to focus: Scry, in a costume from God knows when, talking of a time long past. Scry had fashioned his emergence from a coffin, crowned like an ancient emperor. Was the *Herald of Wynter* firework her creation too? The cards she had dealt included the Emperor. This abundance of connections did not, however, make her sane.

'Where is this place?' he asked again.

'Now is not the time, and don't go looking. Show patience, and your rewards will come.'

Strimmer turned petulant. 'You can't reveal and then withhold the proof.'

His pitiful rebuke decided Scry: he must learn the hard way. 'If you agree to my terms, leave the book,' she said, her voice calm, 'and if you don't, take it – and the consequences. Follow me up after five minutes.'

Scry left the way she had arrived, climbing the steps in the wall.

Five minutes to the second later, Strimmer followed into her bedroom. Her dress lay draped over a four-poster bed; shoes placed neatly on the floor with their owner nowhere to be seen. One of the four floor-to-ceiling windows swung open, banging against the sill. Damp air flannelled his cheeks. He struggled to comprehend: she had removed her clothes and asked him to follow?

He stepped through the window onto a modest platform with carved owls on the corners, no rail and a sheer drop. Moisture misted his spectacles. *Where the hell was she?*

Then he heard a *whoosh, whoosh*, with a *snap* mixed in, like an umbrella rhythmically opening and closing. He crouched at the edge of the platform and peered down into the unlit space between *The Clairvoyancy* and Scry's front door.

The creature did not rise; it soared to face him. In the moment before he fell, every sense was assailed by this mythic horror: the hag from Vulcan's Dance bathed in a putrefying stench: a feathered, beaked face with Scry's cheekbones.

As he hurtled towards the street he felt a violent punch to both shoulders – and blacked out.

Strimmer recovered consciousness draped over the platform like a sacrifice. His glasses were miraculously intact; his sodden clothes clung to his skin. His shoulders ached front and back. He stumbled back to the bedroom. Her clothes were laid out as before; there was no sign of Scry. Descending to the sitting room, he noticed a single framed photograph of a jagged-edged sculpture which must have stood directly opposite. The marks on the carpet confirmed its one-time presence.

He left the book.

He would be part of this unknowable future.

7

Voices from the Void

The following morning Oblong encountered Jones, running from quad to quad.

'Warning signs abound, Obbers, yet we do *nothing*. I'm talking manly action,' declared Jones, puffing out his chest. 'I am taking a trip to the marsh.' He wore his 'knight errant' expression, a known precursor to disaster.

'The marsh is not a marsh, it's a lake, and, even if it were a marsh, nobody goes there, it's far too dangerous.'

'Unguided, yes,' agreed Jones.

Oblong reconsidered. Bolitho's subterranean kingdom must indeed be under threat, and the thought of rescuing Morval Seer tickled his romantic disposition. 'When do you suggest?'

'Leave that to the weather.' Jones paused. 'We shall have change.'

Oblong peered at Jones. His banalities opened doors and triggered solutions. Where had this madcap runner come from? What did he *know*? 'I'm game,' he replied, the same word he had used when accepting Finch's mission.

At first light next morning, the deluge abated. Slates, cobbles and windows had carried the rain's staccato beat for so long that the silence felt both ominous and relieving. Moisture scarfed the town like gauze and penetrated deep, bypassing waterproofs, umbrellas and chimney cowls. Fires sputtered and smoked; and still the river rose.

The quiet woke the South Gatehouse sentry. He flipped open the single shutter above the entrance gate, piled high with sandbags on the landward side. The parapet of the bridge had sunk from view, with only the stone birds standing proud of the flood, fantastical waterfowl caught at the moment of take-off.

But the rain had relented.

He barged open the narrow door to the embrasure above the portcullis. Miniature waves ran towards him at intervals, and from the direction of the Island Field, halos of yellow green light materialised – tube-lights, illuminating featureless silhouettes apparently walking on water. As they closed, the jumbled shapes resolved into boxes and crates stacked high, and a dark line emerged: the deck of a floating platform, supported on barrels, and tall poles rose and fell. Near the Gate, its crew moored the strange craft to a stone griffin, and a single coracle cast off.

A vacuum-driven Lamson tube-system linked the Town Hall to the two gatehouses, but the glass cylinders, sealed with corks, were rimed with dust, so rarely were they used. The sentry struggled to remember the mechanics.

Gorhambury, already at his desk, colour-coded paperclips at the ready, was struggling to deal with reports on flood-levels, food, sand and sacking reserves, methane and barometric pressure. He uncorked a pithy message: *Alien craft approaching South Gate*. Gorhambury, prone to take such reports at face value, dismissed the 'alien' as hyperbole and hailed the Town Hall rickshaw driver.

'Top speed to the South Gate,' he said.

'Ghostly, ain't it,' said the sentry on Gorhambury's arrival.

'It's a raft following a coracle, meaning it's one of ours,' Gorhambury replied. 'Raise the portcullis.'

'But – Mr Gorhambury!' stuttered the sentry as the temporary Mayor started shifting sandbags; Snorkel's lofty rule had imbued civic staff with the belief that Mayors *never* dirtied their hands.

A countrysider, a handsome farmer with a regular market stall, clambered out of the coracle and splashed along the parapet. He wore long rubber boots, an elderly knee-length waterproof coat and a cap. He walked through the Gate and shook Gorhambury's hand.

'We thought you might be needing supplies,' he said, 'so we've fruit and veg and what we could get from Hoy. They've not delivered to the Ten-Mile Post, thanks to the weather. It's been hell on the lower pastures.'

Gorhambury felt humbled. Nobody had spared a thought for the countrysiders, their winter crops or marooned livestock. 'What do we owe you?' he replied, but the farmer shook his head.

'You owe nowt but recognition of who we are and what we do.' He gave Gorhambury a wink. 'Thou'd do t'same for us, no doubt. We've a condition or two: we deal with you and Miss Roc, to be sure of proper distribution. And we do it in The Understairs, not Market Square.'

'Be a good fellow,' said Gorhambury to the rickshaw driver, 'and get Boris and the charabanc, pick up Miss Roc on the way, then find *Sewage & Maintenance*. Last but not least, get the Crier on board – figuratively speaking.' He hated unintended puns; they afflicted proceedings with levity.

Within the hour the charabanc had arrived and the platform was docked and unloaded, while the Crier, bell tinkling, spread the good news in iambic pentameter.

By nine o'clock the mist obligingly eased. Orelia opened proceedings. 'We are in your debt,' she told the countrysiders. 'Hell and high water, and still you remember us. I hope we'll return the compliment.'

The countrysiders, men and women of all ages, dispensed advice to those who sought it. 'You best sow spinach in August, sprouts in April, and parsnips in May.'

'Kale tastes sweeter after frost.'

The Understairs tenants, growers from seed in their high window boxes and rooftop patios, engaged most.

A young man with a wheelbarrow barged his way to the front. 'Order for Mr Snorkel!' he barked. Before he could read out a lengthy list, Gorhambury stopped him. 'No proxies. If Mr and Mrs Snorkel want a share, they can come themselves.'

'I'll get the boot,' whined the servant.

'Tough,' replied Gorhambury, surprising himself.

An Apothecary came next. 'This is unlawful canvassing, Mr Gorhambury, and a disgrace,' she protested.

Gorhambury maintained his forthright approach to dissenters. 'It's *charity* work – *their* charity.' He indicated the countrysiders. 'You or Master Thomes are welcome to help, as is Mr Strimmer – a second delivery is expected shortly.'

She flounced off.

Bendigo Sly dismissed the proceedings as a naïve stunt, with one proviso: Miss Roc had a natural warmth which her opposition lacked. Not as dangerous as charisma, but the quality remained an asset. If Vlad could bottle its essence, his master would benefit from a liberal swig. He concluded that Strimmer remained the greater danger, but Roc should be watched.

8

Phony War

The company had experienced just such a lull approaching Mid-summer, with no visible hostile activity – then enhanced by warm weather, now by dispiriting dampness and a world purged of colour. The Island Fields reacquired its blotchy complexion as the waters subsided, but only slightly. Tangled driftwood rather than riverbanks still delineated the margins of the Rother.

Oblong visited *Baubles & Relics* after closing to find Valourhand ensconced with *Straighten the Rope* and Orelia relaying the fire.

'Yes, Mr Oblong?' Orelia greeted him stiffly.

'No, thanks,' added Valourhand as if dismissing a travelling salesman.

Oblong persevered, achieving a stunned silence as he placed the sphere on Orelia's desk, where it turned and turned of its own volition. 'I thought you should see this.'

'Let me guess,' said Valourhand. 'The moleman gave it to Finch to give to you to put in the mixing-point on the Winter Solstice. He chose you as the man least likely to attract attention.'

Upstaged again, Oblong mumbled, 'Something like that.'

Orelia reappraised Oblong. He had shared his mission, when she had not shared hers from Vibes until forced to. He deserved better. 'We believe it's going to transport Bolitho's observatory to Lost Acre,' she told him. 'Everyone will be on the Island Field for the election result, so it'll be safe.'

'But should I do it?' asked Oblong.

'Any move by Fortemain will be for good,' said Orelia.

Valourhand belatedly entered the fray. 'Well . . . I'm not so sure. He's concerned about the seismic effects, but believes the river will soften the blow. But he's also concerned that if this millennial technology were abused, it could destroy the town. The river, you see, can only absorb so much shock.'

'Well, all things being equal, I've agreed, so I'll do it.'

He's changing, thought Orelia, *slowly but surely, just like Gorhambury – he's more his own man.*

Strimmer, in contrast to the company, was unsettled by the absence of *friendly* action. Scry's transformation validated the mixing-point's existence and, in Strimmer's eyes, its vast untapped potential, but he sensed another transformation. The Apothecaries had been energised, direction added to intellect, but Master Thomes would divulge nothing.

'They were *my* cards, Mr Strimmer,' he parroted whenever they met.

Scry maintained her distance too, so he must again, as with the wretched Oblong, tap the unwary.

The fog swallowed houses and humans alike; only gaslight conferred definition at night, as in the arc encircling the Apothecaries' Guild Hall, Strimmer's chosen point of ambush.

'As a candidate, I'm keen to understand hard-working professionals,' opened Strimmer, but his stilted pitch fell on stony ground, to judge from the target's bewildered reaction. He moved on hastily, 'including neglected academics like Mr Fanguin.'

'You're here a lot these days, Mr Strimmer,' replied Mrs Fanguin suspiciously.

Avoid direct questions, thought Strimmer. 'Your Florentines are irresistible.'

A good-looking man, thought Bomber, wondering how deep the coldness went. 'Mr Fanguin is indeed seriously neglected,' she replied, taking the bait.

Strimmer reeled her in. 'Vlad has opened a small bar on Aether's Way – how about a quick Winter Warmer?' He had no intention of risking an encounter with Mr Fanguin in *The Journeyman's Gist*.

Unbeknownst to him, the offer had a like attraction for Mrs Fanguin. Anonymous at work and excluded from her husband's projects, she felt a visceral pleasure at the prospect of sharing a drink with a stranger – not that he could be interested in her *that* way, not at her age. 'Why not? It's on the way home.'

Vlad's new bar overlooked Aether's Way through ogive windows. The tables for two were each set with a single candle; no beer, Vlad's spirits only. The back wall shelves held a gallery of cut-glass bottles as multi-coloured as their contents. Strimmer decided on sloe gin.

'I'm afraid the Apothecaries are neglecting their duties to the North Tower,' he began. 'They appear to be distracted.'

'They're making as well as designing,' replied Mrs Fanguin. She leaned over a little. 'They're brewing, too.'

'I bet they don't tell you what they're making, they're that secretive.'

'I have eyes, Mr Strimmer. Silver sticks – ceremonial sticks, no doubt, to celebrate your victory.'

'I'm a physicist among many, but Mr Fanguin is the best biologist we have.' Strimmer had intended this offhand compliment as small talk, but a deeper significance struck him, for it happened to be true. When the mixing-point became available, Fanguin would have his uses. Socially, Strimmer loathed Fanguin's tweedy *bonhomie*, but the mind had always been sharp.

'He needs work desperately,' said Bomber.

'Muster me votes, and he'll have it,' he said.

She had nothing else of value to give, but tramping back to the North Tower, he mused on the silver sticks. Thomes might do cheap ceremonial, but Scry would not. *Whose design for what purpose?* he wondered.

Orelia's part in the countrysiders' relief brought more visitors to her shop, and belatedly, policies formed. She would establish a complaints procedure to curb both excessive pricing and excessive criticism of reasonable pricing. Countrysiders would be represented. She chanced on the argument that a falling-out between the two communities would risk an appeal beyond the valley boundaries, jeopardising the valley's very independence; a price *nobody* could afford.

That concern gained some traction. Strimmer, when challenged, refused to engage, while Snorkel, his finger ever to the wind, backed off.

'Not my suggestion,' he said. 'I believe in all for one and one for all.'

Several Guilds combined to present to the countrysiders a life-sized mechanical as a token of their gratitude.

In the marches of the night, a disturbing thought seized Orelia: she might even win.

9

The Thingamajig

After the tandem ride, Miss Trimble's work seemed humdrum and her pokey flat a lonely place. She feared her hesitant performance after the fireworks had closed her horizons once more.

But Boris kept his word. 'Angel,' he had typed, clumsily leaving the 'a' off Angela, 'six-fifteen tomorrow, Travel Company, please. I need you. Boris.'

The ambiguity of the last sentence provoked a tingling sensation, only for Boris to greet her with a disappointingly chaste kiss on the cheek.

'I'm sorry about Vulcan's Dance,' he said. 'I couldn't join you but I can't say why.'

'You don't need to. Your hood stood up on your hair, and your shoulders – well, they're very much yours.' When Boris blushed, she said quickly, 'It's me who should be sorry. I just couldn't face your friends.'

The apology baffled Boris. *Let it settle*, he decided. He seized a tin of *Polk Multi-Purpose* and ushered her to a large shed, the door fastened with a rusted padlock. He rubbed the shackle with steel wool and squirted the oil into the lock. A key labelled *The Thingamajig* completed the exercise.

'I've never seen it myself,' said Boris, picking up a lantern made of multiple tube-lights. Six huge circular leather containers occupied the shed's far wall, each chock-full with stone balls twice the size of a marble. Each set of stones had its own distinctive blotchy colour.

'Votes,' muttered Boris. 'But where—'

Necks craned and they gasped in unison at the bizarre silver device suspended from the ceiling. It resembled two huge wide-brimmed hats sewn together: a central rim with a symmetrical bulge above and below the centre. Four rotors had been fixed to the rim's edge, equidistant from each other.

'It flies?' asked an incredulous Miss Trimble.

Boris had studied his grandfather's drawings. 'And some. Let's bring her down.'

A makeshift system of turnbuckles lowered *The Thingamajig* to within a few feet of the floor. It measured a good six yards across, and had apertures on the side to accommodate piping to feed in the voting balls.

'Where does she go?' asked Miss Trimble.

'She loads up in Market Square and announces in the Island Field.'

Miss Trimble stooped to examine the lower surface, silver filigree honeycombed with glass, but unmistakably a map of Rotherweird.

'It glows,' Boris explained, 'constituency by constituency. And here it shows the total votes.' He pointed to small towers on the circumference, again with coloured glass.

'Wow!' she said.

'She sorts, she counts, she shows,' declared Boris proudly.

Unwittingly Miss Trimble posed a question that had troubled Boris since childhood. 'Does it work?'

She lost him for forty minutes. Strange instruments emerged from his pockets and returned there; pipes were connected and disconnected; two rotors juddered briefly into life. He took copious notes.

Life with him would be like this, she realised, *long periods of immersion*. She approved; he was his own man.

Cheeks and fingers stained with grease, he delivered his verdict, one familiar to those who knew him. 'It needs minor adjustments.' He stopped as a faintly acrid aroma wafted through the open door.

'Aah ... I cooked dinner,' he stammered, 'the works. No worry, Bert's missus does kitchen rescue.'

'No,' she said, 'that's my task.'

Later, with Miss Trimble lying beside him in all her magnificence, he unravelled her reticence about meeting his friends.

'There's a simple cure,' he whispered, 'but promise to do what I say when I say it, just the once, tomorrow.'

'I shall do what you say, just the once,' she replied, flaxen hair sweeping her face.

Most overlooked, hardest-working, oldest, Aggs brought a refreshing directness to her new hobby: canvassing.

'What we wants,' she would say in any ear she could capture, from employers to fellow servants to shop queues, 'is a person what's warm and straight with pluck and bristlin' good sense. What we don't want are pocket-liners and clever-clogs.'

At this point the eyebrows would rise and the lower lip jut forward. 'Anyone sayin' otherwise?'

10

Priming Prim

'As custodian of an institution older even than mine, I come to you.'

Pull the other one, thought the recipient of this uncharacteristic compliment as Master Thomes placed a magnificent silver Thermos, engraved with the motto of his Guild, on the grimy table. A balsawood box followed. Thomes' manicured fingers picked open the greaseproof paper: shortbread and crystallised ginger spotted with bitter chocolate. The corked lid of the Thermos lifted with a pleasing *pop*, but it also marked the end of deference.

'I provide, you pour,' Thomes said.

Head Gaoler Denzil Prim rustled up two cream-coloured china mugs and a chipped milk jug, earth-stained like discarded eggshells.

Thomes ran a silk handkerchief around the rims, his distaste evident. 'You must change your sign,' he said. '"Gaol" undersells. "Hall of Correction" is more *redemptive*.'

'Trouble is, Master Thomes, there's nobody to correct, apart from the odd one-night stand.'

Thomes' goatee beard twitched at the vulgarity of Prim's language. 'On the contrary, Mr Prim, there is much to correct, and soon. Rot sits deep in our very fabric. Consider this an *informal* tip-off. Check locks and bars, secure the keys, sharpen up the record-keeping. Leave guards and finance to us.'

A gold ten-guinea coin pirouetted briefly on the tabletop before disappearing into Prim's grimy fist. 'What's the offence? And how many is "much"? Is we talking bigwigs or smallwigs?'

Thomes ignored the questions. 'After the election, you get straight back here – no pub, no dawdling – with your escort, of course.'

Escort. Prim blinked, then gave a purring smile.

Thomes had one last bauble. 'I also dislike the word "Gaoler". It suggests a grubby man with no finesse. Do as you're asked and we'll promote you to Castellan.'

An acolyte packed away the Thermos and surviving delicacies. Thomes climbed into a pied rickshaw while Prim scurried off to find a locksmith.

II

Shenanigans

As windows and doors opened at first light, everyone caught an insidious siren scent. The stall, a semi-circular structure with shelves of tiny glass cruets with cork stoppers, stood in Market Square, staffed by a swarm of Apothecaries. A purple banner emblazoned in gold with *STRIMMER FOR MAYOR* and *PLEASURE FOR ALL* on the reverse had been stretched between two poles. Every few minutes the Apothecary in charge removed the cork from a huge jar, then closed it, launching wave after wave of delectable fragrance.

Over the course of the morning almost every citizen drifted to the Square to sample the miraculous brew.

The Apothecaries canvassed shamelessly. 'Imbibe Mr Strimmer's election gift!'

'Get it daily and free if Mr Strimmer wins.'

Bill Ferdy came late. For once, the Apothecaries were reluctant to serve and the cork stayed in.

'It's for the electorate,' said the Apothecary in charge, waving the countrysider away, but Ferdy ignored her, seized a cruet and downed it. A palate honed by long experience instantly diagnosed the undertow, a chemical masked by an otherwise natural taste.

They were dispensing addiction, not pleasure.

It resembled a prison classroom: a windowless underground chamber with chairs and desks in rows, paper, pencils and pens at the ready, and blackboards at the head of the room.

The janitor, Bendigo Sly, walked around, dispensing orders: 'More informal; mix it up; change the writing.'

Faking authenticity demanded variety – in manuscript, mode of address (Dear Friend, Dear Neighbour, Dear Fellow Metalworker), phrasing (cruder if from The Understairs), message, and the excuse for anonymity. Sly knew not to overstate his master's virtues: *better the devil you know* and *for all his shortcomings* being phrases of choice. Many avoided any mention of Snorkel.

The themes had predictable targets:

1. Roc the amateur.
2. Roc, who fiddles her taxes.
3. Roc and Oblong plotting an outsider putsch.
4. Roc's countryside friends.
5. Strimmer's dalliance with the Apothecaries.
6. Strimmer's plan to abolish all other Guilds.
7. The Apothecaries' bribing brew is carcinogenic.
8. Strimmer will take over the South Tower too.

Stacks of paper and envelopes of all weights, shapes and sizes sat on Sly's desk. Snorkel facts were ready to launch, a mix of intended lies and accidental truths.

12

Light Show for One

Almost as overlooked (by his own choice), and almost as hard-working, Hayman Salt had exhausted his stock of curses. True, excessive rain in spring and summer did more damage than in autumn or winter, when roots were dormant and there was no photosynthesis to interrupt. But underground, this quantity of rain raised the pH in acid soils and depressed it in alkali, with oxygen and nutrients declining in both. Sediment was harmed too. Salt's body, now a mirror to the health of his charges, was afflicted by a stooping lethargy.

Nobody had visited Grove Gardens for days. The paths were sodden, the branches bare. Early-flowering camellias weighed down by dun-coloured waterlogged buds wore a leprotic look. That after-noon he had wandered over to a sturdy favourite, *Prunus serrula*, and encircled the trunk with both hands. A foreign energy had tickled the palms: a faint oscillation picked up by deep roots close to Rotherweird's rocky base.

Where did this force come from? Lost Acre had been afflicted on the longest day, so might Rotherweird, her connected cousin, face similar extremes on the shortest? *Saeculum*, Ferox had said to him, almost a year ago now.

Now, at two in the morning, he stood in the same place to the inch, staring over the Grove Gardens parapet. This time he had run, after pulling on a heavy jersey over pyjamas and a heavier coat over the jersey, heavy boots over heavy socks, balaclava over head and ears, answering a summons from the air, not the ground. He had heard what others could not: the *crackle* of fine moisture freezing, fracturing and falling. The beads of the water on the underside of the bars were hardening beneath his fingers like strung pearls; his breath plumed. Extreme cold had come in an unnatural rush.

The river below was changing her music to something slower and more sombre; he felt his own blood, and the sap all around him, follow suit. A *clack*, clean as a castanet in the still dry air, was followed by others: windows and shutters closing all over town, her inhabitants too incurious to investigate.

Above Salt's head mauve and green slats of light came and went like deconstructed rainbows: geomagnetic storms, with their ignited auras, should be confined to the magnetic poles, not *here*.

Salt blinked, his eyes stinging at the rapid change in temperature. The damp on the town's exposed surfaces transformed to frost; a world purged of colour turned brilliant white. Above him the light show faded, to be replaced by the Milky Way, its edges sharp as an estuarial map.

Saeculum.

13

Last Chance Saloon

That evening, Madge Brown, Secretary of the Liaison Committee, executed another Rotherweird ritual. She visited Snorkel first as the present incumbent; true to form, he kept her waiting.

'You read the terms and conditions of office, then you sign the declaration or choose not to.' The next sentence she read from a card, as the *Regulations* demanded. '*No penalty or obloquy shall attach to a candidate who withdraws.*'

'Give me the form,' barked Snorkel.

'You must read, Mr Snorkel. I have to be satisfied.'

Bolshy bitch, thought Snorkel, *your days are numbered*. He scanned the litany of high moral dos and don'ts, adherence to which would render the exercise of power impossibly unrewarding, and signed.

Strimmer made Snorkel sound verbose. He read, smirked, signed and dismissed her with a finger-flick, all without a word spoken.

Orelia alone vacillated: such a sea of committees and responsibilities. 'Where is the space to be wise?' she asked.

'There's no duty to be wise,' replied Madge. 'That's an optional extra.'

No penalty might be true, but no obloquy – handing Rotherweird to Snorkel or Strimmer?

She signed.

14

Treading Carefully

In Oblong's bedroom, which faced northeast, body and bedclothes had contorted to defend against the plummeting temperature, knees to groin, chin to sternum, eiderdown pulled over his head.

He dismissed the first tap at the window as a beetle driven by the Arctic blast from hibernation to exercise, but the second brought reappraisal. Swathed like a mummy, he parted the curtains, to be dazzled by a brilliant duck-egg blue sky. Frigid air slapped his cheeks. A dried pea rolled along his sill as he pulled the window open. He was being summoned.

When the weather changes . . . Jones must be waiting. Adrenalin surged. He dressed in double time, as many layers as his feeble wardrobe could provide, and bounded downstairs to find Jones jogging on the spot and waving a pea-shooter.

'Confiscated from Dawson minor,' he declared. 'If you can't beat 'em, join 'em, eh?' In his other hand he held a jumble of webbing with spikes attached and a rope. Water bottles hung from his belt. Jones strode north up the Golden Mean, his pace driving Oblong into an ungainly trot to keep up. The glare narrowed the eyes; everywhere windows pockmarked with ice.

The river had frozen over. Jones ignored the bridge and clambered down to the shoreline, where he fastened the spikes to Oblong's boots and his own.

'Cold dehydrates no less than heat. Slipping is fine on ice, but falling is not. Luck's Landing is our destination.' Jones threw a stone onto the ice from a crouching position. There was a thump and a higher pitch as it bounced on. He moved on to the ice, tapping with his stick, vigour giving way to caution. Frost puffed like smoke around their ankles, the ice beneath smooth as glass. Jones' spikes bit and held. The trees on the western shore lacked the lumpiness snow brings. Hoarfrost accentuated the contrasting profile of alder and willow. The eastern marsh's bare face wore an unshaven look, tiny points of grass and reed piercing the blanket of white.

Aggs' first words of advice to Oblong had included the warning, *Never walk in the marsh*. Even the peat-cutters had withdrawn from the margins in recent decades, leaving behind a few shelves of earth and Luck's Landing, a patch of *terra firma* marked by duckboards and mooring poles.

'Respect a river and you can trust it; not so this place,' declared Jones, producing from a pocket *The Rotherweird Runner*, his bequest from Bolitho, wrapped in a plastic sleeve. A single ribbon marked a double-page spread covered in a blizzard of dots beneath the title *Mired in the Marsh: One Walk NOT to Do*.

'Compare!' he said, and Oblong did, acknowledging that the shoreline at Luck's Landing bore an uncanny resemblance to the starting point of the walk. 'It's all to scale,' added Jones, tapping the vertical lines of dots, crisscrossing like a drunkard lost. 'Stepping stones. They read so.' His forefinger followed the route. 'Up, across, down, across, up . . . They're two steps apart – rest between and you'll sink. Mind on the job, Obbers, and call me Gorius when on active service – less of a mouthful.'

I am the all-purpose traveller, thought Oblong immodestly: *on, under and over ground*, but he found this journey the worst. The other two had hinged on luck – when and whether the earth ceiling fell; how the Fury's arrow struck – but the marsh demanded deftness and concentration. Jones excelled at both. With book in one hand, stick in the other, he probed before executing a double jump, weight thrown forward to the next point of landing, all to a sound like breaking crockery. Oblong, often mired up to his thighs, plunged and panted, the malodorous mud clinging and freezing until he felt like a man in armour.

Jones declared short stops when Oblong's co-ordination threatened to disintegrate. 'One minute, no more – warmth loosens the limbs – and watch that breathing. In, out; in, out!'

The sun rose; their shadows shortened; the glare intensified; the shoreline receded. Two hours later, with Oblong crimson-faced and drenched in sweat, Jones declared journey's end. Ochre stains and shards of fractured ice marked their trail.

Oblong's composure failed. 'Gorius, where on earth are we? There's nothing ahead but more of the bloody same—'

'Finch's fastness . . . where you'll be my eyes and ears,' replied Jones, winding Oblong with a slap on the back. He stabbed the ice, tilted his stick, caught an iron stirrup with its tip and then another. Each connected to a turfed-over half-moon door, heavy even for Jones. A tube-light from Jones' backpack revealed two semicircular shafts, one with rock steps leading to a large empty chamber, the other with no steps and a much narrower opening.

Jones wound the rope through the stirrup on the first door and then about his waist, before bracing himself in a half-crouch, as if anchoring a tug-of-war.

'On you go,' he said.

Oblong walked as far as the steps would go, and then descended on the rope. The darkness had a threatening, cavernous quality, oddly more unsettling than the subterranean pathways. He found the large hole where the moleman had broken through. 'Finch's cell,' he shouted to Jones, 'or should I say, his cave.'

'Try the other.'

There were no steps this time. 'Just a narrow cave with a sheer rock wall,' reported Oblong. 'Ah – and there's a speaking tube connecting to the cell. Poor old Finch.'

Gorius the *speculator* engaged. This had been his particular gift, working out who had passed, how deep their step, armoured or not, the points of spear-shafts or not, transport or not, how many wheels, what discarded food, sourced from where.

A Fury could fly over the marsh, interrogate in human form and then fall through the adjacent open shaft to resume her bird shape. But why construct and disguise the shafts in the inaccessible marsh in the first place? The openings must be centuries old; indeed, they looked older than Wynter's time. His extravagant theory, conceived in the basket during Vulcan's Dance, was looking disturbingly plausible.

His memories of 1017 trickled back: the stooped monk and his upright companion plodding through the sharp-sided hail, the tremor that followed and the great rock henge with its single eye vanishing into nothing: the flight of the winking man. If his theory was right, should he keep history caged, or let her free to do her best and worst?

Oblong's face emerged from the rim, only to freeze in astonishment.

A young woman of striking beauty stood leaning on a long stick, only yards away. She was wearing a patchwork of leather, wool and fur; golden hair hung free. She offered a gloved hand and a smile. Morval Seer; it could be nobody else. She flipped her stick and a silver spike, notched and numbered, protruded from the base. Her smile expanded; such an expressive face, flitting from guarded suspicion to relief to welcome.

'Is it . . . ?' stammered Oblong.

Nervousness before the apparition had lifted the pitch of Oblong's voice and her smile shifted, now enigmatic. She suddenly clasped her stick close and hurried east across the ice, leaping like a dancer at a speed not even Jones could match. She disappeared into the far distance.

'Valourhand squared,' said Oblong admiringly, 'or do I mean halved?'

'She is who she is,' observed Jones. He pointed behind them. Their tracks had disfigured the pristine white of the marsh, but hers left no mark: the footfalls of a ghost.

'I've never seen anyone less spidery in my life – and imagine not being able to talk,' Oblong mused.

'We could try the experience on the way back,' suggested Jones. 'Breathing allowed, of course: in, out; in, out.'

They reached Luck's Landing in half the time, even Oblong achieving a rhythm of sorts. Tiny holes pierced the ice of the river around the miniature jetty – Fortemain must have sent Morval to test the depth of the ice, with cheering results, to judge from her demeanour.

As children acting as criers bore news of the frozen river, a frenzy seized the town, part sporting, part commercial, prompting a mass-retrieval of skates, sleighs, braziers and ice-stalls, long buried in dusty cupboards and forgotten sheds. Young and old polished, sharpened and waxed rusty runners and blades. On the southern tributary beyond the Island Field, barrels in zigzag formation marked out a slalom. Woollen hats emerged in the form of animal heads with a wintery theme: bears, hares and ermine among the most popular.

Vlad's staff prepared a travelling bar, and in The Understairs, cellars disgorged sacks of chestnuts to be cooked and sold at a penny a go.

Gorhambury interrupted his rituals to study the *Appendix* to the *River Regulations*, compiled in 1608 during the first recorded river-freeze.

Jones and Oblong encountered children, hands clasped behind their backs, scarves streaming, as they neared the town. In the distance by the South Bridge figures crisscrossed the ice, delivering pennants and the paraphernalia of outdoor commerce and entertainment.

Apothecaries erected an awning, readying another distribution of Strimmer's vote-winning brew. A horse-drawn sleigh stood half-assembled further north as the river became a street.

'Frost Fair,' whispered Jones to Oblong as if a miracle had come.

Exhilaration merged with physical exhaustion to inspire Oblong. He imagined himself high over Rotherweird, as on the night of Vulcan's Dance, with the town below a pocket watch, the alleys and towers its intricate workings, the northern twist of the river the chain. Words came without effort:

> *'A giant's fob lost in the frost*
> *And now discovered by children.*
> *Its face is leaden and as dull*
> *As spectacles upon a skull . . .'*

They parted at the bridge. Jones looked oddly solemn, but Oblong hurried down the Golden Mean, his mind divided between his burgeoning poem and the image of Morval Seer dancing across the ice.

15

An Excursion

'*I'll come when colour returns*,' he had said, and Everthorne duly appeared at nine at the door of *Baubles & Relics*.

'North Bridge at ten,' he said, hoisting a backpack into place.

Orelia checked the security of *Straighten the Rope*, dressed warmly and gathered her skates. She had not felt such anxious anticipation for years; she craved fulfilment and feared disappointment.

He was sitting on the riverbank close to the North Bridge, sketchbook on knee as he held up a piece of string with a polished peg at either end, mentally framing the view. He wore figure skates with the telltale toe pick at the front; Orelia's, inherited from Roy Roc, had longer blades made for speed.

'We head north,' he said with a flamboyant flick of the hand, stooping as they sped through adjacent arches of the bridge to virgin ice beyond, following the course of the Great Equinox Race in reverse. Orelia, as adept and more elegant, easily kept pace.

'Ever done this?' cried Everthorne. Using his blade like a pencil tip on fine paper, he cut a camel, jumping to break a line or find a curve, spinning to make the animal's eye. This was the Everthorne of their first meeting, playing hopscotch with the moonlight.

Beyond the start of the Great Race, the river contracted, choked with bulrushes, carriers siphoning off much of the main flow. Everthorne led them down a narrow stream which widened into a small lake fringed with weeping ash and rhododendrons. Moored to the largest tree was a houseboat, her prow, stern and side rail decorated with exotic carvings in the best Rotherweird tradition.

'Grandfather's,' said Everthorne, 'and Father left it to me.'

The open stern deck had a rolled canvas roof for protection against sun or rain, and the wall beside the door accommodated a small iron fireplace with a steel flue, serrated at the top like a paddle steamer. Hooks on the side at roof level held oars and a punt-pole. Orelia's shopkeeper's eye gathered detail – the wood recently polished, the fire laid, coal and kindling bought and stored, canvas installed. Everthorne had spent time here.

Not for the first time, he caught her line of thought. 'I came my first morning, and most days since. She's lacked love for far too long.'

Was this a secondary reference to her? If so, he was right. Far from the madding crowd, nothing else mattered. 'Let's get the fire going.'

They knelt and blew, and it caught. He showed her below deck: two hammocks, a galley, a table and four stools. He opened a shallow bench to reveal paintbrushes of all sizes in bundles tied with shoelaces, tubes of oil paints squeezed almost to exhaustion, the labels aged in colour and script. An easel hung on the wall.

She removed her hat. Warmth was already seeping into the room.

'The fire has a back-burner,' he explained. 'All mod cons.' She smiled: not a Rotherweird expression, 'mod cons'. He led her back to the deck and dived into his backpack. 'Castor Everthorne's book of the boat – witness his happy days.'

He handed her a sketchbook with a faded cover and the label of *Alizarin & Flake*, Rotherweird's solitary art shop, still visible. Water-colours, pastels, pen and ink had captured the boat's prime of life, an all-season impressionist's mirror to light, landscape, nature and the easy pleasures: picnics, swimmers with glasses raised, beribboned straw hats, and Rotherweird Church with jackdaws perched on its snow-covered roof. She saw little sign of the madness to come, save perhaps in the occasional ink drawings of gnarled roots, tangled and reaching.

'He's good at straw hats, the way the shadow falls,' said Everthorne.

She liked the way he complimented others, as if art were a common endeavour. 'He's good at smiles too.' She meant it. These long-dead men and women exuded easy contentment.

'I wish I knew their names and their histories – why are we so strangled by rules?' replied Everthorne.

'So we don't pitter-patter, back and back, and find what we shouldn't.'

He took a photograph from the back of the sketchbook. 'Castor,' he declared. His grandfather, a canvas in either hand, was being presented with a carving by an older man, his greying hair discernible. 'Hard to see, but it's the mouse. So, you see, all connects.'

He put down the photograph, produced a bottle of wine and two glasses, and laid out his own pastels, both sticks and pencils. 'It's a Visitors' Book, of sorts. You must join them,' he said.

He worked fast, using the point of the stick, then the edge, his finger and the pencil.

'Pastels have their own language,' he explained, 'hatching, feathering and scumbling. But beware, their freshness risks stridency.'

He moved her hair from a cheekbone, and the weakening physical barrier between them broke. She touched his cheek. He moved her shirt a little – *to show the clavicle*, he said. She held his hand where it was. Minutes later, they went downstairs.

'As a young man I tried making love in a hammock. I don't recommend it.'

'What do you recommend?'

'Rugs, rugs and more rugs.'

Tartan ones, as it turned out.

'How to break the ice,' he said afterwards, 'but was it the warmth or the motion?'

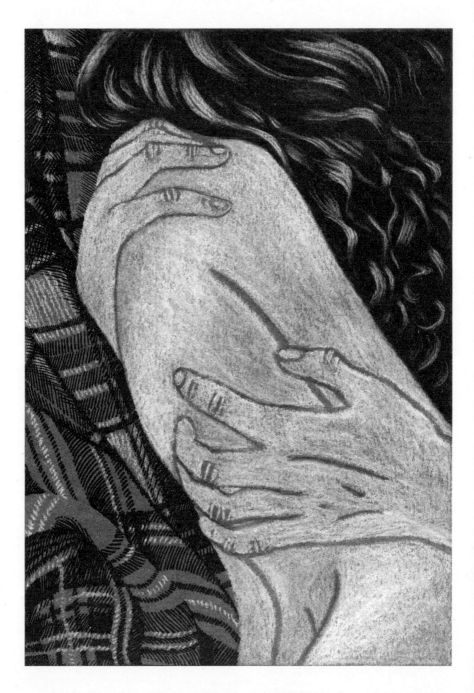

'Rugs, rugs and more rugs . . .'

'Both,' she laughed.

Rotherweird reclaimed them at dusk. He cooked for her in Artery Lane and when she left him asleep at midnight, she felt they had discussed everything and nothing, a magical dalliance.

She glanced for the first time at his sketches of her on the way out; two, unfinished, but detailed around the eyes and mouth, better than a likeness. The first mirrored her strength and frailty; it was affectionate, insightful. The other discomforted her: she wore an expression of puzzlement, a created pose, not how she had looked at the time. What had provoked it? That she had given herself to him so easily? Was she a trophy? Other pages in the sketchbook had pieces cut from them. On impulse, she carefully removed the one she liked: a talisman against the coming storm.

The moment she saw the frozen river, Valourhand understood: the ice would cushion the earthquake, sparing the town serious damage. It was deep enough to absorb the shock of a displaced observatory, but not enough, by Bolitho's calculations, to allow a more ambitious plan. Yet she feared Bolitho was wrong; he had underestimated Calx Bole.

Valourhand did not *do* dither. You decided a course and recruited accordingly; as with Oblong and the tunnels, so now. No alternative stratagem existed; no other companion offered his advantages. He would agree – he had courage. He had known the mixing-point.

She recognised one snag: she was using him as bait, entrusting his life to her unpractised hands. Yet she succumbed to a siren voice: *clarity of purpose is what sets you apart. You* decide, *you* choose, *you* act. She picked up the package and hurried through the School gate into the night.

Orelia could not sleep. Her head swam with contradictions – Everthorne's alternating states, physical fulfilment and spiritual uncertainty, her diminishing interest in the mayoralty set against a passionate hostility to Strimmer or Snorkel holding office; she was caught between hope and despair.

She put on a thick jersey, descended to the rear of her shop and lit the fire. For distraction, she laid three postcards face up on her desk: *Theseus Lost, Incarceration* and the photograph of the wall-carvings in Wynter's cell. She toyed with the notion that the numbered archways in *Theseus Lost* mapped a route through the tunnels of Rotherweird to some unknown destination. The shapes in *Incarceration* had surely been inspired by Wynter's carvings – the title said as much – although they were not the same, and there were more of them.

She decided to count the respective shapes and archways in the two oils and in minutes was cursing her slowness: there were sixteen in each – the same number of pieces that had been delivered to Ember Vine by her anonymous customer. She saw another connection between the two oils: the archways and shapes occupied parallel positions – and a disturbing explanation struck her: the numbered archways in *Theseus Lost* represented the sequence in which the pieces in *Incarceration* were to be assembled. Who had commissioned the oils? Had Everthorne Senior's remarkable spatial awareness solved another's problem – and if so, whose?

She recalled the photograph of Everthorne Senior with a canvas in each hand, being handed a beautifully carved mouse. Her ancestor, Benedict Roc, a woodcarver, had been murdered by Bole. Had the shapeshifter taken his gifts as well as his appearance? Apprehension seized her. Too many threads were converging.

16

Desperate Measures

Salt sat at his desk before a vase of winter flowers, their shadows magnified by the single gas-lamp on the wall behind. He loved plants for their quietness and generosity. Flytraps and sundews might kill for a living, but the balance lay overwhelmingly in credit: beauty, shelter, inspiration, food, breathers-in of poison and out of life. No wonder the Almighty had fashioned them before the sun, moon and stars.

He found it deeply disturbing that on Rotherweird Island, and less tangibly in the valley, trunks and branches were conveying distress; invisible fingers, as yet microscopic but gaining in intensity all the while, were grinding and tearing at their roots. The comet had become more irascible with age.

Salt's ornate door-knocker rapped, the caller insistent and urgent. He expected Orelia, but found Valourhand, warmly dressed, but in white. She carried a backpack and a long, flattish package wrapped in brown paper.

'Come in.'

She shook her head. 'I've been a fool – it's staring me in the face. They *can* do what Bolitho thinks is impossible. '

'Which is *what*?' asked Salt gently.

'I don't know exactly, but it's to do with the river. In 1017 there was a small earthquake, but the effect was limited, thanks, I believe, to the river.'

'It was frozen?'

'There's a record that says so.'

A pending quake? That explains the unease below ground, thought Salt.

'It might be stopped, but it's dangerous.'

'And I'm expendable?'

'You're *different*. Wrap up; we're in for a long, cold night. Wear something colourless.'

Salt, direct himself, respected directness in others. His recent life of husbandry had been dull, if fulfilling, and he felt a need to be back in the action. He obeyed her orders: a knee-length sheepskin coat, two pelts sewn together with the wool on the inside, a sheepskin cap with ear muffs. Valourhand appraised him. 'Barkish colour: that's fine, you'll do.'

'Let me guess,' said Salt. 'I follow you in silence.'

What a refreshing change to Oblong, thought Valourhand. *He gets it.* 'We'll need a way through the walls – a speciality of yours, I believe.'

Salt took a key from his desk drawer. 'Consider it done. But first, a little insurance.' He took a tiny box from a drawer, placed it an envelope and addressed it to, of all people, Aggs.

'What's in there?'

'There's no safer depository for the rare and precious than the honest poor,' replied Salt with an air of finality, and Valourhand did not press him further.

They scurried through Rotherweird's more labyrinthine paths to the hidden door in Salt's potting shed in the western wall, pausing only for Salt to drop his package in a Delayed Action Service post box. They passed his coracle, tied to a willow, redundant in the freeze. The walls occluded the moonlight on the bank, but beyond the entire landscape glistened.

The eastern branch of the Rother had entertained the Frost Fair but here only a few swirling lines, as from a drunkard's compass, marked the passage of skaters.

Opposite the door in the wall, a stand of willow and alder offered cover.

'This will do,' she said. Salt ran his fingers over the bark – the trees' unease was still growing. 'Give a wave,' she added. 'You'll know it's coming before me.'

'"It"?'

'An ice-dragon from the other place – it was kept near the white tile and now I know why: it's coming to seal the river.'

'But it's sealed already—'

'Not firmly enough. A quake is coming; there'll be rocks on the move.'

'That fits,' replied Salt.

'You'll know what to do.'

'If we succeed, won't the tremor's effects be worse?'

'I *hope* they'll only be different.' That Bole had only buildings in town in mind troubled her – how could any of them matter this much? She unpacked the Fury's bow and the single arrow.

'What a wicked-looking thing,' said Salt.

'Wicked does as wicked is.'

'Would you rather I . . . ?'

'No, you take cover. I'll wait on the river.'

He knew better than to waste time on a pointless argument with Valourhand. He sat on a stump, his kind of chair – dead leaves at his feet, brittle and curled by the frost, starfields above – and let Summer's memories wash over him: the bubble careering through the wormhole, the flower entwining his forearm, his few hours as the Green Man. His mind drifted.

In contrast, Valourhand had the stillness, stamina and concentration of a sniper. She strung the bow and crouched, white on white, the weapon resting across her thighs – one arrow, one chance. Across the river she could hear Salt singing quietly to himself, an old Rotherweird folk song about hope and despair:

'Corn has an ear,
The moon a face,
Sadness can cheer
But Hell is a place . . .'

An hour passed before Salt snapped upright, sensing a ferocious presence. He caught what the trees and grasses felt: not the slow chill of frost, but a scything blast of cold. Fish below the ice were cauterised, insects too, as beyond the east wall, a cloud of crystal splintered the air. Salt waved, but he hadn't needed to; Valourhand had already nocked the arrow.

The ice-dragon had come.

Salt watched her in trepidation – *one arrow*? Now a child of the mixing-point, he could feel the creature's progress, skimming low over the river. But if he recognised it, would it not recognise him once in the open? *Of course* – that was why he'd been Valourhand's choice. *You're different*, she had said. *A decoy*. Salt mustered a smile; 'could be dangerous' had been something of an understatement.

The crystal cloud moved on, enveloping the South Bridge. Valourhand was still crouching mid-river.

Salt checked his spikes; a slip would be fatal. The trees, kindred spirits, masked him for the moment. He signalled Valourhand, palms down. The creature had landed by the South Bridge. Gusts came and went as it worked the arches; not an inch of river was escaping its attention.

Moments later, the river ahead turned the colour of lead; flying pins of ice stung the cheeks and blinded Valourhand. Salt edged on to the river, his camouflage slipping as he did so. The smog abated and the ice-dragon prowled into view, head questing this way and that – Salt had achieved surprise. He questioned how this creature with such symmetry and coherence could be from the mixing-point, then moved to the harsher realities: the head looked too armoured for an arrow to penetrate – which prompted him to understand his role. He ran back to the trees, and the ice-dragon turned, following him, exposing the left shoulder.

'Now!' screamed Salt, twisting his head round. 'For God's sake, *now!*'

Valourhand froze, as she had before the blaze in Mrs Banter's tower. The monster was magnificent, *too* magnificent, its hold hypnotic – the uncompromising belligerence, the bone-ribbed face and serpentine body, the glowing meridian line, the glacial eyes: a throwback to a lost age.

'No,' she cried, seeing in her mind's eye the beast reduced to ruins by the acid. Her arm dropped; the arrow fell from the bowstring.

A second time Salt cried out as he clambered up the bank into cover, and too late, Valourhand realised her mistake. She fumbled for the arrow as an explosion of smoke and ice-needles enveloped her. Blue frost-fire belched into the shore and engulfed Salt's stand of trees in a single sweep. *Aim just behind the frost-fire for the head*, she directed herself, but a second blast swept her feet away. She careered across the ice into the roots of a willow, where she found relieving darkness.

She raised her head, trailing a few commas of blood in the snow. She had a bloody nose, a cut cheek, a sore elbow and hip, but nothing worse. From the moon's movement, she had been unconscious for less than an hour. She kicked to disengage her feet from the ice, which had acquired a mottled grey patina, and scanned the sky, horizon to horizon, but found no sign of life.

The bow and intact arrow restored the closing images: the ice-dragon's magnificence, her inertia, Salt's cries, the burst of frost-fire. She rushed to the trees and flailed her way through the ice-panels between them, calling his name. Two boot-spikes lay embedded in the ice. He had been *shivered* to pieces.

She had killed him.

Self-hatred racked her slight frame. She had never wept for

anyone other than herself, but now she did. Rotherweird's election, the Furies, Bole's chosen mask, Wynter or no Wynter, what the spheres might do: these acute concerns shrank to irrelevance. She could not face anyone. After retrieving the bow and arrow, she trudged south towards the dark shadows of Rotherweird Westwood.

She needed the wilds. She fought to suppress a deeper, unrecognised desire: she needed Tyke's reassuring presence.

17

Democracy's Day

At dawn Bert Polk set off from *The Polk Land & Water Company* to Market Square. The charabanc bowed low to the cobbles under the weight of the ballot-balls in their huge leather baskets, while Boris and Miss Trimble wheeled *The Thingamajig* into the courtyard on a chassis designed for the purpose.

'She should fly to Market Square and stop dead-centre,' declared Boris. 'She did last time. There she takes on the votes, then it's off to the Island Field for verdict.'

Gorhambury looked on as the four rotors moved from a low whirr to a gentle high-pitched hum and the machine rose sedately over the rooftops, heading towards the Golden Mean.

Wrapped against the cold, the three of them followed in the vacuum-driven Umpire's chair last used in the Great Equinox Race. The raised bench and telescope made for an ideal observation post. The near-soundless procession woke nobody. Early sunlight silvered the fuselage. Not a breath of wind disturbed the wisps of high cloud. With his brain tuned to the disciplined management of administrative challenges, Gorhambury felt the grip of contrary currents. How would Rotherweird change, for change she surely would? What defined a 'modern improvement'? At moments during his brief interregnum he had privately toyed with what *he* might do.

En route he noted a curiosity: towers on the edge of town had acquired a blue-grey sheen on their outer faces. *A freak hoarfrost*, he concluded.

Boris anchored *The Thingamajig* by wires to grates in Market Square and fitted the four pipes, each running from a different cubicle, one for each quarter of the town: the Municipality (northwest after the Town Hall), the Oasis (southwest in honour of *The Journeyman's Gist* & The Polk Land & Water Travel Company), The Understairs (northeast), and Scholars' Corner (southeast, after the School). Municipal workers selected by Gorhambury for their incorruptibility distributed the three distinctive types of ballot stones, sufficient to accommodate a landslide in any direction, to the cubicles whose light timber construction featured a sprung door in and out and a canvas ceiling as proof against prying eyes.

Gorhambury distributed excerpts from the *Election Regulations* to his chosen few.

'Voting starts at eight and finishes at noon and we adjourn to the Island Field at three,' he announced.

'Time for a good lunch before we discover our fate,' added Boris.

Miss Trimble, by now tuned in to her lover's voice, caught anxiety beneath the bravado. She squeezed his arm. 'The will of the people – we never know. That's the point, isn't it?'

Orelia watched the charabanc and the Umpire's chair pass by, and glimpsed the fleeting shadow of *The Thingamajig*; but stood back, limelight-shy despite her candidacy.

Rotherweird's electoral dynamic requires overhaul, she decided; *one chance, one speech* disadvantaged novices like herself, and with the passing weeks had encouraged the dark arts – poison-pen mail, addictive drinks, funding the Summoned. With no platform for counter-attack, a straight player simply succumbed. *But*, she recognised, *she* had been unimaginative – her exposure of Snorkel had been neither revelatory, nor a policy. The arts, the poor, equality for the Guilds and countrysiders, controls on the North Tower – there was so much more she *could* have said.

At least the election had brought Everthorne, but the physical pleasure, though stirring, had left uncertainty in its wake. She could not see him staying beyond the election. His grandfather had atrophied in Rotherweird; so would he. Restlessness, bordering on mania, bubbled away in his genes; he offered the attractions and downsides of a richly talented drifter.

She lit the fire and made coffee, planning a quiet hour to prepare for Democracy's spinning wheel, but within minutes rhythmic thumps on the shop-front window drew her to the door. Outside, Fanguin was headbutting the glass with his forehead. Even by his low standards, he looked unhinged – unkempt, red-eyed, collar half-up, shirt half-out, buttons and shoelaces undone.

Orelia glared and tapped her forehead. He stopped. She hauled him in like a fish, catching a waft of Vlad's best malt. 'You smell like a distillery.'

Fanguin collapsed into the nearest armchair. 'Huge,' he mumbled, 'bloody *huge*.'

Pieces of paper spewed from his pockets – graphs and a diagram of Rotherweird Island sprinkled with arrows and figures.

'Stay!' she said, as if scolding a renegade pet. Mildly disorientated by his intensity, she seized the nearest cup on display, filled it with coffee and thrust it into Fanguin's trembling hand.

He scrutinised the vessel's incongruous daintiness like an auctioneer. 'Sorry,' he mumbled, 'up since three.'

'What's bloody huge?'

The coffee worked at his scrambled wires. 'My bat detector alarm went berserk,' he stuttered, putting down the cup and tying his shoelaces. 'Not a Fury: miles larger, and faster, with blue flanks like a line of toothpaste.' He paused. 'My machine sits on a neighbouring tower – the town walls blocked my view most of the time, but I saw it fly away south. They sent the ice-dragon to seal the river.' Fanguin paused. 'On my way down from the roof, I slipped and I thought I would fall. For a moment, I wanted to.'

Orelia's gift for compassion buckled. 'Cut the self-pity, Fanguin.

We don't have time.' She picked up the hand-drawn map, where Fanguin had transposed his machine's data on movements and timings.

'Only an intelligent beast would work the arches one by one. And why does it come in from the northeast? The tile is to the south.'

'If you were an ice-dragon, wouldn't you want to come from the north?' said Fanguin.

Orelia followed the creature's course on the map, across the marsh, pausing to seal the ice beneath the North Bridge, then moving down the eastern side and sealing the South Bridge. She stopped, cheeks turning pale, eyes dampening, shoulders hunched. She earthed her despair on Fanguin. 'This is the moment? *Now*, you give up? You really do? Look – *look!*' She stabbed a finger at the western stream.

Fanguin looked. 'So? It paused for a breather to recharge the ice-bucket.'

The unfortunate choice of metaphor passed Orelia by; she felt beset by horror. 'It stops – it turns left – it *moves* left – that's hardly a breather. *What's there?*' she almost screamed at him.

Fanguin followed her finger and shrugged.

'It was only weeks ago, Fanguin – is it really such a fog? You and I?'

Fanguin fumbled and finally grasped the connection: Salt's hidden door lay just above the dragon's halt. 'You mean—'

'The scribbles in *Straighten the Rope* are full of references to the river and seismic forces – Valourhand saw the ice-dragon by the white tile. She knew it was coming in.'

'She's seen my book. She knows the river froze last time, when the monks came,' Fanguin mumbled, head bowed.

'Salt has a key, and Salt's been in the mixing-point. He's the perfect decoy.' Orelia half-regretted her savagery, but her frustrations demanded it. They were all in disarray.

Fanguin, the target, felt an urge to make good. 'We'll go now.'

'I'm a *candidate*, Fanguin. I have to decorate Market Square from nine to noon.'

'Well, that's one contest you will win.'

Orelia would have ordinarily welcomed the warmth behind the remark, but now his flippancy felt out of place. 'They would have stood no chance.'

'She's resourceful – she survived the dragon once.'

Orelia, softening, folded the map and tucked it in his pocket. 'It's not your fault. We should all have foreseen this. And Valourhand – well, she is what she is.'

In truth, fear for Salt ravaged her more deeply. Her curmudgeonly companion in the bubbles on Midsummer Eve and the saviour of Lost Acre had in recent months striven to escape the clutches of the other place, but to no avail.

Sobered by coffee and circumstance, Fanguin began to tackle his shirt buttons and collar. The thought that the enemy had every square covered prompted a change of tack. 'You do have the book?' he asked. '*Straighten the Rope?*'

'Sure – I checked last night. I always check.'

'Check again.'

'You remind me of my aunt,' replied Orelia, happy to open the cupboard at the back of her kneehole desk. Bole would never choose Fanguin as his alter ego. *Straighten the Rope* was lying where she had left it, on a pile of ledgers.

'Check inside.'

Orelia flipped the book open. The printed diagrams greeted her, but then, astonishingly, page on page of virgin white, as if Fortemain's work had never existed. She gaped – so much horror in so short a time – and blurted, 'It *isn't* Everthorne, I promise, I checked it yesterday morning – it was here then. We spent . . . the rest of the day . . . and some of the night . . . Somebody else came in my absence—'

'Nobody is accusing anyone,' replied Fanguin gently. 'May I?'

He took the book, the old Fanguin, wires rapidly reconnecting. 'Same printer, same date, same binding. They prepared this switch centuries ago.'

'You mean Calx Bole did.'

A grotesque thought struck Fanguin. *They want us to think they're only after Fortemain's calculations.* 'Have you a microscope?'

'I've three Bexter-Bunes.' The microscopes, designed by and named after Rotherweird School's Head of Biology in the 1930s, had been ground-breaking in their time and now served as staple tenth-birthday presents. She returned with her best working model to find Fanguin wielding a pen-knife. He expertly removed a sliver of leather from the cover and mounted it between two glass slides. He peered, and peered again. He gathered specks of leather from a nearby armchair and examined them too.

His pale face turned paler as he pushed the book away in disgust. 'It's mainly calf, but there's human skin mixed in with rock powder.'

Orelia shuddered. She spoke more to the room than to Fanguin. 'The *binding* – it's not the *book*, it's the binding. That explains the "unnatural attack" on Wynter – Bole skinned his own master. The cells rebind and Lazarus rises, chrysalis to butterfly.'

'That feels too precarious,' replied Fanguin. 'Surely anyone could go to the mixing-point and obstruct them? And all those particles swirling about – look what happened to Slickstone.'

'Slickstone may have cleared the mixing-point – your theory, remember, at our picnic lunch at Wynter's old house after the Hoy Fair.'

'Or Salt's merger with the Midsummer flower might have cleared it, but every working leaves residue – that's what Slickstone's death suggests. Process toxic waste and what do you get? More waste. And Wynter's other cells – they'd have been cleaned out too. We're missing something.'

Orelia's hand flew to her mouth. '*Vibes* was Bole – he needed to leave the book with someone who would guard it but not suspect.

Remember the mangled cat-boy? Bole has enemies too. I've played the diligent caretaker to perfection.'

'The rock powder – any child of the mixing-point would sense it. Bole wanted us to think the *calculations* mattered most.'

'*Everything* matters, on past form, including the rotating sphere and *Straighten the Rope*. If only we knew what the first does and the second means – we're missing bloody *everything* – the book, the stones, the plot. What *do* we do?'

'First principles,' said Fanguin, 'start with what we *do* know. Scry is one of the Eleusian women. Her questions to Finch prove that she doesn't know who Bole is, although she probably killed his familiar – remember the feather. She's also unaware of the rebound *Straighten The Rope*, which is why she seized the useless copy in Escutcheon Place. Scry *doesn't know* how Wynter returns.'

After this bout of decisiveness Fanguin patted her shoulder and made for the door. Orelia asked *the* question as he opened it. 'Are you saying Bole is one of us?'

'He could be anyone,' replied Fanguin. 'I'll find you in Market Square.'

The Square took time to fill. The countrysiders kept away, and manual workers from The Understairs dominated the early arrivals, excited at being on terms with their masters and suspicious that the privilege might yet be withdrawn. They offered a rich variety in their manner on entering their voting tent: furtive, proud, embarrassed, nervous, serious, talkative or silent – but they all looked inscrutable on leaving. They valued their vote and its secrecy.

At the door to each booth, a municipal worker announced Boris' allocation, his only attempt at subliminal canvassing. 'That'll be light stones for Miss Roc, dark stones for Mr Strimmer and brown speckled stones for Mr Snorkel.'

The teachers came between classes, Guildsmen in relays so their shops were always minded. The self-important came late; the

Apothecaries in groups of twenty. For the first time in years, the Town Crier's bell fell silent, an obscure clause in the *Regulations* not missed by Gorhambury.

The three candidates sat at tables in the lee of Doom's Tocsin in the order of their Parliament Chamber speeches. Orelia attracted occasional well-wishers; Strimmer sat flanked by Apothecaries; while Committee members and placemen afforded Snorkel a permanent audience to whom Bendigo Sly dispensed sloe gin from a trio of cut-glass decanters.

Gorhambury, one eye on his pocket watch, spent equal time exchanging pleasantries with the three tables. A good parent has no discernible favourites. In his habitual overcoat, three-piece suit, blue-black monochrome tie, and shoelaces tied with perfect fairness in four identical loops, he appeared untouched by his new office. Yet Orelia sensed change. Nature's perfect administrator might be the orthodox view, but Gorhambury had ridden unexpected turbulence with dignity and firmness. His face had loosened around the cheekbones; the gauntness was now more imposing than downcast.

Orelia grudgingly admired Strimmer for his unflinching disdain. He held a Rubik's nonagon, which he solved, dismantled and solved again: *Give intellect its chance.*

'They've had bad news,' Sly crowed to his master, who glanced across at Orelia and chuckled at her breathtaking naïveté, engaging in a tête-a-tête with a drunken failure yards from the ballot box.

'One escaped south,' whispered Fanguin. 'The wood looks like a hall of mirrors smashed by a hooligan. I found these.' He showed Orelia the boot-spikes. Casting the narrative between Valourhand and Salt was hardly difficult. 'He was brave. He left his cover and ran back. I'm so sorry.'

Orelia recalled the single syllable of comfort Salt had offered her on Mrs Banter's death: *Quick.* It had been that, at least.

She glanced across as Everthorne sauntered into the Oasis tent, emerging with a small wave, but nothing more. Was he being discreet, or did he not care? He disappeared north up the Golden Mean, sketchbook under one arm and backpack slung across his shoulder; heading back to his boat, no doubt.

The centre cannot hold. She felt threatened by disintegration, her face shaping into Everthorne's second sketch, an ugly puzzlement, wrong-footed at every turn. She could have declined to sign Madge Brown's declaration form: a dignified exit, if only she had taken it . . .

Fanguin had anticipated this, Orelia being the daughter he had never had. 'My first artistic purchase,' he said, placing before her a tiny stone figure with a telltale EV carved on its base. 'I've been saving it.'

Ember Vine had refashioned St Christopher as a woman, an adverse flood surging past her thighs, wading stick in hand, a child on her back. Despite the strain on muscle and face, its message was unequivocal: she and her precious cargo would achieve landfall. *Hope at the bottom of the box; determination gets you through.* Fanguin wrapped her fingers round it and left.

Oblong too came early. 'Virtue sits next to the venal and the vile,' he said.

'Who wants to be virtuous?' Orelia replied, in no mood for compliments, but she quickly thawed. 'My copy of *Straighten the Rope* is missing,' she whispered. 'If you get to the mixing-point, be careful – *very* careful.'

'It's time I cut loose without a chaperone,' replied Oblong, like an adolescent off to his first nightclub.

'I do mean it,' she said. 'Very, *very* careful.'

'I thought you might like to see this,' replied Oblong, handing Orelia a copy of the *Rotherweird Chronicle*'s electoral edition.

'No, thanks,' she said.

'The back, not the front.'

She turned the newspaper over to find Shapeshifter's Winter Solstice crossword solution. She quickly found the clue which had baffled her on the evening of Bolitho's funeral: *Actualité stitched up* (4). The answer could be 'news', or equally, 'sewn', which, on Bole's past form, suggested a hidden third answer. In the event, it was 'news'.

'Thanks, this might be important.'

Oblong smiled nervously.

'Best of British, if I'm allowed to say that here.'

'You are and you may.' She gave him a peck on the cheek, and he ambled off.

She peered at the letters and an idea came. She consulted Gorhambury on his next visit to her table. 'Didn't Valourhand's suit malfunction at Bolitho's funeral?'

'She ended up by the Pool of Mixed Intentions – where the river goes underground. Everyone else landed safely, and to the inch.'

'What's the name of that earthwork in the marsh?'

'The Tower of the Winds. Polk flew the Artefacts Committee there one year in a prototype flying machine. The mound is completely sealed. Typical Boris, we only just made it back.' Gorhambury consulted his pocket watch. 'Sorry, Miss Roc, that's your three minutes. We can't have Mr Snorkel feeling left out, can we?'

The Tower of the Winds – S, E, W, N or N, E, W, S – the points of the compass and Bole's third hidden answer? Was that his final tease, his *news*?

Jones came last, earning a titter from Snorkel's camp and a smirk from Strimmer's: the Roc party of fanatical PE.

Orelia came straight to the point. 'Oblong is going to Lost Acre alone with his sphere. He needs protection.'

His answer was direct and surprising. 'Mr Oblong will be fine; he's learning fast. But please take your skates to the Island Field and keep a weather eye on your old friend, Jones.' The athlete paused. 'Never commit until you see the whites of their eyes.'

And all the while, *The Thingamajig* floated above, gathering and digesting the will of the people.

Marmion Finch, the only disenfranchised citizen in town, took advantage of the emptying of The Understairs to slip into the derelict building he had visited with Oblong. The mysterious carver, flitting in and out of Rotherweird's history, held the key.

Provisioned for a lengthy journey, he dropped through the cavity in the floor, secured the end of an outsize ball of luminous string to a beam and set off into the gloom, tube-light in one hand, the gently rotating metal spool in the other, away from the blocked tunnel.

Unravel, he muttered to himself, *unravel*.

His sojourn underground had sharpened the senses, but his one mechanical aid, a compass, quickly failed, the hand twitching and spinning in all directions. After an hour, avoiding duplication and marking dead ends with lengths of red wool, he reached a wider passage which ended in a generous chamber. Spent fragments of wood and shavings littered the floor. Further investigation revealed wooden nails, a wooden roof tile and a large half-carved head marred by a deep split to the forehead – but no tools, no workbench and no sign of food or drink. *A workplace once, but no longer*, Finch concluded.

Three roads now beckoned – but which to take?

His quandary brought Oblong to mind. He liked the outsider for his hapless integrity and engagement with history. Pray God he had properly equipped himself.

Finch chose the middle way, not as a symbol of moderation, but for its fresher air.

18

The Rotating Sphere

A morning for backpacks: his vote cast, Oblong followed the shore of the river southwards. The Island Field would soon host the declaration and leaving any later would attract undue attention. He ate his packed lunch warily on the edge of the meadow, well away from the tile.

Surveying the expanse of white, he resolved to read the game, all moving pieces and their players, including the ice-dragon, whose presence he had overlooked when accepting the errand from Finch. Would it be waiting by the tile again? Salt had never encountered it; the moleman had never mentioned it and nor had Ferensen. The odds favoured him – and hopefully he could escape back through the tile in time if the beast were there.

Transportation of the observatory struck him as a harmless, even worthwhile, ambition with no risk of collateral damage with everyone gathered on the Island Field.

Above, two building anvil clouds threatened the noon sunshine. *Incarnations of Snorkel and Strimmer*, he thought as he strode to the white tile. Broken ferns and twigs indicated another recent visitor, but Oblong, in crusading mood, did not notice.

Lost Acre greeted him as a friend: the ground hard, the frost, as in the carol, deep and crisp. Dabs of cumulus sat in a still blue sky: no ice-dragon and no sign of other opposition. In the stillness of deep winter, strange chrysalides hung on the taller grasses, and a nearby burrow showed no sign of activity. Lost Acre's creatures must hibernate too. Orion's Lantern shone low above the forest; an occasional streamer arcing up, only to fall like a shooting star.

He soon saw the tree alone in the meadowland, branches spread wide. He identified the mixing-point, a fish-back slippery patch of sky, just as Ferensen and Salt had described it. He sat down in a comfortable niche among the roots as stress, relief and exercise in warm clothes overwhelmed him. His eyes drifted closed, opened, drifted, fought to stay open, and closed. He slept.

Oblong awoke to a double footfall landing right beside him and his head jerked up to meet a quizzical smile in a pretty oval face – the young woman he and Valourhand had met in *The Journeyman's Gist* on Lazarus Night, working Euler's theorem with the fisherman mechanical and a name too unusual to forget. She carried a satchel over her shoulder.

'Pomeny Tighe?'

'Just so,' replied Tighe. A failing sun gilded her face.

In that fluid state between sleep and waking, Oblong found himself shuffling letters.

'Your name is an anagram of eight,' he stammered, wishing to impress.

'I am the eighth. I am the architect. I open the way.' She spoke these nonsensical words as if summoning a fading memory that she did not herself understand.

'Why call you Pomeny?'

Her face loosened.

She wants to share, thought Oblong.

'I was Mel.'

Oblong clambered to his feet, alert now. *Mel – Mel Pomeny*— 'Melpomene, the Greek muse of tragedy,' he cried immodestly, only to hesitate. *Tragedy* – so why was she here? How did she know this place?

'I died here,' she said before the question could be asked, her smile fading, 'all but. One tall, one squat: the men stood here and here.' She positioned herself, seeking exactness, her head turned down to the stream below. 'They watched me roll; they *relished* my agony.'

'They put you in there?' He pointed up at the mixing-point, the obvious conclusion, and she grimaced, still looking down at the stream. 'When did this happen?'

'When I was about as old as I am now. But I didn't look like this then. Growing backwards changes your appearance, Mr Oblong.'

He recalled the third woman's shield in *The Dark Devices*, an old crone with builder's mallet and key in hand. *I am the architect. I open the way.* But *what* way could she open? To *where*? The tall man and the squat man centuries ago had to be Wynter and Bole.

From her satchel, she produced a sphere, much larger than his, but similarly constructed of multi-coloured pieces. She placed it on the palm of her hand and with the gentlest flick, it spun – the same energy too.

'Who told you – this time, this place, this sphere?' When she failed to respond, he said urgently, 'You're being exploited, Miss Tighe. I know who the men were – I know what they're like, what they're capable of.'

She looked incredulous. 'A cure, they say – and they could not say that, unless they knew my condition. It's *mine*, mine to use, only me.'

The sentence echoed her childish possessiveness with the mechanical and the truth dawned: Wynter and Bole had brought her to the mixing-point, somehow spinning her to the last breath, conferring immortality, but reversing for her the march of time. They must have set the moment when her condition would reach its crisis, threatening loss of memory, passion, mind; shrinkage to childhood and beyond to *tabula rasa*. Her condition, and the election, whose timing they had also set, would bring her back.

'But they're the same, Miss Tighe. The men who put you in there also constructed your sphere.'

'Why would they do that?'

'Because . . .' But he had no idea why. It was like talking a would-be suicide off a ledge. He had to *engage*. 'I have a sphere too. It's constructed from local rock.'

She darted behind the tree and clambered up a rope hidden on the other side, hauling it up after her, too quick for him to intervene.

He pointed to Orion's Lantern and did what he could to distract her. 'That's a comet, but it's only visible here. We inhabit parallel worlds, which connect somehow.'

The sun's disc closed on the tangled crown of the forest. Tighe kicked off her shoes and edged along the bough to the hoist. There was no cage, but she did not need one. 'Pray for me, Mr Historian,' she said, before leaping onto the rope and swinging forward and back, once, twice, before disappearing into the mixing-point clutching her sphere.

Oblong called her name, silence. Disconsolate, he hurled Fortemain's sphere in after her – at three in the afternoon to the minute.

Then the ground shook.

19

Tremor

At the twelfth stroke of the great bell, the voting booths closed. Boris disconnected the pipes, returned the unused ballot-balls to the charabanc and sealed the baskets. *The Thingamajig*, high in the sky, floated beyond the reach of all chicanery.

Boris turned to Miss Trimble. 'Now is the moment.' He clasped her hand.

'What do I do?' she asked.

'You leave my hand where it is.'

She glanced down and understood: they would make the most public declaration possible. 'Oh, Boris.' She kissed him on the cheek and they set off, hand in hand.

The Journeyman's Gist reverberated to the tinkle of guineas on wood and the din of betting: the result, the turnout, the winning margin, the length of the winner's acceptance speech; every permutation and combination.

Orelia, sitting alone on the parapet of the South Bridge, pecked at her homemade sandwich. She felt besieged by polar opposites: Salt's death and Everthorne's disinterest. Where the hell was he? Why not wait for her? If ever she needed him . . . Yet Salt's shade proved the stronger, hauling her back. She had gone it alone with him on Midsummer Day, heading into the worm-hole to face the unknown. In his memory, she must do the same at the Winter Solstice. Sod Everthorne. *Be methodical, look, analyse.* She took strength from Vine's small carving.

Sunlight bathed the scene, but on opposing horizons two single clouds gathered in size and deepened in colour. A fickle breeze spun frost-devils along the frozen river. She could not see or hear a single bird. She thought of the two monks, picking their way into the valley. She, like them, faced a millennial moment with stakes *beyond* high, a true tipping-point. She felt a kinship. They had fashioned a church; she must preserve its values.

A hubbub behind broke her chain of thought: *The Thingamajig* was heading towards her down the Golden Mean, a jostling populace following its shadow. In the lead walked Boris Polk, hand in hand with Miss Trimble. Schoolchildren pointed and tittered, but not for long; both were popular, and the alliance enhanced the prospects of attending future test-flights.

Orelia was also pleased; she had admired the porter's pluck in the Great Equinox Race, a sight to cheer.

Close behind strode the matronly Estella Scry, with Master Thomes struggling to keep pace. Apothecaries appeared at intervals in ordered ranks, adopting an unnatural trot, each holding a silver stick. Orelia found their step and formal grouping both absurd and sinister, an organised pack loose among individuals. Strimmer sauntered along nearby, wearing an expression of wry amusement.

Once freed from the constriction of the bridge, everyone from the old and infirm to babies in arms spread out on the Island Field, around and below *The Thingamajig*, an 'I *was there*' moment. The candidates stood apart with Gorhambury before a trestle table bearing the Mayoral chain of office on a plump purple cushion with an open box beside it, poised to receive its lesser relative, *In loco parentis*, when Gorhambury's duties were done.

'How does she declare?' asked Miss Trimble.

'Smoke,' replied Boris, 'white, brown or black – but the electoral districts show first on the underside, anti-clockwise from the southeast. The top glows too, one band for each candidate in their allotted colour. It won't be long now.'

Heads turned skywards, but not only drawn by *The Thingamajig*. The two clouds, roiling with inner life, were closing; only a light ribbon of sky remained between them. Flakes of sleet scurried down from the north, accompanied by growls of thunder. Surrounded by the frozen river and its tributary, the Island Field had turned forbiddingly bleak. Boris reassured the candidates that the machine's inner skin had an insulated lining. In the gloom tiny pinpoints of coloured light, each a vote, illuminated the Scholastic quarter in the map on the machine's hull. Telescopes craned. The three columns on the machine's chimney also began to rise, with black ahead.

'Town and gown,' whispered Sly in Snorkel's ear, 'ever the same – no worry.'

Orelia felt a pang of disappointment. Academe had largely looked after its own. Strimmer had drawn first blood. *The Thingamajig* started to rotate gently on its central axis, not a phenomenon Boris' grandfather had noted. The Understairs came next: a finely balanced contest between Orelia's support from the disadvantaged, augmented by Aggs' vigorous efforts, and Strimmer's from the Apothecaries and those seduced by their addictive blend. Snorkel again trailed, his poison-pen mail of little effect – but Municipal, the constituency of Town Hall workers and Rotherweird's establishment worthies, hauled the ex-Mayor back into contention. The overall position registered in three coloured columns on the machine's chimney; it was still too close to call. All turned on the Oasis, home to a mishmash of different interests, including many shopkeepers and craftsmen.

Boris clasped Miss Trimble's arm. The hull of *The Thingamajig* quivered as if in the grip of terminal fever. The gentle rotation turned jerky, moving now fast, now slow, as the sun succumbed to the encroaching clouds.

Darkness covered the face of the earth.

'It's the ballot stones,' Boris yelled at Gorhambury's staff. 'We have to get her down—'

They looked blank. *How could rock turn animate?*

But *The Thingamajig* did not come down; it disintegrated, top and bottom prised apart, spraying ballot stones in all directions, a height and distance that defied the laws of gravity. A few unfortunates were struck, but shock proved the greater injury. The elements joined the fray, wind rising and sleet thickening into snow.

The ground juddered; feet slipped, slid and stumbled; some fell; children screamed. A cloud of dust swirled above the town.

An amplified voice rang out, an authoritative female voice: Estella Scry. She had prepared for victory or defeat, not a spoiled election, but the plan required little adjustment. 'Citizens of Rotherweird, this moment is ordained. The Apothecaries will collect the ballot stones in due course. Everyone stays here until it is safe to return to town, when, for the public good, a curfew will be in place.'

Gorhambury strode forward and confronted Scry. '*You* have no authority to direct *anyone* to do *anything.*'

A knot of Apothecaries seized Gorhambury and removed his chain of office.

Jones burst through the press, but not to defend the Town Clerk. He whispered urgently to Orelia, 'Look!'

Orelia focused first on the Apothecaries, deploying from the shoreline in an enclosing cordon, arcs of electricity running between their silver sticks – and then on a solitary figure, skating fast upriver.

'After her or him,' he added.

Orelia needed no further invitation. She discarded her bag, clasped her skates and followed Jones back through the crowd. He strode straight at the advancing line of Apothecaries. She had only seen him in action on the night of the fire, but now he showed balance, economy of movement, speed and accuracy. He ducked the first swinging stick, throwing its owner over his shoulder, and disarmed the next Apothecary, skilfully eluding the ribbons of electricity. The Apothecaries resumed their line like well-programmed automata and continued to close the net on everyone else, presumably under orders not to break ranks. Jones and Orelia sprinted to the shoreline, fixed their skates and set off in pursuit of the phantom skater, who had vanished.

'Luck's Landing,' cried Jones into the wind and snow.

Orelia's steel blades transmitted an unsettling movement in the ice despite its thickness and the lack of any visible disturbance. Jones crouched lower. *He must be sensing it too*, thought Orelia, the election now wholly out of mind.

Within two hundred yards of Luck's Landing a deafening crack, as of a giant bone bent to breaking-point, rent the air, and a great shelf of ice reared in front of them. Jones swerved, then again, avoiding a second fracture, with Orelia close behind. No water surged through; the ice-dragon had done enough.

As the river transformed into a disturbed jigsaw, Jones moved along the eastern shore, jinking round the driftwood to the security of the Landing, only to hear a new sound, far deeper than the sundering ice: the voice of the earth. Instinctively they looked up. Columns of dust spiralled high above the town.

Orelia grabbed Jones' arm for reassurance. She had not anticipated this.

The town's skyline was on the move.

Tremor.

20

Straighten the Rope I

The quake tossed Finch off his feet. He had never felt so puny, a mote in the palm of Nature's hand. He bounced off the tunnel wall, shielding his head before smacking into the stone floor. He spat out a mouthful of dust and blood and snorted his nostrils clear. Mercifully, the ceiling had held.

As the groan of ropes under strain, the squeal of gears engaging and disengaging and the rattle of hydraulics echoed down the tunnel, Finch retrieved his tube-light and ran towards the source. He emerged onto a vertiginous open balcony overhanging a deep pit. A cat's cradle of chains, ropes, pulleys and counterweights had come to life and a tower was slowly rising. The sides and window frames were bedecked in carvings. An ornate window passed on its upward journey, almost in touching distance.

Finch fell to his knees, part in awe, part in shame. He had *spectacularly* underestimated the scale of the carver's ambitions. Another pulley snapped into life and still the tower rose, storey by storey.

A new Age of the Eleusians dawned.

Straighten the Rope.

Morval Seer barred the outer doorway of the moleman's quarters, pleading by expression with shaking head and open, outstretched palms: *Stay, stay, stay—*

The tope was pleading too – despite being an expert in subsidence, he could not track this quake to any particular source.

'. . . a tower was slowly rising . . .'

Rotherweird's rock strata moved from time to time, but lightly and only locally.

A second tremor struck, longer and slower, yet more forceful, setting the decanter of Richter 5 bouncing on the tabletop. An unworldly scraping sound followed from the tunnel beyond, distant but distinct, like bricks rubbed together.

Fortemain ignored his companions and uncharacteristically barged past Morval with a self-congratulatory cry. 'I knew it – I *knew* it! But we'll stop the clever bastard.'

The tope could not unravel this enigmatic announcement; Fortemain had kept this to himself. *Right about* what? *Stop* whom? But Fortemain had seized the reins, and the tope could not check his companion's headlong sprint.

Nimble and lithe, Morval would have caught him, had he not cuffed the ceiling and caused a minor cave-in to block the way. She pawed frantically at the cold, granular earth; breaking nails and grazing knuckles, hair matted with soil.

Could he not see what she now saw? Finch had been the unwitting bait to draw Fortemain out.

Fortemain bounded on, oblivious to risk and the tope's calls for restraint. Now all made sense: the other place and Rotherweird Valley mirrored each other exactly, created by the same cosmic impact. The forces he had devoted centuries to calculating had opened the rock wall behind Finch's cell, hence the grating sound. He had to get through before it closed – and before *them*. His private ambition for an observatory in the other place, his one preoccupation until now, receded into insignificance.

Wynter, Wynter, Wynter . . .

He knew *how*, and he knew *where*.

21

Straighten the Rope II

At Luck's Landing Jones and Orelia unfastened their skates. Above them, the town's profile disappeared in a fog of dust and thickening snow. The river looked like burned treacle.

'We're in the wrong place, Jones – Bole spoke of the Tower of the Winds.'

'The wrong place can get you to the right place,' he replied enigmatically, a man transformed, alert and certain. He picked up a pair of skates, abandoned in the frozen reeds, and pointed east. Their phantom skater, too far away to identify, was nimbly traversing the marsh.

'We'll follow the tracks,' Jones said. 'There are stepping stones beneath – but you need to be exact. The ground is treacherous.'

Like free-stepping dancers, Jones and Roc set off in pursuit. When the mysterious skater vanished as if swallowed up by the marsh, Jones plunged on regardless. Orelia gathered the connections between the Rotherweird Valley and Lost Acre, formed by the same cosmic collision, open to similar cyclical disturbance under the comet's dark influence, each with a river and island, joined by the tiles, identical in time and season. She added a shared geology . . . A *shared*—

'Jones!' she screamed through the blizzard, 'I know – I *know*! I know what Bole is about.'

Jones did not respond until they reached Finch's fastness, when he simply said, 'Yes' – a truly odd 'yes', neither question nor answer, more a declaration of shared understanding.

Orelia still felt compelled to say it out loud.

'*Rotherweird has a mixing-point too* – that's why the ancients enclosed it in earth. *That's* why Wynter had himself disappeared. It's virgin, unused. He's here, waiting.' She paused, overcome by nausea from the effort of the journey and the shock. 'Jones, *Straighten the Rope* is bound in Wynter's skin. They've taken it to resurrect him . . .'

Jones did not look remotely surprised. He stooped and lifted the doors to Finch's cell and the narrow cave. He craned his neck into the latter. 'The rock wall has opened. It's responding to the same millennial forces. Question is, how long does it stay open?'

A plangent woman's cry came from the other side. Anxiety creased Jones' face. He moved from one shaft to the other, snared in a hideous dilemma: should he go to the unknown damsel in distress or guard a favourite damsel from danger?

Orelia decided for him. 'We split up: you go there, I go here; you take the tube-light, I have the candle.'

Rescued from indecision, he could only stammer, 'Devilry's afoot, Miss Roc, devilry to the north and devilry to the south.'

He descended by his own rope, still firmly attached to the handle, into Finch's cell and on into the moleman's tunnel beyond. She used a second rope obligingly left by the phantom skater. The rock wall had divided with geometric precision, creating a doorway to a tunnel beyond. Torches with gnarled fingers, coated in a dark, resinous pitch and set in stone sconces, illuminated the way to the first bend, a sharp turn south. From the distance came the echo of two voices, one male and one female; the pitch of the former was mercifully too high to be Everthorne's.

Jones adapted quickly, splaying his feet to minimise the need to crouch: ungainly, but effective. The tunnel surfaces, treacherously zigzagged by cracks, had been sealed by the cold. There had been the one cry, which disturbed him, for it suggested a final cry, a vain plea for help, as well as grief, rage, horror and pain . . .

Scouts, so often the first in, witness more than their share – massacre, the bodies of women with child, victims of torture and fire – but he had never seen a sight like this: a creature, man-sized but half-mole, half-man, had been lifted high into the air, impaled on vicious ribs of shining steel. One had pierced the neck, another had impaled the chest right through to the back. Beneath the disturbed earth Jones glimpsed a pressure plate. In death, the face wore an attitude of pained surprise. He held the tube-light close and recognised beneath the velvety hair and hybrid eyes the features of his old friend, Bolitho.

Only then did he see *her*, crouching at the edge of the tube-light's arc: beauty ravaged by grief. Morval Seer. It could be nobody else.

Jones somehow found words.

'We take him down. We wash him. We bury him with his face to the stars.'

The torch-lit tunnel had the feel of cliché – a thoroughfare for grave-robbers, a secret sold by traitors – and yet nobody had walked this way for a millennium despite the torches and carved sconces. This was old, *old* history.

Orelia ran, steeling herself for confrontation, as at Lost Acre's mixing-point on Midsummer Day. Jones' absence could only mean misfortune behind her too.

The bends had been signalled by flickering torches, but not this one: no torch, only spectral colours dancing in the air like a fine spray caught by the sun. She took the final torch from its sconce and walked into a cavern with glowing walls. The floor sloped down to a huge tree, its trunk as wide as the shop front at *Baubles & Relics*, bursting with leaves. Luminous moss clung to the bark, the branches kissed the cavern floor and the ceiling; roots dived, rose and dived again.

She looked up to an open space, a shimmering patch of air where no branch trespassed: unmistakably a mixing-point.

Above her she heard a rustle: Bole must be climbing up to the mixing-point with *Straighten the Rope* – the bole hiding Bole, the *double entendre* apposite for his protean nature.

Using the branches as a winding stair, she climbed with the torch held away from the trunk. She reached the edge of a wooden platform, greyed by age, with a jetty leading to the mixing-point. She hauled herself up.

To her horror, there stood Everthorne, book in hand. When he spoke, it was not as Everthorne, but in a high voice, an unsettling mix of the obsequious and the assertive.

'Whom would you like to meet, Miss Roc? Which voice would you hear?' Bole smiled, lifting the book, and this time she heard Vibes. 'She's not to be sold, shared or parted with. And take my bag – it's immune to pox, water and sunshine.'

He changed again, a gentle voice suggestive of wisdom. 'Mr Vere, I have an idea. London has a Royal Society – why not a Rotherweird Guild, with scientific purposes backed by proper beliefs; its Hall could be your home.' Bole's own high voice added, 'That was your ancestor, Benedict Roc, a carver of wood beyond compare – with a little guidance from me.' And finally, '*Sum Ferox.*'

Orelia could barely comprehend. 'You murdered them all—'

'I preserved them all, I absorbed them all,' replied Bole. 'As for the killing, Flask killed Ferox in Lost Acre, Ferox killed Vibes near Hoy, Vibes killed Everthorne, sketching near an alpine railway station. Guess who's next?'

Bole has a weakness, Ferensen had said, *he toys with his victims.* 'Let me speak to Everthorne,' she begged. 'Let me hear his voice.'

Bole pondered the request. 'I might, if you tell me why I needed Everthorne.'

Loathing for Bole's arrogance and cruelty revived Orelia. She must play along, wait for an opening. 'You designed a sphere with very particular pieces, to move objects from Rotherweird to Lost Acre – buildings, to judge from my last sight of the town.'

'But my sphere also opens the wall, Miss Roc; above all, it opens the wall.'

Orelia shuddered. They had been blindsided. Whatever Bole had done to the town was secondary, a diversion. *Play for time.* She continued, 'You determined the shape of the sixteen pieces, but you had a problem fitting them together. As the carver, you chance on old Everthorne, an artist with exceptional spatial awareness. You show him your drawings and he paints two pictures which, taken together, show which piece to fit in which order. You gave him a carving of his treasured mouse in return. But the sequence alone might not be enough; I imagine there is twisting and turning – so you gambled on the grandson having the same gift. Next, you wanted an innocent custodian for the book – one who might fall for him, and you chose me. Meanwhile, you commission Miss Vine to make the pieces.'

As Orelia spoke, her analysis felt awry; a piece was missing. Bole as Everthorne could not have arranged all of this.

'Not bad, Miss Roc, but I'm afraid Mr Everthorne can be most assertive. At this particular moment, I would be rash to give him his head. This is not his party.'

'Let me kiss him, then.'

She had chosen skilfully. Refusal would mean a loss of face; acceptance might give Everthorne a moment of control. Bole dipped his head – and, as he did so, she seized the book and kicked him away. She raised the torch, screaming, 'I'm not the fool you take me for!'

One sentence – ten seconds to utter – but the delay was fatal. She should have put the torch to the dead skin instantly. A scything blow from behind knocked her to the floor of the platform and sent the torch spinning from her grasp. She fought to stay conscious as her arms were bound behind her back. Struggling to see, she rolled onto her back – and caught sight of her assailant: the woman skater!

A face came in and out of focus – and she understood.

Madge Brown had alerted them to the *Popular Choice Regulations* and started the road to the election. Madge Brown had sent them to the Hoy Book Fair for Bole to hand over the book as Vibes, the true Vibes being already dead. Madge Brown, hearing Fanguin mention *The Agonies* on their visit to Gorhambury, had destroyed it and the changelings. Madge Brown had chaired the Liaison Committee, placing Everthorne on Oblong's staircase so they would meet. Madge Brown had acquired the invisibility film and attacked Oblong after his enquiry about the Apothecaries. Madge Brown had attacked Everthorne on Aether's Way, freeing the artist of suspicion. Madge Brown had visited her with the electoral form, checking the book's presence and location.

Madge Brown, Assistant Head Librarian, of the mousey looks and retiring character, Madge Brown the leather-winged Fury, stared down at her.

'Time to go, Potamus,' she said.

Head throbbing, blood trickling down her cheek, Orelia could only watch.

With surgical precision Madge Brown stripped away the binding of *Straighten the Rope* with a stiletto and passed it to Bole.

Contrary emotions seized Orelia: had she made love to Everthorne alone, his true body and essence – or had Bole been there too, a manipulative voyeur, even a participant of sorts? Loathing and disgust at the violation was leavened by the hope that, if Everthorne's body survived, she might reclaim him. She worked her hands; the knot was loosening, but not quite enough.

Bole had his back to her as he tendered the binding to the mixing-point, which sucked it in. He took the woman's hand in his. 'Nona,' he said, '*resurrexit*.'

She stooped and gathered a dark cloak from the platform.

A naked male figure stepped from the mixing-point, slim and tall for his time, hair turning silver over a high forehead, the irises strikingly dark.

The man had no issue with nakedness, nothing hesitant in the step or the sibilant voice. 'You have changed, my children, but in ways that do not matter.' He accepted the cloak with languid ease. 'And this woman?'

'An obstructor,' replied Nona.

Wynter said softly, 'Nona, there are always obstructors.'

'You have servants too: a Guild in waiting, true scientists. I set it up – a pretty business with a portrait. Scry is here, but she is envious – she killed Calx's familiar. She does not know her proper station.'

Nona's deference was tangible.

Wynter took another step, more hesitant now.

How, she wondered, *does this Elizabethan view the cut of our clothes and hair? What will he make of Rotherweird Town? 'True scientists' means modern scientists – how will he be able to engage with them?* Orelia caught a nuance, a flicker of anxiety in Wynter's face.

'Now, Calx: the service you were born for. Don't flinch.'

Guess who's next, Bole had said, and finally Orelia grasped the true reach and horror of Wynter's design.

Everthorne moved to face Wynter and his arms rose.

'No!' Orelia screamed.

Even Nona averted her face. Orelia could not see, but heard the glottal whimper of a strangled man. Wynter stooped to inhale Everthorne's last breath, and, as he did so, the living swapped with the dead. Everthorne's lifeless body fell to the platform, leaving Wynter, blinking like an owl, as the knowledge gleaned by Bole in his many guises over the centuries flooded in.

Nona bowed briefly to him. 'We must hurry, Master,' she said, twirling her stiletto before flicking a finger at Orelia. 'What about her?'

'Let her lie with him ... forever.' He kicked Everthorne's body as he passed, a husk of no consequence.

By the time Orelia was free of her bonds, Wynter and his acolyte had left the chamber. She did not follow, instead cradling Everthorne's lifeless head to her chest.

The spectral colours faded and the rocks turned dark, leaving only the luminous moss. Far away, the rock wall ground back into place.

Laying his body against the tree trunk, her knee scraped a small object, the pegs and string with which Everthorne had measured the view on the morning of their one day together.

How all human constructs can be put to good or evil use, she reflected, *an artist's line or a garrotte? What will this new order do to my town, my valley and my friends?*

On the Island Field, corralled by Apothecaries and pummelled by the storm, a knot of children broke away and indulged that childish fifth sense which marries omen with an instinct for what the future holds. They joined hands, chanting as they danced, an old rhyme set deep in their consciousness:

> *'By the pricking of my thumbs ...*
> *The graves are open,*
> *Wynter comes ...'*

Rotherweird and its citizens will return
for one final adventure in

LOST ACRE

Acknowledgements

Having taxed several friends with drafts of *Rotherweird*, I decided on a more solitary journey for this second, darker story. In consequence *Wyntertide* was written with only the literary assistance of my outstanding publishing editor, Jo Fletcher, whose contribution has been immense. But there would be no second volume without the first, so my debt to friends – and above all my agent, Ed Wilson – bears repetition at the outset.

I have at the Bar defended the rights of the citizen critic to speak his or her mind, and it has been instructive to be on the receiving end. I am grateful to *all* who took the trouble to read *Rotherweird*. To those who liked it and said so to others, I owe a particular debt. Unknowns need a following wind.

Critics and supporters often agreed that *Rotherweird*'s multiple points of view presented quite a challenge, early on particularly. I hope this eases in *Wyntertide* with the return of the main players and but a few new arrivals.

Sasha has again excelled herself as my chosen illustrator, even though she is expecting twins the month that *Wyntertide* appears. The book aspires to the mood which her images convey. If the text does them justice, I will be pleased indeed.

Never buy wine for the label – but an entrancing cover sure

helps, so a warm thank you too to art director Patrick Carpenter and artist Leo Nickolls.

I had naïvely believed that books sell themselves. Not so; the energy and commitment of Olivia Mead, with the support of Quercus' sales team, has been exceptional. She also has a gift for earthing authorial *angst*.

There has been one change of personnel since *Rotherweird*. Sam Bradbury's talents moved her onwards and upwards, but Jo's new assistant, Molly Powell, has been a fine successor and a pleasure to work with.

Wyntertide's proofreader, Sharona Selby, excelled with her eye for subtle inconsistencies and spotting Oblong-esque errors in Oblong's code, a face-saver.

Last, but foremost, my family, and especially my wife, could not have been more supportive. Time spent with your head in a notebook is time lost to them. They have borne the recurrent and infuriating writer's '*mind is elsewhere*' look with exemplary patience. Inflicting pain and loss on likable characters, as life alas can do, may be satisfying dramatically, but it is not conducive to high spirits. They have endured that too.